I0632215

A VAGABOND ARMY

A NOVEL OF MARYLAND IN THE AMERICAN REVOLUTION

VOLUME TWO
The Old Line Chronicles

JOHN CONRADIS

FIRESIDE FICTION
2008

FIRESIDE FICTION
AN IMPRINT OF HERITAGE BOOKS, INC.

Books, CDs, and more—Worldwide

For our listing of thousands of titles see our website
at
www.HeritageBooks.com

Published 2008 by
HERITAGE BOOKS, INC.
Publishing Division
100 Railroad Ave. #104
Westminster, Maryland 21157

Other books by the author:
The Willing War: A Novel of Maryland in the American Revolution

Cover painting by Don Troiani
"Trenton"
www.historicalartprint.com

International Standard Book Numbers
Paperbound: 978-0-7884-4620-7
Clothbound: 978-0-7884-7317-3

*T*o the wonderful members of my family.

My dearest friend and second best critic, Hazel Bagwell
Our son and my best critic, Brandon Conradis
My sister Jocelyn Tully, brother Gil Conradis, and their families
&
My parents, Winifred and Albert Conradis

There have been so many people over the years who have been unfailingly helpful and encouraging in wanting to see me realize my dream of publishing an historical novel—friends, and neighbors, and amateur historians like myself; but, in truth, in today's publishing world it takes (besides considerable good fortune) professional writers, editors, and publishers with all their skills. I am profoundly grateful to the following: Roxanne Carlson of Flintlock Press (roxcarl@verizon.net), who years ago wrestled with a 900-page gorilla and changed it into a couple of svelte novels which even possess plots. Roxanne also did some beautiful work on maps and the covers. Then there is Debbie Riley, my editor at Heritage Books, Inc., who not only prepared the cover for printing, but also helped to create what we believe are very attractive cover designs, as well as creating some visually stunning ad layouts for various magazines and newspapers. And I want to thank Leslie Wolfinger, Publications Director for Heritage Books, Inc., for giving me the encouragement and opportunity to have my novels published. Regarding the cover painting by Don Troiani, *Trenton*, it appeared in the August 1973 issue of *American Heritage Magazine*. Finally, *deep* appreciation goes Henry Leish, a leading collector and dealer of Revolutionary War artifacts who has been a great supporter of *The Willing War* and I hope *A Vagabond Army*. Be sure to visit his virtual museum at www.RevolutionaryWarMuseum.com.

A vagabond Army of Raggamuffins, with Paper Pay, bad Cloathes, and worse Spirits.

New York Gazette, October 14, 1776

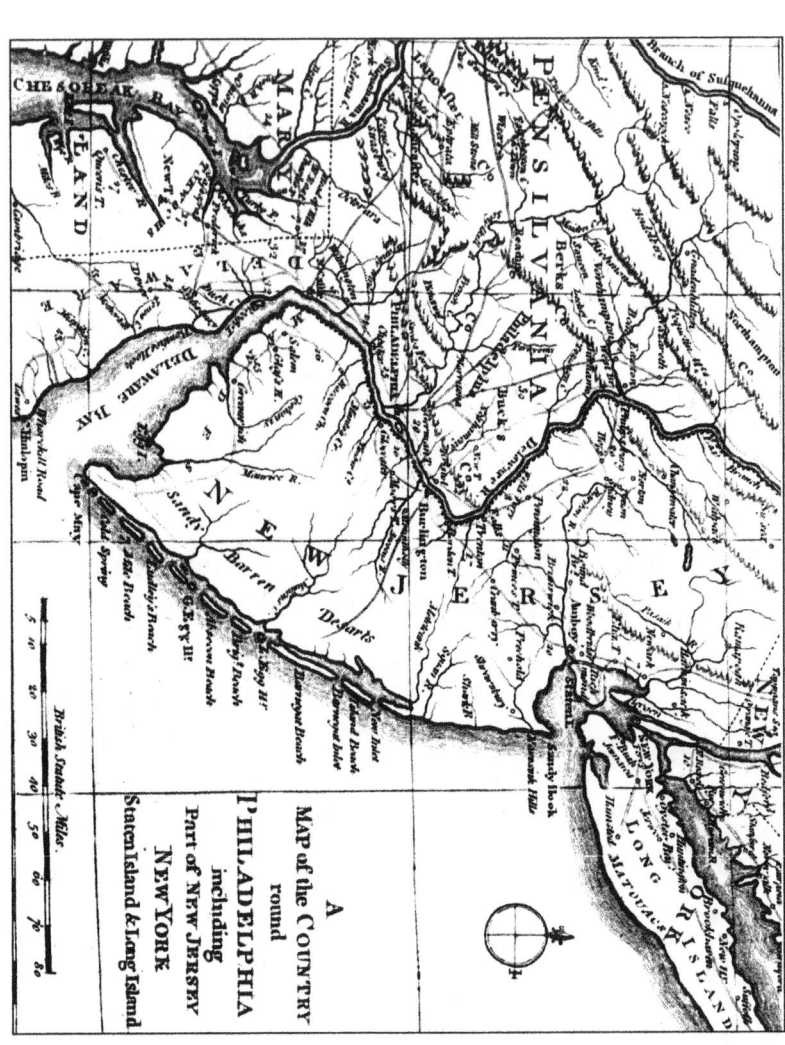

A Map of the Country round Philadelphia including Part of New Jersey, New York, Staten Island, & Long Island.

From *The Gentleman's Magazine*, London, 1776. Courtesy of the Library of Congress, Geography and Map Division.

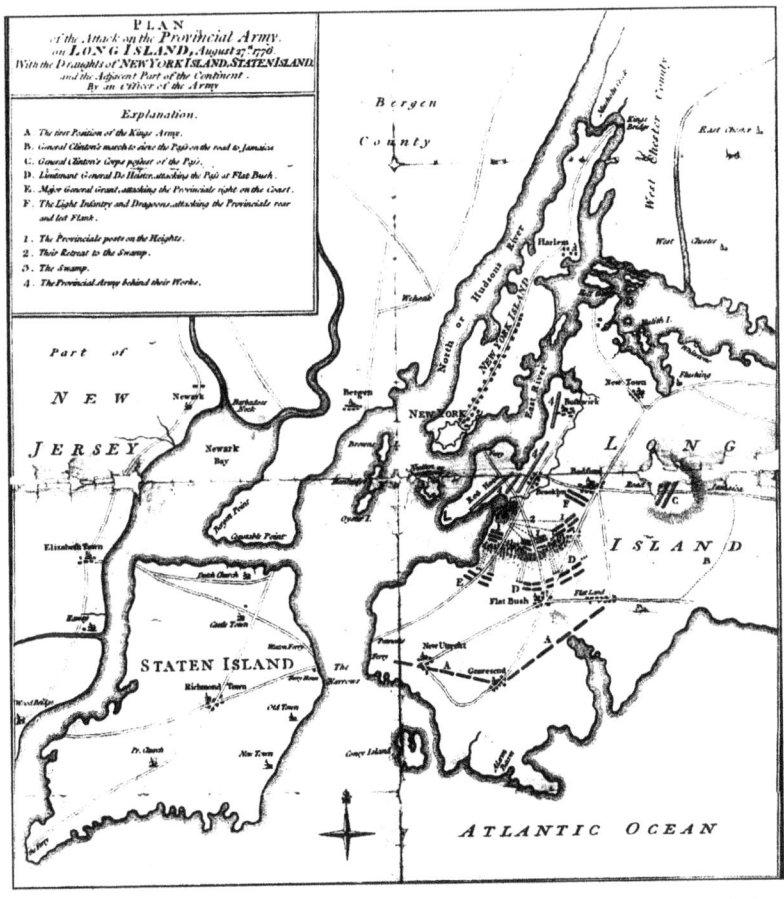

Plan of the Attack on the Provincial Army on Long Island, August 27, 1776, With the Draught of New York Island, Staten Island, and the Adjacent Part of the Continent. By an Officer of the Army.

Printed for J. Bowles, London, 1776. Courtesy of the Library of Congress, Geography and Map Division.

Part One

The Army of Israel

Numbers who a few Days ago were plain
Countrymen have now clothed themselves
in martial Forms—Powdered Hair—Sharp
pinched Beavers—Uniform in Dress with
their battalion—Swords on their thighs—
and stern in the Art of War.

Philip Vickers Fithian,
Journal, 1775-76

1

FRAGMENTS OF HISTORY

Head of Elk, Maryland
July 13, 1776

*The Military Journal of
Christopher Sims
of Frederick County,
State of Maryland,
A Pvt. soldier, Md. Batt.*

*Begun at Baltimore, Maryland,
July 1776*

CHRISTOPHER SIMS carefully considered the title page and decided that he was satisfied with it. It was rendered in a passable roundhand, with fine lines and flourishes except for some blotches where he had begun a stroke. Anyway, it would do—he had already torn out two leaves from his leather journal, the first one because of poor penmanship caused by nerves, the second to change Maryland's status from province to state.

He turned the page and carefully wrote,

Pg.1 July, 1776, Baltimore

Taking a deep breath, Christopher made his first entry.

Thurs 11th   This   Eve.   We   march'd   through   Balt. town to the publick Wharf and there took ship to head of Elk

Satisfied, Christopher then carefully recorded his entry for the next day.

'Fri 12th   Arrived head of Elk this morn ware we est't camp. Join'd sum other compys. Drew Provision and practic'd as a hole.

Terrence Simon, Christopher's friend and now comrade-in-arms, watched as Christopher laboriously made these entries, and though he wasn't invited to do so, made his critique anyway.

"It doesn't quite capture the moment, nor your seasickness, does it? But I do admire your penmanship."

Terry Simon also admired the leather-bound journal and writing set which Missus Goddard had given to Christopher. Along with the journal, she had also presented him with a brass writing set which had belonged to her brother. It looked like a flask, but when the top was pulled off, it contained a glass inkwell, a little sander, and two quill pens.

With such writing materials, a man ought to be able to paint a vivid picture of the campaign, and Terry Simon said as much.

"Chris, the 9th would certainly have been a more memorable occasion to begin your journal. I mean, think about it: the day when the Continental Army officially celebrated *our declaration of independence*, for God's sake, with readings, sermons, and booming cannon. But if you're goin' to begin with the 11th, what about Baltimore's celebration? With the fireworks and the large crowds, and all? Such hallowed events are the stuff of journals, and all you see in it is that we marched through the miry streets of town to the public wharf?"

Christopher looked at Terry and then at the journal, considering what his friend had just said.

Missus Goddard, owner and publisher of *The Maryland Journal and Baltimore Advertiser*, had given him the journal and writing set as a parting gift. In doing so, she challenged him to keep a journal of his adventures during the campaign which would assure America's independence. Upon his return, she said, he could write episodes of his military adventures for her newspaper.

Thinking about keeping a journal in those terms, he realized, meant more than simply listing events.

"Aye, you're right, Terry." He carefully tore out the misbegotten page, wadded it into a ball, and threw it at his friend. Taking a gulp of his ration of rum, Christopher gritted his teeth and applied himself to recording a more compelling entry for July 11.

Having rewritten his original entry, Christopher thought a while before adding,

> *The town celebrated our independence with a lg illumination of blue*
> *white & green colors and the fireing of cannon and grate crowds*
> *cheer'd our solders*

There. Christopher now considered his next entry, for the 12th, and decided that what he had already written would have to do. He would write more expansively for his next entry.

He placed the small quill pen back in its holder and pushed the top down on the stand's base, now thoroughly exhausted by the effort to paint Terry's damn'd vivid picture.

****

Three days before, the leaking old schooner *Harmony* had transported Captain Smith's Eighth Company of Smallwood's Battalion of Maryland Regular Troops from Baltimore up the Bay to the Elk River. Here, it deposited Christopher and his comrades at the very head of the Chesapeake, about a mile from the town of Elk, which was a major shipping point for grains, corn, and fruits between Baltimore and Philadelphia.

Beyond a fine frame house, the home of Colonel Hollingsworth, a local patriot, militia leader, and the unofficial commissary for the province's armed forces being sent north, was a muddy meadow where the Maryland troops would camp.

Shouted orders rang out and men sought their companies, as drummers, most of them younger than John Paul, Christopher's thirteen-year-old brother, beat the Assembly, while Corporal Smith called out in his harsh voice, "Eighth Company here!"

Thus, the companies marked out company streets, raised tents, saw to their cooking fires near the food tents, dug vaults, and watched in anticipation as the sutlers set up their tables.

The next afternoon, for the first time, the entire battalion formed on parade. Here, the Baltimore companies joined those from Annapolis. In addition, several independent companies assigned to Continental service were also marching north with the battalion, and they, too, were paraded.

Standing in the spongy grass, Colonel William Smallwood and his staff welcomed the new arrivals. This was the first time that most of the men from Baltimore had ever laid eyes on their commander, who had a martial air about him despite his corpulence, middle-aged jowls, and small, beady eyes.

The colonel was dressed in the battalion's unofficial parade uniform of red and buff regimentals, as were many of the officers. While the prescribed uniform was the hunting shirt, the officers, in their more elegant uniforms, did present a splendid appearance before the battalion and the public.

Lined up in formation, with brightly uniformed officers astride prancing horses in the rear, and fifers and drummers on each flank, Colonel Smallwood and Lieutenant Colonel Ware stood on foot at the center of the battalion for the blessing of the colors.

The battalion standard was a square of buff-colored silk upon which were painted in red the initials "MB" and the word "Liberty." As the colors were brought forward, the Reverend Daniel Sere, the battalion chaplain, stepped forward to bless the flag with a prayer he had prepared especially for the occasion. It was a stirring prayer, ending with, "*So honor this standard, Dear Lord, which is a brave symbol of the people of Maryland who have just freed themselves from the injurious and destructive bonds of a tyrannical power!*"

There was applause and cheering from the spectators, many of whom had traveled miles to see their sons and husbands off on this historic and decisive campaign against the British occupiers.

Christopher really hoped that Hannah would be among the civilians present for the ceremony. Looking about after his company was dismissed, he searched for her, expecting that she would stand out because of her height. He finally spotted her moving about like a sheepdog herding a dozen children who belonged to the area's leading families.

As he approached her, he reached down and grabbed a small boy who was making a getaway.

Putting the boy down, Christopher spoke sharply, "Soldier!" The boy froze, looking fearfully at this tall man in his rifle shirt and lugging a huge musket with a bayonet attached. "Stand at attention when spoken to by a superior officer! And say 'Yes, sir' when spoken to!"

The little boy stood as straight as he knew how. "Yes, sir!" he cried, his lower lip trembling.

"In our army, soldier, we don't run away. Is that understood?"

"Yes, sir."

"Good, now rejoin your company—fast as ya can!"

Christopher winked at Hannah as the little boy ran back to join the other children.

Hannah, who had been running to catch up to the child, stopped in front of Christopher.

"Well, sir," she exclaimed, breathlessly, "You have certainly proven yourself capable as my second-in-command!"

"I'll accept that as a compliment, ma'am," he laughed.

Tall and attractive enough, Hannah literally stood head and shoulders above all the other women on the field that day; but more importantly, she now stood smiling in front of Christopher, her breasts heaving becomingly as she caught her breath.

"And how are you, Missus Williams?" Christopher asked politely. Wanting to wrap around her like a winter blanket.

"Fine, Private Sims. Jus' trying to catch my breath." She was pressing her chest with the flats of her hands as she said this, taking a deep breath before exhaling. She smiled at him.

They stood looking hungrily at each other, neither making a move. It had been over a week since they had last seen each other back in Baltimore. Things had sure changed since their last night together in Aunt Jane's little blue house on Lovely Lane.

Hannah Williams was a runaway and still hiding out. Both she and Christopher had traveled great distances to be with each other—one always, it seemed, trying to catch up to the other. Finally, they found themselves together in Baltimore, among friends...for what proved to be only a short time.

Then Hannah had to run again, this time ending up in charge of the household of one of the most prominent patriots in Maryland at the family manor near Head of Elk. Here, it was decided, she would be safe from her Tory pursuers.

As for Christopher, he was now a private soldier in the Maryland Battalion and under the watchful eye of every strutting corporal and sergeant in the army. It was, he thought, not much better than courting Hannah under the jealous eye of the Reverend Crabbe, to whom she had been bound out—and still was, legally speaking.

As it now stood, they could only fervently hope the next few months would bring independence to both the new United Colonies and to them.

In the meantime...there was the sudden sound of a drum and the accompanying shrill whistle of a fife, then more and more drums and fifes joined in as each company called for its men to form. The rolls and flams of the drums and the screeching of the fifes reverberating across the meadow as men moved toward the forming lines.

"That's the order to assemble, Hannah. I have to go."

He looked at her. "It won't be possible to meet tonight. Tomorrow—the Sabbath—is possible for me. How about you?"

"Could be. If it is, I'll wait for you from nine o'clock by yon gate."

2

"DID YOU JOIN TO FIGHT
FOR INDEPENDENCE?"

Head of Elk, Maryland
July 13-14, 1776

THE MEN WERE NOT GIVEN LEAVE that Saturday evening to visit the village of Elk, which sat beckoning on the hills above the meadow; but the sutler wagons were open and dispensing great quantities of poor quality liquor at a price most of them could afford.

The men of the battalion drank and strolled around the camp satisfying their curiosity about their new comrades, who came from throughout Maryland—from such faraway counties as St. Mary's, Somerset, Frederick, and Anne Arundel. For most of them, this was the first time they had heard of these other counties, much less met someone who lived there.

"I was just wanderin' around talkin' to some of the men from the Annapolis and Eastern Shore companies," mentioned Caleb Hayes, a member of Christopher's undersized four-man mess, as he returned from one of his forays.

"Nice fellas, with interestin' things to say. Did ye know the corn they grow near Cambridge in Dorchester County is different from the corn we grow in Cecil County? God's truth! They say it's not Indian corn, that the cobs are longer and the kernels sweeter. That's what they claim. Call it 'high bird' for some reason."

Caleb was a man of the land, whose dream was to own his own farm, so soils and seeds fascinated him.

"That is...if I understood 'em right. But that's the trouble talkin' with strangers—I couldn't hardly understand a word of what those boys from the Eastern Shore said. The Annapolis boys are fairly understandable, but those eastern shoremen babble like idiots."

"Did they understand a word of what you said, Caleb?" asked Davey Lynn with a deadpan expression.

Caleb had a shocked look on his face. "What?—whaddaya mean by that?"

The next morning was the Sabbath. Camp chores were relaxed and the men waited in a tolerably good mood for eleven o'clock and the Sunday sermon. The sermon on this day referred to the duties of the soldier and dwelt a little more on politics than the normal sermon. The preacher, a little man spewing fire and brimstone, spoke from a platform made of drums, which seemed to echo his every word.

The reverend's impassioned sermon was followed by the reading of orders, roll-call, assignment of light duties, and instructions for the next morning's march to Philadelphia.

While the great plunge into independence was accepted with surprisingly little controversy, not everyone favored it. Some of the officers even saw fit to resign their commissions in protest and left for home with long faces, knowing that life-long friendships had ended.

And there were men among the enlisted ranks who had grave doubts about the move. Unlike the officers, though, they could not simply up and quit.

Stepping out of the ranks at roll-call that evening, just hours before they were to march to Philadelphia, an agitated Private Robert Gassaway loudly declared, "I say it is better for us poor people to lay down our arms, and pay the duties and taxes laid upon us by the King and Parliament, than be brought into slavery and to be commanded and ordered about as we are."

The lines rippled, and heads turned. There was a murmuring. A few might have agreed with Private Gassaway, but most did not. But all of them were impatient with the disruption in routine because of the gill of rye whiskey awaiting their dismissal in celebration of their march to Philadelphia tomorrow morning. Captain Smith quickly came over to confront the recalcitrant soldier. Angrily, he demanded who the private meant when he said the people had been brought into slavery.

"Why, a parcel of great men, that's who. They destroyed the tea at Boston, and then knowing they had done wrong, they didn't know what to do to save themselves. So they ordered all of America to be brought under arms and now say 'my brave boys, fight away' just to save their own necks."

Ignoring Captain Smith's order to be silent, Private Gassaway carried on. "I am convinced I am right and only wish the eyes of the multitude were open. The only way to resolve this dispute is for us to lay down our arms and petition Congress to petition the King and Parliament…and if Congress won't do this, why then, people should petition the King direct."

Upon hearing this, Captain Smith ordered a sergeant and four men to arrest Gassaway and take him away.

"What's goin' to happen to Gassaway, Corporal?" Christopher asked Corporal Jeremiah Smith, as the men, now dismissed, were standing around talking about the man's outburst.

"I reckon he'll be taken before the Council of Safety, which'll decide what should be done with him."

"Not that I agree with Gassaway," interjected Terry, "but I'm not sure I agree with a man being punished for jus' speaking his mind. That doesn't seem to be in the spirit of what we're about, Jeremiah. What do you think?"

"Terry," said Corporal Jeremiah Smith wearily, "*I think* soldiers should obey orders—that's what I think. The time for discussion has come and gone. Whether we made the right decision or not, I leave to you philosophers."

With that, Corporal Smith strode off.

Back at their tent, Terry and Christopher discussed Congress's declaration.

"…it's not just men like Gassaway," Christopher pointed out, "it seems that a lot of people are not particularly in favor of independence."

Unlike Christopher, Terry was not surprised—or discouraged, for that matter. "When you think about it, it's quite a step. A man ought to be a little sobered by it, don't ya think?"

"I suppose," was Christopher's slow response. "I just thought people would be…well…feelin' more free, if you know what I mean. There're even those who say they would fight for their rights as Englishmen, but not as separatists."

"Christopher, declaring independence isn't the answer—it's only the result of not getting what we want as a part of Great Britain. That confuses a lot of folks. But what *do* we want? Remember Missus Goddard sayin' the other night that all this had started out only as a desire to have our rights returned to us? But somewhere along the way we acquired a different vision of what we want. That's how things happen, Christopher—we start out wanting one thing and then, much to our surprise, we end up deciding on something altogether different."

Terry then asked rhetorically, "So, what do we want? Liberty? Certain rights? Or do we want to start the world over again as Mister Paine says? If ye think about it like that, then the idea of declarin' independence isn't all that comfortable."

Christopher was thoughtful. "Well, you might be right, , but *I* say it's a fight between the overseers and those overseen, and what that relationship will be like when all is said and done. It's really as simple as that. Our 'betters' can call it what they will, and maybe look forward to something else; but, truth is, this revolution ought to be a victory for the common man."

****

On the eve before they were to march off to fight the regulars, the men who did not have further duties relaxed, wrote letters, read their Bibles, or furtively took swigs from their rundlets. Christopher hoped to have other plans.

Hannah had told him that she and the Alexander family were staying at Colonel Hollingsworth's manor. Sunday, all would be attending a reception and dinner for battalion senior officers in honor of their departure for the theatre of war. After putting the children to bed, Hannah was sure she could steal out later that evening.

Christopher prayed that their plan would work out as he approached their agreed upon assignation a little after nine o'clock. But the camp fires in the meadow and the brightly lit manor house up the hill did not reveal her waiting at the gate. Christopher felt a surge of disappointment...when out of the darkness came a woman's figure.

As Hannah approached him, she said apologetically, "I should have known the children would have been too excited to sleep!"

Without another word, they came together, almost colliding, both laughing at their clumsiness; they then clasped each other so tightly neither could speak even if they wanted to.

They loved how their bodies fit together—like a design cut from a single folded piece of paper, Hannah once suggested. She was almost as tall as him; in fact, she had always been almost as tall as him, going back to the time when she was sixteen and he was nineteen and they had first embraced. They had happily agreed a long time ago that it was a very comfortable feeling being together like this.

They did separate enough to talk. "The Tattoo will be beat at ten o'clock, so I have about an hour. And you?"

"I told Missus Alexander that I would like to take a walk when the children had been put down, and she was agreeable.

"They're a wonderful family...oh Chris!—"

"Keep talking, Hannah, I'm listening." He was nuzzling her neck at her hairline, smelling the rich oils and lapping at small beads of sweat, which tasted like the inner moisture of a woman.

"Well, anyway...oh, that does feel good..." Breathing heavier now, Hannah interrupted herself, "Don't stop!...ah, the Alexanders are a wonderful family. Mister Alexander is very polite and easy going. Missus Alexander is a lot like Rachel—strong-willed but caring in a sort of defensive way, if you know what I mean.

"And the children are...well—they're like any children, needing a mother...or someone who they can trust like their mother—"

Christopher saw the suddenly distressed expression on Hannah's face and knew she must be thinking about the Crabbe children, whom she felt she had betrayed by running away. He wanted to say something comforting, but did not want to chance enlarging *that* wound.

Instead, he asked about Mister Alexander, curious to know something about the private side of a man many Marylanders considered a remarkable person. Lawyer, businessman, gentleman farmer, Robert Alexander was an early leader of the patriot cause. He was elected to the Maryland Convention, the province's extralegal political body before independence, then selected to be a member of Maryland's delegation to the Continental Congress. He would surely have been a signer of the Declaration of Independence had he not badly injured a foot which forced him to retire to his family manor at the Head of Elk.

"...So we won't be going back and forth between here and Baltimore," Hannah sighed. "I'm told it's because of Mister Alexander's poor ankle, but I really haven't seen it pain him that much...ah, well, hopefully, you'll be returning in a few short months."

After a few more statements regarding her new life as a house manager for the Alexander family, Hannah was finished with most of what she wanted to say to Christopher on the eve of his departure. She had thought about this a lot in the last few days, wanting to say something special, but having no idea what that might be.

What she ended up saying was, "It's selfish, I know, but I don't want you to go off to war."

Christopher, too, had practiced his goodbye speech, meant to be rich in feeling; but like Hannah, it didn't work out the way he planned it.

"'Tis worth it, Hannah. Independence means you'll be free, perhaps as soon as this fall—or early winter at the latest. I spoke to a lawyer friend of Missus Goddard, who said the new state court can declare your bond null and void because the Reverend Crabbe is a traitor to Maryland. As soon as I return we will petition the court in Baltimore."

As they continued to talk quietly, with Christopher's departure lying in wait in the darkness of this night like a child's demons, Hannah suddenly stopped talking in mid-sentence. Her lower lip quivering, she looked like she was about to cry, but then gathered herself, even as Christopher was trying to comfort her.

"Enough said now, Chris Sims," and she placed two fingers on his lips. "I'm not goin' to have ye remembering me as a bawling girl when you're off campaigning. I want you to remember this goodbye in such a way that the next time you think ye have to make a decision on goin' without me—you'll never, ever leave me again!"

Hannah chuckled as Christopher fumbled with hooks and eyes. "Here, let me do that...."

3

MARCHING OFF TO WAR

I should not choose to march, but as I am engaged in this glorious cause, I am willing to go where I am called.
Christopher Sims,
in a letter to Hannah Williams

On the Road to Philadelphia
July 15-16, 1776

A T FOUR O'CLOCK IN THE MORNING, the signal was given for the battalion to begin its march to Philadelphia. Groggy, the sleep not even out of their eyes, they marched up the road leading from Elk River, through the town of Elk itself, which turned out to be a small cluster of less than a hundred brick houses braced on a steep incline, and out onto the main road to Philadelphia.

The battalion marched by files, two abreast. They were allowed to march at ease, which inevitably meant that the columns began to ripple back and forth like a field of wheat moving to the vagaries of the wind as men began to ease their way up or down the column to be with a friend or relative.

Despite the efforts of the noncommissioned officers, men horsed around, left the ranks to relieve themselves, or otherwise began to fall out of formation. In addition, hundreds of feet kicked up clouds of choking dust on this hot, dry July day, and thirsty men sipped increasingly on canteens or flasks filled with spirits. But despite the lack of proper discipline, the column made rapid progress on a road which was wide and in good condition.

They soon crossed into the newly independent state of Delaware, which appeared no different in appearance from the newly independent state they had just left. The road took the battalion through the small villages of Christiana and Newport. In these villages and all along the route, people flocked to see this handsome unit from Maryland, with its pretty square standard snapping in a fine wind, the sounds of soft fifes and cadenced drums, and the men stepping out to impress all the girls, who stood by the roadside to offer them cool milk to drink, as well as a little ambiguous talk.

In late afternoon, the battalion came to the town of Wilmington, a port town in Delaware, which lay precariously on the side of a steep hill overlooking the Delaware River. They marched down Market Street through the center of town, which struck them as having no particular appeal—just a scattering of houses, mostly of brick, braced on the sides of a hill, with no notable public buildings. Just outside of town, they camped for the night.

Continuing their march the next morning, they soon crossed into Pennsylvania.

Christopher found marching easy. While Terry was already footsore, it seemed to Christopher that it took less time traversing Delaware than it used to take to walk from his home to Hungerford's Tavern. The day was beautiful, the milk cool, and the girls pretty. His only complaint was the smothering dust raised by the hundreds of slogging feet in front of him tramping over a road whose surface was now ground to a fine powder.

By afternoon they came to a high ridge overlooking the Schuylkill River. From this vantage point, they saw a quiet brown river, not very wide, below a makeshift bridge beside a ferry. Looking toward Philadelphia, which was largely hidden by forest and orchards, Christopher could see a vague outline of the city four miles away.

Terry was excited by the prospect of seeing this grand city. "Philadelphia is second only to New York in size and population. I've heard that upwards of twenty thousand people live here."

Twenty thousand people in one place was simply beyond Christopher's comprehension. "What on earth do so many people do there?"

"Oh, everything." Terry said expansively. "It's a great port that lies near the center of the north-south trade routes and within fairly easy reach of the western settlements. And just look at the forests and farmlands around it—a man with a knack for commerce can get rich here." Indeed, Philadelphia was a successful town because it excelled in merchandising most of the staples of colonial trade.

Just then, orders came to descend to the riverbank by companies, crossing by squads over to the other side. The bridge turned out to be constructed of floating logs which supported a walkway of rough planks. They bounced across, while the planks bobbed in and out of the water, soaking their shoes and stockings. Laughing and jumping up and down to make sections wobble and buckle, they tried their best to submerge planks upon which one of the other squads was treading.

Once on the other side, Corporal Smith ordered them to wash their hands and faces, brush their clothes, and see to their equipment.

"We'll be marchin' into Philadelphia as proud Marylanders and proper soldiers. See to it."

The battalion, refreshed and stepping out in proper order, turned onto Market Street as it came to the outskirts of Philadelphia. Marching down this wide paved street, which at some point became High Street, they all looked in wonder at the magnificent residential and public buildings. All were made of brick and seemed to attest to the success of the city's entrepreneurial spirit. Further down High Street, they glimpsed the State House two streets over—again, an elegant brick building, adorned with paned glass and topped with white cupolas—where representatives of the United Colonies had recently declared America's independence from Great Britain.

A little further on, they passed by the City Market, a cavernous roofed brick structure, situated in the very middle of the street, bustling with activity. Walkways of stone on each side of the street were crowded with people. The residents, especially the women, were fashionably dressed, much more so than the people of Baltimore. Christopher and many of his comrades also saw their first church spire.

The battalion turned left on Front Street, near the Delaware River, and before long was halted in front of a building. They learned that this was the Bank Meeting House, belonging to the Society of Friends, and rumor was this would be their billet during the battalion's stay in Philadelphia.

"The battalion will be billeted here, Sergeant Major," Major Gist informed Sergeant Major Older.

"Here, sir? In a church?"

"Yes. Those are the orders. Battalion headquarters will be in the meeting house and the troops quartered in the back. There is an outbreak of the smallpox amongst the troops in the city and it has been deemed prudent to set us and other newly arrived units apart from those infected, who are encamped on the public squares."

The sergeant major looked toward the meeting house with a pained expression. "I hope this is not intended to punish the Quakers, Major."

Major Gist stopped and stared at him. "It may very well be just that, Jonathan. I don't know. But remember, *we* are at war, and there are only us and the enemy." The major saw no shades of gray.

4

AWAITING ORDERS

**Philadelphia, Pennsylvania
July 17, 1776**

"EIGH," EXCLAIMED ONE OF THE MEN. "Step to it, boys. This be prime duty, for sure." Christopher and his messmates, in deed, looked forward to the ration detail because it offered them the chance to wander around and enjoy the city.

As they followed the cart hired to carry their purchases onto Front Street and headed in the direction of High Street, the men were keen on seeing as much of this town as they could. They were trying to convince Corporal Smith, in charge of the detail, that it was worth the extra distance to go to the New Market down on Second Street to stretch the company's rations allowance.

"'Tis that a fact, now, Private Simon? And just where did you pick up this important intelligence since we arrived in town?"

Actually, Corporal Smith proved agreeable to 's suggestion since he, too, was interested in taking a tour of the city.

The detail plunged after the cart, which was parting the crowds on Front Street like Moses had parted the Red Sea.

The city was wide but had no depth. Even though Philadelphia had been carefully planned, it obviously had not developed exactly as its founders had envisioned it. The settled part of town ran inland only about a half mile. On the other hand, it extended upwards of a mile and a half along the Delaware River bank, and was packed with wharves and warehouses.

Still, the streets were straight as a plumb line, and even if the city wasn't the green city imagined as part of William Penn's holy experiment, it was a town of substantial brick buildings, wide streets and public greens.

The city was crowded with small houses of similar size, all built of the same rose-colored brick, and all looked alike except for doors, windows, dormers, and cornices, which differed remarkably, and, in fact, claimed, denoted social status.

In contrast to the comfortable residences, all of the homes crowding the alleys in this part of town were small, ramshackle dwellings, and the neighborhoods were chaotic. A large number of women were out on the doorsteps doing their house chores, having left their gloomy little houses for the light of day. Not all the streets were paved or had street lamps…and the air on this sunny July day was heavy with the stench of garbage, urine, and excrement. It was a different view of Philadelphia than they had seen marching down elegant High Street.

Their work done and the men thirsty, Corporal Smith allowed the detail to stop in for a mug at the Bag of Nails Tavern on Front Street, an establishment which reputedly had attractive barmaids with loose bodices.

The Bag of Nails tavern was a typical waterfront tavern which catered to seamen, ocean voyagers, and local sparks, and did not turn away any man as long as he had ready money. The group of men in hunting shirts drew no particular interest as they entered, though the barmaids closely watched the T.I.P. box.

"It stands for 'To Insure Promptness,'" explained Corporal Smith as he ostentatiously waved a coin before dropping it in the box. This brought a surge of service before one of them noticed that these men intended to pay in Maryland provincial currency.

In the colonies almost any form of money would do— shillings, pennies, dollars, pistareens, sous, johannes, even cut bits of some of these—as long as they were coins. When a lack of coins drove the colonies to print paper currency, their value was open to argument.

"A Mary-Land dollar? Well...I don't know," stated one jade, whose uncertainty caused her to send flying a hand belonging to one of the finest families of Maryland which had been roaming over her plump haunch.

This brought the barkeep, who, after examining the bills in question, reluctantly agreed to accept them—at a considerable discount, of course.

The Marylanders then happily spent what money they had on cheap, watered-down drinks and the placing of half-pennies deep down the pits of barmaids' bosoms. The women were round and soft enough, even if they weren't very pretty.

Mister Paine Pays A Call
July 18, 1776

From his room across Front Street, Thomas Paine had watched the column of soldiers stop in front of the Bank Meeting House. He could not make out the unit's standard and wondered if they were from another province. *Province,* he smiled and shook his head. *We are not provinces anymore! So what are we?* To be truthful, Paine had not given a lot of thought to this question. *Later,* he thought disinterestedly—later, there would be time enough to consider this.

Curious as to the identity of the soldiers, Paine put aside his work, and, leaving his room and bottle of brandy, walked across the street to the Bank Meeting House.

Christopher and Terry were on guard duty in front of the meeting house when they saw a tall, somberly dressed gentleman approach the gate. Mistaking him for a member of the Bank Meeting House congregation, Christopher intercepted him as he passed through the gate and informed him politely that the grounds were now under military authority.

The plainly dressed gentleman smiled, realizing what these young soldiers were thinking. "No, no—soldier, I'm not a Quaker, but a Philadelphian and a Patriot who wishes to welcome you to our fair city. Where are ye from?"

"The State of Maryland, sir," Christopher said proudly. It was one of the first times that he had used the term "state" to describe his homeland. "We're the Battalion of Maryland Regular Troops under Colonel Smallwood."

"Mary-Landers, by God. Isn't that wonderful," exclaimed the gentleman in true happiness. He used the old way of pronouncing the name of the province—meaning "Mary's Land"—the way it was used by the papist founders. It was said that this name actually referred to the Virgin Mary and not King William's Queen.

"Is your Colonel present?—Smallwood, did you say? I would like to pay my respects. The name is Thomas Paine."

Upon hearing the name, both of them stared at the man. The visitor was not an attractive man, but he did have a presence about him. In addition to being tall and plainly dressed—actually, poorly dressed—he had a great hooked nose, a small sensuous mouth, and ice blue eyes which could bore through metal.

"Sir," asked Terry sheepishly. "Would you be the Mister Paine of *Common Sense* fame?"

"Indeed, I am." Thomas Paine appeared delighted that his reputation was known to two Maryland privates. A common man who genuinely enjoyed the company of common people, he stopped to talk to these soldiers.

"You have read *Common Sense*, have you, lads? Well, we've now created this splendid new nation of America, with all the promise in the world. But the British resist our Congress's decision with force. So, what think ye, men, can we defeat the sixpenny soldiers of the tyrant?"

"Aye, sir, indeed we can!" Both Christopher and Terry were quickly caught up in Mister Paine's infectious enthusiasm.

"Mister Paine," Christopher ventured, "What do you believe independence will bring us?"

Paine leaned back and looked seriously at the two soldiers, as if he recognized that it would be upon men like them that the success or failure of the revolution would be decided.

"Independence provides you, and all Americans, with the opportunity to create a civilized society which will determine its government, rather than vice versa." In stating this, he became the stern lecturer who had penned the now famous pamphlet.

"Nations should be nothing more than a sovereign body of citizens who collectively govern themselves. How this is manifested is debatable, but the principle of *self*-determination is *not!* Such a civil society is not subject to the dictates of monarchs or birthrights.

"Americans don't need a government to allow them to do what they want to do anyway! If government does not serve the common good, why, then, the people ought to replace it."

Just then Major Gist walked up. "Major Gist, sir," said Christopher, as he saluted. "May I introduce you to Mister Paine, the author of *Common Sense*." Major Gist stopped before the group with a quizzical look on his face.

"You don't say? Are you indeed Mister Paine? My pleasure, sir," said Major Gist, doffing his hat.

"Your servant, sir. I came to pay my respects to the colonel of the regiment."

"Pray, allow me to introduce you." With that, Major Gist directed Paine to the front door. Paine turned and, with a smile, waved. "God bless you, men."

As Paine entered the meeting house, Christopher looked at Terry and said, "Mister Paine talks like he writes, don't you think, Terry?"

"Certainly does. Odd man—I wish I had a great passion..."

"Friendly, though," Christopher noted. "You'd have thought such a man would have no time for ordinary soldiers."

"Who's an 'ordinary' soldier, if I might ask? I'm a most extraordinary private, I am." Terry laughed and poked Christopher playfully in the stomach with the butt of his musket.

5

THE FLYING CAMP

We're headed for troble"
Lieutenant Joseph Hodgkins

Elizabeth Town, New Jersey
Late July 1776

AT ONE O'CLOCK on a late July afternoon, the Maryland Battalion marched out of Philadelphia on the Post Road to New York.

Five days later, foot weary from marching twenty miles a day, they arrived at their destination, which was Elizabeth Town, the largest town in New Jersey, located on a river with easy access to Newark Bay and the shipping lane to New York City.

"Where's the Flyin' Camp?" Terry asked in confusion, as he viewed a sizable town—but one bereft of a large military establishment. It seems he had envisioned a grand encampment with flags flying and large marquees for all the generals standing on a hill, with row after row of little white tents below for the rank and file. This was the vision of grand encampments he had in mind based exclusively on an engraving he had once seen of the English encampment on the eve of the Battle of Blenheim.

None of them was exactly sure what a flying camp should look like, and they had no ready answer to his question. Later, Corporal Smith would inform them that *they* were the Flying Camp, and, with the exception of the local militia, the only troops in the town.

Most of the regiment was billeted in the numerous houses abandoned by their owners who had fled to the interior when the British Army landed on nearby Staten Island. Captain Smith's Company, however, was barracked in St. John's Parsonage, a low-slung brick building situated on the river. The parsonage and St. John's Church had been abandoned by its Anglican rector and many of his parishioners, who remained loyal to the Crown and had fled to British-held Staten Island.

"I just hope we don't get in the habit of billeting in places of worship," sighed Davey Lynn, as he staked his claim to a bench for his bed, guiltily removing a dozen or so books of Common Prayer which he placed on the floor.

"Amen to that," was the chorus.

As if to warn them that they were in a theater of war, the British batteries on Staten Island fired on the American fortifications at Elizabeth Point, opposite the small bridge that connected the island to the mainland. The hollow boom of cannon were followed, for those close enough to hear, by the sound of whirling balls as they flew toward the American works, followed by a smacking sound as their impact threw up a splash of muddy water and spume when the heavy balls hit the marsh flats.

Far too close, the cannonading caused the Marylanders to drop what they were doing and scramble to form a line of battle. Wide-eyed, pulling on hunting shirts and slinging cartridge boxes over their shoulders, the battalion nervously huddled in a semblance of order expecting imminent attack, anxiously awaiting orders from officers, most of who were in a similar state of confusion.

Not knowing what to do, they stood uncertainly in ranks, until a New Jersey militia officer arrived to advise them that the British were not mounting an attack, but appeared to be firing their cannon for the simple purpose of "amusing" their foe.

"Only the damn'd English would come up with such a word to describe harassment," accused Terry.

Laughing, the Jersey officer said, "Whether you find it amusin' or not, 'tis nothin' to concern yourselves about. Good Jerseymen caught every single one of those balls after a hop or two just to make sure not a-one would bound into one of our brethren from Mary-Land. Just wanted to let you know." And off he went, still chuckling to himself, as his old horse clopped down the road, its tail swishing angrily at huge black flies.

Shaken, Smallwood's Marylanders drew down, stowing their muskets and accessories, and returned to their fatigue duties. They did so with a great deal of relief, but with the sense that their time was coming.

"They say the King's ships are so thick in the Bay that their masts resemble a forest of trimmed pine trees."

"'Tis also said that the British army on Staten Island numbers thirty thousand," Christopher noted, now with a hint of awe, remembering his rather casual reference to the same figure at Aunt Jane's party. It's amazing how proximity greatly inflates the importance of an enemy's numbers.

"And all that separates us from them is that ferry down by Halstead's Point and a few small cannon," he remarked with a nervous voice—in effect, admitting that British cannonballs could make a considerable dent in a man's head without even hitting it.

"But there's also the Battalion of Maryland Regulars which is here to stem the tide," offered Terry, with a wicked smile on his face.

"*That's* exactly what I'm worried about, Terry...."

****

The battalion would spend almost three weeks at Elizabeth Town, much to their joy and despite the close threat from the British on Staten Island. Elizabeth Town was known as a town of pretty girls, and it quickly became clear that they found the men from Maryland intriguing, with their easy Southern ways and soft speech.

"There must be something amorous in the very air of this town, Jonathan," noted Major Gist to Sergeant Major Jonathan Older with good humor. "I fear that there is a soft infection here which will lay all of us low!"

"Nicely put, Mordecai," Sergeant Major Older laughed appreciatively. "I've never seen so many bare asses beneath quaking bushes as I've seen here. It must be the uncertainty of war—it certainly can't be the ladies' Puritan instincts," referring to the town's New England character.

Beyond this happy plight, Elizabeth Town was a pretty place of perhaps three hundred dwellings and twelve hundred inhabitants, founded by New Englanders, who brought with them not only their insufferable Congregationalist ideas, but also a charter of liberties that gave them a republican outlook on government.

A soldier's time here was not all taken up with the tender passions or quaffing. Indeed, knowing that a battle with the British was now inevitable, there was a sense of urgency to the twice-daily drills—which made them all queasy as hell.

Sufficient ammunition was finally distributed so that each company could actually conduct a live firing, and they badly frightened themselves with their first volley *en masse*. Each platoon fired as instructed, the sharp, concentrated popping striking their ears like the sound of pebbles pelting a coffin; then bilious gray clouds of gunsmoke enshrouded them in an evil darkness, as the volleys rolled in succession down the line. Very few of them had ever experienced such a hellish fury.

With their nerves shaken, they left the drill field, changed forever.

"Good Gawd almighty! Are we expected to stand up *in front* of that?"

6

THE BOAR GETS HIS CHANCE

Our Enemies have been but too successful
in employing a Sett of Villians...
Isaac Sterling, in a report to
the Maryland Council of Safety

Elizabeth Town, New Jersey
July 29, 1776

ON THOSE INCREASINGLY RARE OCCASIONS
when the battalion was allowed a little free time, groups of
them would wander around the town, mostly honeying with the
girls or drinking at the local taverns.

During those brief afternoons of freedom and nonchalance,
Christopher would enjoy walking past the modest Dutch houses
with their graceful gambrel roofs, waving at the girls sitting on
their porches, as they walked from the parsonage to their
favorite watering hole, which was named the Red Lion Inn.

The Red Lion was next to a screeching but picturesque old
mill, served reasonably priced drinks, and had a pretty barmaid
who appeared to like Terry. She was chief among a couple of
local girls on whom had his eye; but, to be sure, he had to hurry
since more and more families with their attractive young
daughters were loading their possessions on wagons or carts and
heading inland to escape the coming battle.

"I like this town," Terry announced contentedly as he sipped
on a beer on one of their outings. "It's...well—it's...an elegant
town." He said this as he watched the girl of his immediate

desire carrying mugs from table to table, giving him a smile every time she caught his eye.

"Terry, there's nothin' to this town except a swarm of lovelorn women."

"Why, Christopher, you wouldn't be accusing me of being an amatorculist, would you?" Terry Christopher a pained look.

"If that means a 'rake,' certainly not. I know you to be a man of high moral standards. It's just that these Jersey women are so in need of the soft ministrations of a Marylander—I don't want them takin' advantage of your desire to please people, Terry," Christopher said tongue-in-cheek.

Sparring such as this went on until the two of them returned to barracks or Terry would casually excuse himself to pay a call on nature—a double-edged sword if ever there was one.

On one of those evenings when Terry became otherwise occupied, Christopher, his mind mellowed by drink, returned alone to the barracks. He walked past the Presbyterian Church, the largest and most stately structure in town, momentarily pausing to admire its high spire and clock tower, when a group of three men came out of the shadows ahead of him.

Assuming they were some men from the battalion out carousing, he was about to pass them with a comradely greeting when two of them suddenly grabbed him by the arms—while, at the same time, the third man stepped up and drove a fist into his stomach.

He didn't recognize the two who grabbed him, but was very much aware of their foul odor and the stench of gunpowder. For some reason the only thought that came into his mind was, *"Why, they must've been at the practice firing the other day."*

Doubled over, gasping for breath, his head was then violently knocked back by an upward blow which caught him clean under the chin. His head snapped back, then forward in an unnatural nod. Now semiconscious, he tasted blood and felt like puking. The men pinioning his arms roughly prevented him from falling, and a hand pulled at his neckband, fingernails tearing down his neck, his chin was forced up, and his shirt torn.

His glazed eyes were barely able to focus, but in a dreamlike stupor he was able to see a face thrust against his, smiling contemptuously.

"Before I kill ya, farmer, I just wanted ya to know I killed that woman of yours—"

Christopher tried to understand, his head swimming. Did he hear right? "What?" he asked stupidly.

Now impatient, the man spoke carefully, as if speaking to an idiot. "I killed your woman. Fucked her good, then killed her. Ya understand now?"

"Hannah...?" Christopher couldn't believe what he had just heard. "Hannah?" he repeated.

"Hannah? Who tha hell...?" The man turned to one of his confederates. "Knock some sense into this man."

The man happily sent a well-aimed knee into Christopher's groin, then a bare knuckle blow to the temple—

The pain was furious and the last blow caused an explosion of swirling colors behind now sightless eyes...with the faint sound of men's voices somewhere in the distance, he finally spiraled into complete unconsciousness.

"Aw, shit. Ya hit 'im too goddam'd hard, ya idiot." The man was beside himself. He had taken out his huge pocketknife, ready for the coup de grace, which he envisioned as a graceful upward arc, slicing skin and muscle—but not now.

"I can't carve 'im up like this," he complained.

"Wake the bastard," he ordered.

****

Thomas Boarman, alias The Boar, hadn't joined the damn'd army to kill the Sims fella. It just turned out that way. In fact, Boarman had been given a choice by the town authorities: join the army *or* go to jail. He had been caught and charged with a couple of petty crimes in Baltimore and folks who knew—and fear'd him wanted him put away. Actually, Boarman considered himself lucky. If the authorities knew half the things he had got away with so far, they'd have hanged him for sure.

One of the things he'd gotten away with was murdering Alma whatshername. Ah, but that was sweet—fucking, killing and a cash re-ward....

So, instead of being punished for his transgressions, The Boar joined the army. And joining the army, he discovered, wasn't all that bad. Being in the army offered the possibility of killin', rape, and plunder, same as crime.

Thomas Boarman had enjoyed thinking about killing Sims, just as he had enjoyed thinking about killing the cunt. He wasn't called The Boar because of his appearance—he was not unattractive; no, he was The Boar because of his shiv. Like the boar, he used his knife same as those razor-sharp tusks in a powerful upward arch to whip through sinew and muscle and organ, blood flying everywhere. It was a thing of beauty, he always thought.

A while back, he had been contacted by a "Mister Benjamin," who made it clear that he was a man of mystery. 'Pears "Mister Benjamin" knew he had been friends of sorts with The Vulture. "Mister Benjamin" informed him as to who had killed The Vulture, then offered to pay him in Spanish milled dollars if he could prove he killed a slattern named Alma Lynch and her squeeze, Christopher Sims, both murderers of a good man—as "Mister Benjamin" referred to The Vulture with a straight face—as well as being enemies of the Crown.

Easy enough. The Alma woman could be found at St. Paul's Church. One night he simply abducted her as she went from church to rectory. He took her to a bad part of town, where he had his will with her, then put her out of her misery and tossed her carcass into the Basin. He showed Mister Benjamin her St. Christopher medal, which had her name inscribed on the back, and collected his re-ward.

Nailing her man was more difficult. He had got her to tell him his name, Christopher Sims; and where he lived, a rooming house on Lovely Lane; but it took him a while to realize that this Sims fella was also a soldier in the battalion, with Captain Smith's company here in Baltimore, and, he reckoned, easy prey. He had an opportunity when he thought Sims and one of his comrades frequented a gin shop on the Basin. He and a couple of his mates attacked 'em one night. Much to his disgust, though, turned out it wasn't Sims at all, but two of his messmates.

Starting over, The Boar was working on an opportunity to strike when all the troops were confined to camp and shortly thereafter took ship to Head of Elk. Chances to take care of Sims became hard to come by after that, until the battalion was quartered in Elizabeth Town.

****

"Did he say something?"

It was the next day, and a worried Terry Simon had been hovering over Christopher for the better part of the morning. Christopher had been brought to the camp hospital, a vacant house with a few straw pallets for the sick, by some of Veazy's men.

One of the orderlies had alerted Terry to the incident. Hurrying to the hospital, he found his comrade bruised, bloody, and semi-conscious, mumbling about Hannah's untended garden and how it needed tending.

Vying with a jumble of thoughts, Christopher had heard the question but could not identify the questioner. He desperately wanted to tell the person to talk to him direct and not ignore him as if he wasn't there at all. He tried again to speak, but his words were muffled by the wad of cloth stuffed in his mouth.

"Hey, his eyes are open—Christopher! *Christopher!* Can ye hear us, man?"

Coming somewhat to his senses, he realized that it wasn't a rag in his mouth which interfered with speech, but a hugely swollen jaw. Pursing lips that were as dry and cracked as ancient leather, he tried to make his words smaller—small enough to fit through the pinhole he had managed to form through swollen lips—and, with an effort, expelled them.

Exhausted, he lay quiet, breathing heavily, wondering if he had said anything at all.

Terry did not really understand any of the noises dribbling out of Christopher's mouth along with some bloody spittle. But a broad smile appeared on Terry's face as he exclaimed, "He's fine. That's one of the more intelligent things I've heard Chris Sims say."

Turning suddenly serious, Terry looked down at his friend, noting the swollen face and lips, marked by deep purple blotches and dried blood, and a nose now battered.

"Chris," he said, "Do you know who did this?"

He nodded and tried to shoot the name through the pinhole. It came out as "Barman."

"Barman?" Then it came to : "Boarman, you say? Thomas Boarman!" Noting Christopher's nod of agreement. "Well, now...he and two of his confederates have gone and deserted. Yup...disappeared yesterday. Discovered missing after Taps."

Caleb gave his usual snort. "Told 'em so...told 'em he was responsible for my and Walker's beating. The man should've been put down like a crazed animal a long time ago. Now he's someone else's problem."

Christopher tried to add some detail to the incident. "Alma...killed. Me...Alma..."

"He what? Alma? He killed her?" Terry shook his head, not sure that he had heard Christopher right. He wanted to ask more questions, but noticing his friend's discomfort, Terry cautioned, "Don't you try to speak, Christopher. You took a bad beating and you need to rest." The others nodded in agreement. Feverish and tired of trying to talk sense, Christopher relented and drifted off.

Christopher had indeed taken a beating. Besides deep bruises and a broken nose, he had also suffered a cracked cheekbone. But that was just his head...additionally, he had some sore ribs and a pair of balls the size of melons.

With all that, he considered himself fortunate—indeed, very fortunate. He was badly hurt and would undoubtedly carry some scars for the rest of his life, but he was alive and it looked like he would recover.

A little while later, he realized that his Spanish milled dollar had been taken—more accurately, ripped from his neck, as he felt the burning pain and rubbed a nasty welt on the back of his neck.

Despite the loss of his lucky coin, his comrades agreed that he was lucky indeed. "No doubt you'd have been dispatched to eternal oblivion if it hadn't been for some of Cap'n Veazy's men, who came upon the scene and scared off your attackers."

Yeah, he'd been lucky. Right now, though, he had to get well enough to march with the battalion. Doctor Dashiel was of the strong opinion that this wouldn't be possible, given the lack of time. Glancing at Terry and Caleb, he stated matter of factly, "Oh, I suppose Private Sims might be able to march—say, *next spring.*

That same day, Terry reported to Mordacai Gist, the battalion's second major. Gist, along with Christopher and , and with the help of Alma Lynch, had played a major role in thwarting what was a major loyalist plot to undermine Maryland's support for independence by kidnapping one of its members to Congress.

"...but Christopher is recovering, though he will not be able to march with the battalion to New York, sir."

"I'm sorry to hear that, Private Simon—oh, let's dispense with military formality, Terrence." Gist sighed. "...This whole affair has been costly. Well, we know now what happened to poor Alma and who was responsible. I'm sorry this man Boarman escaped but I'll have an advertisement put in the Pennsylvania and Maryland papers and, hopefully, he'll be apprehended. We don't know who put him up to this, do we?

"No, sir. Obviously someone involved in the plot, perhaps one of those priests with the S.P.G.

"Shows they're still active, too. I'll send word back to the Convention, warning them to remain vigilant."

Gist rubbed his forehead, a gesture Terry and everyone who knew Gist recognized as a change in mood.

"Well, then...we've done all we can to defeat our enemy's chicanery at home. Now it's time to concentrate on winning our independence on the battlefield. That will be all, Terrence. God be with you."

7

MISSUS McBRIDE COMES TO THE RESCUE

From Elizabeth Town to New York,
On the Post Road
August 9-10, 1776

SEETHING, Christopher was finally able to speak his mind and be understood on the subject of being left behind. "No, I will not allow this to happen! I am marching with the battalion."

"You're not marchin' anywhere, Christopher," Terry said patiently. "You need to stay put here and then catch up to us later. What difference will it make?"

"Terry," Christopher said quietly, "I didn't come this far to miss the great battle that's coming. I'll be ready—I swear I will."

"Christopher, you can't march with us, you know that…and riding with the wagons will impair your healing. That's what Doctor Dashiel says. It's as simple as that."

"To hell with that! I'm goin'…Now leave me be, Terry…."

To his bitter disappointment, Christopher was assigned to the invalid detachment which would remain in Elizabeth Town. During the ten days following the attack, he had made notable progress; but Doctor Dashiel was adamant that he was in no condition to accompany the battalion.

Christopher did not accept this situation with any grace at all. On the ninth of August, Smallwood's Battalion was ordered to New York City; and on that same day, he as good as blackmailed Terry into helping him absent himself without leave.

"Terry, I know that I can't march with the regiment, but I sure as hell can travel by wagon. Don't argue with me on this, Terry. I need your help. Now, I know you and Missus McBride—damn it, Terry, I'm not criticizing your morals—just listen, will you? All you have to do is convince Missus McBride that I gotta ride in her cart...Do that, will you?"

Mary McBride was a lively young woman who was married to a dour private in the Fourth Company and was a woman on the rolls, receiving half-rations in return for cooking and washing for the officers of her husband's company. Terry and she had been *afoutering* back in Baltimore, and Christopher was desperately hoping that he could parlay their lewd behavior into an unauthorized ride to New York.

"Christopher, you're putting me in an awkward position here. Now, Mary and I are on good terms, but I can't ask her to put herself in a position for which she might be court-martialed for insubordination."

"Terry," Christopher said in exasperation, "all I'm askin' is that you and Missus McBride look the other way. See? Neither of you know anything about this—understand? On the other hand, I can't have her thinking me a common thief and screaming bloody murder if she sees me skulking around her cart."

Terry considered this, and decided he would help. "I'll have a word with Mary this evening."

Terry was apparently able to convince Missus McBride to go along with this mad scheme because she consented to hearing Christopher out on his plan....

"...So ye can see, Missus McBride," he explained to her, "I won't be any trouble; and if—understand, just if—I happened to be discovered during the trip, you'd only have to deny any knowledge of my errant behavior."

"And when we arrive at New York City, what are your intentions, Private Sims?"

"Why, to turn myself in to Corporal Smith. The whole point is to get up to New York. After that, I figure there's no reason I can't rejoin the company. They'll surely need fighters."

Mary McBride looked hard at him. With her arms folded across her breasts and an upward tilt of her face, she looked at his eyes, measuring him. Finally, with a snort indicating her reservations, she decided in favor of his sincerity.

"Aye, Private Sims, be at me cart as soon as the drums sound the March." She nodded curtly to Terry and walked away.

Mary McBride agreed to help get Christopher to New York because she believed him. Mary McBride might have been of the poorer sort, uneducated and using low speech, and she might have had low morals; but she was a passionate revolutionary who looked upon the provincial gentry—patriots though they be—and their rules with the same disdain she held for the English and their damned rules…all of 'em meant to deprive the common people of their right as freemen to do as they chose. For the good of the Cause, rules had to be broken. After all, she would say, the Cause was all about breakin' rules, wasn't it?

Well before sunrise, the drums beat The March and the regiment moved out. Christopher quickly made his way to the wagon park and found Mary standing behind the cart. Motioning him to get in the back, she threw a tent leaf over him and before long, the cart lurched forward.

He felt the cart, bumping and jolting along, moving across a rough field and then the slipping of the wheels as they bounced into the furrows of a defined road. For a time he heard the wheels grinding against the ruts and felt the frequent nudges in the laden cart's direction as its wheels hit against the ridges in the road.

Shortly, Mary lifted the canvas and motioned him to come out. She was perched on a folded tent, her back against the side of the cart. The driver was walking with the single horse which was drawing the cart, carrying a switch which he used sparingly to prod the horse to keep up its pace.

"Don't mind old Joseph there. He's been hired to haul this load for the battalion and he don't care beyond anything but his old nag, the cart, and the coin he's paid." She thrust a water bottle at him, which turned out to be rum. Their ensuing conversation was intended to occupy them as the cart slowly covered the miles to New York.

"My man joined up back in January. He sorely needed a job and bein' a common soldier at more than five dollar a month was prime work. But I could see him spending his pay on likker and gamblin', leavin' me with little choice but to sell men a sniff o' me rosier for a penny or two. So I thought to myself, 'Why not join up yourself, Mary, you've got nothin' more pressin' to do'—oh, I know you gentlemen don't understan' this."

"Missus McBride—Mary, then…and I'm Christopher—I'm no gentleman. I'm a sot-weed farmer from Frederick County who moved to the city."

"Good," Mary said, "'cause gentlemen mostly aren't worth a turd. Anyway, I made my mark on the paper—why, sure, Christopher, I enlisted jus' like you. Each company in the battalion is allowed three women on the rolls to wash and cook an' such. No whorin', mind you—women on the rolls don't fuck for blunt."

Christopher had no experience with women such as Mary. She came from a different world than his and he could only make a stab at establishing a common interest.

"At first I thought you didn't approve of what I was doin', Mary."

Mary glanced at him with the hard, appraising look which she saved for questionable situations. "I don't hold with a man who won't do his patriotic duty—shirkers, cowards…can't abide 'em. You, though, appear'd different. I took a chance on you, I did.

"And I thank you for it, Mary."

"I believe mightily in the Cause, Corporal Sims," she stated formally, reminding him of his military status and duty. "Creatin' a country where plain people have a say in things—jus' like the well-off—who aren't their betters any more…jus' richer, which I don't mind. 'We hold these truths to be self-evident…that all men are created equal.' That's in our Declaration of Independence. Now I know that isn't true—men aren't created equal…and probably the men who wrote it don't truly believe it. But in statin' in such bold terms that the people have the right to choose their own government, why us common people are bound to have a better chance in life."

Acting the sophisticate, Christopher asked, "You've read *Common Sense*, then?"

"Nay, I haven't. Can't read. But I heard enough so I can support every word of it. Tom Paine's his name, right? And he's a Britisher?" Looking questioningly at Christopher and getting his nodding approval, she went on. "Well, if a Britisher has to leave his own country and family and come to America to obtain a better life, then you know we're on the right track. Right?" She didn't look questioning at him this time.

Bouncing along in that little cart, his injuries throbbing, unsure what tomorrow would bring, Christopher wondered at the shared radicalism between an illiterate slattern, the well-off son of a Baltimore merchant family, and a backcountry tobacco farmer....

It was neither a long nor difficult trip to Paulus Hook and the regimental wagon train arrived at the ferry landing over to New York by midmorning. The companies were already boarding a small fleet of flat-bottomed boats which were plying back and forth across a wide river, referred to variously as either the North or the Hudson River.

From the bank, Christopher looked across the water at his first view of New York City. He could not make out much from this distance; but he did see a remarkable concentration of buildings, as well as Fort George with the governor's house looming above its stone ramparts. Standing there on the Jersey bank, he was surprised to count seventeen—*seventeen!*—church spires, since he had heard New York was supposed to be the most sinful city in the New World. He said as much to Mary, who retorted disgustedly, "And I expect that's exactly what you're lookin' forward to, Corporal Sims."

****

After arriving in the city, Mary gave her appraisal: "Ain't a pretty town," sniffed Mary, as their cart clacked along the cobbled streets. "Not grand like Philadelphie, and there be no excitement."

The city was strangely quiet. They had seen only a few merchantmen with their tall masts tied up at the wharves, their decks and the landings empty of freight. It also lacked the strange, exciting smells and people in odd garb which characterize a true seaport. There were enough people and carts out and about, but instead of bespeaking a rich commerce, they were plainly townspeople, their carts loaded with household possessions, preparing to flee the city. And a goodly number of stores and houses were boarded up.

It hadn't occurred to them that an impending battle could snuff out the life of a great seaport.

They continued their journey across town, passing the Commons, a vast triangular field in the middle of the city filled with troops drilling in front of the city barracks and a large, handsome brick building which was, in fact, the city jail. Shortly thereafter, they arrived at a vacant lot near Bowery Road, which had been assigned as the campground for the battalion.

As the cart rolled into camp, the regiment was already busy marking company streets and erecting tents, the standard of the regiment streaming proudly in a soft summer breeze.

All Christopher could do was thank Mary for her understanding and help. With her rather curt blessing, which was more a stern lecture on his patriotic duty, he went in search of the company and Corporal Smith, to whom he reported with as much dignity as possible, seeing that he had been absent without leave.

"Private Sims did *what?*

"Good Lord, Jeremiah, what do we do with this? He absented himself from his assigned unit to accompany the battalion to the theater of war! Why can't this Private Sims follow orders?" Sergeant Major Older pondered this one, and finally stated, "He ought to be punished—if not...." The sergeant major let his intended threat of a court-martial trail off because he simply did not know what to do.

Major Gist, who had been listening to Corporal Smith's explanation as to just why Christopher Sims had insisted on following the regiment to New York, piped up. "So, Corporal Smith, if what you say is true, Private Sims absented himself without leave in order to be with his company for the upcoming battle? Is that correct?"

Corporal Smith agreed that, indeed, that was the case.

Worried about deserters going the other way, Major Gist found this particular situation refreshing, and he was actually chuckling when he asked, "So, do we have him shot for *not* malingering?" He winked at Captain Smith, who grinned back.

Not at all happy with the major's cavalier approach to insubordination, Sergeant Major Older retorted, "Wasn't it you who told me, Major, that we can't wait until we're on the battlefield to instill discipline?"

A pause. "Right you are, Sergeant Major," the major admitted. "But do look at this with a sense of humor, won't you?" He grinned at the sergeant major.

This calmed the sergeant major down enough so he could put things in proper perspective: 'Well, then, Corporal Smith, I understand that Private Sims has shown a talent for rolling cartridges, so let's again assign him to that duty. In addition," the sergeant major paused dramatically, "let's have him not only roll cartridges, but also do duty as the major's runner, which is even more onerous work."

Jonathan Older smirked at Mordecai Gist.

They all had a good laugh over it.

Corporal Smith could hardly keep a straight face when he informed Christopher of his punishment...and admonished him to obey orders in the future.

Christopher took this with a fair sense of humor in front of his comrades since it appeared that it would not preclude him from rejoining his company.

"Hell, the rate I'm goin', I'll have rolled every cartridge fired by the army in the upcoming battle."

New York City
Mid to Late August 1776

Even as Christopher was kept busy for long hours doing his punishment, the American army was overflowing the city of New York. Other city lots around their encampment were being used as campgrounds by various American regiments, while still others, more fortunate than the Marylanders, were billeted in vacant houses: There were troops from New England, Pennsylvania, New York, New Jersey, Delaware, and Virginia here. They wore a variety of clothing—some in hunting shirts, the militia in their civilian suits, while a number of units were actually uniformed in regimental coats of brown or blue trimmed in various colors.

Truthfully, it was a motley horde that filled up the greens and vacant lots and houses of the city. Not only did they not look warlike in their appearance, they didn't appear particularly martial in their activities. While some units drilled, most of the men seemed to spend their time in their ragtag camps playing cards or ball, or, more usually, drinking.

Christopher had no idea what he expected to see, but the Continental Army he saw did not fire his martial ardor.

The battalion was assigned ground next to a fine-looking regiment from Delaware. The Marylanders were immediately jealous of their smart uniforms of dark blue faced in red, white smallclothes, and jaunty leather caps with high peaks ornamented in gilt. Their nickname was said to be "the Delaware Blues," but Caleb and David soon learned different.

"They actually call themselves the 'Blue Hen Chickens.' Can ye believe that? But, in truth, 'taint a bad name for a regiment," noted David, "'cus they got these fightin' hens—I swear to God!—which are nigh unbeatable. According to one of the Delawares, these hens go for the balls an' there ain't a cock'll stand up to 'em—er, so to speak."

"Sounds like most women I know'd," said one of the men, and the group laughed, slapping at their thighs.

Now this interested almost all of the Marylanders, because they fancied themselves great lovers of cockfighting.

"Say, can we see these hens in action?"

"Sure. Every night over at the Delawares' camp."

While bivouacked in New York City, the regiment continued to perfect its martial skills. In between the constant drilling, though, they were allowed to wander around the nearby encampments. Surprisingly, perhaps, the soldiers in general showed very little interest in meeting their brothers-in-arms from the other provinces; and they had little contact with any of them—that is, other than the Delawares.

One of the more adventuresome Delaware men they met noted this phenomenon.

"You'd 'ave thought all of us would be clappin' each other on the back and being brotherly, but that ain't the case. 'Tis singular, indeed, but many of the men won't even talk to those from their own province lest they be from the same county. Of course, we generally aren't much better but that doesn't make it understandable, does it?

"I can say," he went on, "that the Connecticutters—they be right o'er there," and he pointed to a disorganized campsite across the way, "are considerable imbibers. Speaks well of 'em and they do offer a swig to a stranger, but they don't sing even when quaffing. Queer men," the Delaware concluded, shaking his head in perplexity.

"And we call ourselves 'The United Colonies?'" Christopher asked, understanding exactly what the Delaware soldier meant.

8

THE COMING STORM

And I hope we shall be able to give them such a Reception as shall show Mankind that there is a difference between Troops that fight only for their Masters and 6d. Sterling a day, and those that fight for their Religion, their Laws, their Liberties, their Wives & Children & everything else that is dear to them.

Captain Smith in a letter
to his father, August 22, 1776

New York and Brooklyn
August 22-27, 1776

MAJOR GIST ENTERED, hurriedly ducking under the rolled-up sides of the marquee tent.

"Jonathan, we're being sent over to Long Island." He made this statement with a calmness he did not feel, as he seated himself on the canvas camp stool at his field desk.

The interior of the tent, despite a light breeze, was stuffy and smelled of hot canvas, crushed grass, and mud. Sweating, the men stripped to their shirts, as small flies flittered about them.

The sergeant major gave Christopher a distracted but not unfriendly nod. Major Gist interrupted what he was saying to ask Christopher for paper and pen, as well as cups and the bottle of whiskey, before resuming his conversation with the sergeant major.

"Aye, Jonathan, His Excellency has made up his mind that the main British attack will be made on Long Island, not Manhattan. He views the situation there as 'dangerous.' We're being sent over to join General Alexander's brigade, which I understand is holding an advanced position outside the Brooklyn defenses, and even now is skirmishing with a large enemy force."

"Outside the defenses, Major? What are the dispositions?"

"As it was explained to me, we've established a defensive line on western Long Island where the island forms a neck closest to the bottom of Manhattan. We've constructed a line of forts across this neck which runs from the East River on the north to a place called Gowanus Bay on the Hudson River side."

He hurriedly drew a rough sketch, showing the Brooklyn line roughly shaped as a horse's head. Outside of that he scribbled in a line running across Long Island itself, which he indicated was a line of hills forming an abrupt rampart, impassable except by a few narrow defiles. "Something like that—I'm not a cartographer." Gist smiled self-effacingly at the sergeant-major. "But, anyway, we're afforded a second, natural outer works." Jamming the pen in its holder, he said, "What really matters is that it appears we're goin' to fight the great battle there.

"So," he went on, "General Alexander's brigade has been placed *outside* the defensive lines of Brooklyn Neck, and our regiment and the Delawares are being sent over to reinforce him. This is supposed to be an honor. His Excellency wants the best troops in the army to man the advanced positions."

"It's what we've prepared for, Mordecai."

"Aye, Jonathan, but sobering enough now that it's upon us."

With flags flying, the regiment was soon marching proudly through a quiet, near empty city to the embarkation point on the East River. Their route took them south down Broad Street, a wide avenue lined with shops, warehouses, and high brick residences, many with their windows and doors boarded. They soon passed through the older part of the city, that nearest the southern tip of Manhattan; a part of the city which had retained the flavor and appearance of a Dutch commercial port, most noticeably in the style of having the gabled ends of the houses rather than the fronts face the street.

The regiment finally arrived at the bottom of Maiden Lane and the Manhattan terminus of the Long Island ferry. Other troops, including the Delawares, who waved and shouted friendly insults at the Marylanders, were standing in loose formation waiting to embark in the boats that would take them over to Long Island.

As each vessel pushed off, the soldiers onboard gave three huzzahs which were returned by the raucous crowd of laborers, bawds, apprentices, and urchins who lined the water's edge.

As they neared the stone steps down to the ferry slip, they saw up ahead several unheaded casks and men reaching in as they passed by.

"Sea bread, men," said Corporal Smith. "Take as much as you can carry. Who knows when we'll get our next rations."

"Sea bread? What is it?" Christopher asked.

"Well, lad," explained a man from another regiment, "it actually be made of canel and pease meal and it's somethin' ye can eat if you're hungry enough. If not, ye can use it for a gun flint." The man and his comrades laughed knowingly and moved off.

With a shrug, Christopher and his comrades stuffed handfuls of these crackers in their haversacks. Moments later, someone was heard to say, "Hey! The man was right...they is good for flints." This was followed by the distinct splashes of hard objects hitting water.

Following the crossing, the regiment quickly formed near the old Ferry Tavern, which most of them passed longingly as they marched up the steep ascent to Brooklyn Heights, then through the tiny village of Brooklyn Parish.

Beyond the village, they looked out over a small plain which was the campground for thousands of troops—formed into numerous regiments and even more numerous companies, each marked by colorful standards and pennants. Beyond the drilling formations, the canvas tents, and the lines of cooking fires was a commanding hill upon which stood a small fort with three cannons, and beyond that, mounds of fresh earth and more cannons which stretched as far as they could see. This, Christopher thought, was the encampment of a great army.

The regiment was told to rest, while Major Gist would go in search of General Alexander and further orders.

"Private Sims, you will report to Major Guest," ordered Corporal Smith. "Move out, smartly now."

He found Major Gist dressed in his red and buff regimentals. "Sir, Private Sims reporting."

"Ah, Christopher. Keepin' out of trouble? Well, that's good." Gist smiled at him. "We need to search out General Alexander and find out what we're to do to win this war."

Once away from the fortifications and military debris, they were afforded a spectacular view of Gowanus Bay and the Hudson River on the right, both sparkling below in the afternoon sunlight. In front and to the east were gently rolling meadows parceled into neat little squares by thickets of trees and hedges, which stretched up to dense wooded hills dotted here and there with stone farmhouses.

They soon found General Alexander's headquarters at a house located where the Port Road—the road they had been riding on—crossed the Shore Road. This latter road, also called the Gowanus Road, followed the curve of the bay with the same name and, a little further south, pierced a rugged ridge, covered with woods and hedges, thick with laurel and summer foliage, which loomed before them.

The general's headquarters were in a handsome stone house, a local landmark which everyone referred to as the Old Stone House at Gowanus. Like most of the dwellings north of the ridge, it backed directly against a hill. It was constructed of fieldstone with two chimneys at each end, a steeply gabled Dutch roof, and an attached kitchen of wooden shingles, now worn to a weathered gray by the salt air. The house was surrounded by poplar and pear trees, which offered shade for a table and chairs set on the small lawn.

As they dismounted, an officer passed them with a distracted glance, intent on some assignment. Major Gist called for him to stop.

"Lieutenant, I'm Major Guest of the Maryland Regiment reporting to General Alexander for orders."

"That should be General *Stirling*," the lieutenant informed Major Gist in a rather brusque manner.

"Am I to understand, sir, that Generals Alexander and Stirling are one and the same? And, *Lieutenant*, I am a *major* in the Continental service and I will be treated as such by junior officers—is that understood?" Gist's remarkable eyes had turned hard and penetrating, the anger giving them a disconcerting glow.

The young lieutenant, brought up short by Major Gist's demeanor, stammered, "Yes, Sir! I…ah…I'll inform the General immediately, sir." The young officer turned to go, but abruptly turned again to face the Major. "Sir, I meant no disrespect. The general prefers to be addressed as General Stirling—in acknowledgement of the peerage he claims."

"The what?" But the lieutenant had already disappeared inside the house.

An officer soon came out of the house and walked toward Major Gist. He wore a well-tailored uniform coat of midnight blue turned out in a rich red, with plenty of gold lace, and across his vest wore the pink sash of a brigadier general.

"Major Guest, is it, of the Maryland Regiment? General Stirling at your service, sir! What a fine afternoon and no damned mosquitoes for once. Why don't we talk here?" And the general offered Major Gist a chair.

They settled themselves on chairs around the small table set prettily in the front yard under a pear tree, which provided some cooling shade.

The two officers seated themselves, sweating heavily in woolen uniforms. "May I offer you a refreshment, Major? Perhaps a glass of Madeira."

General William Alexander fascinated everyone in the rebel army. Addressed as General Stirling, or even more to his liking as *Lord* Stirling, he was no lord at all; but his disreputable claim to a Scottish peerage was good enough for most folks, so they respectfully referred to William and his wife as Lord and Lady Stirling.

Admittedly, Lord Stirling's claim was a curious conceit for a general of a revolutionary army attempting to overthrow its king. But then, it appeared that many American revolutionaries were so only in part, while another part still yearned for the theatrics of a monarchy.

"I have heard good things about the Maryland Regiment and warmly welcome you to my command, Sir."

"Thank you, Sir. I trust we will earn the good reviews. Unfortunately, Colonel Smallwood, who commands the regiment, and his second-in-command, Colonel Ware, have remained in New York to attend a court-martial, so I am temporarily in command."

Before General Stirling could reply, a small knot of horsemen drew up in front of the house. From their uniforms, it was apparent that they belonged to the Delaware Regiment and also were reporting to General Stirling for orders.

The Delaware officer who came forward was Major McDonough, and, like Major Gist, he was the acting regimental commander because their colonel was also occupied with the same court-martial in New York.

"Colonel Haslet, too? Ah...just this morning His Excellency told me that the Brooklyn defenses would receive his personal attention. *Now* I am informed that *someone* believes that my colonels have more important things to do than lead their regiments into battle?" General Stirling was clearly irritated.

Shrugging this off, "Gentlemen, let me explain our situation to you...," and he explained that while they were badly outnumbered, they were in a very strong defensive position, not only with the string of forts on Brooklyn Heights, but also the daunting ridge that loomed in front of them, impenetrable by troops in formation except through three passes—all of them, according to General Stirling, heavily defended by the best regiments in the American army. "It is, gentlemen," he said emphatically, "as if designed by the Almighty to protect the defenders of Brooklyn Heights."

All of them looked as the general turned and pointed down the Shore Road toward the ridge, and, as if making a speech, dramatically said, "One of the passes is right there—and that will be ours to defend!"

General Stirling downed the remainder of his drink. Beckoning the two officers to remain seated. "Then, gentlemen, while you finish your wine, I will write out orders to bring your regiments up. Then we'll go take a look at the other side of the ridge."

Less than two hours later, the two regiments were marching down the Port Road to where General Stirling's aide was waiting to direct them to their campsite in one of the little meadows, sweet smelling and springy to the step with cut grass.

Fires were quickly made and the normal duties of a camp seen to; they ate what little food they had, some even resorting to the sea bread (soaked in spirits); and with no sutler's watering hole, they sat around playing cards and talking. There was no foreboding of what was to come the next day; and so, bored on this hot Monday evening, they bedded down early to sleep on the soft grass, expecting tomorrow to be a day for catching up on the food and drink they had missed today.

****

Around three o'clock in the morning, Christopher and every other sleeping man in the camp were awakened by the sound of the drums beating To Arms, an angry rolling noise of paired strokes which signaled an alarm.

"Get yourselves dressed and ready to parade under arms now, Goddamit!" yelled Corporal Smith. "Ye heard me—now!"

"Jeremiah! What's happenin'?"

"Scouts report that the British are advancin' up the Shore Road with several fieldpieces. Can't ye hear the firing?" It was hard to tell with the drums and all the yelling and noise...but, yes, there were the chesty cough of smoothbore muskets and the sharper crack of rifles on the other side of the ridge.

As the men hurriedly put on their shoes and donned their equipment, Corporal Smith was yelling out additional orders.

"No packs—leave 'em here...but bring your necessary bags and any food you got. Also, water bottles. *And no likker!*"

After a pause, the drums sounded the Assembly, and the men began to form, ready to march.

Just them General Stirling rode up, dressed perfectly in his general's uniform. Generals may not always be properly prepared for battle, but they are always properly dressed for battle.

Saluting Majors Gist and McDonough, he gave the signal to march. Orders were yelled out and the fifes and drums of the two regiments played a tune for the quickstep.

The morning was still dark and chilly; there was a slight mist scudding along the ground and among the thick trees and bushes along the narrow road on which they marched. The moon was hidden behind clouds, and they were enveloped in a darkness which caused them to trip on rocks, or roots, or stumble as they made a misstep on the ruts in the road.

They marched toward sporadic firing ahead, somewhere beyond the ridge, starting at each report. These were greatly exaggerated in minds muddled by the suddenness of the alarm.

Heads aching from interrupted sleep and stomachs rumbling from lack of food, the men were confused and uncertain. There's no such thing as bravery in the early morning hours, a time when instinct and habit, at best, serve the place of courage. At four o'clock in the morning, fear prevails…so there was a constant murmuring of voices as frightened men sought reassurance for their fears.

"'Tis said the enemy is small in number—only a foraging party."

"But I heard they were thousands strong."

"They say there's Hessians among 'em, who are seven foot tall an' they be paid by the number of ears they take."

"Quiet in the ranks!" bawled Corporal Smith.

"For God's sake, Jeremiah," hissed Terry. "Leave it be, will you? We're tired and hungry and scared. It doesn't hurt to talk a little amongst ourselves, does it?"

Corporal Smith glared at Terry, but only ordered, "Close up, men. We're lagging."

And the Maryland and Delaware Regiments marched off to battle.

9

THE DAY OF THE SURPRISE

The enemy advanced towards us, upon which Lord Sterling,
drew up in a line and offered them battle in true English taste.
An American soldier, in a letter

The Heights of Guan, Long Island
August 27, 1776

THEY SAY THE SUN ROSE that day with a red and angry glare. It seemed as if the very heavens were awash in blood—or, perhaps the skies above Long Island were simply a sordid reflection of the landscape below.

Even as the sun rose, men lay dead or wounded south of the huge pile of rocks called the Heights of Guan. They lay in the tall grasses of little meadows, on the rolling knolls, beneath the stands of ash, chestnut, and tulip trees, on the roads and paths, in the fruit-laden orchards, and among the ripe watermelons in the patch near the Red Lion Inn where the fighting had first begun.

General Stirling formed his two new regiments to defend the pass through the Guan Heights. They formed a line of battle across the road, the men standing silent and tense, gripping their muskets so hard their hands seized up, while night insects swarmed around them.

There was sporadic firing of muskets and rifles further down the road, as well as the hollow boom of cannon. In the mean light of early dawn, groups of men below could be seen darting from copse to hedge, from stone wall to split rail fence, working their way toward them—shadowy figures in the dim light, some with their backs turned to them, others facing them, all moving closer and closer. Every so often one or two of these figures would pause and a puff of smoke could be seen, followed by the cough or crack of a discharge.

Soon the retreating Americans came in, gasping for air, their eyes dilated. Some stopped to look back; one man pumped his fist at those hounding him, but he, too, quickly turned and continued his retreat. These were Atlee's and Hand's men, amateur soldiers not long ago, but now blooded veterans. They passed through the lines of Marylanders and Delawares.

"Damn'd regulars shoot high." The man who said this had huge rings under his eyes, and the right side of his face was burnt black from the ignition of his flintlock. He said matter-of-factly that he had fired his rifle seven times this morning.

All was now quiet. The firing had stopped and there appeared to be no movement on the road below. The soldiers stood nervously along the crest of a ridge which rose to some woods at the top of a steep hill, directly below the rocky ramparts of the Heights, staring intently to the south. The Maryland Regiment had been placed on the right nearest the water, which undulated and foamed below, and across the road itself, with the Delawares placed on their left. Beyond them, Christopher saw a little hill upon which two pitifully small cannon were being unlimbered.

Looking at Corporal Smith, who was prowling the line, Christopher asked nervously, "So we'll just stand here and wait for 'em to attack us? *Is that the plan?*"

Corporal Smith stopped in front of Christopher, took a long swig from his canteen, and only after leisurely wiping his mouth on his sleeve did he answer. "Yes," he replied simply. He began to explain about military formations such as "kettle" and inverted V's, but then came the sounds of fifes and drums and the skirl of bagpipes.

Men suddenly turned to stare down the road, their survival instincts alert, like a dog tensing, its nose quivering, testing what the air had to tell, ears laid back and eyes wide open, its whole being focused in the direction of immediate danger.

Tense with anticipation, their minds too open to suggestion, fatigued beyond belief, and more scared than most of them had ever been in their entire lives, the bagpipes spooked them.

"It's like the screechin' of the damn'd," yelled one man, hands protecting his ears, and terror in his eyes. Men began to stir in the ranks, like horses at the start of a race, ready to bolt at the first opportunity.

"Easy, men, easy," said Sergeant Major Older soothingly, as he walked down the line. "'Tisn't a sound to be compared to the war hoops of the savages—now, is it?" He saw that some of the men were nodding in agreement. Looking up and down the line, he said, "And didn't we learn from that experience that as fearsome as their noise was, it couldn't deflect a musket ball?"

Of course not, men nodded in agreement.

"Well, same thing here—right, lad?" The sergeant major looked at a soldier who was trembling from head to toe. The man nodded in agreement, and might have meant it.

"All right then, now let's calm down..." And he moved on down the line reassuring fearful men.

General Stirling, seeing the ripples of fear and uncertainty moving up and down the ranks, spoke to his troops:

"Patriots and soldiers! The time for battle has come! And I thank the great Jehovah that I command men such as you, in this our country's time of crisis! I know you will do your duty!

"The enemy before you is commanded by General Grant. It was this very man who, in the year 1774, while a member of Parliament, boasted that Americans *won't* fight, and with five thousand men—*five thousand men, no less!*—he could march from one end of this continent to the other.

"It appears General Grant may have his five thousand men with him now, if reports are to be believed. We are not so many—but I think we are enough to prevent his advancing further on his march across our continent than that mill pond over there!"

And General Stirling, in a theatrical gesture, threw his arm out to point at Gowanus Creek and its surrounding marshes, which lay between them and the Brooklyn defenses to their rear.

Then they heard the band playing. It was the quick-stepping, arrogant *Grenadiers March*, and many of those Americans who heard it knew this was the beat used when the British Army was advancing to charge an enemy.

Here come the Grenadiers, my boys, who know no doubts or fears,
Singing, Tow row row, with a tow row row, to the British Grenadiers.

Peering intently, they saw through the leaves of ash and oak trees, which were temporarily obstructing their view, the glint of burnished metal and the flash of red. Suddenly, up the road appeared the British Army in all its intimidating splendor: light infantry moved swiftly ahead of columns of heavy infantry, marching behind in stately fashion. Bands playing, flags whipping in the breeze, resplendent officers on fine horses, rank after rank of colorfully uniformed soldiers marched up the road. Their red uniforms splashed with bright facings of yellow, blue, black and green. It was, as it was intended to be, an awesome display of professional arms.

With a dramatic flourish of drums, the whole British force, now in open view of their enemy, suddenly stopped; and, at the renewed sound of the drum, regiment after regiment deployed gracefully into a perfect line of battle, three deep.

Once formed, they stood at shoulder arms, the officers with swords resting on shoulders and numerous standards flapping in the light wind. Thousands of men stood like this in dense ranks for some minutes, nearly motionless, as if giving their enemy time to reconsider their rash decision to resist the might of the British Empire.

Then officers shouted orders, repeated by non-commissioned officers down those immaculate lines, drums began a different beat, and the British ranks went to fix bayonets with a hollow thud as boots and musket butts hit the ground in unison, and then came the sweeping flash of bright metal. Christopher and his comrades could almost hear the rasping sound of metal fitted to metal.

More yells, followed by beats of the drum, and muskets were brought to advance arms, and there suddenly appeared a thicket of steel three hundred yards in front of them.

Christopher had naïvely thought his battalion and the Delawares were real soldiers; but that, he realized, was only in comparison to the morbidity of the rest of the Continental Army. Facing off against the regulars, they were laughable.

The spectacle of the British advance was unnerving enough for green troops, but then the British artillery began bombarding them, and that began to take a grisly toll.

They actually saw balls shot out of the muzzles of cannons, and men could even dodge them, which even brought some laughter. But then the first four-pound ball bounded into the ranks, badly mangling three men, who lay writhing and screaming on the ground. Another ball, on the fly, hit a man in the front rank just a few files over from where Christopher stood: the man's head suddenly exploded in a burst of blood and brains with a sound like a ripe pumpkin striking the ground, showering gore on half the company.

Then there were the bombs tossed up into the air by two British howitzers. These would explode who knew when or where—sometimes in the air, sometimes in the soft turf, throwing up clods of earth and grass and rock fragments; or they might not burst at all, and lay smoldering on the ground.

Christopher lost his nerve because of the cannonading. He took to closing his eyes tight upon each discharge, but what he desperately wanted to do was run. He had seen a few bolt, and others throw themselves to the ground. He felt compelled to do one or the other. But no one around him ran, or even threw himself to the ground; so he stayed standing in line, clenching his bowels and bladder.

The two lines—one ragged and flinching, the other beautiful and steady—faced off against each other. Sporadic skirmishing continued, mostly off to the left, and there was the artillery fire, of course; but the massed ranks of infantry just stood, watching each other—for four miserable hours.

Time stood still. Tired Marylanders and Delawares stood on the rocky ground, tending to crowd under the partial shade of poplar and oak trees, leaning heavily on their muskets. In the ill-defined shade, all of them suffered immensely from the heat. Christopher was miserable even in his light linen smock and the cover provided by his hat. Looking over at the Delawares, he wondered at their fortitude, standing there in their leather caps and woolen coats, now noticeably mottled with sweat. He thought about how jealous they had been of the Delawares' dashing regimentals.

They were finally allowed to stand at ease, which meant that they could talk among themselves, slake their thirst, piss in line, and chew on the sea bread issued yesterday. Those who needed to move their bowels were also allowed to slip away and seek relief in the dense laurel thickets behind the line, squatting amidst the dark green shrubs with their aromatic leaves. And (thank God) casks of rum had finally been brought to shore up their frayed nerves.

Though men continued to die violently, the battlefield remained disconcertingly quiet throughout most of the morning. The only startling sounds—and those, while disquieting, were also entertaining—came from the British battalion bands.

Then, at ten o'clock in the morning, all hell broke loose.

That was when a signal gun sounded somewhere off in the distance and seemed to have come from the American rear. Echoing with a preternatural loudness, it made the men uneasy—as if it were a foreboding of some great evil to come.

This was followed moments later by the sound of heavy musketry from the east, which definitely came from their rear *and* from the other side of the Heights, which was not possible. Officers and men turned in confusion, first toward the sound of battle, then quickly back to look at the enemy arrayed in front of them.

They heard General Stirling call out orders. "Major Guest and Major McDonough, see to the readiness of your men. I suspect that may have been the signal for a general attack." The general's voice was almost conversational, although he too had turned, and turned again on his horse, trying to figure out what was happening. He looked anxiously toward his front.

Yet Grant's Brigade in his front showed no signs of hurry. More time passed and nothing seemed to be happening.

"What…for God's sake…?" General Stirling muttered half-aloud, swinging around on his horse in front of the line. He rubbed his chin in perplexity, felt stubble, and realized he had forgotten to shave in all the excitement that morning. Then more sounds of fighting erupted in the direction of the American center, which guarded the pass for the Flatbush Road, and Stirling jerked the reins and knocked his knees against his horse's ribs to urge it in a different direction, now toward the rear.

As if the situation suddenly dawned on him, Stirling bellowed out, "I'm going to the other side of the ridge to see what's goin' on." Kicking his horse on, he galloped up the road and disappeared over the crest.

Meanwhile, cries to *form up! form up!* rang up and down the lines.

"Check your pans!" Corporal Smith hollered out as he checked arms and equipment. As he watched, Christopher pushed up the frizzen and showed him the powder in the pan of his musket. He nodded and moved on as Christopher snapped it back down. Christopher looked for Terry and saw him several rows up intently priming his musket. Shifting his gaze, he saw Caleb standing at order arms. He could not see Davey.

"Fix...bay-o-net! Shoulder...firelock!"

"I guess this is it," the man next to Christopher whispered.

Christopher took a deep breath. "I reckon so."

Less than a quarter of an hour later, General Stirling returned, both he and his horse in a fine lather. The troops saw him talking animatedly to his lieutenants.

As soon as they dispersed, there was a hasty gathering of captains and lieutenants, then sergeants and corporals. Finally, word was passed down to the ranks.

"Men, we've been played for the fool! A large enemy force is on the other side of the heights and comin' down between us and the Brookline defenses. We must retreat immediately, or be caught between that force and the enemy in front of us."

Soon the drums sounded the signals which prepared them for movement to the rear and they began a purposeful retreat.

It wasn't until they crested the hill and started down the north side of the ridge that they realized how precarious their situation was. This vantage point provided them with a panoramic view of the prospect below, and as they took in the scene, the entire column recoiled as if fending off a physical blow.

At the summit of the Heights, they stood in the midst of a wilderness landscape, a bold, rocky rampart with dense foliage and moss-covered ground sprinkled with red and yellow flowers. Below, a middle ground rolled gently downhill, crisscrossed with paths and country lanes, as well as the hard-surfaced Jamaica Road, and checkered with small pastures and clearings bordered by fences, stone walls, and shrubs. Beyond, the terrain climbed again, this time up to the defenses on Brooklyn Heights. All of this was squeezed between water to the west and swamps to the east.

A shocked voice was heard above the din. "Good God Almighty—will you look at that!"

Temporarily spectators, they could actually see the British plan unfolding successfully before them.

Below to their right was a melee of men hurrying in their direction, down a hard, level road to the east. This was the Jamaica Road which paralleled the heights and was supposed to serve as an interior line of communication. Instead, it served the British as a ready means to cut off the American outer defenses from the Brooklyn Heights fortifications.

Along this road they now saw a phalanx of red-coated troops advancing rapidly, driving large, disorganized groups of American troops in muted colors before them.

It was a pathetic sight…few of the fleeing Americans appeared to put up any fight at all. They could plainly see the British—who had no time to reload because of the precipitous American retreat—bayonet, club, and even tackle these fleeing men. All of those retreating soldiers were trying to make it to the Brooklyn defenses.

"Well, there goes our chance for a proper withdrawal…" Corporal Smith was disgusted as he realized that Stirling's Brigade, and, indeed, most of the fleeing Americans, wouldn't be able to reach the bridge over the causeway before the British.

It was at this crisis in the battle that General Stirling made the decision to attack the oncoming British in a last-ditch attempt to save as many of the fleeing Americans as possible.

He quickly had six of Smallwood's companies counted off, including Christopher's, and they remained formed on the Shore Road, while the rest of the battalion and the Delawares wheeled off and formed to meet the British force under Grant, that they expected would be coming over the pass behind them.

"What the hell is goin' on?" Christopher asked no one in particular.

"Haven't the faintest idea, Sims," replied the man next to him. "But I don't expect we'll be returning by the route we came—"

Another man thought he knew. "God help us. We're goin' to attack 'em Britishers over there!" And he pointed to a large number of redcoats moving toward a stone house which sat at the crossroads below Brooklyn Heights.

Christopher looked in the direction the man was pointing and saw a stone house with a twin-chimney gable roof, and British soldiers swarming around it like a colony of red ants. Damn'd if the man wasn't pointing at General Stirling's headquarters—he remembered it referred to as the Old Stone House—the very house where he and Major Gist had been just...when?—was it really only yesterday?

Commands rang out and they formed into line of battle. General Stirling and Major Gist moved to the front of the line. Upon the former's signal, the drums began to beat The March at the quick, and some four hundred Marylanders stepped off to stem the tide.

10

SACRIFICE

*The horrors of battle then presented themselves
to me in all their hideousness.*

Joseph Plumb Martin,
His Narrative

Gowanus, Long Island
August, 1776

THERE WERE THE NEVER ENDING COMMANDS to
Close up! Close up!

This particular command would torture Christopher like a
migraine headache for the rest of his life. Many battle-hardened
veterans will say that the order to charge bayonet was the most
fearsome command in the military lexicon. But others, including
Christopher, would swear that the command to *Close up! Close up!*
was far, far more frightening—because it meant that the man
who used to be fighting beside you had now become a bloody
carcass.

Numbed by exhaustion and rum, they dumbly went through
the motions of marching forward or retreating...loading and
firing...and dressing to the center—always dressing to the
center—*Close up! Close up!*—and they would make those little
stutter steps to the left or right, as their battle line grew more
and more feeble.

They had stepped off proudly enough, bravely enough. Dressed, the six companies had moved forward in two lines, which straddled the Shore Road and extended on either side. They found themselves on soft ground and in high meadow grass, the pale green blades swishing at their calves. The air smelled heavily of sun-baked soil and plants, and there was only a whiff of burnt powder. Gnats, attracted by the men's sweat, danced around them like dust motes.

Then the two opposing lines clashed and the destruction began.

There were shouts and drum signals. Captain Smith howled, the timbre of his voice showing that he too was anxious, "Halt!...Front rank!...Make ready!...Take aim!...Fire!" There was a horrendous crash of noise and smoke in front of them.

Then, "Rear rank!...Make ready!" Christopher brought his heavy musket up to his shoulder and leveled it. It shook and he tried to steady it.

"Take aim!" he sighted down the barrel at the crossbelts of a burly British soldier, who seemed to be staring straight at him, even as he calmly went about reloading his musket. His musket bobbed as he tried to take a bead on the Britisher.

"*Fire!*"

He pulled the trigger and there was a burst of sparks, and a backfire which scorched his brow, then an explosion as the musket discharged. He was enveloped in swirls of gray smoke. When the eddies of smoke cleared, he saw that the British line was wavering, with several men on the ground and others leaving the ranks, their officers frantically trying to rally them with the flats of their swords. He could not see the man he had shot at.

Then the drums beat the signal to charge bayonet.

Dry-mouthed, Christopher tried to huzzah with the others and went forward.

Then they retreated.

Breathing heavily, trying to catch their breath, they moved back and forth across the meadow. They marched through the grassy field trampled by their previous advance. This time, as the pale green blades of grass swished against their calves, faint red streaks were left on their stockings.

Once, they almost reached the Old Stone House itself—the house suddenly looming out of the pall. Christopher passed the very table upon which he had placed glasses of Madeira for General Stirling and Major Gist, now laying on its side, one leg broken, the pear tree which had offered shade just hours before was now shorn of pears and leaves, its trunk chipped by shot.

Then they were blown back as if by a strong wind.

The sights and sounds of battle soon became only a confusion of discordant scenes and noises to overwrought minds. Christopher was aware with terrible clarity of the smoke and bright sunlight, the crushed grass and dandelions that gave the ground a brownish cast, and the debris of battle: the meadow around the Old Stone House strewn with muskets and hats, and many shoes; tripping over a cannonball; the blood and entrails, and numbers of his comrades lying grotesquely in the field, mutilated, either writhing or still. And more powerfully, the stink of battle: burnt powder, burning grasses, the metallic odor of fresh blood, human waste, and the palpable smell of fear.

The last attempt to take the Old Stone House ended, not in another bloody repulse but by default. Exhausted and beaten, the Marylanders stopped their advance well beyond musket range. As solid shot and grape began to play on their pathetic little line, they just stopped and simply admitted defeat by refusing to go forward another step.

It didn't make any difference since they were surrounded on three sides. In fact, they were lucky to have checked the British as long as they did. As it was, they had succeeded in providing for the escape of hundreds of their fleeing comrades.

Now, the saviors just wanted the chance to save themselves.

11

"LOOKING LIKE DROWNED WATER RATS"

What brave fellows I must lose this Day!
General Washington,
while viewing the battle
from Cobble Hill fort

Brooklyn Heights, Long Island
August 27, 1776

THE TEPID, BRINY WATER brought Christopher back to his senses. Gasping for breath and snorting water, his throat and nostrils stinging from the salt, he was confused and not sure of his bearings.

Sitting in water to his chest, Christopher looked around in confusion. He realized he was in the upper mill pond, because the tall structure of the old sawmill with its decaying clapboards stood off to his right, the high tide lapping at its crumbling stone foundation.

Taking in more of his surroundings now, he saw numerous other men splashing and flailing about in the shallow water, while a small number of others were milling around the edge of the pond, uncertain what to do, or finally plunging into the water, as all tried frantically to escape death or capture.

It was coming back to him now—the battle, the charges, and the rout...and, finally, madly running toward the shimmering water.

The sounds of battle also returned. Groggily, he considered his surroundings, realized with a shock that he was not out of danger and frantically sought safety.

Looking around, he spied an old skiff tied to a pole about ten yards from him. He tried to stand up but could not gain his balance as his feet sank in the mucky bottom. Crouching rather than standing, he duck-walked his way over to the craft, which turned out to be barely afloat, untied it, and pushed off towards the opposite side of the pond. Hanging on the side, he used a rowing motion with his other hand to propel the boat forward as he pushed into deeper water.

By now, fleeing Americans by the dozens were trying to cross the water. The mill pond was deep in places and a man had to swim if he was to make it to the other side—it wasn't that far. Those who could not swim and were without something to buoy them, simply sank.

He grabbed one man about to go under and helped him to obtain a firm hold on the skiff's rail. Knowing that he had almost been a goner, the man, coughing and gasping for breath, expelled his name, which was Tom, and would have gone on and on in appreciation, except that Christopher cut him off. "Tom, save it for later—just paddle."

Together, the two weary men pulled at the water and the skiff moved hesitantly across the pond. Finally, feet scraped bottom. Slipping in the mud, they pushed the boat toward the shore and felt it ground in shallow water, wobbling wildly now as its bow sat out of the water.

Friendly hands reached out to grasp and pull them bodily out of the black mud, dragging them through the thatch grass and salt hay to solid ground, where they lay stretched out, retching up salty bile, and trying to catch their breath, physically spent.

"Ye looked like drowned water rats, you did, comin' outta that pond," said one of the men who had pulled Christopher from the water. "But I gotta say you Maryland gentlemen did us proud over there. Here, have a little of the good creature—it'll get your blood circulatin' proper-like." The man talked in a careful nasal twang which seemed to purposely muffle the expression of any emotion.

"Name's Joseph Martin—Douglas's Connecticut Levies."

"Christopher Sims—Smallwood's Marylanders. Much obliged to you." He drank freely from the flask offered him. The raw rum tasted so damn good and restored a measure of strength.

This Martin fellow was hardly more than a boy, with a mischievous grin and a thatch of straw hair. But he was tall and well built and had the appearance of a soldier in his brown regimental coat.

Thinking of Martin's reference to him as looking like a drowned water rat, Christopher took stock of himself. He was missing musket, belts, necessary bag, cartouche pouch, knife—in fact, everything he owned. He had even lost his shoes and a stocking...the remaining stocking was down around his ankle and thick with mud. His once elegant hunting shirt and breeches, sodden and filthy, hung on him like sackcloth.

Martin looked out across the pond at the enemy, and then back, to consider the disorganized mass of unarmed, waterlogged men who were now a beaten rabble.

"Drubbed us good today, they did." Then, looking up at the sun, he added, "—and it didn't take long either." Christopher looked up at a cloudy sky and was surprised to see that the sun had hardly started its westward descent.

"My comrades—I need to find out about them."

"Well, Christopher Sims, some of your people made it over to this side. I hope ye didn't lose too many of your friends."

Christopher thought of Terry, and Caleb, and David, and wanted desperately to learn their fates. But he was tired, and just the effort of worrying about them drained him of the last of his energy. Exhausted, he fell asleep.

He awakened some time later to find Joseph Martin sitting nearby, chewing on a length of onion grass, looking at him curiously.

"Never met a craw-thumper before—don't believe we allow 'em in Connecticut."

"Craw-thumper?—"

"You know, a papist...like you Mary-Landers."

"I'm no papist...I'm Church of Eng—*hell*, I don't know what I am...."

"I'm a Congregationalist, I am," Joseph Martin stated with self-satisfaction.

Then, changing the subject, "There, you'll be needing that." He pointed to a musket he had placed beside Christopher. "It'll need oiling. You'll also be needing those," and he motioned to a sodden cartridge pouch and a wooden canteen. "Sorry, but I didn't find no shoes for you," he apologized, adding, "When the tide went out, some of us went in and took out a great number of arms and such. Also pulled out a number of corpses—"

Distressed at hearing this, Christopher said, "I gotta search out my friends. I'm much obliged to you, Joseph Martin." Shaking his hand, "Now, you take care and God bless. Be seeing you."

"Aye, Christopher Sims, fare thee well...ye take care yourself.

Christopher found the battalion up on the plain, trying to pull itself back together. There was confusion and disorganization, but the men seemed to be game enough.

"Where's the Eighth Company?"

"Not many remainin'," Christopher was told with simple honesty. "I know Corporal Smith is at the hospital—Naw, he's alright—just lookin' after the wounded."

His hopes buoyed by this news, Christopher walked to Brooklyn Village, where he had been told the battalion hospital was to be found in one of the vacated houses. Finding it, he entered as only those who had never been in a field hospital would.

It was awful inside. Screaming and moaning...blood...the smell of urine and feces...men in rent and bloody clothes laying on foul straw...and nurses moving mechanically about. He saw the battalion surgeon Doctor Wisenthal and Surgeon's Mate Doctor Dashiel elbow deep in gore grappling with a wounded man. Christopher suddenly realized they were in the process of sawing off the man's leg. He gagged and vomit rose in his throat.

Sickened by the sights and sounds, he looked wildly about and spotted Corporal Smith squatting down by a still body.

"Corporal Smith," he gasped.

Pivoting around on his heels, Jeremiah Smith recognized and greeted Christopher with what might have been a smile.

"Christopher Sims—I'll be damn'd." He was genuinely relieved to see him. The trace of a smile quickly disappearing, he motioned him outside.

"I thought we might have lost you too, Christopher. We lost so many—"

"Corporal Smith, the others—Terry, Caleb, Dav— Christopher suddenly stopped talking as he saw the expression on the corporal's face.

"Terry and David are missin', Christopher. Both have been reported as being felled by enemy fire—but we can't confirm it, so there's hope…" Corporal Smith was uncomfortable and couldn't quite look Christopher in the eye. Suddenly he blurted it out: "Caleb's dead, Christopher—I saw it—he was struck in the throat by a grape. I'm—" Corporal Smith gave a helpless shrug "—I'm sorry…."

Christopher wasn't listening as Corporal Smith ticked off the others who were killed or wounded or missing from this battle. *My God. Terry and David missing…Caleb killed…*his head was pounding, and his temples throbbed…*this is not the way it was supposed to be!*

****

"What are our casualties, Mordecai?" Colonel Smallwood asked this question with trepidation, not really wanting to know the answer. He had hastened over to Long Island, throwing a hunting jacket over his parade uniform, as soon as he had heard about the British attack; but he arrived too late to do any more than watch as half his battalion hurled itself futilely against the British, and, then, help haul survivors out of the pond.

"Hard to tell, sir. Initial returns—and these are woefully incomplete—are that the battalion lost upwards of three hundred men. *But…*" and here Major Gist tried to be optimistic, "men are still straggling in, so it could well be less."

"Three hundred men." Smallwood repeated the number in a daze, it was so shocking. He paced back and forth under a canvas awning which protected them from a tumultuous sky, his riding boots grinding the grass into the earth, forming a muddy path around the small camp table.

"What a disaster! Generals Sullivan and Stirling captured, whole regiments swallowed up, our vaunted outer defenses pierced with no more resistance than that involved in wheedling the parson's daughter—good God!"

"Colonel, what on earth happened?"

"Well, it appears Lords Howe and Cornwallis with a force of some fifteen thousand troops and a great number of field pieces circled to the east and got between us and the Brooklyn defenses by a route we never dreamed of."

Colonel Smallwood took a swig of his Madeira. "Now, half the army is here and separated from the other half by a river which would be controlled by the enemy but for the capriciousness of the winds, behind fortifications which remain unfinished, and which are right now being invested by the enemy." He shook his head.

Finishing his wine, the colonel gave Major Gist some instructions and then excused himself to hurry off to a council of war called by General Washington.

Left alone, Major Gist, infinitely tired and depressed, reflected on yesterday's losses. *A costly defeat, but hopefully not a crippling one. And all morning we've been talkin' numbers. But it's not just about numbers—it's about three hundred comrades, friends, and relatives.* He thought about that: many of the officers killed or missing served under him in the Baltimore Cadets, and a few had been boyhood friends…and there was Sergeant Major Older—a noble man, Jonathan—who was crushed by a cannonball…and then, so many others—

With an emptiness he had not felt since the deaths of his wife and infant daughter, Major Mordecai Gist went in search of arms and equipment for what was left of his mortally wounded battalion.

12

EVERYTHING HAD DISAPPEARED IN VAPOR

In the history of warfare, I do not recollect a more fortunate retreat.
Colonel Benjamin Tallmadge, Memoir

Brooklyn Heights, Long Island
August 28-30, 1776

DESPITE THE FORLORN HEROICS of the Marylanders, it was really the weather that saved General Washington's army on Long Island, now crammed perilously into Brooklyn Neck.

On Tuesday, August 27, the day of the British grand attack, and through the next day, unfavorable winds prevented British warships from gaining the East River and cutting the Americans off from Manhattan Island. Then, late Wednesday afternoon, a great storm came over Long Island, bringing high winds, rain, hail, thunder and lightning. Though a blessing in disguise, this cold nor'easter cut through Christopher and his comrades, as thinly clad as they were, like a serrated knife.

They looked out toward the British lines, which lay beyond the killing field. Standing ankle-deep in the muddy water filling the trenches, and lashed by a cold rain, which the wind whipped across them with the viciousness of a cat-o'-nine-tails, they surveyed the tree line for signs of movement. The British were digging their own trenches, as well as approaches toward the American defenses in anticipation of a formal siege. There would be no repeat of the arrogant British attack on Bunker Hill.

The day after the battle, Smallwood's battalion was marched off to the extreme left of the entrenched line, where the men took up positions in the trenches as part of General Mifflin's Brigade. Posted immediately on their left was the Fourteenth Continental Regiment of Foot, better known as Glover's Marbleheaders, who were Massachusetts mariners before they became foot soldiers of the Revolution.

Among the men who served in Glover's Massachusetts regiment were Negroes, strong, robust men whose self-confidence and easy dignity offended many of the Southern troops.

"The officers are saying it's unseemly to have Negroes in the ranks."

Many of the enlisted men agreed, but not all. While Maryland was a slave state, a good many Marylanders—most notably those from the northern and western parts—had no use for slaves and were more like the Easterners in their thoughts on black slavery.

"Why do they think that? The Negroes be free men and volunteers. The New Englanders accept them as equals and fellow patriots."

"Those damn levelers don't have to deal with Negro slaves like we do, that's why."

"What're ye talkin' about, Tom? We're talkin' about free men, not slaves."

"Nigras is nigras, I say."

"Well, I don't know about that. If a man's free, he's free. If he's bound-out, he's bound-out. If he's a slave, he's a slave. I didn't realize there was any more to it than that."

"Just so," said one of the other men. "And, anyway, I thought we were doin' away with all that by fightin' this war."

The man named Tom would have none of this kind of talk. "Well, by damn, no man should have the right to fight for freedom if he ain't free...."

The Retreat,
August 29, 1776

The fog lifted enough to reveal empty trenches. "What's up?" Christopher said out loud, "pretty soon I'll have to shout at the top of me lungs to talk to the man next to me."

Jeremiah Smith rushed over and made a movement as if to strangle him. "The army's being taken off the island and we're to stay to cover 'em. I'm not to tell you that, but"—looking distraught—"there're no officers around."

So, they remained in the trenches, leveling their muskets every time one of them heard a suspicious sound.

Tired, wet through, and feeling forsaken, they stood watch as the rest of the army fled.

It was not until the early morning hour, as a vague gray tinge appeared on the horizon, that they were finally ordered out of those miserable, water-filled holes.

"Don't talk—don't even cough…follow the orders of your officers and do not ask questions…now let's move."

They arrived at the ferry landing to find, to their great relief, that boats were waiting to carry them off. There were not many men waiting their turn to embark—Smallwood's Marylanders were among the very last to leave.

The very last man to leave, however, would be a Virginian. His Excellency General Washington was standing on the stone landing, wrapped in a cloak, quietly watching the last of his army safely off Long Island, a tight smile finally playing upon his tired face as he realized that his preposterous plan had actually succeeded.

As Christopher climbed into a small flat-bottomed boat, he saw that the men at the oars wore the seamen's garb of the Marbleheaders from Massachusetts.

Two of the oarsmen pulling his boat were black men, to whom, if all went well, he would owe his freedom, if not his life. One of these men even gave him a helping hand as he lurched into the swaying boat, along with a reassuring smile and a comradely "well done."

Remembering the earlier conversation about the Negroes, he wondered about the inconsistencies in this revolution. The Cause was about equality under God and a rejection of dependency based on artificial hierarchies. The most extreme form of dependency was bondage, and of that, the very worst was slavery. What, he wondered, was the moral justification for allowing black slavery in a nation of free men?

Though he put some thought into it, he couldn't come up with an answer...and it bothered him.

Their oars muffled by rags, the Massachusetts rowers pushed the boat quickly over the choppy water. They established an easy rhythm. As one of the men softly sounded "Pull," the oarsmen would grunt and the boat would shoot forward...coasting as they recovered, then shooting ahead again as the heavy oars thrust through the water—the litany repeated over and over until the bow gently bumped the stone jetty at the bottom of Maiden Lane, where they had begun their ill-fated adventure just days before.

Disembarked and awaiting orders, one of them asked, "Where do ya think we'll be goin' next?"

"Don't know—word is up Manhattan way to the north o' here," offered Christopher.

"Yeah? Well I just heard that Manhattan is an island—jus' like Long Island. What do you want to wager the British'll go and land a grand army way up there and come down on us from behind?"

"Hadn't thought of that. Do ye suppose our generals have?"

"Well, Jim," volunteered Christopher, "in my estimation, this army doesn't think to look over its shoulder 'til we know there's something awful behind us."

Concluding that Christopher might well be right, the man named Jim said, "The British will be up to some sort of deviltry, for sure. They do seem to take advantage of our untangled way of thinkin', don't they?"

The battalion was told to rest in place as officers awaited orders. Looking around, Christopher saw men from other units busily throwing up breastworks along the East River wharves facing Long Island. Spars and logs were being piled atop each other and filled with stones and any old junk at hand. Among those engaged in this duty was Joseph Martin, the Connecticutter who had helped Christopher after the late engagement. "Joseph Martin!" Christopher yelled over the din.

Martin looked up from his work. "Why, if it isn't the Marylander, hisself! How be ya, Christopher?"

As Christopher walked over, Martin sat back and admired his handiwork. Turning to Christopher with a grin, Martin noted "Ye know, Christopher, if the Britishers send a cannonball into this thing, it'll kill five men when the ball alone would kill only one."

Looking critically at the makeshift breastwork, Christopher had to agree. "Tis probable, for sure. Look ye here, Joseph, here's some Maryland tobacco for ye. As a way of saying thanks, you know."

"Well now, I do appreciate this." He took the pouch and sniffed at it. "Don't use the stuff meself, but a lotta men chaw tobacca. I can trade it fer food and such. Thank ye, Christopher. And where are ye off to?"

"Don't know—they're sayin' north above the city."

"Appears we're going to stay here for awhile, behind these well-constructed barricades, allowing you Southern men to frolick in the countryside."

The two men shuffled about, before Martin spoke again. "His Excellency General Washington…men are sayin' that we didn't do very well by him over there on Long Island…and maybe, they be thinkin', he ain't fit to be our commander. Now, I don';t know, but here we are, on another island with a man who maybe don't know much about islands. I know he's a Southerner, but…well, don't it concern ye?...

"Conern me that His Excellency is a Southerner? Why no, it doesn't, Joseph." There was an edge to Christopher's voice. "Just like it don't bother me that the generals His Excellency depended upon on Long Island were New Englanders."

"No, no—I didn't mean it that way…"

Noticing that his battalion was forming, Christopher waved off this clash of provincial cultures and, with real fondness, bade goodbye to Joseph Martin, a Connecticut soldier who didn't mince words.

13

LICKING WOUNDS

Harlem Heights, New York
Early September, 1776

THE CONTINENTAL ARMY wisely fled New York City for consolidated positions further north on Manhattan Island. The commanders decided upon Harlem Heights, located at a point where the long, narrow island was pinched by the Hudson and Harlem Rivers, before they converged to separate Manhattan from the New York mainland. Harlem Heights was a rocky plateau perched upon steep bluffs, more than fifty feet high in places, which stretched from one broad river to another. It was the type of terrain much preferred by the Americans.

Smallwood's Regiment made good use of the two peaceful weeks following the Battle of Brooklyn to recover. The sick and those on detail were returned to the ranks; arms and equipment were found to replace that which had been lost on Long Island; and good food, rum, and a little clothing was found and provided for the men's basic needs.

As soon as he had the chance, Christopher went in search of his belongings left with the heavy baggage when the regiment went over to Long Island. He desperately sought his extra pair of shoes and stockings, in particular; but he also wanted

George's old wool suit. The unseasonable chill had warned him that his linen hunting shirt and tattered breeches would provide no warmth against a cold northern autumn.

He finally found his possessions in one of the regimental wagons, collected the small pack, and was about to hurry back to camp—now carrying the added baggage of newly resurrected memories of home along with his belongings. Then he saw Mary McBride, the free-spirited woman who had helped him accompany the regiment to New York.

"Missus McBride—Mary! It's me, Christopher Sims!"

"Well, Christopher Sims! How are you? The last I saw you, ye was preparin' to face the wrath of your sergeant. They didn't hang you, I can see that—so how'd it go?" She looked hard at him. "Ye did report yourself—did you not, Private Sims?"

"Aye, I did—and rolled cartridges and ran errands for Major Guest as a reward, I did. How are you, Mary?"

"Fair to middlin'. I heard I lost my man on Brookline Heights—no, it ain't no great loss—but I never ever wished him harm. You were in the battle?"

"Aye, Mary, I was—and as a result wish'd it was my last, but I reckon I'll see another battle or two before my enlistment is up."

Figuring that the death of her husband had changed things for her, he asked, "And what will you do now?"

She looked surprised at this question. "Why, remain with the army. I'll not be goin' back to the old life—even with a husband, I wouldn't be doin' that. The army is my home now—the 'Continental family,' we call it...I'll do fine. Besides, I be an enthusiast for the Cause."

"The Cause...ah, I'd almost forgotten about that." And truly he had—the rigors of campaigning...the battle...the emptiness over the loss of his messmates...the fear and longing he now felt ... yes, indeed, he had almost forgotten what this was all about.

"Don't you *ever* forget that you're fightin' for Liberty, Christopher Sims!" Mary glared angrily at him and was about to say more when her face softened. She looked at him and obviously saw a tired and dejected man, shivering as a cool sun set, his clothes threadbare, his bare feet caked with dried mud.

"Christopher, you've spare shoes and clothing in that bag? Then go off and change. And why don't you clean yourself up a bit—there's a stream over there"—she pointed toward a wooded area—"I'll wash and mend those rags you're wearin'. And I've got a little pork and drink for you. After that, 'tis certain you'll be feeling like a ragin' Patriot again."

Mary McBride was prepared to pick up a musket and fight battle after battle for the revolution she believed in. Prevented by her sex from doing so, she demanded the most from the men who, by default, must fight the good fight for her; and, in turn, she gave what succor she could to her heroes.

****

"Private Sims," said Major Gist, "join the rest of the men over there." Christopher had reported to Major Gist's tent as instructed and was surprised to find a rather large gathering there. Major Gist looked over the group, which included Corporal Smith and a number of other enlisted men.

"Colonel Smallwood and Colonel Ware are present—*ah-ten-shun!*"

Colonel Smallwood strode forward. "Men…I have the honor of informing you of your promotions to ranks of higher responsibility in this regiment. I have to admit, it's with a sense of sorrow that I mention some of these promotions—we lost many a good man on Brooklyn Heights. But each of you have been selected to follow in the footsteps of these heroes because of your own deeds on that day and the diligence you have shown in serving the regiment."

He then began to call out the names of those promoted: "Promoted to regimental sergeant major; William Smith…congratulations, Billy. Promoted to sergeant, Captain Smith's company, Jeremiah Smith…congratulations, Sergeant Smith." Colonel Smallwood went on to announce the names of several more men promoted to sergeant, before announcing those promoted to corporal…and then further down the list: "Promoted to corporal, Captain Smith's Company: Christopher Sims…congratulations, Corporal Sims." Concluding the list, Colonel Smallwood informed the gathering that these promotions would be read by the adjutant at the evening formation, and dismissed them with, "Once again, well done, soldiers."

Captain Smith was there to congratulate Sergeant Smith and Corporal Sims. Smiling, the captain informed them that they had thirty minutes before noncommissioned officers' call.

"Well, *Corporal* Sims," said Jeremiah, "Who'd have thought you'd *ever* be a respected soldier of this man's army? Undoubtedly, this never would've happened if we were able to win a battle."

"That's for sure. It requires a peculiar kinda man to be a corporal in an army which keeps goin' backwards—fast. And congratulations on your promotion to sergeant, Jeremiah." It was the first time he had ever addressed Corporal Smith using his Christian name.

"What do ye plan to do with the extra two-thirds of a dollar you're to receive each month, Christopher?" Jeremiah asked this with a wry smile, which they both understood too well.

"Why, the same as you, Jeremiah—imagine it jinglin' in my pocket along with the rest of my imaginary pay. Better yet, I can now *imagine* spending it at the sutter's on a drinkable whiskey befittin' my new status."

Jeremiah laughed appreciatively. "Well, at least you'll not have to dig shitters any more."

"Right you are, Jeremiah—now I'm in charge of 'em."

14

TO LOSE AND YET FIGHT AGAIN

I trust that there are many who will act like men,
and shew themselves to be worthy of the blessings of freedom.
General Washington, in a letter
to Congress, September 16, 1776

Harlem Heights, New York
Mid-September, 1776

LOOKING AT THE ROCKY WALL all the way up to its rim some fifty feet above, all Christopher wanted was to be up there at the top. Instead, he was down here below, looking out over a flat approach just perfect for the regulars.

Smallwood's Marylanders had been assigned to defend the Post Road, the only road that ran the length of Manhattan Island and represented the Continental Army's only viable line of retreat.

On September 15, a bright, sparkling clear Sabbath, they had heard the deep boom of many cannon to the south that morning; and hours later they began to see the effect of that cannon fire as crowds of American soldiers fled toward their positions on the Post Road.

Among the passing rabble, Christopher recognized Joseph Martin helping a flagging comrade, and he was one of the few among the scurrying mob still carrying his musket.

"Joseph Martin! Over here, man." Seeing Christopher waving, Joseph Martin struggled over to where he stood. Breathing heavily, he dropped his musket and gently helped his comrade lay out on the ground, "Lemuel ain't wounded, just sickly. He's a nigh neighbor of mine back home and I'm loath to leave him."

Turning his attention to Christopher, Martin said, "Well, well, here we are, together again, Christopher Sims! But this time, I'm the one who's been hurryin' away from the enemy! You're probably wondering what's goin' on. Well, not to exaggerate a bad situation, Christopher, the whole damn'd British Army is fast on our tracks—which, I can tell you, are well-marked by many a nervous bowel."

"What happened, Joseph?"

"The British landed at Kip's Bay, which is a few miles south a here. Thousands and thousands of 'em. I gotta tell you, we didn't behave well, but there was no way we coulda held them." Martin stated this apologetically, but also with some defiance. "We had no field-pieces and there was only about four hundred of us....

"We ran," he ended simply.

Wearily picking up his musket and helping the sick man to his feet, Joseph said, "Christopher, I should be gettin' along. We're supposed to regroup on the heights above."

Christopher watched as Joseph Martin limped off to safety.

Later, after a short scuffle with lead elements of the British advance, the Maryland battalion also moved up to the Heights. As Christopher wearily climbed the steep incline, all he could think of was, *Thank the Lord for creating piles of rocks for us to hide behind...."*

On September 16, there was a significant skirmish below the Heights and at evening Retreat the battalion was informed that their comrades had driven the British advance back several miles. "And," the adjutant added proudly, "participating in this action was Brigadier General Beall's Brigade from the Maryland Flying Camp, which won great praise for themselves in this engagement; and, in fact, His Excellency has honored them in today's General Orders, making the parole 'Bell' and the countersign 'Maryland.'" There was a loud cheer from the assembled men.

"In honor of our fellow Marylanders' gallantry on this day," the adjutant paused for effect, "Colonel Smallwood has ordered an extra gill of rum for the battalion!" The cheers were even louder.

As he sat down next to Jeremiah to enjoy his drink, Christopher asked, "A brigade of Maryland troops?—where did they come from?"

"They recently came over from New Jersey. Part of our quota for the Flying Camp. I'm told there is a battalion of troops from Western Maryland with 'em—under a Colonel Griffith. That's from your neck of the woods, isn't it, Christopher?"

Christopher bounced up, excited by this news. "You don't say!—It surely is. Colonel Griffith was once captain of our local militia company. Why, there must be neighbors of mine with 'em. I need to get over and see them!"

News from Home
Harlem Heights, New York
Late September, 1776

When Christopher asked for the Maryland Brigade, he was directed to the center of the first line, just above the rim overlooking the fields and clumps of woods below. There, he spoke to a man from the Southern Maryland Battalion who pointed vaguely off in an easterly direction and said he thought the Frederick men might be over there. He walked among these Marylanders, ears pricked for the familiar western Maryland accent or the sight of a familiar face.

"Hey, Christopher! *Christopher Sims*. It's me—Mike Callum!"

Christopher started and stared dumbly at his sister's beau, before breaking into a wide smile as Michael Callum rushed up.

"Hey! *Mike!* What for God's sake are you doing here?"

"Youthful folly, your sister says. Long story—I'll tell you later."

They slapped each other on the back, before Michael Callum stepped back, looking critically at Christopher.

"Well, I suppose I can say you're still alive; but, good God, Chris, what do they feed you in this army?"

"The hell with you, too!" Christopher retorted good-naturedly. "When'd you depart home? Did you and Mary get married. How—"

"Whoa there, Chris," Michael interrupted. "Let me answer one question at a time!

"No, Mary and I decided to postpone the wedding until after the campaign. We want you and Aunt Jane there.

"I left with the battalion on the thirteenth of August. We spent a week in Philadelphia to equip, came up to Jersey, and were finally sent here a week ago."

At this point, Michael blurted out, "Chris, I've been so concerned for you ever since we received the news about the terrible losses suffered by Smallwood's Battalion on Long Island. We heard about it on our march here from Philadelphia...no doubt your family and all are mad with worry."

Christopher hurried through a narration of the battle—to get that out of the way—so he could ask about family and friends.

"Wonderful news, Chris. George and Susan have a strapping boy. 'Twas born in mid-July, I believe—yeah, they're doing fine. Mary and your little brother are well...John Paul's still carrying that damn'd wooden sword everywhere he goes.

"But, more importantly, I called upon Hannah while I was in Elk. Good heavens she's lovely. Doing well with the Alexander family, but I can only imagine her panic upon hearing of the Brooklyn battle."

Christopher assured him that he had written to Hannah, his brother George and sister-in-law Susan, and to their Aunt Jane in Baltimore.

Michael went on to recite the latest gossip—nothing interesting there—and more neighborhood news, noting that the war had yet to really affect them: "Crops have been good and many are selling their wheat and corn to the army. George is plantin' all wheat and sellin' it to the Convention at a goodly price. Life is good.

"But all the neighborhood women, of course, are concerned about us men goin' off to war.

Michael told Christopher that his family had received his letter informing them of Hannah's escape and joining him in Baltimore. "It was a tremendous relief, and we were hoping to have a double wedding, until the fightin' moved south. She was full of bravado when I saw her less than a month ago. And hey! She penned you a letter along with a package which she gave me to deliver. I got 'em here in my trunk."

In a few minutes, he produced folded sheets of paper with a seal impressed with a rose and the letters "H" and "W." and Hannah's girlishly rendered roundhand addressed *"To Mister Chris. Sims,"* as well as a small package tied with twine.

Christopher took the letter and package from Michael, looked longingly at Hannah's handwriting, and put both in his pocket.

By this time, they had moved to Michael's tent to continue the conversation.

"Good Lord, an officer's tent." Christopher looked with surprise at Michael.

"Why, yes—I'm an officer and a gentleman," Michael said smugly, pouring whiskey into two cups and handing one to Christopher. "It's a Rock Creek Hundred company, and"—he waved airily—"my father did something to obtain me a commission as an ensign."

"Well, I haven't attained such an exulted rank in the regular forces, but I was recently promoted to corporal." They drank heartily to their success in the martial arts.

Christopher refilled his cup. "Who's here from the neighborhood, Mike? I don't see many familiar faces."

"Well, the battalion's got two companies from the lower county, but I'd say there's only a dozen or so from Middle Potomac Hundred. Let's see—there's Ben Crisp, George Winston..." Michael ticked off the names, all of whom Christopher knew to some extent. "Ben was just wounded in the buckwheat field—he'll be all right." He also named several men who had taken sick and were in the general hospital. "Lotta men sick in this army. Somebody said it's due to bad water."

Christopher changed the subject. "Now, tell me about this recent battle you were in, Mike. I heard Griffith's Battalion did us proud."

"We did! 'Twasn't as much as they're making it out to be, though. But a bunch of Maryland militiamen did charge the regulars with the bayonet and sent them flying, Chris! Swear to God! I saw a British officer throw away his sword when he saw me coming down on him and run. I went back to get that sword but, dammit, someone—no doubt a Yankee—had already grabbed it.

"Anyway, we sent the bastards flyin' an' left the field as victors *and* with two of their cannon! Come on, I'll show 'em to you." Michael took him over to the brigade headquarters area and proudly showed him two three-pound brass cannon, now standing under the Maryland standard, which was flapping proudly in the wind.

Returning to Michael's tent, they found another soldier there, leaning over the camp desk, studiously writing a letter. The man looked up as the two entered.

"Ah, Pace," said Mike, "this is no other than Mary's brother, Christopher, who is serving with Smallwood. Chris, this is Pace Anders, a fellow officer from Frederick."

Ensign Pace Anders stood up, ignoring the piece of cloth in Christopher's hat which clearly identified him as a corporal. "My pleasure, Sir."

"And mine, Sir," Christopher said.

Respectfully, Ensign Anders had Christopher repeat his narrative about Long Island, as all three men drank rum and relaxed, before the ensign excused himself to see to his duties.

Christopher noted, "The ensign seemed to favor his left arm. Wounded?"

Michael nodded, "The buckwheat field. Hit by a ball in the arm. Fortunate for him, it was spent by the time it struck him."

The two men continued to talk, when Michael suddenly exclaimed, "Oh yeah—I almost forgot...." Reaching into his trunk, he pulled out a small purse which he handed to Christopher. "From your brother...he was worried that the paper script you're being paid in won't sustain you—ye know that the Continental money is depreciating even faster than the state paper."

"That right? I wouldn't know—it's been about two months since I got paid. Thanks, Mike." He hefted the small purse and felt hard coins. "But how about you? Officers are not receiving their pay either—do ye have enough cash for yourself?"

"I'm fine. Now, let's get something to eat—and I'll tell you the latest stories about lewdness and infidelity in the Lower Potomac Hundred...."

...A bottle of rum and hours later, with the night already dark and the camp quiet except for the sounds of men snoring and coughing in their sleep, happy and slightly tipsy, Christopher returned to his camp. He threw some sticks on the fire and soon had enough of a flame to provide reading light.

He took out Hannah's letter and her package, carefully setting aside the latter. Considering the letter, he stared at the handwriting, then tenderly broke the seal, but only after stroking the elegant rose and initials as if the curved wax impression was the woman herself. Leaning towards the fire, he read:

August 16th, 1776

My Dear friend Christopher,

I had the pleasure to write to you knowing that Michael Callum will make every effort to deliver this letter to you, and I hope it finds you safe and in good health — It was so good to see Michael again and hear news of the old home The latest intelligence we have is the Md. Batt. Is in Philada which I would envy you with all my heart if it wasn't for the War, 'though Mr Alexander informs us your batt. as well as Michael's will be sent to N. York to fight the British thear.

It is our lot to live in a time of remarkabl trouble and, I fear, danger; a time wherein we see dear friends off as warriors to defend our Liberty: I think of this constantly and, 'May heaven's guardian arm protect my absent friends from danger guard them, and from want defend."

Now that the great question has been decided, we all must protect and nurture our new and suffering country. To this effect, some of the women hear in Elk as well as myself have created a little circle the purpose of which is to spin flax for shirts, knit stockings and collect lead for our soldiers. As I'm certain you'll guess, this endeavor does not wholly satisfy my need to be

a useful Patriot, but I am told that women do thear duty by suffering,
admiring our army, and maintaining our innocence—

At this point I should assure you, all is not a rage for politics or
the military here: The flowers bloom as usual, and appear for some reason
more colorful than in years past; the fields are prettily planted in wheat and
corn and not tobacco weeds. War has not tested us yet; people are satisfied;
Friends and loved ones spend days together without a hint of politics. I know
some of this will change as a number of our men go off to join you with
General Washington's army but, God willing, this will be brief in duration.

You will know from Michael that your sister-in-law Susan and
brother George had a wonderful baby boy born on the 4th of July. His name
is Richard after some General I'm told, he is healthy as can be and
practically perfect.

I have nothing more to entertain you with, unless it is to regale you
with tales of domestic life which is comfortable but cannot be of much interest
to a brave soldier on campain.

I have been setting stockings on the needles for the army. I have sent
you my very first pair.

You, Dear Sir, will forgive my saying no matter how important is
your service to our country how happy I shou'd be if I cou'd see you soon.

May the Almighty keep you under His protection.

I am your Most obedient and affectionate

Hannah Williams

He had to smile. Between the prim "My Dear Friend" and
the proper "…obedient and affectionate" was a vibrant woman
who demanded his full attention, war or no war. Her signature,
writ large and carefully, fitted her perfectly. How he missed her!
Pensive, he folded the letter, tucked it and the package of
stockings in his pocket, and went off to bed.

Tripping into the tent, he squeezed himself in to lie beside a
softly snoring Mary, who had lately sought shelter from the
elements with him, Jeremiah and three other men in their small,
crowded tent. The nights were now cold, the blankets thin, and
the heat of another warm body next to you was a necessity.

He went to sleep that night with the most intimate thoughts
of Hannah, sleeping contentedly through a cold, blustery night,
even while the wind slapped loudly against the sides of the tent.

15

THE SEASON IS FAR ADVANCED

Harlem Heights
Early October 1776

IT HAD TURNED SUDDENLY COLD following an afternoon rain, and there were few in the American army who were comfortable in their worn clothes—or satisfied with their equally worn courage. They huddled over their small fires, trying to keep warm, and in the fire's light and warmth perhaps bolster their courage.

> *"Keep still!" said the thrush as she nestled her young,*
> *In a nest by the road; in a nest by the road.*
> *"For the tyrants are near, and with them appear*
> *What bodes us no good, what bodes us no good."*

With low morale came low esteem, and Captain Smith was among a growing number of officers who believed that General Washington couldn't lead this army competently and should be replaced by General Lee.

Christopher asked Major Gist about this, as he occasionally asked other such questions which corporals undoubtedly should not ask officers. Sometimes Major Gist would point that out to him; on other occasions he'd simply answer Christopher's questions without so much as a glance—which is what he did in this case.

"Perhaps the critics are right. But there is a nobleness in General Washington which leads me to believe he is the right man for this command. The idea of untrained militia standing up to regulars in the open field! Any commanding general of *this* army will have to work miracles.

"But miracles aside, it would just be a happy change to have the rest of the army tarry a bit to fight beside us—don't you think? But do the slaves have the courage to fight their master?"

Wanting only to hide in the fortress they were now frantically constructing atop Harlem Heights, the American army fervently hoped the campaign was coming to a close.

Christopher had happily traded his musket for a fascine knife and had set to work constructing as good a barrier as he could between the regulars and his freedom. He too was hopeful that the campaign was over.

Looking out over the intricate earthworks now being thrown up, Sergeant Jeremiah Smith thought it was possible, but said unenthusiastically, "I'll believe it when the British retire to winter quarters in New York City and we receive orders to construct huts."

Christopher chopped at a thicket that obstructed the view from the trench his men were now digging at the edge of a comforting precipice. He glanced at Jeremiah. "The men are counting the days of their service, and are anxious to get home—with good reason," he added.

"They have no good reason to go home until the war is won." Jeremiah had already decided to reenlist and was adamant that every other veteran in this army ought to do the same.

"Jeremiah, the war won't be won this year...*but it might be lost.* Let's see an end to this campaign, for God's sake. Let the men who believe they've done their part go home, and a new army be recruited for next year's campaign."

****

The American hope that the British Army soon go into winter quarters became more problematic when Christopher and his comrades watched in fascination as the city of New York went up in flames.

It was near midnight, and the sentries' yells and a few shots in the air awoke men from their nervous sleep. For those who crawled out of their tents at the first sounds of alarm, it appeared as a small flame far below, dancing in the wind like a candle. Then another flame appeared, and then another...and as more men crowded the rim, they all saw a city aglow.

Once thought strategic to a patriot victory, the American evacuation of New York City now made it expendable. Or so the generals claimed. From their defensive positions on Harlem Heights, the American army cheered wildly, willing the flames to make the city uninhabitable for the enemy. Watching the flames as they grew and spread in the distance, they drank to the real or imaginary patriots who must have set the fire. Strategic or not, it had turned out to be a Tory city, anyway.

So bad was their plight that they considered the burning of New York, the greatest city in North America, a victory.

As 1776 drew to a close, all their high talk had proved empty, and their less than skilled efforts had put them on the verge of utter defeat. They were now convinced that only an end to the campaign could save them.

Kingsbridge, Manhattan
October 15-18, 1776

As usual, they were digging fortifications. Raw, reddish-brown trenches were appearing everywhere around the bridges, the excavations creating mounds of protective dirt. Working in shirtsleeves, Christopher's crew was tamping gun platforms for artillery that didn't exist.

"Let's fill these gab-beans, men, then we'll help the others finish up on the abatis." Shovels thrust at the rocky soil, while fascine knives flashed in the early morning sun, chopping brush and sharpening branches.

Christopher was looking over the Harlem River when Jeremiah Smith came up, both men wiping dirty sweat from their faces with rolled-up sleeves.

"What's over there?"

"New York mainland—Westchester County."

Smallwood's Regiment had been augmented by the four remaining independent companies raised by Maryland in January 1776, and was now the largest regiment in the army. It had just been sent to Kingsbridge at the northernmost tip of Manhattan against a possible British landing in Westchester County. The two bridges here provided a crossing from Manhattan over the Bronx River to Westchester and were a vital line of retreat to the New York mainland. The need for defensive positions here was obvious and the Marylanders threw themselves into their digging with a passion.

"Goddammit! Only the village idiot and our Commander in Chief could miss the strategic significance of having navigable water around the whole of Manhattan. Of course the damn'd British have outflanked us and made all this"—Captain Smith waved dismissively toward the substantial fortifications on Harlem Heights and then included those his men were even now industriously throwing up around the bridges to the New York mainland—"a damn'd exercise in futility."

A large British force had landed in Westchester County on October 12 at a place called Throg's Neck on Long Island Sound; but it was met by stiff resistance from a handful of Hand's incorrigible Pennsylvanians, who, when not acting up, were savage fighters. The British gave up this attempt and it was not until six days later, when General Howe moved his forces three miles further north to Pell's Point, that they landed and established a secure beachhead.

Despite a spirited defense by Glover's Marbleheaders, the British were now advancing westward across Westchester toward Kingsbridge to threaten the Continental Army still enwombed in its defenses on Manhattan.

So much for an end to the campaign. As a disgusted Captain Smith put it, "We're between the hawk and the buzzard." And so they were.

"His Excellency has ordered the army to evacuate Manhattan, with the exception of those forces at Fort Washington—which apparently will be held by order of the Congress—to obstruct navigation of the Hudson at 'whatever expense,' I believe was the wording." Captain Smith had his doubts about their ability to hold Fort Washington.

"What is our destination, Sir?"

"White Plains, which is about a day's travel north. It's said to offer good defensive positions. Trouble is, we have valuable supplies to take off, but lack sufficient wagons and horses to do so in one haul—so we have to do it in stages."

Jeremiah shook his head. "Captain, our duties will be?"

"The usual," Captain Smith stated matter-of-factly. "Cover the retreat and defend the army's most valuable supplies." He put up his hand in anticipation of the objections he knew would come. "I know what you're going to say, Jeremiah. Once more this will separate us from our own baggage."

"Sir, while protecting the baggage of others, we ourselves have lost a considerable amount of baggage during this retreat up Manhattan. It's getting cold and we have insufficient tents, blankets, and winter clothes, even medicines, all because of thievery."

Major Gist understood and approved an increase in the guard. The task of guarding the company baggage fell to Christopher and Jeremiah, who were given a detail of eight invalids. As soon as the regiment began moving out early in the morning, the civilian followers, wagoners, and the guard detail loaded tents, camp equipment, and medical supplies into the wagons and started on their slow journey to White Plains.

After crossing old King's Bridge over the Harlem, the train continued on the Post Road toward White Plains. Mild weather had delayed the signs of autumn; it had just recently turned cold enough to daub the trees with the crimsons, oranges, and yellows marking a crisp autumn day—a beautiful day to be traveling.

Christopher walked with Mary McBride alongside a heavily loaded cart. As usual, Mary did most of the talking.

"Doin' some nursing now in addition to the washin' and cookin' chores," Mary noted with pride. "Good thing, too, 'cause there's not much in my line a work. Lord! If the Cause wasn't so important, I might be tempted to return to me old ways."

Christopher had never asked about Mary's "old ways," but did ask her if she still intended to remain with the army. She nodded in the affirmative and said, "I've decided I want to be a sutter—Why certainly, women can be sutters, Christopher. And just why not, if I might ask? There's nothin' to commercing in booze, for goodness sake—it's bosoms and arses and befoggin' men's minds with cheap drink—simple as that...who do you want entertainin' you when you're having a drink—the barkeep or the barmaid?"

Bantering and laughing, they walked on, as the wagon train plodded toward its destination. By early afternoon their progress had been painfully slow. They would have to stop soon and unload their cargo by the wayside, so that the wagons could turn around and return to the regiment's abandoned camp for more baggage.

Jeremiah spied a farmhouse off in the distance, "Christopher, we'll dump our load at that farmhouse over there." The wagons and carts turned off the road and followed a narrow, rutted lane to the house, which appeared to be deserted. It was a substantial wood-framed dwelling, likely the home of a prosperous farmer; but the door was splintered and a number of the glazed windows were broken.

Jeremiah and Christopher went inside and found the interior a shambles—broken furniture and crockery, the pungent smell of urine coming from the corners of the room. Mary then walked in, having investigated the detached kitchen. "I'd like to prepare ye gents a proper home-cooked meal, but"—she laughed derisively—"it'll have to be thin ration stew and yesterday's bread."

"Christopher," said Jeremiah, "ye stay here with the baggage and the women, and I'll return with the teamsters for the rest of the stuff."

Following supper, Jeremiah set off with the wagons, cautioning Christopher to be alert to deserters and marauders. "These environs are a haven for lawless bands and such, Chris—take care."

16

A RUN-IN WITH THE REFUGEES

Westchester County, New York
October 21, 1776

TWILIGHT HAD SET IN, and a cold sun had left the skyline stippled in washed pinks and grays, when a voice called out from a locust grove in back of the house.

"Who's there?" the sentry cried. "Advance and be recognized." A single man, dressed in civilian clothes, came out of the shadows, holding his musket above his head. Christopher came up as the guard demanded, "What is the countersign?"

"I don't know today's countersign," the man admitted and stood still, continuing to hold his musket above his head. "Name's Jerred Samuels—private soldier with the Westchester County militia. We weren't in the lines last night, so weren't given it."

Christopher motioned for the man to approach.

"I'll take your weapon. Now, what can we do for you?"

"Not much, a little to eat or drink if ye can spare it. I was out scoutin' with a patrol, working around the British advanced positions near New Rochelle, when we was attacked by a party of 'em. During the fightin'—which was hot, I can tell you—I got separated—so, I'm headin' up towards Wepperham."

Christopher looked the man over. "Private Samuels, you are welcome to share our supper with us, such as it is. Missus McBride over there might even be able to find you a bit of rum." "Thankee, Corporal," he said with a smile, as Christopher directed one of the men to take him over to the kitchen.

Christopher was involved in checking the baggage and walking around the house lawns, and did not talk to Private Samuels. Immersed in his duties, he was surprised when Samuels approached to thank him for the hospitality. "I best be moving on, Corporal. Much obliged for your comradeship."

After Private Samuels's departure, one of the men came over to Christopher. "Corporal...now, I'm not sayin' this Samuels fellow is a liar, but I don't fully believe his braggin'."

"Why's that, Jim?"

"Well, he didn't seem to know that we have a line of troops further east that he should a come through if he was coming from shadowin' the British."

Christopher considered this. "Could be a deserter...could be a militiaman—it's hard to tell the difference." He gave the other man a tired shrug and went about his business.

****

"There's three or four men—armed—that I saw, and a couple a women," the man called Jerred Samuels reported.

"Women, ye say? Ripe?"

"Ripe enough." Samuels responded, and looked curiously at the man asking the question, thinking a gash is a gash, ain't it?

"Hmm...don't like the idear of hittin' on wagons guarded by armed men," the leader of the gang said. "Who be they?"

"Mary-landers," said Samuels. He rubbed his runny nose on his rotten sleeve.

"Marylanders, you say? Well, now..." Thomas Boarman looked up from the knife he was sharpening.

Thomas Boarman, aptly named The Boar, had joined a small band of Refugees soon after he deserted Smallwood's battalion in Elizabethtown back in August. The band had tried their hand at thievery between Elizabethtown and further north in Jersey, but found it unprofitable and risky. Then they realized there were opportunities in the growing confusion of retreating and advancing armies in New York, and fortuitously found themselves in Westchester County when the armies were scrambling around in October. The isolated estates there were fair bursting with family silver, cellars full of French cognacs, and pretty wives and daughters. To date, however, pickings had been slim, mostly because the men lacked enough firearms and ammunition to strike it really big.

This disappointed Thomas Boarman. The gang's leader was a gutless wretch with no vision for profitable rampagin'. His sorry men were satisfied with robbing the solitary traveler or two, or raiding the occasional house, all of which provided them with a bare few coins, booze, and the occasional woman. It got so bad, his two comrades from the battalion gave it up and turned themselves in to Continental authorities. Living a life of crime *was* risky business and Thomas Boarman truly believed he deserved to get a lot more out of it than he was getting.

"What d'ya think, Tom?"

"There's only three or four of 'em armed? I say we take 'em. We need muskets and cartridges, Dan'l, not to mention spoils— and a woman would be nice. With, say, four guards, no more than two will be standing guard after midnight, and more likely just one."

The gang's ammunition had been wetted by the recent rain, and three of the five men were without muskets and carried makeshift spears. Guns, ammunition, food, booze, and the smell of women were driving them to overcome their natural cowardice and decide in favor of attacking the party of Marylanders.

Still, Dan'l was not convinced.

"Jerred, did they believe your story?"

Certain, they did! Gave me a good meal and a slug of whiskey to boot. Why, one a the cunts even let me feel her titties!"

That was enough to convince even Dan'l. "Let's do it."

Laughing and rubbing their crotches in anticipation, The Boar and his confederates made their plans.

****

Late that night, the guard was surprised when Jerred Samuels carefully approached the house and respectfully announced himself. He claimed a bad limp as reason for his return. Indeed, he leaned heavily on his musket, which he was using as a crutch. Jarred was practiced at this and went forward confidently.

The ploy worked perfectly. The guard was the same one who had challenged him earlier that evening. Recognizing Samuels, he welcomed him familiarly, and upon hearing his explanation, clucked in sympathy with his plight.

"Bad luck, Samuels. Here, just ease yourself down by the fire."

"I was thinkin' maybe your corporal would allow me to ride in one of the wagons nearer to Wepperham."

"I don't see why not. Lemme call Corporal Sims."

"Is he restin'?—Well, then, don't go botherin' him now. I'll just bed down here until the morning. Maybe keep you company for a spell—if you'd like?"

"Why, that'll be fine. Gets lonely about this time a night."

"It does that," Samuels said with good humor....

Christopher heard this exchange standing silent as an Indian in the darkness outside the gloomy light of the fire. He had indeed thought to nap, but there was something about their situation which kept him wide awake. Rather than toss and turn, he thought he'd do the rounds of their little perimeter.

It was a good thing, too.

As the sentry turned away from him to tend to his duties, Samuels, who was not the least bit interested in taking his ease, carefully rose to a crouch and seemed to poise himself for some sudden action.

When Christopher saw the knife in his hand, he realized Samuels's intentions and quick as he could ran over and tackled him, pinioning his arms to his side and knocking the knife out of his grasp.

Picking up the knife, Christopher held it to his throat and demanded in what he hoped was a whisper, "Now, tell me, 'Private' Samuels—how many other bravoes are out there?" He made sure Samuels felt the point of the knife blade as he punctured the soft skin under his chin. He felt blood, warm and sticky, dribbling on his fingers as he pushed the knife in a little further.

"I'm not goin' to ask you one more time, *Private* Samuels," he threatened.

"Fi—four others," the man gasped. "For God's sake don't shive me."

"Five or four, which is it?" He twisted the knife just a little to make his point.

"Four, I swear."

"What's the signal to bring them in?"

Samuels was silent, and Christopher pushed the knife in a little further, hissing, "The next thrust will spear that silent tongue of yours."

"A little powder thrown into the fire to make it flare up. *Please*—"

"Good." Christopher turned to the sentry, "Bind him and gag him good."

Minutes later, the fire near the wagons flared suddenly but distinctly. Seeing the signal clearly, the rest of the gang quietly but quickly advanced and were in the fire's light when shots rang out.

Immediately, two of the Refugees fell—the other two turned around in confusion. One had a spear and went to the ground searching for one of the muskets dropped by the others, while the other man stepped back into the darkness in an attempt to conceal himself.

There was another shot and one of the Refugees staggered back into the darkness. The soldier who had just fired charged frantically with fixed bayonet to stab the other bandit, who had by then found a musket and was beginning to raise it—the musket flashed with a loud report and the soldier fell with a sharp cry of pain.

The one remaining bandit, surprised by the man charging out of the darkness, reversed his direction and ran across the area illuminated by the fire—straight toward Christopher, just as he stepped into the light, his bayonet-tipped musket pointing at the man's throat.

The man stopped short. Realizing there was no escape, he raised his musket and cried, "I'm a Marylander! I'm a Marylander! For God's sake, don't kill one of your own!" He immediately began to explain that he had been captured on Long Island and then impressed into service with British partisans.

Seeing the man clearly for the first time, Christopher started. Could it be? he asked himself in shock.

Then, masking his surprise. "Well, Thomas Boarman. Welcome back to the battalion. Ever since that night in Elizabeth Town, I've been hoping for an opportunity to come across you again—and what do ye know...."

He saw recognition dawn on The Boar's crude features. He looked calmly at Christopher. "Well, shit, if it ain't the farmer. So, you've been waiting for an opportunity to get even with me, have you? Now, here's your chance—*if* you're man enough, an' I don't think you are."

The Boar had quickly decided that challenging Christopher to a fight was his best hope of finding some advantage; perhaps this ploy would put his captors off guard and he might manage to escape into the night.

"Sure, you and the rest can shoot me down in my tracks, but then"—he looked at the men surrounding him, calling on their sense of manhood—"Sims here won't be able to brag to that skinny-arsed whore of his back in Elk how he won a manly fight!" Looking straight at Christopher, The Boar laughed obscenely as he said, "Oh yeah, Sims, I been told to kill her too!"

He had judged his man right. Christopher was in a rage and itching to go after him. He was actually torn between shooting him down in his tracks—which he should have done without a second thought—or taking him on, which is what both men wanted.

Christopher was on the verge of making a decision when an unexpected shot rang out, followed almost immediately by the discharge of a second musket.

The first shot had been fired by the bandit who had run off; the second shot had been fired by Mary, who, armed with a musket, had thrown up a shot in the direction of the muzzle flash. Neither shot had any accuracy to it, but the exchange caused everyone to duck.

Everyone except The Boar, that is. He took advantage of the momentary confusion and fled into the darkness. Christopher saw him pick up a musket lying on the ground as he darted off.

"Dammit," Christopher cried and started into the darkness after him.

"Chris! Don't you go out there!" Mary's voice was high-pitched and insistent.

"Don't!" She repeated, now screaming. He hesitated, looking in her direction. She ran over to him and grabbed his shirt. "You'll get yourself killed."

Mary was right. But the killing madness had hold of him.

Firmly removing her hand from his sleeve, Christopher turned to one of his men. "John, c'mon." And the two of them ran off in pursuit of The Boar, who could still be heard crashing through the underbrush.

The night was cold and silent and any noise should have resounded like glass breaking in an empty room—but there was no noise, except the wind swooping through the trees. The earlier noises caused by The Boar thrashing around in the brush had died away and all around them was quiet.

Christopher and Private Jamison, motionless in a stand of trees, began to move forward in a semblance of Indian stealth in the direction they thought The Boar might have fled, the silence suggesting that he had gone to ground nearby.

Suddenly there was a shot. Jamison let out a grunt and Christopher heard him crash to the ground. Over the moaning, he could hear the crackling and swishing of a man pushing through the brush. He foolishly aimed and fired his musket in that direction.

Furiously, he rushed wherever he imagined The Boar might be. He tripped over bushes and fallen tree limbs, struck out at tree trunks and shadows, and froze because of every noisy leaf. But The Boar had just disappeared. Nothing. After too many wasteful minutes, he concluded The Boar had gotten away for good. Then he heard Mary's worried voice calling for him and knew it was time to call it quits. He carefully withdrew and went to find Jamison, whose painful sounds he could hear nearby.

Jeremiah and the wagon train returned around noontime the next day. They were quickly filled in on last night's events. Jeremiah looked at Jamison's arm and was satisfied that Mary had done a good job of patching him up. Then Christopher took Jeremiah around to see the corpses laid out in the back field.

Jeremiah looked at the bodies, a bloody hole in the gray linsey waistcoat of one, a bough covering the shattered head of another, and the suggestion of a surprised look on the pale face of the last. The Maryland soldier who was killed in the attack had been laid off to the side.

"Well, good riddance. And you say The Boar was one of 'em? Pity he got away." With a final look at the bodies, "Did ye strip these of any valuables? Good. Now place Private Weedon's body in a wagon—I want him buried with his comrades—and then have these scum buried in a hole shallow enough for the animals to find 'em."

Jeremiah hesitated, and a peculiar look came to his face. In a quiet voice, he asked, "Ye say this Samuels fellow put his hands on Mary?" Christopher had mentioned to Jeremiah that Samuels had gone to grope Mary and had got a bit ugly when she rebuffed him.

"Nothing outta the ordinary, Jeremiah. He just seemed...well, more demandin' than most, that's all. Y'know Mary don't take too well to men takin' liberties with her and she'll tell you that the words they had had nothin' to do with the physicalness of it. It's the principle of the thing," Christopher said.

Jeremiah scratched his stubble, the look still on his face.

"Well, that might be. But I guess I'll jus' go and have a word with this Samuels."

17

"THE BRITISH ARE ON THE CAMP, SIR"

White Plains, New York
October 28, 1776

EVEN AS THEY CLIMBED CHATTERTON'S HILL, they heard the sound of cannon, booming sounds echoing thickly among the soft, rounded hills, ricocheting among the thickets of trees, or lapping like sea waves over the steeply-angled meadows. Near the crest, they were met by fleeing militiamen.

Jeremiah looked at them in disgust, not even bothering to try to stop their flight. One of the militia officers, shoulders sagging in disgrace, was explaining in a whining voice that a cannonball had struck one of the men in the hip and that had sent the rest fleeing in terror.

"Ye know," Jeremiah said calmly. "I'm convinced I was shot dead on Long Island and have gone to Hell for my sins, where I am to spend eternity watching militia forsake the Revolution."

"Naw, Jeremiah, if you were really in Hell, you'd *be* one of those militiamen."

"Good point, Chris. Shall we venture over t'other side of the hill and see what awaits us?"

Reaching the hilltop, they had a spectacular view of the unfolding battle. Down below and across the river, the British

Army had approached the American lines around White Plains in eight columns. The massed formations flowed over fields and hills, moving in stately procession, and then formed in line of battle with the precision of a ticking clock.

"Will you look at that!" Christopher exclaimed in awe, staring in the direction of the British Army, watching in fascination.

The pomp was magnificent. A coppery autumn sun reflected on burnished arms and equipment, making them seem to burst into violent flame; officers and men were uniformed in scarlet and blue, but with colorful facings and spotless white crossbelts, some wearing great bearskin or shiny brass grenadier caps. Silky Grand Unions and brightly colored regimental standards waved languorously in a slight breeze, while several regimental bands discordantly blared forth martial music.

"Guess what, Jeremiah"—Christopher posed this as a statement of fact, not a question—"We're goin' to bear the brunt of this attack. Know why?—Just take a look."

They saw a detached force moving toward the east bank of the Bronx River in the direction of Chatterton's Hill; while the rest of the British army simply sat down in place, as if it expected to be the audience at an entertaining farce.

"Isn't that something?" Jeremiah whistled, appreciating the ceremony. "I do admire the way Europeans turn war into a show." Looking around, he added, "But there's us, an' the Delawares, and some New York regulars—so perhaps we don't have to act the fool to hold their attention."

****

They actually fought well—well, many of them did, and that included some of the much maligned militia; but, as usual, they were out-maneuvered and out-generaled…and, of course, defeated.

They held their own for a while, trading volleys with the advancing enemy, puffs of smoke like storm clouds hung over the field, smoldering paper wadding littered the ground in front of them; the acrid stink of black powder, the collective shout of *"hut"* as the British prepared to deliver another volley; the yelling and screaming of men who were afraid or hurt. What seemed like an eternity lasted only minutes.

Sooner or later it was bound to happen…and it did when the militia broke. Without support, the Marylanders began a graceless retreat. Christopher did not feel compelled to urge his men to stand and fight. Slinging his musket, he grabbed a man wounded in the thigh, and, like a four-legged animal making do with three, awkwardly hopped away from the advancing British line as fast as they could.

Drums beating The Retreat soon relieved them of any guilt.

****

General Washington tried to anticipate the next British thrust. Assuming that Fort Washington, the last American outpost on Manhattan, could withstand a British siege—it was impregnable, wasn't it?—he assigned Major General Heath and a goodly number of Eastern troops to guard the New York Highlands; Major General Charles Lee with an even greater force was to remain here at North Castle to respond to any contingency, while His Excellency would cross into New Jersey with the Southern troops to protect Philadelphia.

On November 11, Christopher and his charges were put aboard an old fishing shallop stinking of rotten fish and ferried over to Haverstraw in New Jersey. They were happy indeed to be going to New Jersey, which they thought of as a stage stop on the way home.

"It's good to be heading in the right direction," they said to each other. "In three weeks our enlistments will be up."

The Cause, it seemed, was no longer their greatest concern.

18

"YE SHOULD NEVER FIGHT AGAINST YOUR KING!"

What was called their flying camp was literally so.
A loyalist with the British Army

Newark, New Jersey
November 23, 1776

IT WAS A RACE NOW. If it had been Lord Howe who led the pursuit, Christopher and his weary comrades very possibly could have strolled across New Jersey to the safety of the Delaware; but Howe had appointed a huntsman who was intent on bagging the fox. Charles, Earl of Cornwallis, now on a long leash, knowing that this rebellion survived only because of His Lordship's rather leisurely offensive pricks, was inclined toward swift and daring strokes.

Following the fall of the last American stronghold on Manhattan and the fall of Fort Lee, across the Hudson, in New Jersey, Lord Cornwallis was free to take off after General Washington and the main army, and the chase across the Jerseys was on.

The weather had turned cold and wet, the days gray with a misty foreboding. Men who had set out with the promise of spring were not prepared for the bleakness of winter. Most were summer soldiers…and only a few of them would find it in themselves to become winter soldiers.

Smallwood's regiment was now a shadow of its former self, numbering perhaps two hundred and fifty in all. Major Gist was now in command. Colonel Smallwood had been invalided to Philadelphia, while most of the other senior officers were seriously ill and had also been evacuated from the theater of operations.

"Unfortunately," Major Gist told the remaining officers and non-commissioned officers, "while the army has improved its fighting capabilities to the point where we can stand up to the enemy, we now have virtually no army left standing."

What was left of Smallwood's regiment had been in Newark several days and finally under canvas, the first time in weeks they had shelter from the cold nights. Here, temporarily safe from Cornwallis's threat, they rested. Going about their camp duties, they watched Newark's women and children evacuate a doomed town.

Two days of mild, dry weather, some pork or beef and good flour, and a little rest had done wonders for their morale. Mary spent this time patching and washing clothes, and cooking meals with the sparse rations available. After two days of mild weather, on November 26 came a hard, cold rain which wet them through and chilled them to their very bones. Too wet to make a fire, all they could do was sit shivering in their leaking tent.

That is, when they weren't mounting guard.

"Goddammit"—Christopher's use of profanity had now reached prodigious proportions—"Could we've had guard duty yesterday? Or the day before? No, of course not. We have to have it tonight." The rain was beating on the tent like drum taps, as a gusting wind, which sounded cold, punched at the duck cloth. "All right, then, let's go."

The detail set off in the darkness pelted by a wind-driven rain on an intolerably bad road, their bruised feet crunching on the frozen, crusty mud. Hours later and thoroughly miserable, they came to a farmhouse which served as the command post; here they relieved the guard on duty, provided password and countersign, and wearily assumed their duties. After posting the first watch, Christopher returned to the house.

Reluctantly, the Wente family had acquiesced to the military use of their house but only with the understanding that the soldiers would confine themselves to the kitchen. Christopher entered the room, a warming fire in the great hearth, and saw Jeremiah sitting at the plank table talking with the father, a garrulous, opinionated old man.

Speaking in the careful English of one who learned the language late in life, the old man was wagging a finger at Jeremiah. "Ye should never fight against your King! Rebels—ye be rebels, and will be drawn and quartered, and your very hearts torn from your bodies while ye're still drawing breath!"

Jeremiah looked up at Christopher, with a wry smile. "The old man here is a king's man—like his son-in-law, who I gather is with the loyalist New Jersey Volunteers."

Christopher walked over to the fire and poured himself a cup of coffee, then sat down at the table.

Christopher should have ignored the old man, but, instead, exploded. "Old man, *we* are not rebels...*we* are Patriots— revolutionaries. Your king is not our king. *We* are buildin' a new world in which there will be no kings. Now, begone, lest I tear out your shriveled heart while you still breathe, and eat it before your daughter's very eyes—because *I am a starving revolutionary.*"

The old man looked at this foul, rotting rebel and saw the devil—just like he had seen the devil when the creek overflowed its banks higher than anybody could recollect and had flushed out a coffin, its top off, and a bloated, white corpse, smiling evilly at him, floated downstream, swirling around the rocks.

And he was frightened more than he could ever remember.

Trembling violently, the old man rose and shuffled as quickly as he could from the room, passing his daughter, who no doubt had tried to keep her father away from these hard, angry men, knowing he would cause their ruin with his talk of kings an' such.

Looking beseechingly at the two rebels, the woman held out her hands as if asking forgiveness. "He doesn't mean any harm—"

Christopher was in no mood to hear her sniveling. "Ma'am, I beg your pardon, but he does mean us harm," he said harshly. "More importantly, he means the Cause harm."

The woman stepped back as if physically struck.

Suddenly surprised at himself, Christopher shook his head, as if trying to regain his senses. He had not intended to brutalize the poor woman, so he added gently, "Ma'am, we're not goin' to hurt the old man, nor you, nor your family—an' we'll honor your house, and we thank you kindly for your hospitality."

The woman began to babble in her relief. "We're obliged to have ye here with us, Captain—'cause of the bandits, y'know ...and we was paid—in Continental paper, but I don't mind that...an'—" She suddenly stopped talking and left the room, only to return with a squat green bottle in her hand. Putting it on the table, she confided, "'Twas my husband's, and is only half full." Finding that this gesture pleased them, she departed.

Jeremiah considered the dusty bottle, then reached for it, pulled the cork and took a sniff. "Why that smells like good brandy." He took a swig. Nodding appreciatively, he took another pull on the bottle before handing it to Christopher. "It is good brandy."

He watched as Christopher angrily took a swig, looking like he needed the alcohol and not the taste.

"Chris, ye seem to be in a black mood. The weather?"

"Oh, I don't know, Jeremiah," Christopher said wearily and handed back the bottle. "It's not being beaten by the British that discourages me—we're getting the hang of fightin'. Trouble is, as I see it, there might not be enough interest in continuing this war. Why, we're fightin' for our lives and whole regiments are goin' home. An' those of us remaining are naked and starving—in a country which is rich and fat. Is this a popular uprising or not?"

"Christopher," Jeremiah began in his careful way, "Many of these men have been servin' since April of '75. They enlisted in the Continental service for six months or maybe a year—believin' that the war would have been over long ago. Now, those who are family men have the care of their families heavy on their minds. They need to get home, Christopher."

Christopher really thought he had set out to serve a noble cause. Now he was not so sure. If the very people for whom the Cause was meant to embrace despised you, what on earth were you fighting for?

He said as much to Jeremiah, whose explanation was simplicity itself: "The people are disappointed in the army. We've not exactly been the Righteous Host people had in mind, now have we? Not only do we suffer defeat after defeat, we steal, and cheat, and use the Lord's name in vain.

"The fact of the matter is, Chris, the British can't govern us—but it might take some time and suffering for them to realize that—an' it's this army's job to further convince 'em."

Christopher could discuss his doubts with Jeremiah, but not with Mary, because she had no doubts of her own. She'd told both of them in no uncertain terms that she'd never surrender.

"If we can't win…why, we'll simply run away to a better land." In a soft voice, she then sang a stanza from "The American Liberty Song," a popular army song:

> *With the beasts of the wood*
> *We will ramble for food*
> *And live in wild deserts and caves,*
> *And live poor as Job*
> *On the skirts of the globe,*
> *Before we'll submit to be slaves!*

"But that's only if we *have* to flee, Christopher," she said sternly. "Right now, we needs must stand and fight it out. We have our country to defend!"

Mary had asked him what he planned to do when his enlistment was up, and he was honest with her. She looked at him, anger etching her dirty face.

"What d'ya mean 'someone else's turn?' What does that mean?—is liberty worth only six months or maybe a year of a person's labor? Now, I'm not saying that you or any other man doesn't have reason to leave the army…what I'm saying is that either you believe in the Cause or you don't; and if you do believe, you give it your all—whatever that might be; but ye accept it at its face value, not like you'd assay a worn coin."

19

JUST KEEPING BODY AND SOUL ALIVE

Moving Fast on the Post Road, Across New Jersey
November 28-30, 1776

"HERE YE ARE, Chris, that ought to hold you for a while," said Mary as she handed him his hunting shirt. By now it retained little resemblance to the one given him by Rachel Jones just five months ago—the cape had disappeared for patches and the handsome fringe had long ago gone for thread. Tattered as it was, he wore it over George's old suit of clothes, more for its warlike appearance than for the slight warmth it provided.

Even though he looked like a tatterdemalion, he was still well-clothed compared to most of his comrades. Almost all of the enlisted men were dressed in summer clothing, which were now threadbare at best—at worst, they had no proper shirts or waistcoats. In the case of more than a few men, they were reduced to wearing linen drawers in place of pants. They were all desperately cold.

Worse, the regiment to a man was without stockings and wore broken shoes with soles like paper. After losing his sturdy shoes in the mud of Gowanus Creek, Christopher had been wearing his pumps, the ones with the silver buckles. He would joke that these light shoes enabled him to fly in the face of the enemy with the fleetest militia; but, in truth the pumps might be the death of him: his feet were poorly—terribly bruised, cracked and crusted with blood—feet which might not carry him a great deal further across New Jersey's razor-sharp roads.

There was also a shortage of food and drink. The campaign, particularly this precipitous retreat, had outstripped the army's rudimentary supply system. Sutlers had decamped; and the civilian wagoners, those whose worn horses could still stumble along pulling a wagon or cart, had called it quits, leaving the army with virtually no means of transporting what little supplies it had left.

A soldier of the regiment put it about as well as any of them could: "An' a course, we ain't been paid in—what is it now, boys—near three month?" All snorted in unison. "An' His Excellency—who, I suspect, ain't down to eating goddamn turnips like us—tells us not to *presume* upon the civilian population for firewood and food an' such."

This was both a common accusation regarding the public's lack of appreciation and a common excuse for their depredations against the civilian population. Christopher was as indignant as his comrades, but the money given him by Mike Callum tempered his inclination toward abusive behavior.

Several days earlier, he had given Mary the small purse of coins to use as she saw fit. During the past several weeks both Jeremiah and he had come to depend upon her frugality to keep them fed and clothed.

"This be a monstrous sum! Why, there must be near two pound in *real money* here!" Mary carefully counted the coins, and bit one or two for good measure. "An' ye want me to use this for the three of us, Chris? Well, then," she sighed happily, "the first thing I gotta do is nab some beeves' hides and find that shoemaker I know in the Fourth Company; then…I don't know about stockings—but I might be able to have some blanket coats made if I can lay me hands on a few pieces of stuff or duffels…an' certain we'll still have some left over for belly-timber." Mary then added, "And maybe even a peg or two…How's that?"

On November 28th, the Continental Army hastily evacuated Newark just as Lord Cornwallis's vanguard arrived.

"Burn the tents and whatever else we can't carry off. That's an order!"

Jeremiah bridled, knowing how much they were already suffering in this wet and cold November weather. But Captain Smith was adamant. "Burn the damn things!—now hurry." They set the duckcloth and canvas on fire and watched miserably as their worn little shelters went up in flames and black, oily smoke.

Captain Smith winced. "It's better than leaving equipment to the British, men...."

Tent poles, which had been carried individually by the men, were happily tossed. Then they started to think about tossing other items, not all of which even this fleeing army considered expendable.

"Private Rees, what the hell do ya think you're doin'?" Christopher stared in amazement as he saw Private Rees throw away his mess's cast iron kettle.

"Corporal, what's the sense in luggin' this thing around? We haven't had any food to cook for days—and runnin' off as we are, won't have any for God knows how much longer. Besides, the damn'd thing stinks."

"Stinks? Whaddaya mean, stinks'?"

"Jus' what I said, it stinks...probably because of the meat's been in it for—oh, I dunno...for awhile."

"For a while? Why didn't you and the others eat the meat when it was fresh, for crissake?"

"Well, because it's been foul from the very start, an' we thought we'd save it 'til we were awful hungry."

"Rees, toss the carrion, keep the kettle. Got that?"

So, that much lighter in load, the regiment fled.

Above freezing weather had made the tracks a muddy mire, but walking on the edges wasn't too bad, and it was soft on sore feet. Added to this, Christopher and Jeremiah were shod in new shoes, and while the wet would harden the raw, untanned leather to rivel'd iron, Mary had also managed to procure them some woolen stockings. Best of all, she had somehow obtained coarse woolen coats which protected them against the damp coldness.

Mary, herself, looked like a bumpkin. A rough coat made from her worn blanket covered her thin shift and bodice of cheap ticking; she was down to one bedraggled skirt, the hem stained black and ragged; to top off her outfit, she wore a formless slouch hat secured with a strip of cloth beneath her chin, giving the brim the look of a pair of bedraggled wings.

"Well, here we are beating hoof again, and, as usual, actin' surprised." Mary was thoroughly disgusted. "You'd think an army which retreats as much as this one does would've developed a little *flamboyance*—is that the right word?—in the way it flies from the enemy."

They were on the New York-Philadelphia Post Road, moving fast, hearing sporadic gunfire in the rear. Looking back, Christopher saw several of the regiment's companies marching doggedly in retreat. Remnants, he noted sadly, remnants of a once proud regiment. The little group of men looked like scarecrows, all for the most part clothed in foul-smelling rags, without stockings and in broken shoes; heads, many of them bare, bent to a sharp wind.

But they marched like soldiers and their arms were burnished and shone in the cold sunlight. *Bent but not broken—not yet,* Christopher thought... *but I wonder for how much longer.* He sighed and, turning around, marched doggedly on himself.

Mile after painful mile, the dispirited men of Washington's army marched with no purpose other than flight. Vanquishing the enemies of the revolution was not their purpose; defending the capital of their new nation was not their purpose; their sole purpose was to survive; and the knowledge of their abject plight did not encourage them to do anything but flee from the enemy.

So on they hurried, the clay muck sucking at shoes with flapping soles, now caked in heavy mud, their legs tired, their feet cracked. The day was raw and misty, a hint of ice in the air, and the harsh wind swirled through thin coats and breeches. The Post Road wound through fields of corn stubble, lined by gnarled trees and deserted hamlets, the narrow track a reddish-brown weal on the barren winter landscape.

Finally they crossed the bridge over the Raritan and trudged into Brunswick, a substantial river town lining the western bank of a turgid, brown river.

"Word is that the British intend to move on Philadelphia before the end of the campaign," noted Jeremiah. He was roasting a chunk of meat, the fat bubbling and spitting, on his ramrod over the fire they had built outside the neat whitewashed barn which served as their quarters.

Chewing on his piece of tough, blackened beef, Christopher said, "Don't tell me—there's some who still have expectations we'll defend the city." He licked his fingers, savoring the grease.

"Naw…Captain Stone is talking about makin' 'em pay dearly if they try it; but 'tis empty talk—we all know this army will disappear tomorrow when the enlistments of the Flying Camp regiments are up."

"Just look at the damn'd officers, Jeremiah. They've all gone off to recruit for their next year's command. But what about *this* year?"

"Chris, you know we don't need all those officers. Now is the time to recruit for the next campaign, or we'll have no army next spring."

"So our officers are back home handing out our uniforms and back pay as enlistment bonuses to men who might not have a cause to fight for next spring."

Dissolution
New Brunswick, New Jersey
December 1, 1776

The army was still in Brunswick when the first of December dawned, overcast and threatening, the date the army experienced yet a further dissolution. This time it was the Pennsylvania, New Jersey, and Maryland battalions of the Flying Camp who left camp in droves.

"Damme if Bell's entire brigade isn't goin' home!" This was a reference to General Beall's Brigade of the Maryland Flying Camp. News of its wholesale departure shocked the officers and men of the regular regiment. A bunch of the regulars were discussing this while sitting in the relative warmth of a barn, smelling of old hay and horse manure.

Jeremiah refilled his cup from the keg of rum Mary had produced two days ago. Sitting back in the hay, the dim lighting masked his disappointment. "I understand some of 'em have enlisted in the Sixth Regiment under the new establishment, but it's true that more than a thousand are leavin'."

"Well, don't forget, men, the term of *our* regiment is up and quite a few of us have also decided to call it quits."

"I'll be goin' home tomorrow, too," James Nolton said softly. "But it's not because I'm quittin'." James was a much-respected sergeant who had fought valiantly in all their fights and always stood up for his men. They would miss him, but they knew also that James had a newborn and a sickly wife, who needed him more than a dying army needed him.

"Will you be comin' back in the spring, Jim?"

"Might."

A dozen others in their company also departed. Christopher and Jeremiah knew all of these men and loved them dearly; they were good men, willing to fight and sacrifice; but they had become convinced that there was no fight left in this army...and thinkin' that their family needed them more, they intended to set out for home.

None who elected to stay held it against those good, steady men who felt the need to leave. In fact, they didn't hold it against all those men who left simply because they felt their country had forsaken them.

The night before, Christopher had sought out Michael Callum to see if he was staying or leaving. They had run into each other on several occasions, but had never discussed this particular subject—perhaps because neither of them was quite sure what he would do on the first of December.

"Goin' home, Chris. And I don't make any excuses for it, either. I'm starved, stinking foul with the flux, and I'm gettin' the dry cough. I could stay on to the end of the campaign, yes—and likely die of camp fever, for what? We're not going to fight—we're goin' to retreat until the British go into winter quarters.

"Chris, this army is not disintegrating on the battlefield from shot or bayonet, but in camp from starvation and sickness. For every man we've lost in battle, we've lost ten to the camp or hospital. As for desertion—why, who can blame a man? The plight of this army, Chris, is not worth my life, nor yours.

"So, I intend to march off to Philadelphia tomorrow to see to the pay and discharge of my men; then I'm goin' to seek out a good physician; then buy me some clothes; then have a sumptuous dinner at the City Tavern—then I'm goin' home."

Michael's voice, which showed his anger and frustration as he explained his reasoning for leaving, calmed noticeably as he described his plans after being mustered out. "And you?"

"Mike, I'm stayin'—at least until the end of the campaign. I can't see walking away now—oh, everything you say is true, and I oughta have sense enough to know when enough is enough, but somehow," Christopher shrugged lamely, "it doesn't seem right."

"Come with me, Chris," Michael persisted. "Don't convince yourself that you carry the Cause on your shoulders. I've said the same thing to Pace—Ensign Anders. Sick as he is, he intends to stay, too." Mike shook his head in perplexity. "There's surely enough three-year men to keep the army together until next spring. The rest of us should be goin' home."

"No, Mike, I'm staying." This was not a spur of the moment decision, but one which Christopher had agonized over for days now. More and more, he had sought escape from his sense of obligation to this dispirited, pathetic rabble in thoughts of home and family and friends...but it seemed the more he yearned for home, the more clearly he saw his duty.

"I have some letters for you to take home." He handed Mike three short letters, one addressed to Hannah, one to his brother George, and the third to Aunt Jane.

"And Mike, tell everyone I'm fine. Tell 'em I've just gotta stay until the army goes into winter quarters—it can't be long, maybe a couple of weeks."

20

"WE SUSTAINED AN ORDERLY RETREAT"

On the Post Road,
Approaching the Delaware River
December 1-6, 1776

MAJOR GIST RETURNED to the camp from an early morning staff meeting and announced "Here we go again." Everyone understood: the army was retreating once again.

Christopher happened to be the duty sergeant that day and as the officers of the regiment crowded around the major, he inched himself up to hear what was said.

Turning to Captain Stone, Major Gist announced, "We'll be breaking camp and evacuating Brunswick immediately. General Washington has received intelligence that the British have been loading wagons, collecting livestock and dressing rations in preparation for continuing their advance. He wants to get all our troops and supplies over the Delaware as quickly as we can."

General Washington's flagging army now consisted of perhaps three thousand men, mostly Virginians, Pennsylvanians, the Delawares, some New Englanders, and, of course, the Marylanders. This was not the only American army, but it was the main army and desperately needed reinforcements to hold off Lord Cornwallis's persistent army of fourteen thousand supremely confident regulars. They were told that reinforcements were on the way, but they would have to arrive soon to be of any use since the enlistments of most of the army would expire on December 31.

Captain Stone's face was expressionless. "So, Mordecai, on the very day that half the army is marching home, the other half is once again fleeing for its life."

"John, there is nothing to be gained by such complaints. We must continue to fight for the Cause with what we have. To not do so means it is ended—there is no starting over...." Gist looked fondly at Stone. "This is not what you and I and the others had in mind when this all began, is it, John? But if we don't believe in this army, how can we expect others to, eh?"

With nothing more to add, the officers dispersed to give the appropriate orders to the men.

Christopher was left standing alone in the presence of Major Gist, who looked at him quizzically. "Well, Christopher...what think the soldiers? Will they continue the fight?"

He gave the major his best corporal's look, screwed up his courage and said, "Continue what fight, sir?"

Major Gist was caught short by this response and looked hard at Christopher. "Why, the Cause, of course. What else are we fighting for?"

"We're not fightin', sir," Christopher replied stubbornly. "We're retreatin'. For a man who has a family and winter comin', retreating is not worth soldierin' on."

Major Gist frowned and shook his head—he might have done this in perplexity over the audacity of a corporal, or frustration at their plight. In any event, he abruptly dismissed Christopher.

"Well, it doesn't take much to pack up this army, I can tell you," exclaimed Jeremiah. Then, facetiously, "Hey, Corporal Sims. You got all those tents packed—and the kegs of rum stowed—and checked each of your men to make sure they have their complete issue of clothing and extra pair of shoes as ordered by the Congress—and three days' cooked rations?"

"Why certainly, Sergeant. Just look at these well-shod men in their warm winter uniforms, with their bulgin' packs." The men listened to this exchange with bemused expressions and snorts of disgust. Christopher looked at them and saw men barely covered in rags, shoes with exposed toes, some bound with strips of cloth, and empty packs on their backs.

When the brigade drums began beating the March, Jeremiah simply said, "All right, boys, let's get going."

And shortly after noon, the Continental Army trudged out of Brunswick just in time.

The Maryland Regiment was toward the rear and actually saw the British column appear on the other side of the Raritan as they moved hurriedly down the road.

"Look well-clothed and *fat,* they do," muttered one Marylander, who was cloaked in a thin blanket and hadn't had a real meal—even a real army meal—in weeks, as he turned tiredly away from the river.

They did not flee in panic from the enemy—nor did they march away from them with any semblance of pride. There were no columns with standards flying, no drums or fifes, no martial spirit; instead, the men walked dejectedly, as a boy would walk off his mother's tongue-lashing or a rejection by a pretty girl. It was a long straggling line of sullen men, each of them angrily dealing with his own devil as they set off for the Delaware River on that gray December afternoon, stumbling along on the sharp, brittle road.

In addition to the thousand or so ill-clad, despondent soldiers, the column included less than two dozen pieces of brass and iron cannon, and a few limbers, most dragged and pushed by hand, all part of the ill-equipped, ill-trained Corps of Continental Artillery—a ludicrous caricature of the Royal Artillery.

The column also included the rest of the Continental community, an uninspiring sight indeed: there were creaking wagons and wobbling carts drawn by worn-out horses or bony oxen which carried the army's meager supplies; these also carried the wounded and the ill—those who hadn't been evacuated to Morristown in New Jersey, hidden behind the rugged Watchung Mountains; there was also a small herd of cattle which represented the army's entire food supply at the time—gaunt, skinny beeves which couldn't provide enough meat for the average family; and finally, there were the camp followers—sutlers, women, Negro slaves, as filthy and bedraggled as the soldiers, who provided some service to this woebegone army.

The entire column stretched perhaps two miles and moved in no particular order, except for the precious artillery and the small amount of army stores. Troops would be sacrificed to prevent the loss of these. Though there was precious little to lose, it was all the army had, or was likely to obtain any time soon. There was enough ammunition to stand and fight if necessary. But as for the rest, there was no vinegar or salt, no vegetables or bread; there were no tents or even blankets, no medicines or palliatives…and there was no rum or cider.

While flat gray clouds lingered overhead, blocking the sun, the haggard column marched on a red clay road now thawing into mud, sucking at feet and wheels. On they marched over a flat landscape, broken only here and there by knolls and ridges. Mile after mile the Continental Army tramped, marching all day and through the night, resting only periodically. Resting meant foraging. Like locusts, they swarmed over the countryside consuming all in their wake: fences, hay, shriveled winter vegetables, nuts, feed corn—anything that could conceivably feed or warm them.

And continuing on, always continuing on, the retreating columns finally reached the banks of the Delaware and began crossing, always looking over their backs, never feeling safe until they reached the other side.

It was the end of an ignominious retreat, but one that would prove to be an epic success for an amateur general and his amateur army.

21

THE END OF THE CAMPAIGN?

**Encampment on the Banks of the Delaware,
Bucks County, Pennsylvania
Early to Mid-December, 1776**

THE LAST OF WASHINGTON'S ARMY reached
Trenton—the unattractive transshipment town which the
regiment had passed through on its march to New York—on
December 17; with the army crossing over to the Pennsylvania
side that afternoon and into the early morning hours of the next
day. Boat after boat skirted the crystalline rocks of Trenton Falls
to carry the troops over to the other side.

The Marylanders crossed with the rear guard and most of
them were carried across in a local river craft called a Durham
boat. Up to sixty feet in length, and eight feet in beam, this flat-
bottomed boat carried loads of ore and pig iron from the
Durham Iron Works downriver to Trenton and returned with
manufactured goods and whiskey. Entire companies were loaded
on these boats; and propelled by sweep and setting poles to the
far shore.

"Steadiest damn boat I ever been on," exclaimed one of
Christopher's men. "Why, it's like walking across the water!"

Company by company, the regiment disembarked on the
Pennsylvania side, scrambling out of the large Durham boats and

up the low, bushy embankment to mill around, waiting for orders to assemble. As Christopher and Jeremiah lolled on a patch of grass watching the boats going back and forth, Jeremiah suddenly sat up, looking intently at a splendidly dressed officer standing on the bank. They heard the officer utter a loud exclamation as if in surprise and walk quickly toward a boat off-loading men.

"Say, I know him!—be right back." and off Jeremiah strode.

Some time later, Jeremiah returned, puffed with self-importance.

"Do ye know who they are?" he asked in the manner of a person who had just met somebody important. When Christopher admitted that he did not recognize them, Jeremiah enlightened him. "The scruffy lookin' one is James Peale...you know him—ensign in the Seventh Company. The other man—I reckon ye can see he's an officer—is none other than Jim's brother, Charles Willson Peale."

When Christopher did not respond as expected, Jeremiah snorted in disgust. "Christopher, Charles is a famous face-painter. Why, he's even studied in London. Born and raised in Maryland and now lives in Philadelphia. Before he became famous, he used to paint portraits of ordinary folks, including my esteemed family, that's how I know him. Used to go tippling together in Bal'imer. Now, he's serving with the Philadelphia Associators—that's why he's here. Hasn't seen Jim since July and has been mighty worried about him. Jim's also a face-painter—an' a good one too."

Christopher thought to himself that he'd have to see if Ensign Peale, whom he knew slightly, would be willing to do a painting of Hannah after this business was finished. The thought of having a portrait of Hannah pleased him—that is, until it occurred to him that the man painting her portrait would be able to feast his eyes on her as only a lover would, intently studying that wonderful face of hers, giving a sparkle to her eyes, stroking her hair and bringing a smile to her face, and boldly caressing her breasts as he fondly recreated them on canvas. It was a curious jealousy, he knew, but the pangs kept him awake at night.

****

"A day of fasting and humiliation, they say? Have I missed something?" Jeremiah pretended to look around in confusion.

The Congress had declared December 11 a day of "solemn fasting and humiliation." This had just been announced at evening roll call, and the troops were trying to square this added burden with their daily condition.

"Mark me if I'm wrong, here...I thought Congress had already starved us and humiliated us enough to forgive *all* the many sins they may think prevail among the ranks, and with credit to spare, I'll wager." Jeremiah wasn't about to allow the Congress to lay the blame for the failure of the Cause on the army.

"You don't understand, Jeremiah," pointed out one of the other sergeants, who seemed to have a good understanding of these things. "It's the New England way of thinkin'...that our profane swearing and immorality have angered Almighty God; which is why we're gettin' whipped, so we must repent to save the Cause."

"Does regretting havin' joined this damn army count as repentance?" asked another of the men.

"Actually," one of the Maryland officers volunteered, "General Mercer said we can count yesterday—or today, for that matter—as our day of fasting, and then pick any day we want to count as a day of humiliation."

The men laughed. In fact, they weren't offended at hearing this nonsense from Congress. Most of the men were deeply religious and had long ago come to terms with their God. No, they knew for a fact that it was not immoral behavior which had reduced them to this—but poor leadership, inadequate supplies, and the indifference of their fellow countrymen.

So what were their sins? Surely it wasn't illness or starvation or sacrifice. No, in fact it was the sin of defeat—and defeat, all knew, was unforgivable....

In truth, though, other than Divine Intervention, there was little else Congress could call on for assistance, apprehensive as that body was that the British would continue the campaign and end this sorry little affair once and for all.

Then, on December 13, 1776, Divine Providence did indeed intervene. On this day two events, one considered by patriots as good and the other as very bad, occurred which affected the course of the Revolution. If ever there was a single day that should be celebrated by American revolutionaries, it should be this day.

The first was General Howe's decision to end his dignified pursuit of the rebels and retire to comfortable quarters for the winter. As he pointed out, armies did not campaign in the winter; besides, his army was far from its base of supply—no small concern in the New World, or any other world for that matter. Lord Cornwallis, aggressive as he was in his pursuit, often had to halt his advance until his supply line caught up to him.

"It's the only drawback I can see to having a sufficiency of supplies," muttered Mordacai Gist, now a colonel under the new organization. It was true, though, that those who spent most of the month of November being chased hungry and naked across the Jerseys had their own opinion.

The other event, seen by every patriot as a devastating blow to the cause of American independence, was the capture of General Charles Lee as he breakfasted that morning with his dogs at White's Tavern near Basking Ridge in New Jersey.

General Lee had dazzled patriots and they had placed incredibly high hopes in him. His capture, seen as a calamity portending final defeat, turned out, however, to be the only occasion in which he ever made a significant contribution to the Cause.

The ordinary Continental soldier was quick to agree with Lord Howe that the campaign was finally at an end, and he began settling in along the banks of the Delaware.

Disheartened, cold, hungry, ill-clad, penniless, they tried to make the best of a bad situation. With no pride in their service or in their army, and no confidence in their officers or civil government, the men went through the motions of daily drill and camp routine, and were animated only when seeing to their creature comforts.

Days were spent constructing "huts." These were crude affairs, mostly lean-tos; but with Jeremiah's help, Christopher insisted on hacking away at the hard earth to dig a large hole in the ground, to which they added low walls of logs, and covered it with a peaked roof of saplings and boughs. This provided good insulation against the cold.

They caulked the chinks between the logs with mud, and Mary, who had rejoined them after being sent off with the wagons during the retreat, spread straw, unfortunately damp, on the floor and strew some rue around so they wouldn't catch the camp fever. "A woman's touch," noted Jeremiah in appreciation. After they fumigated the inside with gunpowder smoke against the noxious night air, the finished shelter turned out to be quite snug for its five inhabitants. "And so help me God, don't piss in the fire."

Next, they saw to their personal cleanliness, which required considerable work. It was too cold to bathe, but when a little bit of soap was issued, most of them bit the bullet and scrubbed themselves with buckets of river water. With soapy water and a newly sharpened knife, they scraped off scraggly beards. Mary insisted on hacking away at their hair, which had grown long and infested during the last month or two. Teeth which had become covered in a verdigris patina were finally cleaned—a twig, the tip pounded to form a rough brush, was used to scrape the teeth with an abrasive made from pulverized wood coals rendered savory by a few drops of oil of lavender procured by Mary.

There was little that any of them could do about their clothes. The commissary still had not delivered promised supplies, so they had to make do with the remaining bits and pieces of clothing they had been wearing for the entire campaign. Mary boiled, mended, and patched, but at best they looked like scarecrows in a poor tenant farmer's field. Jeremiah wore his blanket coat over a bare torso and a pair of long linen drawers. Christopher's fine hunting shirt was in shreds, literally—what remained of it was tied around his neck to close the lapels of his blanket coat and the remaining scraps donated to Mary and some of the other women for their months. Mary herself was reduced to one thin petticoat under her short gown, and remarked with an exaggerated shiver that every gust of wind "felt like the cold fingers of an old man on me quaint."

More or less groomed and cleaned, and ointed for the itch, Christopher, Jeremiah, and Mary's other charges presented themselves before her. Standing back and admiring her handiwork, she indicated her satisfaction: "Well, ye ain't much, for sure, but you're the only men I got."

As for food, the safety of the broad, boatless river finally allowed foodstuffs to be brought up in quantity. There was plenty of salted meat and pork, occasionally some winter vegetables, vinegar, and fresh wheaten bread; there was even rum and gin obtained from McKonkey's Tavern. The effect of this bounty promptly gave most of them the runs, which they accepted happily: "Hey, George! At least wi' that great rent in your breeches, ye don't have to worry about dropping 'em when you feel the surge comin'."

****

Thus the remnants of Washington's army squatted among the bushes along the Delaware River, the foul camps reeking of excrement and urine, the rotting carcasses of slaughtered animals, and the miasma of sick men; while thick gray smoke from damp wood fires rose to mingle with dark storm clouds. The weather was miserable, gray, and ominous, and lay siege to the camps with a barrage of cold rain, or sleet, or cutting winds, pummeling men who were losing the will to resist.

Colonel Gist, too ill to remain in the field, had been sent back to Baltimore to recruit reinforcements. Christopher did not have a chance to say goodbye to him. Captain—now Colonel Stone, commanded all the remaining Marylanders.

By this time, the daily company roll calls were brief indeed.

22

"IT'S TRULY GOOD TO SEE A NEIGHBOR"

McKonkey's Ferry, Pennsylvania
December 20, 1776

A S CHRISTOPHER RETURNED from a burial detail, his attention was drawn to a strange character leaving McKonkey's tavern. Even in an army where the uniform was nakedness, and a full suit of clothes had become a rarity, there were always one or two men whose dress was so surprising, so fanciful, as to be remarkable.

This particular man was wearing Indian leggings made of a Continental-issue blanket; while his head poked through a hole in another blanket which was tied around his waist by a strip of leather, his bare arms showing between the folds; the man's feet were covered by cowhide moccasins and his head was covered with a bright piece of calico.

Amused, Christopher watched the man as he came towards him with a hunter's easy gait, looking almost graceful despite his queer garb. As the man passed, he had a fleeting image of a backwoodsman holding him spellbound in Hungerford's Tavern so long ago.

"*Dugan Fife! Dugan Fife*, is that you?"

"Huh?" Dugan Fife looked unknowingly at the man who had called out his name. "Who's that?"

"Dugan, it's me—Christopher Sims from Potomac Hundred. We'd see each other occasionally at Hungerford's. Remember?"

"Why, I think I do…but it don't matter since it's truly good to see a neighbor. How be ya, Christopher Sims?"

As Dugan Fife approached, Christopher stepped back as if his nose had been tweaked.

Fife noticed this and understood. "Tain't me, but the 'coon grease I'm wearin'. Not as effective as bar grease but keeps a body middlin' warm."

"No offense, Dugan, it's just—powerful."

"Ain't that the truth! An' I might add that ye don't smell so sweet yerself."

Christopher had actually grown used to the smell of hog's lard and brimstone which Mary had slathered on him to cure the itch. Dugan reminded him that it did make a devil of a stink.

"Ointed for the itch…."

"Know it well, but 'coon grease takes care of that as well. Good thing—if I stank any more of animal flesh I'd be shot for food by this army."

Both of them laughed.

"Who're you with?"—Christopher asked.

"Rawling's Rifle Regiment. How 'bout you?"

"First Maryland—used to be Smallwood's."

Dugan whistled appreciatively.

"The last I heard, Dugan, you were goin' up there to Boston."

"Right ye are. I did that, and me an' most of the other riflemen spent most of the time in the clink.

"Why, ye ask?—well, I'll tell you. Me an' the rest of the boys thought we was there to kill redcoats, so we'd go outta the lines and shoot at 'em. Seems, though, the Eastern Continentals didn't appreciate this 'cause it aggrieved the British. Said there was a proper way to fight a war and we weren't doin' it proper— somethin' about the rules of war. I have me doubts 'bout them Easterners.

"Well, we decided to come south where they know what fightin' is all about. Then Mike Cresap, God bless him, died along the way and Tom Price had already gone off to join ye Maryland regulars. A good many of us joined Stephenson's Rifle

Regiment and most of us ended up at Fort Washington under Colonel Rawlings."

"*You* were at Fort Washington, Dugan?—during the fight?—what happened?"

"Thrashed us fair and square, they did. At a proper distance, we was pickin' 'em off like tom turkey—Hooshians, they was; but they kept comin' and pretty soon they was so many of 'em our officers decided to surrender the fort.

"So me and the other boys decided it was time to hoof it....

"But then we was told by our officers, '*Hold!* Ye can't do that!' And jus' why not, we ask'd. 'Because,' these same officers say, 'Colonel Magaw, our commandant, has surrendered all of us, and you can't run off because he gave his word.'"

Dugan broke off his story to explain, "Ye see, Christopher Sims, it's an agreement among gentlemen that we private soldiers mustn't resist being made prisoners of war.

"So what happens now? we ask'd. 'Why,' says one of the officers, 'I suppose the officers will be exchanged and you men will go to prison.' That's when it occurred to us—me an' the boys, I mean—that a gentleman's agreement ain't exactly fer us—so we skedaddled.

"I took off running like a deer, leapin' and slidin' down this steep hill towards the river way down below. Lost me dear girl along the way, also me fine fur cap and me necessary bag, but I got to the bottom in one piece.

"At the water's edge, I saw some of our boys pulling a boat into the water and quick as I could joined 'em. We pushed off and was on our way when I noticed that one of 'em was an officer! Goddamn, I says to him, I thought ye officers had a gentleman's agreement not to run away like us miscreants. 'God's balls,' he says, 'I ain't no gentleman—I'm a barber'...a barber, fer crissake—even offered to chop me hair."

Christopher laughed. "Dugan, you're makin' all this up."

"God's oath, I'm not. We got to the other side and made for Fort Lee, where I joined what remained of the regiment.

"Well, it weren't long before the damn British attacked us there; but this time we was smart enough to run off before they arrived. Those Continentals ran off so fast, I kin tell ya, that they left ever'thing—including kettles full of hot food.

"Well, I knew the British weren't *that* agile; so I calm-like et breakfast, found a coupla potcompanions to have a swaller or two of spirits with—and then collected a bunch of blankets before I *walked* outta camp. Thought about headin' di-rectly west, but decided that the Hooshians owed me a rifle—and maybe some loot; so here I am.

"I plan to git me one a those yay-gar rifles, I do. Ye know, the rifle carried by those Hooshians who wear the green coats? To replace me girl. Ain't as fine, to be sure—kinda stubby, ye know, and it don't throw a ball as far—but it'll have ta do 'til I can have a real American rifle made fer me."

"So you've reenlisted for the next campaign?"

"Haven't reenlisted fer anything," Dugan said indignantly. "I'm jus' waitin' fer the next fight. I told ye, I'm goin' to git me a yay-gar rifle—then I'll be heading west. So fer the time being I'm what they call a 'volunteer'—don't git paid nuthin' fer fighting, which means I git paid the same as a Continental."

"An' without the grief—but Dugan, this army isn't goin' to fight anyone—it's goin' to disappear in ten days."

"*What?*" Fife was truly agitated by this intelligence. "Why, I hear'd the General is planning to attack one of their outposts across the river."

"That's just rumor. I suspect you'll get no closer to a Jaeger rifle than the width of yon river which separates the two armies."

"Well, I cain't head west with a musket, fer crissake, 'cause I cain't hit the broadside of a barn with one." Dugan Fife bit his lip in concentration, worrying the problem. Then his eyes lit up as if he had figured it out.

Looking confidently at Christopher, he said, "No, we'll attack—because we hafta. Ya jus' gotta have a better reason fer havin' an army than runnin' away from another army. *Now,* His Excellency knows *that*—so, we'll attack...I'm certain of it!"

It made perfect sense.

23

DESPERATION

*A universal dissatisfaction prevails, and everybody is
furnished with an excuse for declining the publick service.*
Christopher Sims, Journal

Encampment along the Delaware,
On the Pennsylvania Side
December 20, 1776

WITH FAR MORE ANGUISH than Dugan Fife, General
Washington had indeed concluded that he must attack
before a last opportunity was lost and his army slipped away.

*Even a failure cannot be more fatal than to remain in our present
situation; in short, some enterprise must be undertaken in our present
circumstances or we must give up the Cause.*

The general reread these thoughts, written to him by Colonel
Reed, his adjutant general.

No! We will not give up the Cause. Not yet, anyway.

He had reinforcements; two thousand veteran Continentals—
New Englanders, including John Glover's Marblehead mariners,
men who were not ready to give up. Together with his Southern
troops, he had the strike force he needed. Trouble was the
enlistments of almost his entire force of Continentals would be
up the last day of December. He had to attack.

General Washington walked among his men, judging their
mettle. He gave them encouragement, offered them hope, and
practically begged them to give him one more chance. It helped,

but what was really needed was an emotional appeal to their patriotism which would transform all their suffering and resentments into a white-hot iron with which he could thrust at the enemy.

And just such an appeal did come…in the form of an astonishing ode to resistance called *The American Crisis*, which had just been published by none other than Thomas Paine.

Colonel Stone informed his officers that Paine's essay would be read to the entire army on December 23. "This man Paine," he noted, "has an uncanny knack for mixing words on paper which have the same effect on a flagging revolution as pouring hot oil on a dying fire."

Later, Christopher, feeling self-important, noted, "Jeremiah, this must be what Mister Paine was workin' on when I spoke to him back in November. Remember me tellin' you about it?"

Christopher was referring to a November afternoon, the sky streaked in grays, pale pinks, and gunmetal blues, when he had seen a man, a familiar figure he thought, bent over a drum, using it as a makeshift writing table, chilled fingers writing furiously, his great beak of a nose looming over the drumhead like a vulture ready to pounce on a hapless phrase.

Sure enough, it was Mister Thomas Paine and Christopher had stopped to say hello. The ensuing conversation had been about sacrifice and defeat and hopelessness.

Because he was writing an essay on this very topic, Paine took the time to reassure this despondent soldier of the revolution that now was not the time to shrink from the service of his country. "…this panic, I assure you, will bring out the best in us. Remember this: what we obtain too cheap, we esteem too lightly."

Impatient to get back to his writing, Paine gave Christopher a quizzical look. "So, Corporal Sims, have I convinced ye to stay the course—or at least 'til the end of the campaign?"

Christopher had replied that he would truly think upon it…to which Mister Paine had said, "Very good, Corporal Sims. Now if you'll excuse me…like you, there are several thousand of your comrades yet to be convinced."

Mary McBride looked in awe at Christopher. "Ye *helped* Mister Paine with his scribblin', Chris?"

"Why, I certainly did, Mary," he exaggerated. "Not only that—but remember when you told me about paying a fair price for independence?"

"Why, I believe I do remember that conversation, Chris."

"Well, I told it to Mister Paine and he liked it so much, he wrote it into this very piece which is to be read to the army."

"Oh my Lord!" Mary almost screamed this as she slapped her hands to her cheeks, unable to believe her role in history. "And did you tell him what I said about not assaying freedom like you would a coin...an'...."

Following Retreat, Christopher read *The Crisis* to his comrades, which included Mary and a few other camp women.

These are the times that try men's souls: The summer soldier and the sunshine patriot will, in this crisis, shrink from the service of his country; but he that stands it NOW, deserves the love and thanks of man and woman.

"Hey, Meg, Peter is standing now, and methinks deserves your love and thanks!" The man who said this slid his hand up the woman's leg, as she laughed and squirmed away.

"Shut up, ye miserable lobcock," snapped Mary, who was stirred by Mister Paine's words.

After staring down the wisecrack, Christopher continued, *Tyranny like hell is not easily conquered; yet we have this consolation with us, that the harder the conflict, the more glorious the triumph. What we obtain too cheap, we esteem too lightly: 'Tis dearness only that gives every thing its value. Heaven knows how to put a proper price upon its goods; and it would be strange indeed, if so celestial an article as FREEDOM should not be highly rated"*

"Aye, that be the truth!"—Mary sang out as she heard her very words ringing in the cold December air.

Britain, with an army to enforce her tyranny, has declared that she has a right 'to BIND us in ALL CASES WHATSOEVER' and if being bound in that manner, is not slavery, then there is not such a thing as slavery upon earth. Even the expression is impious, for so unlimited a power can belong only to GOD.

"A-men to that!—" The group was listening intently now.

I thank GOD that I fear not. I see no real cause for fear. I know our situation well, and can see the way out of it.

Here, Christopher had been instructed to conclude the reading. *I...can see the way out of it...*His Excellency—according to Colonel Stone—wanted the men left with this thought on their minds. He wanted everyone to believe in their arms, the righteousness of the cause, and God's Providence.

A Bold Stroke
December 23, 1776

Bad morale...too few good men...time running out...and now the river....

On December 20, there had set in a spell of intense cold that had frozen the river above the crossing points. Now, as desperate generals met, there was a slight thaw, and chunks of ice, like crystal battering rams, were skittering down the river. Commanders whom His Excellency depended upon questioned the practicality of attempting a crossing.

General Washington noticeably grimaced upon hearing this assessment. *God is certainly testing our will to be free,* he thought wearily.

He looked at the men crowding the room, and saw uncertainty.

"Gentlemen, this army is used to treading on thin ice,"—he smiled his thin smile to let them know he was not discouraged— "Surely the ice on the Delaware River is no more treacherous...."

He looked quizzically at his senior officers, hoping for support.

Amidst the ensuing silence, Colonel John Glover gruffly spoke up. "Your Excellency, the river at Eight Mile Ferry"—by which he meant McKonkey's—"is only seven hundred yards across and pole-bottom deep. By Providence and those stout Durham boats, my mariners will get ye across the Delaware."

Washington stared at Colonel Glover and saw resolve. *It all comes down to resolve, doesn't it?* he realized.

Looking again at his commanders, this time with authority, he stated, "Then, it's decided, gentlemen. We will cross."

****

It was Christmas Day and they had ample forewarning that the four o'clock parade would not end with the usual dismissal at day's end, but would be the beginning of a risky expedition. "This must be it," they figured, and readied themselves for the anticipated order to march.

That morning, Lieutenant Fisher had instructed them to turn out for the afternoon parade with arms, accoutrements and ammunition in the best order, as well as a blanket and provisions enough for three days.

"What? For three days—where do we find rations for three days?"

"Why, ye take what's left of yesterday's ration and cut it into three pieces."

"At ease, men," ordered the lieutenant, before proceeding. "Also, the ambulant sick or wounded and those without serviceable shoes will come forward now to be assigned other duties in camp."

"Lieutenant, *none* of the men have serviceable shoes, including yourself—sir," Christopher pointed out respectfully.

"Ah…well then—those men *without* shoes will be dismissed from the formation." The lieutenant, referred to by some of the men disrespectfully using his Christian name, was younger than most of his men. Lieutenant Fisher was from a prominent Baltimore family and had received his commission based more on that than his martial skills. The lieutenant was a nice boy, but not yet a leader of men.

Upon being dismissed, the men went about their preparations for what they sensed was going to be desperate business. Preparing rations was easy, being nothing more than heavily salted meat and hard bread; but a man also had to have something to drink along the way and, with little or no money, this required imaginative foraging. While Jeremiah was off seeing to their provisions, Christopher went around the company issuing cartridges and new gun flints.

"Make sure you keep your cartridges dry, boys, and don't go snappin' your firelocks with the new flints, d'ya hear me?"

As the men cleaned their muskets and saw to their equipment and packs, or in some cases scavenged for shoes or something that would pass inspection as shoes, they considered the possibilities. Counting out cartridges and handing them out to the men, Christopher was asked the question soldiers preparing to march always asked.

"Where we goin', Corporal Sims?"

"Don't know."

"Are we retreatin' or advancin'?"

Before he could answer, Private Brewster pointed out, "Don't recollect us ever *plannin'* a retreat. You'd see the damn'd redcoats and then you'd jus' run—so we must be advancing—that's my thought."

"That's the rumor, anyway," admitted Christopher. "But, in truth, only the first officers know for sure. My feelin' is that anything is better than this."

"What would truly be better than this, Sims, is for our officers to tell us what's goin' on, and give us the right to have our say—that's what we plain people are fightin' for, isn't it?"

Christopher looked at the man, who, he knew, was in the habit of complaining. A good soldier, but difficult because he was a revolutionary who actually believed in a perfect revolution.

"We don't always know better than our officers, Roberts, and in most cases we do best when we do what they tell us to do. That suit you, soldier?"

The regimental chaplain, more sick in spirit than in body, had gone home, but there was a lay preacher who saw to their spiritual needs; that afternoon he was making his rounds to give them encouragement in their time of need.

"Trust in General Washington and he will lead us to victory! Remember how the Israelites doubted Moses when they said to him, 'The LORD look upon you, and judge; because you have made our savior to be abhorred in the eyes of Pharaoh.'

"And Moses asked the LORD, 'wherefore hast thou so evil entreated this people? Why is it that thou hast sent me?' Ye see Moses was perplexed that he had failed his people.

"But what did the LORD say to Moses? Why, He said I am the LORD, and I will rid you out of their bondage—and He did! And He did it through His servant Moses...now didn't he?"

It was something for all of them to think about.

And as they all looked toward the cascading, ice-choked Delaware River, which they were pretty sure they would have to cross soon, one of them said hopefully, "And didn't Moses also part the waters?...

"'Tis time, Jeremiah," Mary said gently. "No doubt the army will be crossin' the river to attack."

Looking at the boats being collected behind the island above McKonkey's, she said worriedly, "It doesn't seem to be startin' out as too secret a venture...I fear the enemy knows the plan all too well, Jeremiah."

There was concern on her face and tears in her eyes. She looked so endearing, as she stood woebegone in her patched garments, which now included a dark blue regimental coat missing most of its plain pewter buttons, obtained from who knew where.

"Mary, the Hessians are no doubt stupid with drink as we speak. We must depend upon that—or have no likely chance. 'God will care for his children.' "

"If He has a mind to," she replied almost distractedly, "but that isn't fixed yet. Not knowing His exact wonts, ye and Christopher will take care of each other, won't you?"

"We surely will, Mary."

"Well then, fare thee well, Jeremiah Smith!" Mary said with false bravado.

"Fare thee well, Mary," he said gently.

Mary gave Jeremiah a long hug, clinging to him, not wanting to ever let him go.

Finally, he disengaged. "I must go now, Mary...."

For the time was now upon them.

24

"READY, EVERY DEVIL OF THEM"

Near McKonkey's Ferry, Pennsylvania
December 25, 1776

LOOKING AT THE SOLDIER'S FEET, young Lieutenant Fisher noticed that they were wrapped in rags with straw stuffed inside and asked curiously, "What are those?"

"Why, Lieutenant, sir, these are jus' like the shoes worn by the clodhoppers in Talbot County. Better'n leather, they say, and warm as can be."

The lieutenant resented being treated like a young fool. "So help me God, Jenkins, if you drop out of line because of those damn feet of yours, I'll have you charged with desertion."

The few remaining officers met, and dispersed, and Lieutenant Fisher, coming over to the company, motioned Jeremiah and Christopher aside. They were all that was left of the company's noncommissioned officers.

"Gentlemen (the lieutenant actually treated them as his equal), our brigade is assigned to General Greene's Division. We are to assemble with the brigade in the valley immediately over the hill one mile in back of McKonkey's." The Lieutenant pointed vaguely beyond the trees as he spoke, then went mechanically through the orders, concluding with,

"Quartermaster Talcott is at the assembly point and will guide us to our spot. Any questions?"

Of course there were questions, beginning with, "Where are we goin'?" Instead, Jeremiah asked, "Lieutenant, what's that piece of paper in your hat?"

Lieutenant Fisher touched the twisted piece of paper. "Oh, that. Each officer was instructed to put a piece of white paper in his hat as a field mark. Instruct the men in that regard, sergeant."

"Ah, of course, sir," responded Jeremiah.

"Any other questions? Good. The password is 'Victory or Death!' Now let's move off—and God bless our Cause."

At the assembly point, they waited and waited. It was cold, very cold, and all of them, dressed as they were in their thin clothes and split shoes, stood around in ranks stamping their feet and jumping up and down to stay warm, waiting for the order to move out. Their brigade, Mercer's, was the second to go across, but even with that it must have been after six o'clock by the time they were marched back down the ferry road, past McKonkey's Tavern, the stone house now filled with officers warming themselves, before turning off into the yard above the riverbank, where they were halted—once again to wait.

As Christopher took a grateful swig of rum from Jeremiah's swigler, he looked in fascination at the activity around him. To all appearances, everything seemed to be in disorder, and far too noisy to be stealthy.

Directly below at the ferry landing, reluctant horses, their hooves clacking and clattering on stone and ice, were being pulled and pushed onto the low ferryboat, its bow-end lowered on hinges to act as a ramp. Nearby some small cannon, three- and four-pounders it looked like, were being dismantled in preparation for being stowed in the bottoms of Durham boats, while two heavy howitzers awaited the time to be rolled onto the ferry boat.

Scores of troops were milling around waiting their turn to cross.

All this activity swirled around the landing in a pale, shadowy light cast by a few fluttering torches.

Finally their order to embark came and they tripped down the bank and into the Durham boats, which appeared black as tar against the vaguely defined river bank, to stand unsteadily in the rocking boat until, packed in by companies, the boat was filled.

"Wouldn't sit down, soldier," warned one of the boatmen. They looked down and saw that accumulated snow and ice in the boat's bottom had mixed with the ore dust and other debris from past trips to form a thick sludge in which they now stood. All of them took his advice.

The boats were manned by John Glover's Marbleheaders, who were well known to a good many of these Marylanders.

"Hey! We've done this before!—remember? So, have ye gents moved your ferryin' service over from New York to this backwater? Thought you were real sailors!"

"We'll be real mariners as of the thirty-first; after that, the next time I step on a boat it'll be for plunder—not to take the likes of you across yet another creek."

Nestled as it was against the bank, the boat still rocked crazily and the river, made frothy by a strong wind, was full of chunks of ice.

As they swayed high and low in the boat, many of them also questioned the practicality of crossing this particular "creek."

"Say, are you *sure* you boys can get us across this raging water and safe to the other side?"

One of the sailors, his movements hardly affected by the bucking boat, spat out a stream of tobacco juice, and grinned. "Reckon."

Leaning heavily against each other, they braced themselves as the boat pushed off. It was the devil of a trip. Chunks of bobbing ice slammed into the boat, and a strong wind and racing gray wavelets pushed the boat in every direction but toward the opposite bank. The boat lurched and plowed, a cold spray thoroughly wetting them. The wind was from the northeast and scraped across a man's face like the pull of a dull razor.

With arms entwined to steady themselves and hands gripping muskets, they could only lower their chins tight against their chests to ward off the cold and wet. The polemen, who had to stand on a narrow running board atop the gunnel, fought the current, wind, and ice floes from their precarious perch, though not always successfully: One of them lost his balance and toppled over—luckily into the boat and the sludgy mess on the bottom, in a tangle of flailing arms and legs and lost pole.

Eventually, with the sharp ringing sound of breaking glass, the boat ground against the icy rim jutting out from the New Jersey riverbank. Similar sounds could be heard up and down the river as scores of other heavily laden boats shattered brittle ice before running up against the riverbank.

The Marbleheaders swung the side of the boat around to allow their passengers to disembark. The men leapt from the gunnel to grab saplings and roots and pulled themselves up the low embankment at the river's edge, though a few had their feet slip out from under them on the muddy bank and slid to their waists in the slushy water.

Thankfully, Christopher managed to scramble up to the top of the bank without getting wet. Jeremiah was less fortunate: "Godammit, can you believe this!—what the hell am I goin' to do now?" He looked disgustedly at his soaking wet feet and legs, already feeling them grow numb with the cold.

"We'll have time to build a fire and get you dry, Jeremiah—and some of the others who also got wet. Let's gather the men and get them to the assembly point."

They quickly gathered the company, made certain all were present and marched them along the bank to the road. The landing below was awash with awkward sounds and jerky movements as the army struggled ashore: The grinding of wood against ice as boats landed, the noise of confused soldiers disembarking, of others clearing away the ice, the rattling of wheels on the frozen ground, the peal of many orders being given.

Amidst all this, there were guides with lanterns who directed them to move quickly up the road to the assembly point. "How far? they asked. "About a mile up," came the reply.

"Lord," complained Jeremiah, "My legs will surely freeze to ice and be shattered by whipping branches."

Their company joined a long column marching single file up the road, past the ferry house tavern, with its Dutch roof and white clapboards with red trim, where generals and their staff supervised the landing, and into the woods beyond.

The noises from the landing faded and now there were only the sounds of sleet striking wood and leaves, the wind strumming tree branches, and a hundred feet crunching in the snow. The sleet changed to small, stinging snowflakes and then to dry, feathery flakes. Even as the snowstorm increased in intensity, a harsh wind buffeted miserably cold men.

They trudged up a gradual incline, the narrow road winding around the trees, its verge marked by thickets and vines. Though it was not a sharp climb, men were constantly slipping on a roadbed worn to a roundness, made treacherous by a dusting of snow covering a carpet of frozen leaves.

The assembly point was at the top of the slope leading up from the river, at a road junction where Bear Tavern stood. They came out of the woods and saw the fields around the tavern ablaze with fires. Coming closer they saw that the assembled force here was crowded around these bonfires, trying to keep warm as they awaited the arrival of the rest of the attack force.

"Jeremiah, you and the others see if you can't find some warmth near one of those fires while the rest of us get our own started." Christopher then hurried off with some of the men to pull down fence rails and make a fire. This was accomplished with some difficulty because the wind had increased greatly and a mixture of snow, freezing rain and sleet wetted everything.

As he stood before the blazing fire, Jeremiah, smiling wanly, said, "Ah, this is much better—now I'm unfroze and just wet and cold to the marrow."

The wind-whipped fire consumed the wood as fast as it could be thrown on, and it spread little warmth among the crowd of men huddled around it. Bitter cold, rain, sleet, snow, wet clothes smelling foully of singed wool, cold meat, little enough rum— you would think there could hardly be a man among them who wanted to be on this expedition. Yet, as miserable as they were, they grinned and joked and horsed around a little as they waited for the rest of the army. Morale was high and the men in good spirits, much to the surprise of the officers. It seemed that having suffered so much in defeat, suffering for a chance at victory was...well—invigorating.

Bear Tavern, New Jersey
Four o'clock in the Morning, December 26

By then, they knew that their objective was the Hessian outpost at Trenton.

They were actually looking forward to it. For some, it was out of righteous conviction; for others, it would be revenge for the grinding humiliation they had suffered since last August; for still others, it was simply the possibility of liberating a warm coat, or a pair of shoes, or eating a meal fit for a man.

Lieutenant Fisher informed them officially that the objective was indeed the enemy outpost at Trenton, and then briefed Jeremiah and Christopher on the situation. "Now to the business at hand. The corps has been divided into two divisions. Our division will be the left division and will take the Upper Road—I believe it's also called the Pennington Road—to Trenton. We have local men to guide us. I understand it is about nine miles to our objective. The right division, under General Sullivan, will veer off somewhere up ahead and make its way to Trenton by a lower route nearer the river, the distance being roughly the same. The two divisions will converge on Trenton from opposite directions.

"Oh, and His Excellency General Washington will accompany our division."

They marched on snow-encrusted roads, the furrows frozen and sharp, poking at poorly shod feet. They moved past farmhouses, silent and dark, over hills and past barren, snow-swept fields, or through stands of hickory and black oak, their rounded crowns and spreading branches glistening with icicles. There was a constant falling of snow and sleet. Torches stuck in the exhalters of the brigade's fieldpieces up ahead sparkled and wobbled in a swirling wind, the dancing light reflected in mirrors of frozen ice, the dim shadows cast by the column giving the impression of a ghost army marching into the nether world.

They marched and marched, trudging along the road with the sleet hitting their faces like buckshot. It was still dark but there was now a hint of gray in the sky, indicating that daylight was just below the horizon. It also indicated that the attackers were way behind schedule: they knew that you surprise an enemy in the dreary early morning hours, not after the sun rises.

General Washington rode up and down the column encouraging them to hurry their pace as best they could, his voice betraying a growing sense of urgency.

"Press on, soldiers, press on!"

With all eyes on the hairline of light appearing along the eastern horizon, they tried to respond. But the weather was violent and, try as they might, they found they could do no more than move forward one slow step at a time. The mind was willing, but the body just wasn't.

By this time there was no longer any pain or suffering in the army's exertions...for it is said that freezing is one of the most gentle ways to die—you simply drift off to sleep—forever...and it was apparent that many of the men were now freezing to death. Only the intense mental effort of taking one step and then another prevented many of them from falling into comfortable oblivion.

Slow as the pace was, there was the need to call a halt at Birmingham, where the two divisions would separate and take different roads. Though it was intended to give cold and exhausted men a little rest and time to eat something before the final push, it had the unintended effect of allowing men to die in their sleep—as if they were weary old men and not soldiers on the verge of a desperate battle.

"Wake up, Bill! C'mon, man!"

"Get up on your feet, Private! Walk, that's it! keep walking!"

Christopher spotted Lieutenant Fisher sitting on a stump by the side of the road. He was in quiet repose, arms resting on his lap, hands hanging limply between legs, his head bowed. Looks a lot like John Paul, Christopher thought, feeling a sudden affection for the young lieutenant as he thought of his little brother.

"Lieutenant," Christopher said gently. "Lieutenant," he said again, this time with more force and a light prodding of the lieutenant's shoulder. Still no response. *"Lieutenant!"* He quickly grabbed the young man under his armpits and forced him to his feet.

"Jeremiah! get over here and help me wake the Lieutenant." Together, they manhandled the young man and tried to get him to walk his way back to life. It was no use. The lieutenant was deadweight in their arms.

Deadweight...dead. Lieutenant Fisher had died as unnoticed as he had served. In this, he was not so different than most of the men and women who had already died or suffered terribly to build a new nation.

"Oh, Goddamn," Christopher cried, regretting those times when they had made fun of him. With the tears freezing on their cheeks, they laid the lieutenant on the ground by the side of the road, and went off to inform the Colonel and to arrange for one of the carts to collect his body.

Even while numbed hands were exposed to the bitter cold, men had carefully wrapped handkerchiefs or rags around their musket locks, but this was not enough to keep priming powder dry. General Sullivan sent a messenger to General Washington during the march informing him that his muskets had been rendered unfit for service by the wet. To this General Washington calmly replied, "Tell General Sullivan to use the bayonet. I am resolved to take Trenton."

This conversation took place as the Maryland Regiment was passing, and the cold air carried General Washington's response to their nearby column. Upon hearing this declaration from their Commander in Chief, the Marylanders calmly reached for bayonets in scabbards and twisted them onto the muzzles of their muskets. Without a single order being given, company after company fixed bayonets as they passed His Excellency.

The general watched approvingly, a faint smile appearing on his concerned face.

"Press on, soldiers, press on!"

25

VICTORY OR DEATH

*...he who is afraid to follow me, let him
stand behind and take care of the packs*
Quoted by John Greenwood,
in his manuscript

**Trenton, New Jersey
Nine o'clock in the Morning,
December 26, 1776**

THE BATTLE WAS OVER. A skeletal, emaciated American
Army had won a victory which would surprise most of the
world. In less than forty-five minutes, it had defeated three of
the finest professional regiments of Europe.

It later appeared in the press that Lord Howe, upon hearing
the news, had remarked, "That three old established regiments,
of a people who made war a profession, should lay down their
arms to a ragged and undisciplined militia" was incompre-
hensible.

"Militia, my arse"—was the American retort. Tired, weary
Continentals would agree with the ragged part of Lord Howe's
description, but undisciplined militia?—no, your lordship: those
hirelings of yours were defeated by *better* soldiers, by god!

The Marylanders were among the line of Continentals who
had raised their muskets to fire point-blank at the Hessians in
the orchard when the latter had surrendered just in time. Less

than sixty paces away at the time, Christopher could see the fear and resignation in the eyes of the enemy.

As they dipped their standards and grounded their arms, Christopher advanced with the others, their bayonet-tipped muskets leveled, to confront the defeated foe, eyeing them up and down in curiosity. Some of the Marylanders and Pennsylvanians yelled at them in the Dutch-English used back home.

Even in defeat the Hessians were well-formed and soldierly. The grenadiers, in particular, still looked ferocious, with their tall pointed caps and great waxed mustaches looking like hawks' wings. The others, however, looked ordinary-like. Most were clean-shaven; some were old, some were young; some were fat, some were thin. "'Lot like us," most of the Americans thought. "But better fed 'n' better clothed."

Looking closely at them, however, Christopher realized with surprise that they were wearing summer uniforms!—uniforms which were worn, faded, stained, patched: "Could look like us in another month—less, depending on the weather and their chores," he mentioned to no one in particular. They would have been amused to know that just days before, the Hessian commander had reportedly dismissed the need for winter clothing for his men with the quip, "I will soon run barefoot over the ice on the river and take the city of Philadelphia."

Well, those scruffy Continentals could have told Colonel Rall a thing or two about running barefoot over ice….

An order was given in German and the young Hessian grenadier in front of Christopher removed his hanger from its scabbard. Instead of putting his sword on the ground as he was apparently instructed, he held it out to the rebel soldier looking so intently at him.

Surprised, Christopher accepted it. He had sometimes imagined himself receiving the sword of a general surrendering his army; and while this was not quite what he had pictured in his mind, it did seem to bring a fitting close to the battle for him.

Christopher's company, now under the command of Sergeant Jeremiah Smith, no less, ended up acting as the regimental guard ordinary for the Provost Marshal.

"We've surely died an' gone to heaven!—exclaimed one of the men. "Jez, where do we start, Sergeant?" This was not so much a question as it was a confirmation of license. In principle, they would maintain order among the troops, which included preventing desertion, looting, crimes against civilians, drunkenness, petty theft and such; in reality, it meant they could, within reason, of course, indulge in some of the same misconduct themselves. Not a bad deal.

"What are we waitin' for?—let's get goin' on our rounds."

The town of Trenton consisted of over a hundred houses, mostly crowded along King and Queen Streets. On their appointed rounds, they entered house after house, only to find each devastated, furniture used as firewood and family belongings carried off, leaving most of the town's houses mere wooden shells. Occasionally, a family would be found wandering around rooms strewn with debris and filth, but more often than not, the houses were empty except for the belongings of enemy soldiers.

Which were fair game: food, drink, blankets, occasionally a shirt or stockings, even a pair of overalls—all were "acquired." Christopher acquired a blanket, dirty shirt frayed at the neck and cuffs, a worn pair of stockings, and a tin canteen which he promptly filled with good Jamaica. Jeremiah claimed much of the same, and also a woman's short jacket and gown pilfered no doubt by a Hessian from some inhabitant, which he rolled in a blanket for Mary McBride.

It was during their guard rounds that Christopher spotted a soldier strolling up King Street dressed in a handsome green jacket faced in crimson, and a short rifle cradled in his arm. One look at the man's headcovering—a kerchief, which he had seen before—and he knew it was Dugan Fife.

Christopher grinned. "Well, Dugan. I see you've got your Jaeger rifle."

"Hey there, Christopher Sims. Ain't she a beauty? And how d'ya like me rig?" In addition to the jacket, Dugan wore a buff waistcoat without a shirt, and the same leggins he wore when Christopher ran into him near McKonkey's.

"You're somethin' to behold, Dugan—no doubt about it. Is that a Jaeger coat?"

"Aye, 'tis."

"Never seen one close up. Can I see your rifle?" Dugan handed Christopher the rifle and he raised it to feel the heft and straight butt against his armpit. She was a short firearm and light, but fired a hefty .60 caliber ball. She had brass furniture and a long-range rear sight; there was fine raised carving on the butt and along the forearm, and she had a nose cap made of polished horn.

Handing the weapon back, Christopher whistled in appreciation. "She's a beauty. This isn't issue, is it?"

"Naw, she's a family piece, I'm told."

"Well now, Dugan, have a pull o' this and tell me your story."

Dugan looked conspiratorial. "Well, now...me and some a the boys from Rawlings' Regiment was behind the houses on tha north side like ye was; but seein' how things was goin' good there, we thought we might do *more* good, y'know, if we was to dash down to the old barracks where we heard a large force of yey-gars was puttin' up a devil of a fight."

Dugan was talking about the old sandstone barracks down on the River Road. This beautiful building was constructed during the French and Indian Wars, but was now decrepit and used only to house the Jaeger company and some loyalist families. Similar barracks, Christopher knew, existed in upper Frederick County.

"Well, when we got there we discovered Sullivan's men had chased off the yey-gars and there weren't nobody else there but Tory wimmen and children an' men who didn't take up arms...or so they thought, and off they went to chase Hooshians—leavin' a threat to their rear, me an' the boys suspicioned. So we decided to search the whole damn place, top ta bottom.

"Well, good thing—one of the Tories soon sidled up ta me and quiet-like told me some of the others was hiding a yey-gar in their midst. Said she didn't want no trouble on account of this, an' that's why she tol' me. So I go and cut this here yey-gar outta the herd. Hard ta tell 'im from the others 'cause he was dressed like a farmer, y'know. But he knew the game was up.

"One of the Tories spoke Dutch and we conferred. I tells 'im—through the Tory—that if he turns over his yey-gar rifle to me, I'd leave him be. That's what I told 'im. He gets all teary-eyed and starts jabberin'. The Tory tells me that the rifle belonged to this yey-gar's father and to his father's father, and givin' it up would be like givin' over his wife to a marauder. Well, says I, ye're goin' to be marched off to captivity and may never return—what do ya think will become of yer yey-gar rifle then? Why, I'll tell ya what—some Yankee farmer will take her home and hang her over a fireplace, to gather soot and grow rusty.

"Then I goes on to tell 'im, I'm a fine hunter jus' like you and I want yer rifle for to replace my dear girl which was lost 'cause of ye Hooshians in the first place. We talk some more—through this Tory, ya see—about our love for these rifles...I'm describing my girl to him and the years we spent together in the far frontier, both of us cryin' like littl'uns, and he suddenly sees I'll be a good man to his rifle. With that, he leads me to her hidin' place and that of his coat and vest. See, that's how I come to be rigged out in this Hooshian costume here, but don't have no new breeches nor shoes—'cause he's still wearin' them."

Enjoying Dugan's tale, Christopher asked, "So you didn't kill a hundred Jaegers to get this rifle, Dugan?"

"Naw," Dugan replied happily. "Jus' had to per-suade the man to see the reasoning of me argument. An' since I don't talk convincingly in Dutch, I kinda made the point with me knife at 'is throat."

"Ah, I see now," Christopher laughed. "But you still let this man go, Dugan?"

"Why, sure I did. He's still there amongst the tories lookin' like a clodhopper, same as the rest of 'em. Now don't go gettin' him caught, Christopher Sims—I gave me word."

"What'll you do now, Dugan, head west?"

"Sure am—as soon as we recross the Dullerway. Thinkin' of headin' to Caroliny."

"North Carolina—really?"

"'Pears ta be too much warfare along the Alleghenies. Western Caroliny is said to be prime huntin' and livin'. So, that's where I be headed. And ye, Christopher Sims?"

"Goin' back to Baltimore."

They looked at each other, each comfortable in going their separate ways. "Well then, Dugan Fife...God be with you."

"Aye, and you too, Christopher Sims."

Trenton, New Jersey
Noon, December 26

The drums sounded the Assembly and the troops, most of whom had sated themselves on rum, beef and biscuits, and then more rum, managed to form for the march.

"The men have had too much rum," noted Colonel Stone, shaking his head. This was said to Jeremiah and Christopher, who were both a little tipsy themselves. "His Excellency had to order scores of hogsheads stove in just to ensure that the army was able to march."

Jeremiah wore a pained expression. "Aye, good Jamaica that was, sir, not the New England swill we usually get."

"We'll need to check the men's water bottles and rundlets," Colonel Stone concluded.

With his own newly-acquired tin canteen full of the good creature, Christopher was not inclined to be *that* strict.

"Well, sir; in fact, it might not be a bad idea for the men to carry a little rum with 'em. Look at the weather, sir—marchin' back in this cold 'n' wet, an antifogmatic is jus' what the doctor would order, I'll aver."

The Colonel looked closely at Christopher, his eyebrows raised in suspicion. After a little hesitation, he said, "*Corporal Sims,* I'm willing to concede that a little rum might be medicinally required during the upcoming march; but *you* will see that there will be no over-imbibing—is *that* understood?" Christopher heard Colonel Stone mutter, "Antifogmatic, indeed," as he strode off.

The Banks of the Delaware
Five o'clock in the Afternoon, December 26

They finally reached Johnson's Ferry at darkness. The river was choppy, and fierce little whitecaps flowed over great chunks of ice. The boats were gathered in ranks at the water's edge, tied to tree trunks and roots, bobbing crazily as waves slapped against the bank.

When the time came for them to cross, they found it a tortuous journey. The bottom of the boat was a foot deep in ice-cold water and slush. The river was rough and threw them about, and splashes of water from the waves hitting hard on the sides of the boat drenched them. The polemen fought against the current but the boat was still pushed downriver and away from McKonkey's. As the boat laboriously drew within ten feet of the shore, and making little headway against the current and the ice, the men simply jumped out into the waist-deep water and waded ashore.

"Goddamn"…was all Christopher could expel from between chattering teeth and quivering jaw. He had never been so cold in his life. Once ashore, his small company quickly formed and almost ran the mile to the encampment, where Jeremiah and Christopher threw themselves into their little hut.

Ah…but it was warm. They tore off their wet rags and Mary was there to wrap them in blankets. "Welcome home, my heroes. Here's some hot beef broth and fresh bread, and—believe it or not—a hot toddy."

She watched as her men began to thaw out.

"I heard the news from Trenton and I saw the hirelings herded up the road, lookin' like beaten curs with their tails between their legs. Now y'all tell me about this glorious victory of ours."

And they did. They told her about the crossing, and the agonizing march through snow and ice and rain, and Lieutenant Fisher freezing to death; and they spoke in proud voices about the battle, of men fighting and dying in the frozen streets of Trenton, of bewildered Hessians running, of mindless charges and cannons belching dirty smoke, of American soldiers standin' tall and vanquishing a mighty foe, and of fighting and winning for so noble a cause.

Christopher showed Mary his Hessian hanger and said he was goin' to give it to his little brother John Paul in place of that damn wooden sword he was always carrying around. Mary looked at Christopher as though he was delirious…then

Jeremiah proudly gave her the jacket and gown, sayin' it was from the both of them.

All the time they were drinkin' Jamaica and gettin' warm. The men were now comfortable—and tired...so damn'd tired—and a little drunk...now giving in to their illnesses...the warm hut and blankets and all lulling them into a pleasant feverishness.

And Mary sat there, sipping the rum being passed around, and listenin' spell-bound, fingering her new clothes—the finest she ever owned, she stated simply.

There they sat, their backs against the dirt wall, the harsh wind rustling the thatch roof, contently sipping their rum, falling asleep, the warm air of the hut heavy with the odor of strenuously worked men and the taut stink of battle, mixing with the smell of green wood smoke, strong rum, gunpowder, and fresh evergreens.

How Dreadful the Odds
December 28, 1776

"Ensign Anders—Pace, I'd appreciate it if ye would take some letters back home for me...and this." Christopher handed him the hanger he had captured from the young Hessian at Trenton. "It's for my little brother back in the Lower Potomac. No, no," Christopher quickly said, grinning, "I know you're not passin' through my neck of the woods—I meant, if ye would kindly deliver it to my aunt in Baltimore town."

Ensign Anders accepted the letters and the small sword, and said graciously, "Be pleased to do it, Christopher. Now, while I plan to go through Head of Elk on the way home, I can't promise you that'll happen. In such a case, should I give the letter to your woman to one who is goin' there?"

Christopher thought before saying, "Nay, if that's the case, it might be best to also deliver the letter to Hannah to my aunt in Baltimore. Appreciate this."

Pace Anders, ensign in the Maryland Brigade of the flying camp, was finally leaving camp for home. Like Christopher, he had stayed on when the rest of his unit marched on December 1 to Philadelphia to be discharged. Now, too sick for the rigors of a winter campaign which was not yet over, Pace was going home to Frederick Town for a spell; and then, having accepted a second lieutenant's commission, would recruit his quota of men and report to Colonel Mordecai Gist in Baltimore.

"My pleasure, Chris." He turned to go, then stopped to add, "You know I'd be marchin' with you if—" he hesitated, his lips pursed…"if I thought I could do my duty…ya know," he trailed off lamely. He knew the enormity of what the brave little army he was leaving was embarked upon.

"I know you would, Pace," Christopher replied, adding "sir" to emphasize his respect for the man. "But ye need to recover…we need you for the next campaign."

With that, the two men parted, both hoping they'd see each other again.

26

"CRUSHING A FRIGHTENED, TREMBLING ENEMY"

Just East of Trenton, New Jersey
January 2, 1777

FLUSHED WITH VICTORY, the Americans had recrossed the Delaware River several days earlier, and now they were in terrible trouble.

In a battle line along the Assunpink Creek across from Trenton, they watched as the main British force began to collect opposite them. It was seven o'clock in the evening, and only nightfall and European military convention had saved the army—and likely the Cause itself.

But for how long? There was neither the time nor means to recross the Delaware to safety...and to retreat toward Bordentown to the south with Lord Cornwallis and his angry legions dogging them would lead to rout if not destruction.

"We should've stayed on the other side of the river and celebrated the New Year with Hessian rum and rations...and satisfied ourselves with what we had already done."

And as our life is but a span,
Let's touch the tankard while we can,
In memory of that day.

They could see cannon muzzles blowing tiny jets of yellow flame and showers of sparks, followed by their hollow reports. Cannon balls and howitzer shells then arched through a black sky, their tails a fiery streak, passing each other to land on opposite sides of the creek. Christopher and his comrades could see shells burst, some in the air as a fiery white blossom and shower of sparkles, while others fell behind houses where the explosions outlined structures in a momentary white light. Small fires burned among clusters of buildings on both sides of the river.

Christopher coughed deeply and spat out a glob of phlegm big as a musketball. Still suffering from the ague caught during the attack on Trenton, he felt feverish and ached all over. The night had turned bitterly cold once again and he drew nearer to the large bonfire, fed by the sturdy cedar fences of the surrounding farms.

Christopher turned to Jeremiah, who was also coughing and hacking. "I think they might fix our flint on the morrow. What do you think?"

"Reminds me of Long Island—problem is, there are no Marbleheaders to carry us off." Colonel John Glover's sailors, true to their word, had refused to serve any longer and had set off to seek their fortunes as privateers.

The army was stretched thin as a thread for three miles along the ridge above the Assunpink, from the Delaware River all the way east to Phillips Ford, where Mercer's brigade and the Maryland regiment held the extreme right of the line.

Looking at the numerous campfires across the river, Christopher asked worriedly, "Jeremiah, do you really believe we can prevent the enemy wading across this brook? You realize we don't have enough men to defend all the crossing points."

He was pointing out an obvious fact. Instead of the twenty-eight hundred Continentals who attacked Trenton, there were now only about fifteen hundred. Like Glover's Marbleheaders, many of the Continentals had refused to stay on past the end of their terms. Indeed, it took the officers considerable prodding and a promise of ten dollars in coin to retain as many of those remaining Continentals as they did.

****

On December 29, General Washington crossed the Delaware—this time with ice floes as big as houses—into enemy territory, having no idea how many men he would have two days hence.

Once again, they found themselves in Trenton. As they marched through the town, they looked with curiosity at the scene of their recent victory. Few of the inhabitants had returned and the town was shattered and empty.

Signs of the battle, however, had already faded: The scattered remains of clashing armies had been so thoroughly picked over by military and civilian scavengers that nothing recognizable remained; and snow, rain and a thaw had obliterated the spoors of war in the streets and lots. Only the mounds of raw earth in the churchyard were left as a reminder of the men who had fallen here; and while the shattered windows, splintered doors and broken fences throughout the town attested to a recent violence, it was hard to say that a battle had taken place here, much less to say which army might have won.

Nightfall, Colonel Stone had emphasized, nightfall was the key, as he looked worriedly at a sun which seemed to hang unmoving in the middle of the sky.

"What will night really do for us, Jeremiah—other than postpone the inevitable?" Christopher was thinking about their situation, shivering miserably on the creek bank, wondering where he could find safety if worse came to worst.

"Night brings us a reprieve, Chris, and time for our generals to collect their thoughts and come up with the right answer."

Frequently they looked up at the sky. As the sun, a pale disc behind scuttling gray clouds, began to set, they measured the success of their resistance by the growing darkness.

With flags waving and bands playing, three columns of British and Hessian troops calmly marched on the bridge, across which lay what remained of the main army of the revolution.

It could all end here....

The enemy charged confidently in column and, much to their surprise, were rudely thrown back. Even as the enemy prepared to make another charge, cheers and huzzahs and taunts came from the American side. Hearing these, the British and German attackers hesitated and their officers had to beat them back into line with the flats of their swords.

From the American side of the creek, a tremendous rumble of angry yelling and shouting greeted the enemy preparations.

"Come on, you bastards!"

"Hey, there's the bridge and here we be—try to cross it, by damn!"

The taunting came not from any certainty that they could hold the bridge against this onslaught, but from a desire to have the matter decided then and there.

Twice more the enemy advanced on the bridge, only to be thrown back again...and then again, the narrow bridge now strewn with blue and red bodies. After the third attempt, which was met by every musket and cannon within range, the enemy had enough. The resolution had been delayed until tomorrow.

"If we stay here, we're sitting ducks," Christopher noted matter-of-factly.

"I'll agree with that," admitted Jeremiah, obviously discouraged.

Around midnight, having just checked their decimated company and its guard detail, Jeremiah and Christopher were hunkering near the fire when Colonel Stone came up. In a hushed voice, he informed them that the army was moving out.

"Moving out?"—they repeated in surprise. "Where to, sir?"

Colonel Stone ignored the question. "Everything is to be done in the utmost secrecy...the adjutant will give you directions for the march...make certain the lock of every musket is half-cocked...no torches, no pipes. An' see that these fires are heaped with wood. We're to create the illusion of an army encamped. Militia will continue to feed the fires and make appropriate noises throughout the night."

As the colonel moved off, Jeremiah grinned and said, "What did I tell you. His Excellency has found a way to get us out of this mess."

So, like a footpad in the night, the Continental Army, artillery and wagon wheels swaddled in rags, gingerly crept away from the enemy and set out on the road south.

Their route was not so much by road as it was along a series of paths joining neighborhoods and farms. Initially, the column moved through serried woods of oak and pine and scalloped stands of stark cedar. Here, they marched on sandy paths, drowsy men tripping over jagged stumps.

After chopping away at some stumps with a small belt axe so that one of the gun carriages could pass, Christopher surveyed the route and noted, "Had we tried to pass along this route yesterday when the weather was mild, we never would've made it." Shaking his head, Christopher continued to march on a roadway which had become as hard as cobblestone, thinkin' that just a few hours earlier it would have been like squishing through freshly churned butter.

Once on the road to the Quaker Bridge, the march was easier but more fretful since they were passing through a wilderness known as the Pine Barrens—more simply called "The Barrens" by the locals.

Moving along a white road matted with years of pine needles, they emerged from the pine-studded woods to find themselves in an eerie landscape of strange little trees—dwarfish oaks no taller than a man, with gnarled trunks and twisted branches. Outlined against the skyline, a long, dark line of these trees might appear to the weary minds of the passing men to be a battle line of soldiers with bayonets at the ready—or...could it really be....

..."Hessians! Oh good God almighty, The Hessians are upon us!"

Hearing the cries, Christopher, as near to being asleep as a man could be and still walk, was shocked to wakefulness just in time to see the line of advancing Hessians.

More surprised voices screamed out in panic.

"Hessians?"

"They're upon us! Over there!"

Only half-awake, Christopher tried to focus. He heard no gunshots, but the Hessians would attack using only the bayonet, wouldn't they? Surprised and confused, his fear exploded and suddenly, he ran.

He ran as fast as he could, throwing away his musket and wrestling desperately to pull off his knapsack. Dodging anything in his way, he made for the nearest forest. Stumbling through some underbrush, he became entangled in a dense clump of sheep laurel and fell. Flailing about, he regained his footing and shot off like a ball on a full charge of powder. He heard screams and shouts all around him...and the pounding of feet. He ran even faster....

...Christopher didn't know how far he had run—or how close behind him the enemy was. He glanced over his shoulder and saw one, maybe two figures chasing after him. He tried but couldn't run any faster. His chest was heaving and his mouth was dry. His flailing arms were so heavy he could hardly lift them. His legs began giving out and now he seemed to be running at a walk.

It was then that he was hit, the force literally lifting him off his feet. He vaguely remembered hearing someone yell, *Chris! Chris!* before the impact hurled him to the ground.

"I surrender, I surrender...."

"Chris, what for God's sake are you doin'?" The voice sounded disembodied—a voice which was angry, yet also concerned, like the time when he fell from a tree and his brother George hovered over him as he regained consciousness, anxiously talking to him. He struggled to make sense of this. Was it the confusion of dying?

"Chris, it's me, Jeremiah. What's wrong? Are ye all right?"

"Wha—? But the Hessians...."

"Chris, there aren't any Hessians. Some of the Pennsylvania militia panicked for some reason and ran off. Why'd you run off?"

Christopher was still struggling with reality. Shaking his head, he said confusedly, "Why, I don't know, Jeremiah. Those Hessians were so real, y'know what I mean?"

"You were having a nightmare, Chris. C'mon, take a slug of this." He put a flask to Christopher's mouth.

Spitting out the liquid, Christopher waved the flask away. "Jeremiah, if I have a drink of rum, I'll be a goner for sure. I'm all right—let me up."

More or less back to his senses, Christopher looked around. He saw the column continuing its march less than two hundred yards away. *Good Lord,* he thought to himself, *I didn't cover but a few rods and it seemed like I was runnin' forever.*

Now on his feet, Christopher brushed himself off, and with a sheepish look at the men around him, reclaimed his musket from the man who had picked it up, and then hurried off to find the company.

Catching up to him, Jeremiah continued to look at him curiously as they cut across the field back to the road. Tired and physically spent, Christopher, like many of his comrades, had fallen asleep even while marching. In this state the real and the imagined merged, and the dark recesses of an overwrought mind conjured up all kinds of goblins and bugbears out of the shadows. He knew Jeremiah understood this—indeed, Jeremiah had admitted that exhaustion and this strange land played tricks on his mind too; but he wanted to make sure his comrade wasn't on the verge of mania.

"I'm fine, Jeremiah—truly."

Satisfied, Jeremiah told him, "Chris, word is we're goin' to attack the British garrison at Princeton."

This made Christopher fully alert. "The hell you say! Well, then, we better check the men's arms," and he broke into a wobbling trot.

To Jeremiah, Christopher looked like a drunk trying to hurry home after last call as he made his fitful way toward the road.

27

IT CAME DOWN TO PUSHING BAYONETS

Princeton, New Jersey
January 3, 1777

IT HAD BECOME a clear frosty morning, and the rising sun sparkled on a countryside made opaque by hoarfrost. It was the kind of snow-still, very cold day in which a man might get the feeling of warmth from just looking at the evergreens.

Standing in drab ranks that blended with the trees and brush, the men breathed out thick white puffs of vapor which were quickly dispelled. They almost seemed to be part of the surroundings. The alarmed noises of towhees and bluejays, however, sounded an accusatory cry against the quiet men collecting below, whose crackling footfalls, muffled coughing and clanking equipment disturbed the natural order of this quiet neighborhood.

The serenity of the morning was interrupted by lowered voices giving commands, which stirred the men into action. Accompanied by the sounds of equipment being adjusted and arms ordered, the men formed up and prepared to march.

Alarmed, the birds flew off, screeching angrily.

The American Army had been halted about two miles from Princeton at a fork in the Quaker Road. Here, the men patiently awaited further orders, watching a cold sunrise above the group of conferring officers. There was the brigade commander, General Mercer, his second-in-command, Colonel Haslet, whose Delaware Regiment now consisted of himself and eight men; Colonel Stone was also there, as were the other regimental commanders under Mercer's command.

The group soon broke up and Colonel Stone strode over to where Jeremiah and the other company commanders had collected. After a short meeting, they too broke to carry orders to the weary rank and file.

"Men, our commanders have decided that we must take advantage of the present situation, which is this: Lord Cornwallis with the main army is sixteen miles away. According to reports, Prince Town is garrisoned by three regiments of the Fourth Brigade—in all, only about twelve hundred men. And none of 'em know we're here. The idea is with surprise and superior numbers we can defeat them, just like at Trenton."

There was little reaction from the men—most of them were just too exhausted to be demonstrative one way or the other. However, the way Jeremiah described it to them, it did have a certain appeal: wouldn't it be something to vanquish both a Hessian brigade *and* a British brigade all in the span of a few days—*well, what the hell*, they thought, *let's give it a try.*

"Men, we're about two miles from Prince Town. From here the army will be split into two main divisions: Our brigade will lead General Greene's Division. We're to break down the bridge on the main road and delay Lord Cornwallis's force should it come too smartly to the garrison's relief. The rest of the division will continue up the Post Road into town and attack from that direction. The other division, under General Sullivan, will turn right at yon meeting house and circle around to attack the town from the southern edge."

General Mercer's brigade, perhaps three hundred and fifty men—deathly sick, utterly exhausted, clad in the remnants of their summer clothing, with bloody and blistered feet poking out of broken shoes—trudged up the hill toward the Post Road. They fully expected to meet an enemy ill-prepared for an attack—perhaps breakfasting or otherwise engaged in routine camp duties.

Instead, the Americans and the British stumbled into each other.

Two of Mawhood's three regiments, after their breakfast of biscuits and brandy, were marching to Trenton to join in the long sought-after destruction of Mr. Washington and his army; even while the American Army was chancing its very survival on surprising an entire brigade of regulars who they thought would hardly be out of bed, much less on the road.

But out of miscalculation and inexperience came yet another surprising victory.

Through the swirling fog and dense growths of trees, the two forces seemed to have spotted each other at roughly the same time. And each then raced for the high ground.

That Mercer's brigade would reach neither the high ground nor find safety with Sullivan's column was decided when it entered a thick orchard and a volley of fire broke out on its left from behind a fence. Musket balls whirred overhead to rattle among the tree branches and send a shower of twigs falling among the rapidly moving column.

As the opposing forces closed, they each touched off awkward volleys. Here and there a ball hit flesh or bone with a smack, like the sound of a child's kiss. Artillery was quickly brought into play and several pieces on each side threw grapeshot into the other's ranks, adding a weird screeching sound over the battlefield, even as the spreading iron balls blew gaps in both lines.

The two forces now stood within fifty paces of each other. The gunfire had momentarily ceased as the two sides gathered themselves, like two rutting rams about to clash.

"Dress ranks, men." Christopher repeated the order going down the line.

"*We'll* dress you, ye damn'd rebels!" came the response. And the British delivered a platoon volley that crumpled the American line. The British then charged with the bayonet. The Americans managed to get off one more hasty volley at the surging line, but it had no noticeable effect.

It came down to pushing bayonets. Some three hundred British soldiers charged, a horde of savages, screaming like demi-devils—and the effect on the Americans was devastating. Their ranks quickly became disorganized. Soon convinced that it was every man for himself, they broke—then turned their backs and ran....

...For Christopher, the fight became a blur of violent, disjointed scenes. Amidst wild yelling and screaming, men running or falling, or engaged in hand-to-hand fighting, muskets and even hands parrying jabbing bayonets, his actions reflected the frenzy around him.

He tried to conduct himself as a proper noncommissioned officer, hoarsely urging the men to fight back even as they ran. But he, too, was overwhelmed by the horror of being bayoneted and joined the rest of Mercer's brigade in headlong flight.

There were cursing British soldiers everywhere, herding American soldiers in front of them like cattle when they were not driving bayonet-tipped muskets into breast or belly. And there were the shrill sounds of men dying or about to die, mocked by the enemy who skewered and clubbed them.

Then, when defeat appeared certain, up came Hitchcock's New Englanders, God-driven, furious soldiers, who raced by their bewildered comrades, charging over and down the hill to throw themselves upon the 14th British Regiment of Foot. Following a volley at thirty yards, the British broke and a once proud regiment fled down the Post Road toward Trenton, with General Washington leading the pursuit, shouting "It's a fine fox chase, my boys!"

The charging New Englanders, as well as General Washington chased by the sprawling bodies of valiant men who had tried and failed to stem the tide, men who lay still or writhed in pain—and among them lay Christopher Sims who had been struck hard in the head by a rifle butt, a blow which left him for dead.

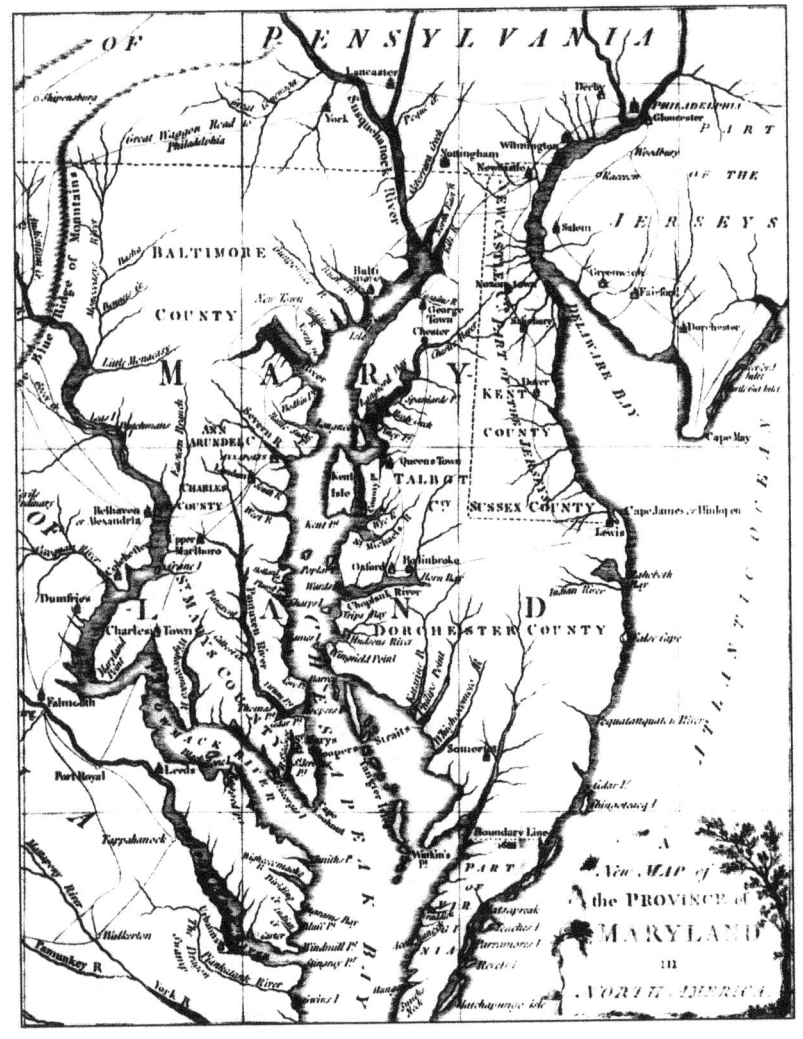

Detail of *A New Map of the Province of Maryland in North America, 1780*, by John Hinton.

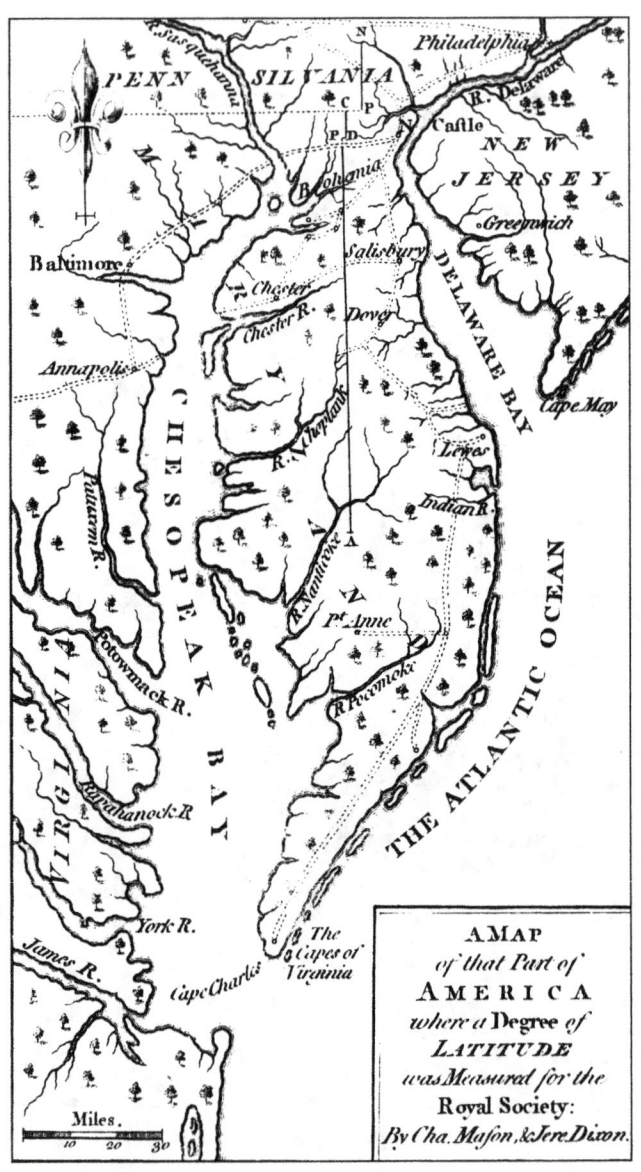

The Eastern Shore of Maryland in 1775

Charles Mason and Jeremiah Dixon, *A Map of that part of America where a Degree of Latitude was Measured for the Royal Society*. From *The Gentleman's Magazine*, London, December 1769. From the author's collection.

Part Two

The Inner War

Every man must be a soldier.
John Adams, May 1776

Not every man can be a soldier.
John Adams, July 1776

Women [should] not be bound by any Laws
in which we have no voice, or Representation.
Abigail Adams to John Adams,
March 31, 1776

28

YEAR OF THE HANGMAN

Prisoners are men, and unfortunate.
Emmerich Vattel,
The Law of Nations

Princeton, New Jersey
January 3, 1777

IT CAME TO HIM slowly that he heard no sounds of battle: no crackling pops or throaty booms, no balls whirring by like a swarm of bees, no high-pitched commands, or the ugly sounds of many different causes of pain as lead or iron shredded muscles, or perforated bowels, or shivered bones; no, it dawned on him, he heard none of the sounds associated with the great din of battle.

Curious to know what was happening, Christopher saw only darkness and could not tell if his eyes were open or not. He tried to lift his head to look around and it exploded.

He lay still, willing the pain to subside. Damn, a head wound. *Next time*, he thought, *I'll just try to use only my eyes.*

It turned out his sense of smell and not his sight told him where he was. It smelled of stale hay and warm animal droppings, and he realized he was in a barn.

Overcoming his stunned drowsiness, head thundering, he gingerly moved his hand to the back of his head to check his wound. He pushed through a stiff wad of lint and fingered wet hair, and a stickiness which he knew was blood—and...thank

God! he felt solid bone. His skull was not cracked open, nor his brains spilling out....

A voice said: "Well now, back amongst the living, are you! You've been unconscious for most of the day.

"It doesn't appear," the man went on, "that your head wound is serious, tho' you may have your doubts about that right now. Ye also have a bloody rent in the seat of your overalls which somebody will have to take a look at; and you have a trifling wound under your arm—maybe from a grape. Other than that it's hard to see what's wrong with you!"

Christopher carefully moved his eyes to look at the speaker. He saw an older man, dressed like a farmer, who obviously wanted to put Christopher at his ease, despite his wounds.

"I should introduce myself. Name's Samuel Pell. I own a farm down the road from here—this be Clark's barn you're in—came to help the wounded who were abandoned." The man saw Christopher's look and quickly said, "Your army had to leave a number of you behind...because of the pursuit, ya know."

Just then, Christopher saw two British soldiers carrying in a wounded man, an American from his appearance.

Glancing back to Mister Pell, he started to ask, "Wha—?"

"There's no good way to tell you this, soldier," the man said almost apologetically, "but you're going to live to be a prisoner of the Crown."

"Or perhaps, we'll just hang ya now, ya damn'd rebel!"

The man making this threat wore the green and white uniform of a loyalist.

"How 'bout that, ye scum?" The soldier then mimed being hanged, which brought laughter from his comrades.

Christopher cringed, but this was not the first time he had cause to think about a noose around his neck....

...Idly drawing shapes in the light dusting of snow which fell that late December afternoon, Mary's finger formed the numbers "1777" on the rock upon which they were sitting. The gray numerals were in stark contrast to the pure white snow.

"A few days and it'll be the year of the hangman," she said quietly.

Christopher had glanced at her, knowing her penchant for signs. The three sevens represented the gibbet in many minds, a year long reminder that they were rebels in the eyes of their lawful master.

"Don't mean anything," he had said with false confidence.

With a wan smile, Mary swept the date into a little pile of soft snow, scooped it up and licked at it, just like they did as children.

...Now, looking at the loyalist soldier looming above him, Christopher glared at the man. "I am your prisoner, sir, and you surely have the advantage of me. You are free to show how to subdue a helpless enemy."

Swearing, the man angrily yelled at Christopher, "Goddam'd rebel, you shall be hanged tomorrow," and he strode out of the barn.

The British were not in a good or kindly mood, Christopher soon learned. Delighted to hear of the overwhelming victory at Princeton, he soon wished that the British had been left with some pride.

But while Christopher was constantly abused verbally and threatened with physical punishment over the next few days, he was not actually harmed, and no attempt was made to steal the few personal items in his haversack or the clothes on his back—*most likely*, he thought, *because I look worse than a tatterdemalion.* Fortunately so, because he had thirteen silver coins hidden in a money belt that he had stripped from a dead Hessian at Trenton. For assurance, he periodically felt for the belt around his waist, tucked under his torn and filthy overalls.

There wasn't much in the way of medical care. Mostly they were left to their own devices; but this also included the British wounded, so it wasn't punishment for being a rebel. In addition to Mister Pell's best efforts, a Quaker woman and her son also visited the improvised hospital each day to administer basic first aid to the wounded and provide some food.

Christopher and several other wounded but ambulatory American prisoners were taken to the Stony Brook Meeting House, the same fieldstone meeting house their stealthy columns had passed on their way to attack Princeton. The building was hardly more than a cabin, the small interior taken up with crude pews which were now being used as fuel for the small wood-burning fireplace. The meeting house was being used as a makeshift prison hospital and was crowded with injured prisoners.

A British ensign, in the uniform of the light infantry, was in charge of the prisoners. He proved to be a fair and reasonable jailor. He saw to the medical needs of the prisoners as best he could and provided full rations to all who could eat.

At the same time, Ensign Walters made it clear that "so-called Continentals"—professional soldiers in the minds of the British, could count on spending the rest of the rebellion in prison, even while 90-day militia were being paroled.

"Unless, of course, corporal-rebel Sims, you agree to take the oath of loyalty and enlist in His Majesty's army."

"No, sir, I can't do that."

"Ah, well then, Sims, you'll suffer being a prisoner in New York, and"—the ensign paused to give emphasis to what he next said, "you'll find the jailors there do not respect their enemies' courage…as I do."

"I understand, sir, and thank you."

****

Less than a week after the engagement, prisoners who could walk and those who would likely survive the trip in swaying, banging wagons, set off across New Jersey for New York City. They arrived at Paulus Hook several days later. The prisoners were then transported by lighter to their permanent confinement—which rumor had it was an old ship anchored off a Long Island beach.

As they passed along the Long Island shore, the prisoners craned their necks to see the prison ship, which still wasn't in sight. Their boat continued up the East River and finally rounded a point and before them was Wallabout Bay, where lay a great derelict of a boat.

"There, ya damn'd rebels, *there* lies the *Whitby*. Don't think of it as a floating cage, gents, think of it as a floating tomb!"

The winter twilight gave a ghoulish look to the hulk. The gun-metal gray sky merged with the brackish water, casting the ship in shadow. It was a large ship but fragile looking, without masts to give it purpose, its hull rotting, and great iron cables tethering it to the shallow waters of the bay. Gray seagulls, screeching hungrily, circled the ship.

As they approached the gangway ladder, Christopher and his fellow prisoners could see arms extended through portholes, furiously waving hats, as if to warn them away from the evil that lay within.

As the lighter hauled alongside the prison-ship, Christopher was struck by the effluvium literally blowing out of the air holes cut out of the hull. It was as if the dead were exhaling their rot, he thought, and suddenly he felt very cold.

On deck their belongings were searched for valuables and weapons, and their names and units entered on a ledger. They took Christopher's pen and ink set, but left him with the rest of his pathetic belongings.

And there was enough swearing and not a few blows delivered to the newly arrived prisoners.

The man who greeted them on deck said it succinctly: "Damn'd rebels, ye'll be here 'til yere executed or die of some awful disease, either of which is better'n you deserve. Now git below!" And he literally threw the first prisoner down the main hatchway.

29

"FRESH FISH"

Wallabout Bay, Long Island
January 1777

"DEATH HAS NO RELISH for such skeleton carcasses as we are, but he will have a feast upon you fresh fish." The man who uttered these words was old beyond his years—wrinkled skin and prominent bones showing through his rags, a sallow, blotchy face—in appearance, a man hardly alive.

But Card Way Whithousen had been a prisoner since August 27, 1776, held in one of the sugar houses until late October, when he was transferred to the prison-ship *Whitby*; and here he was, still alive in January 1777 to tell his tale.

As the new prisoners descended the hatchway ladder to the deck below, they were overwhelmed with questions.

"Was it true that we defeated the Hessians at Trenton and that thousands of the bastards were killed and captured?

"There have been rumors of another victory at Prince Town in the Jerseys—'tis this true?"

There were other questions for the newly arrived: What regiment? Is Philadelphia safe? How is morale? The questions went on and on.

In turn, the new arrivals were anxious to learn of their condition: how long would they be prisoners? Had there been exchanges or a general cartel for exchange of prisoners? And looking around curiously in the murky light, they asked worriedly about living conditions and food.

Such talk lasted well into the early morning even as daily needs were attended to. The new prisoners were each assigned to a six man mess. There was an attempt to match up neighbors with neighbors, though this didn't always work out. Christopher was assigned to a six-man mess that did not include any Marylanders.

He was told that most of the men taken on Long Island back in August '76 were "land" prisoners, held in York City. After the great fire, though, more and more were being sent to a growing number of prison ships. Most of men in the old *Whitby* were surrendered at Fort Washington, and, indeed, there were Marylanders among them—might even be some from Frederick.

It was believed that the Marylanders who were captured on Long Island were being held in New York City itself. Sometimes news of prisoners (and even those dead) was obtained, and names and regiments circulated. "Haven't heard anything about Smallwood's men for months," Christopher was told by one of his new messmates.

The emaciated man named Card Way Whithousen, serving in the 19th Continental Regiment when he was captured, was also a member of the same mess. He was one of the original inmates of the *Whitby* and was onboard when it had been towed to its present mooring in Wallabout Bay.

"Thought I'd died and gone to heaven when I heard I was being moved from New Bridewell, bare of everything including window coverings, blankets, fuel and any other necessity ya can think of. So bein' sent to a ship sounded...well, warm and comfortable, it did. Didn't take long to learn my mistake!" Whithousen told this almost humorously.

"There's 'bout 250 prisoners last I heard, and more coming every day." Then Whithousen angrily brushed aside the figure, adding "But we don't know how many of those 250 are dead or alive."

Just then, the grating over the main hatch was pulled open, and a gruff voice rang out. "Rebels, send up yer dead!"

There was a commotion, the sounds of moving masses, cussing, and then…one…two…and finally three bodies, wrapped awkwardly in worn blankets, were hustled up the stairway.

As all of them stared at the procession climbing the stairs, Whithousen said sadly, "Death is not a burden for the dead, but it surely is for the living. God has liberated those fortunate souls through death," he pointed emphatically towards the stairs. "Here, you live to suffer untold hardships. If ye cain't stand the idear, I suggest you start dying now, peaceful-like."

Christopher and the other new arrivals listened intently, suddenly realizing that their survival would rest on how well they learned their lessons from survivors like Card Way Whithousen.

"There be no physicians or medicines. Jail fever and the smallpox are rampagin' throughout the ship. Scurvy, the dry cough; in fact, every disease known to man is present here in this damn'd hell hole."

Then there were the guards: most of the prisoners said the British were generally indifferent but occasionally would taunt and even beat men. Surprisingly, the Hessians turned out to be genuinely humane, "probably because they're treated like offal by the British," remarked one prisoner. The worst were the loyalists, who were brutal. Story after story was told about loyalist jailers thrusting bayonet-tipped muskets at men on the stairway just for amusement.

The hulk itself was a man-eating monster. Below deck, it was dark and wet, the rotting wood spongy and slick. There were a few oil lamps and a limited amount of oil to provide light. So dear was the light from these lamps, each was allowed to burn only a short while in the evening.

It was so cold in winter that the flooring was often covered in ice. There was no wood or coal for heat; the rags they wore, threadbare blankets, and raging fevers provided their only warmth.

Little air circulated below decks, except wisps through air-holes cut into the hull, the air so foul, the newly arrived instinctively held their last taste of fresh air until their lungs were about to burst. Christopher's mess was fortunate (thanks to Card)—they occupied space beneath one of the air-holes.

The living death between decks was only occasionally relieved by short periods on deck. For a few precious minutes they could breathe fresh air, look at the sun shining in the sky and imagine what it was like to be free.

"Pudding Day"

They learned early on that there would be little food. Some days they were given food, some days they were given no food. Oh, sure, there was a promised ration, but, in reality, they might receive food to last three days consisting of one-half pound of biscuit, one-half pound of pork, half a gill of rice, half a pint of pease, and one-half ounce of a substance called "sweet oil," which substituted for butter. "And even that's 'pretend rations,'" they were told. In truth, the pork was old and unsavory and everything else was full of worms and very moldy. Even the water was foul.

But most of them actually survived on such an allowance, occasionally supplemented (or substituted) with rats, mice and various bugs. Some of the frontiersmen among the prisoners actually enjoyed these little luxuries.

Each member of the mess served his turn going to the galley for their ration, real or imagined, and returned to the mess to give each his share.

There were special days. One day was referred to as "peaday" for which the ration issue was a soup dish of brown water and a few floating peas.

"Pudding day" was also special, when each mess received three pounds of infested flour and one-half pound of bad raisins. These ingredients would be mixed into a pudding in a cloth bag and then put in boiling water. This was usually accompanied by a half pint of rum for each man. But sometimes, just for spite, the officer of the guard would order the rum thrown overboard.

There was also an old woman that came alongside the prison ship in her little sailboat to sell food items to those lucky prisoners who had money. Hearing about this, Christopher offered his silver shoe buckles to the mess.

"This'll sustain six souls, Christopher," Card exclaimed. "Why, this will keep us in fruits and soft bread for months, I'm thinkin'—the fruits to stave off the scurvy and the bread because…well, because there just ain't nothin' better'n fresh bread!"

Christopher looked around at all the other men crowding the deck, a distressed look on his face. Card saw this and said gently, "Christopher, all of us understand that some of us will eat, some of us won't; some of us will die, some of us won't; some of us will be set free, some of us won't…it's a poor prisoner's rendition of Ecclesiastes, Chapter 3. Then there's,

> *Wherefore I praised the dead which are*
> *Already dead more than the living which*
> *are yet alive.*
> *Yea, better is he than both they, which*
> *Hath not yet been, who hath not seen the evil*
> *Work that is done under the sun.*

Card Way Whithousen looked at peace. "Our joy is to suffer as we create the perfect society for our children and their children!"

While others wanted only to live to enjoy this perfect world with their children….

****

Once Christopher got over his shock at being a prisoner on board a ghost ship, he received another, more threatening shock. He realized that men were dying all around him of the smallpox. Christopher had never had the pox and wondered how he could survive this.

"How does a man avoid the smallpox, Card?"

"He doesn't," Card stated matter-of-factly. "I was inoculated after joinin' my regiment in the camp around Boston. Passed through the disease in the most favorable manner. See! I have only a few pockmarks to prove my ordeal" And, indeed, he had only a few pockmarks and even those were faint. "Ought to get inoculated, Christopher."

Christopher was thoughtful, "How do I go about that?"

"Well, ye obtain the infectious matter from someone having the pox." He looked around the deck, "No problem there…then you cut a small incision on your palm or between your thumb and forefinger and deposit a small amount of the matter in the cut.

Christopher looked hard at the numerous men in the throes of the disease. "If it's so easy, why didn't all of these men accept inoculation?"

"'Cause, Christopher, some think it's the work of the devil intendin' to spread the disease, others know there's a risk to it and don't want to take the chance.

"Now, this doctor who inoculated us obtained the matter from another inoculee, not from a sufferer of the natural pox. He also advocated a strict diet bordering on starvation. So I'd suggest, Christopher, that you are in damn near the perfect situation for bein' successfully inoculated against the smallpox! What say ya?"

Christopher finally agreed to the procedure and after looking around some, found a man in the proper stage of the illness who had been inoculated. The man was encouraging: "The disorder has come on but lightly."

The only instrument available was a common pin. Christopher punctured the skin on his hand and then inserted the pin with the infected matter, then wrapped his hand with a cloth.

Two days later he found that his hand had begun to fester, a sure sign that the application had taken effect.

He soon began to show the early symptoms: headache, backache, vomiting, and a general malaise. This was followed by fretfulness and then anxiety.

Will I survive this? he wondered, as if in a dream. Time would tell.

30

SHE BROUGHT GRACE AND CHARM

"Friendship"
At Head of Elk, Maryland
February 1777

UNCERTAIN TIMES, everyone was saying. The newspapers and pamphlets were filled with such pronouncements, and sermons rang from church pulpits proclaiming the verity of this condition in loud, damning voices.

The war is at a standstill, independence is at a standstill—my life is at a standstill, she concluded dismally.

Hannah Williams was restive. This morning she yelled at the younger Alexander children, something which was uncharacteristic of her but recently growing in frequency. This latest incident caused a concerned Missus Alexander to put down her reading and have a talk with her house manager, whom she had become quite fond of. Now, however, Isabella Alexander was becoming alarmed that Hannah's unhappiness might be affecting her reason, perhaps a dangerous prelude to insanity. There were those who related independency to a crisis of reason and sanity in the colonies. Could Hannah become yet another victim of this disorder, she wondered.

"Hannah, dear, are you quite all right?"

Hannah looked helplessly at Missus Alexander and started crying.

At first, she had really not concerned herself about what Christopher was doing during his absence; it was bad enough that he was gone. She received two letters from him that were filled with reassurances and fascinating descriptions of his adventures.

Then word of the Battle at Brooklyn brought home to her the reality that the man she loved had gone to war and men were killed in war.

Distraught for weeks, she finally received a letter from Christopher assuring her that he was all right and not to worry, he would be home soon.

She heard no further word until Michael Callum had visited her in mid-December on his way home. In addition to giving her a letter, he assured her that Christopher was well and in good spirits. Again, she was led to believe he would be home soon; but, according to Mike, Chris agreed to remain with the army until it went into winter quarters. After that, no word until news was received about the Battle of Trenton in New Jersey. Was Christopher involved in that affair? This renewed her worries about him. Did he survive this battle?

Before she had the answer to that, further word was received that yet another battle, at a place called Prince Town, had taken place. Had Christopher participated in that battle, too—or had he already been mustered out?

These were questions which remained unanswered to this day, and they grated on Hannah's nerves. Where was Christopher? Was he even alive?

Isabel Alexander would constantly assure her that, yes, of course, Christopher was alive, and likely on his way to her as they spoke.

In the meantime, Hannah was the indispensable housekeeper of "Friendship," the Alexander estate in Cecil County, Maryland. The house, twelve rooms in all, had two great brick chimneys, and a great staircase dividing two parlors. There were wide windows everywhere, and three dormers from which Hannah and the children would look spellbound out over a wide expanse of clear countryside which seemed to encompass the whole county.

Hannah's duties relieved Missus Alexander from the drudgery of ordering household goods, marketing, seeing that the table was properly set both for family and visitors, and everything economically used. She also cared for the younger children when the older children were busy with school lessons or chores.

Hannah enjoyed her work and grew to like the Alexander family very much. Though she was not on a first name basis with Missus Alexander, both enjoyed the company of the other, and often would just chat about nothing in particular. Isabella Alexander was an elegant and sophisticated woman who was thoroughly captivated by Hannah's adventures.

"...So you were locked in this awful...this awful shed smelling of rotten shellfish and tidal mud? Good Lord, Hannah, and in nothing but a shift?"

They giggled at the absurdness of it all.

"Well," Missus Alexander would finally say, "I'm so delighted that you survived that terrible trial to be with us today, Hannah."

Hannah also enjoyed the six Alexander children, several of whom were almost as old as she. The eldest son, William, a budding ladies' man, was infatuated with her, as all knew, while the only daughter, Araminta, thought of her as an older sister.

Both Isabella and her husband Robert Alexander appreciated the professional accomplishments Hannah brought to her employment as manager. Robert Alexander, of course, knew her entire background from Mordecai Gist. He did not offer the details of this sordid affair to his wife, who was naturally sympathetic to Hannah's plight anyway; but he knew that the truly aggrieved party was not Hannah, but a useful though misunderstood social system.

Throughout the summer and fall, there had been the constant movement of troops through Head of Elk on their way to join General Washington's army—Marylanders, Virginians, even some Carolinians. The numbers of troops marching to join Washington became fewer and fewer as winter approached, and the numbers of troops returning home grew more and more as ultimate defeat approached.

Morale could not have been worse when news of the American victory at Trenton was received. The holiday season was not joyous, even the children were subdued. Hannah and the Alexander family were dining with their guests Colonel Hollingsworth and his family in the huge dining room with its seven doors, trying to be festive, when a rider brought the news of the victory. Everyone met the announcement with cheers and smiles and toasts, as well as noticeable sighs of relief; except, Hannah noted with surprise, Mister Alexander, who seemed almost chagrined—or, perhaps a better description might be "less than happy" by this news. But she soon dismissed this odd judgment when Mister Alexander quickly assumed his usual, jovial demeanor.

In late February, Hannah received a packet from Aunt Jane that included the letter Christopher had entrusted to Ensign Pace Anders. The letter was folded into a tight wad, tied with twine and was filthy dirty. Ensign Anders had apologized for the condition of the letter, assuring Aunt Jane that it showed the scars of war much more so than did Christopher! He also mentioned, wrote Jane, that as he passed through Elk he was unable to divert his route to deliver the letter personally to Hannah at the Alexander manor.

Unfolding the letter, Hannah looked at the words written on crinkled, soiled pieces of paper, the left side of each page showing ragged tears.

She read,

Dec. 27th 1776

My Dearest Friend

I writ this with a ball I hamered into a point, I have no ink I entrust this letter to Ensign Pace Anders a frend of Mich. Callum from home I have chosen to stay with the army til winter Quarters You have no doubt herd of our victory at Trenton it was victory complete and few of our men were kill'd; the march back was terrible I was assigned to escort Hessin prisoners across the Delaware River: they are of a moderate stature and lite complexion ther hair is cued tight and as it was wet and exceeding cold

froze straight back like the handle of an iron skillet I captured a Hessin
hanger for John Paul which I sent back with Ensign Anders: I recev'd your
stockings: They are so warm Ther is talk of our Commanders asking us to
remain one month more I shall agree to do this if ask'd and I ask, dear
Hannah, that you understand and forgive me this when I should be hurrying
back to you.

Your Eternal Friend, Chris. Sims

The handwriting was thick and bold and faint—lead, Hannah thought, doesn't make a particularly good writing instrument, thinking how odd it is that a ball manufactured to take a life had the effect of enlivening hers.

Hannah returned to Aunt Jane's letter. She quickly read over the war news that she knew first-hand from those returning soldiers who passed through Elk on their way home. She did carefully read news about Baltimore and Jane's notation that Rachel was looking forward to the day when Hannah returns to Baltimore and can help her run her girls academy. She added that Rachel, who had been in Annapolis, intended to write her.

Jane described Ensign Anders as a nice young gentleman, very entertaining and outgoing. She said that Rachel was quite "taken" with him, adding that Hannah should not "quote her." Jane added that that it was so kind of Ensign Anders to carry Christopher's Hessian sword all the way from a war just so a young boy could play soldier.

Hannah sighed. She looked down at Christopher's letter in her lap, wondering how many more tattered little letters she would receive before they would finally be together again.

Hearing the younger children rough-housing upstairs, she made the effort to put aside her worries and went to impose peace on the Alexander house, intent this time on keeping her temper.

31

SURVIVAL

This morn found my wound festering;
with the blessing of Divine Providence,
I will recover & with few scars I hope.
Christopher Sims, *Journal*

The Prison Ship *Whitby*
Wallabout Bay, Long Island
March-April 1777

IT WAS twenty-seven days after his last entry before
Christopher brought himself to make a new entry in his
journal. He could have done so earlier, but didn't, "likely
because," Card announced—"he passed the smallpox with fewer
pains than ever expected and feels guilty about it."

"No! That isn't the reason," Christopher said petulantly. "I've
been a sick man, for chrissake, and have exhausted myself
recovering my strength!"

"Here ye go, Christopher," said another of his messmates,
"here's some poor pork and moldy biscuit we saved for you.
Also some of the good creature to get cha feelin' prime after
your ordeal."

The good-natured banter was simply relief that Christopher
had survived the pox. Inoculation was risky business and no
guarantee that the patient would not succumb to this dread
disease.

As it was, Christopher had suffered from a pretty high fever,
bad pains and some ugly eruptions. As soon as he realized he

wasn't going to die from the illness, he started worrying about each and every one of his scabs (which were ugly and still contagious) and spent days wondering about the scars they would leave.

Fortunately, he avoided major scarring, a scar on his nose and one on his hand where he inoculated himself. All in all, not bad, he admitted.

Now he had to turn his attention to surviving imprisonment. The prospects were not good. Men died every day…of festering wounds, from sickness, from poor food, starvation; some were even murdered by cruel and spiteful guards.

This was made abundantly clear each morning with the curt call, "Rebels, deliver up your dead!" What became of those dead was even more revealing of the worthlessness of rebel lives. During those brief occasions when he was permitted to take a walk on the upper deck with other prisoners, many of them shrunken and decaying, Christopher would occasionally observe the bodies of the dead, barely covered in rags, loaded on boats for burial on shore.

Eventually, he was assigned to a burial party and was one of those whose job it was to take the dead ashore and bury them.

The dead were loaded like cordwood on a boat and, along with a guard and the working party, were rowed to a beach, which was only about 200 yards from the hulk. Extending out from the narrow beach was a small dock owned by a Mister Remsen, who also owned a house sitting on the hill above and beyond that a mill.

They tied up at the dock and unloaded the bodies, which they carried a short distance to a ravine. There the dead were as good as dumped in the natural depression.

"All right, rebels, no need to dally. Just lay 'em down and cover 'em up—no need to be respectful, they're goin' ta burn in Hell, anyway." The duty sergeant was in no mood to put up with the stench, not only from the current crop of bodies, but also those older internees whose parts had been flushed out of the shallow trench by recent rains.

"Can't imagine this duty in the summer...bad enough now," said one of the prisoners between dry heaves, the smell of decomposing flesh mingling with the stink of the salt marsh.

They were not given leave to say prayers for the dead, but one man intoned the Prayer for the Dead as he shoveled sandy soil over the grave.

One of the loyalist guards quoted from some unforgiving philosopher,

Certain offenses can be forgiven in this world, whereas certain others will be forgiven in the world which is to come.

They finished their macabre work after several hours and returned to the hulk, feeling guilty that they had almost enjoyed the outing.

"We lay them to rest slightly buried," was the way a distraught Christopher described his burial duty.

****

For men who used to be strong and independent, their physical vulnerabilities and helplessness was intolerable; but perhaps their worst affliction as prisoners might have been the moral degradation.

"I remember having to surrender—found some Britishers to surrender to. Didn't want to fall prey to those Hessians, who would skewer you to a tree and leave ya to bake under the August sun," said one man, apparently describing the events of August 27. "Didn't fare much better with the British, tho'...they stole all me valuables and bruised me badly with the butts of their muskets."

All of the men had stories to tell of their capture, and all expressed the panic and then the despair they felt.

"And it only got worse!"

Then they would recite the litany of unspeakable experiences that went with being rebels and prisoners of the British: usually it began with being "pinched with hunger" and ended with "an' all the while living in the dark and breathin' foul air until ya stop breathin'...."

"I'm afraid most of us will surely die in this den of misery."

New arrivals quickly learned the poor odds that they might survive their stay in prison.

"Ye got one of four ways to end confinement—short of death, that is.

"There's parole...you a ninety-day man or three years? Oh, lord, enlisted in a Continental regiment, did you? Well, too bad, lad, only ninety-day men get paroled.

"Exchanged? Naw, they'll say to you, 'Why, rebel, you're too healthy to be exchanged!'" The sickliest listeners laughed the loudest.

"Oh, yeah, enlistment in the British Army. You'll be offered that, in a manner of speakin'. 'Die or enlist.' Suspicion is that all the hardships we have is for the sole purpose of gettin' us to enlist with the British Army!"

The new men would look aghast at the mere thought of going over to the other side, and ask if any American had been so dishonorable that they actually did so.

Yes, indeed, they were told without rancor. "Do what you have to. I've heard that some of the men enlisted in the British Army and deserted as soon as they could. Trouble is, ya could be hung by both sides for desertin'! I'm not tryin' it."

None of these opportunities for freedom appealed to Christopher.

That left only the fourth way: Escape.

Escape, then, became a matter of necessity.

"Escape now, Christopher, while you're healthy enough to do so," Card told him.

Escapes had been attempted, and had been both successful and unsuccessful. "A successful attempt will require conviction and genius. On a more practical side, it also will require a considerable ability to swim."

Card and most of the others couldn't swim. "Can ye swim, Christopher?"

"Aye, I can."

"Well, I and some of the boys will help you and any others who want to escape.

"Now, here's my idea. Tell me what ya think."

A Plan to Escape
Late April 1777

"If you think all ya have to do is drop into the water and swim a few rods to freedom, you'll surely be recaptured or killed. Escaping from a ship isn't that easy, oh no!

"Where do you swim to? After you reach shore, where do you go? And how do you get there? Just where is freedom? There? Over there? Or there? Or perhaps there?" Each time Card pointed to a different point of the compass. "Every bit of land you can see from here, Christopher, is occupied by the British!

"Makes escape a little more challengin', don't it," Card smiled. He had a distant look as he continued. "Keep myself on the straight and narrow by memorizin' the Bible; keep myself amused with planning my imaginary escape." Card winked at Christopher, who gave him a broad smile.

"Why don't we do this together, Card? Maybe steal one of the rowboats that are tied up alongside."

"Naw, Christopher. I meant it when I said ya had to be strong and healthy to escape. I couldn't go 200 yards even if I could walk on water. No, my best chance to see freedom is to be a good bargain for the British so they offer me in exchange for a healthy grenadier!"

In the days to come, Card carefully described the various escape routes once Christopher reached the shore. He also coached Christopher in how to evade the military authorities and deal with civilians whose assistance he would need.

Of course, the most practical impediment to escape was getting off the *Whitby* without being shot. For this, Card furtively showed Christopher and the other men in the mess an old, dull jackknife.

"We'll gouge out the bolts holding these iron bands across the air holes, which I judge are just large enough to allow a skeleton like Christopher here to slip through."

So, that night the mess began the task of cutting out the bolts from the hull timbers.

"Easy, easy, men. Don't break the blade." The wood had been protected over the years with coat after coat of paint and proved hard to carve. A chisel or like tool and hammer would have greatly reduced the labor, but the noise was unacceptable.

So they quietly scraped, and chipped, and cut away almost every night for weeks.

May 27, 1777

Their plan to escape was nearing completion. A few more nights of cutting and chopping at the wood holding the last bolt and their exit from the hulk would be open.

What occurred next took them by surprise and put an end to their attempt to escape.

Early that morning they were ordered to gather their possessions and be ready to leave the ship.

"Don't get excited, rebels, you're not being freed. You're being transferred to 'finer quarters.' Now hurry up, or you'll go without your miserable possessions."

The men reluctantly did as ordered, wondering what this meant.

"There's rumors that the British are sending captured American soldiers to the Caribbean to labor as slaves on the plantations."

"If they intend to do that, we must revolt!"

"We'll see…."

The prisoners were crowded on lighters which, when full, cast off and moved towards two large transport ships that had recently been moored in the Bay.

32

"IT MUST SUCCEED THIS TIME!"

Although many prisoners were sent on board,
and none exchanged, death made room for all.
Quoted in a Contemporary Newspaper

The Prison Ship *Liberty*
Wallabout Bay, Long Island
June 1777

"HERE'S MY OPINION why we was moved. The damn'd *Whitby* has become so notorious throughout the civilized world, it embarrassed the damn'd British so much they had to get rid of the proof of their perfidity!"

"I think we got moved because the stench became too much for the crew and armed guard to stand!"

Whatever the reason, in early May the prisoners on the *Whitby* were transferred to another recently moored hulk, an old transport wittily renamed the *Liberty* in celebration of its resurrection as a prison ship for American rebels.

The move not only interrupted Christopher and his comrades' planned escape, it nearly brought an end to it.

One of their messmates, a man named Jenkins, simply went mad. While on the main deck for his half-hour of fresh air, Jenkins started yelling crazily, screaming that he had to get ashore because he needed to follow the plan. Fast as he could, the man ran to the gangway ladder, where they were carrying down the morning dead to the rowboat. Pushing men and bodies aside, Jenkins was furiously working his way down towards the smallboat when a guard calmly shot him. He tumbled down to the platform. After a short silence, orders were casually given to toss Jenkins's body in the boat to be interred with the other dead. Nobody knew whether he was dead or alive.

Some weeks after their transfer to the new prison ship, two American officers arrived carrying packages and letters for the prisoners. These officers, from Maryland, were on parole and had used their limited freedom to collect letters from Maryland prisoners way back in January, with a promise to deliver them to family and loved ones, and return with packets and letters as soon as they could.

Just captured, Christopher had hastily written a letter to his Aunt Jane and another to Hannah, both short, describing his situation as best he could. At the time, he was hopeful of being exchanged shortly, so he sounded an optimistic note in his letters.

One of the officers, Captain Wise of Rawlings' Maryland-Virginia Rifle Regiment, was from Monocacy and had promised Christopher that he would deliver his letters to either his aunt in Baltimore or his family in Lower Frederick.

To his surprise and delight, Captain Wise, with a huge smile, handed Christopher a small packet bound in twine, addressed to *Chris. Sims of Maryland abord HMS Whitby berthed in N. York harbor.*

"Handed it to your aunt personally, sir. And ye can't imagine how happy she was!"

He recognized the handwriting of Rachel Jones, and almost in a frenzy pulled off the twine and unwrapped the packet.

March 15th, 1777
Baltimore

My Dear Sir:
Your Aunt & I recev'd the disturbing news of your internment abord the Ship Whitby from Captn Wise, who inform'd us he met you briefly on Jan'y 23 instant.

We thank the Lord that You are safe and in good health – this came after the terrible news that you were missing after the action at Prince Town.

We have sent 10 dollars in coin in the hope this will aid & give you comfort as we are told that money will ensure good treatment We are told the British authorities have been very kind to our men & we can only hope this is true.

Your letter to Hannah was sent immediate by post to Her. We have recev'd no word from Her on this Subject and I will go to Elk in several days to see her.

Our Love and prayers are with You, my Dear Friend.

Your humble & Obedient Servant,

Rachel Jones

He fondled the letter from Rachel, remembering so many good times in Baltimore. Hopefully he would soon be able to return there with Hannah. No more campaigning, he promised himself.

There was a short note from Aunt Jane, who was not much of a writer, but tried her best to buoy his spirits. He hefted the tightly wrapped coins, appreciating their value. He would need a few dollars to make his way to freedom, and a few dollars for the dear comrades he would have to leave behind.

Attempted Escape
July 13, 1777

Poor Jenkins had not given away their secret before he was shot; and the remaining members of the mess almost immediately resumed their efforts to effect an escape.

Thanks to Card's seniority, his mess was given a storeroom on the middle deck. This room had a gun port which, while cross-barred, was large enough to allow an adult to pass through. Looking thoughtfully at their new challenge, Christopher thought of Hannah and the last time he held her. He sighed dejectedly, looking at his messmates, "these should be the best days of our lives—and look how we'll be spending them...and for God knows how long. Well, boys, let's get to work."

The privacy afforded by the little storage room allowed them to work longer at digging out the bolts holding the bars across the porthole. This was the easy task. It didn't take long to loosen the bars sufficiently so that a good tug would wrench the bars off.

"Now, we'll wait for a dark night for the attempt. It has to be done late at night when the watch is nodding off."

But as Card said, getting off this hulk and making it to shore was just the beginning. The bay was large and escapees had first to swim across a formidable expanse of water and slither through mud flats just to reach solid ground. Then, if a prisoner managed to negotiate the bay somehow, he still had several other bodies of water and heavily populated areas under enemy control to traverse in order to reach freedom in New Jersey, the nearest safe haven.

Escape from the Wallabout prison fleet was not impossible, but it would require quite an effort by a very determined man.

Five men would make the attempt. In addition to Christopher, there would be two from his mess, and two other men, one who provided the jackknife, and a young boy whose father had died in his arms at Fort Washington, and whose mother was now alone.

All of them inventoried their possessions. Sad as they were, there were a few items each wanted to take. For Christopher, it was his journal, lead "pencils," and the few letters from home he hadn't lost along the way.

"Well, Christopher, the lead ain't heavy enough to pull ya under, but we gotta problem keeping that journal of yours dry. In the end, they found a frontiersman who knew how to wrap it in oil cloth to make it waterproof. He would put his few valued possessions in his small haversack, the one found for him by Joseph Martin, the man from Connecticut who helped him out after he was dragged from the pond following the battle of Long Island. "This'll do fine," he concluded, nodding his head approvingly.

A dark night came. Off came the bars, and one by one they were lowered as quietly as possible into the water below.

The young boy was the third to be lowered into the water. "Paddle like a dog, Johnny, and don't break water," Christopher cautioned. "I'll be right behind ya coming down, and we'll swim together. Got it." Christopher could see the boy was scared but he seemed collected.

Then, it was Christopher's turn.

"Go with God, Christopher Sims." There was a catch in Card's gruff voice as he said this.

The two men embraced. "We'll be seeing each other again, Card."

And Christopher was lowered into the water.

The water was cold and it took his breath away. He got his breathing under control, and soon used to the water temperature, began to slowly swim away from the ship, searching for young Johnny.

He heard Johnny's heavy breathing and, unable to see the boy, followed the sound until the two touched.

"Easy, Johnny. It's Chris," he whispered. "I know it's cold, son, but you got to slow your breathin'. There, that's better."

As Christopher and Johnny readied themselves to swim off, they heard the sounds, fortunately very faint, of the other two men already in the water and moving away.

As they began to swim towards the beach, the fifth and last man to escape made a noisy entrance into the water, which became louder as he struggled to tread water.

The noise brought a guard to the railing. Immediately there was a shout, a lantern was thrust over the railing, and seconds later the sounds of two muskets being fired.

"Quick, Johnny," Christopher uttered as distinctly as he could without yelling, "swim hard as ye can, but quiet as ye can. Now, go!"

The boy started paddling frantically and whipping his legs like a frog to propel himself as fast as he could.

Realizing that the shots were aimed at the last man in the water and not at him, Christopher quickly started to swim. He thought he would quickly catch up to Johnny, but could not even hear him, much less see him in the darkness. He stopped a moment and listened for sounds of someone moving in the water. He did hear the sounds of the other men some distance away as they had reacted to the alarm by frantically swimming to the shore.

By this time, Christopher realized that the guard had lowered boats and were searching the waters around the hulk, swinging lanterns casting a bobbing illumination over the water. He could hear shouts, cursing, and the tension of wooden oars pulling against iron locks. He swam harder, hoping that the noise of the pursuit would mask his.

There was more firing. Still no sign of the young boy, Johnny.

Christopher continued his jerky movements toward the shoreline, when he saw a boat headed in his direction. Actually, the boat was headed towards the other two men, still making too much noise, who were now between him and the beach, near Ramsen's dock.

He abruptly changed direction to stay well away from the oncoming boat, swimming somewhat parallel to the shore. This maneuver was hindered by an incoming tide, but which also brought to his ears the sounds of labored movement and sharp gasps for air. He had been buffeted against the boy.

The boy was hacking and coughing up water, his movements weak and ineffectual.

"Johnny, Johnny," Christopher was gasping himself. "Relax…I've got ahold of ya. Lie on your back, son, and float. That's it. Good!"

They made their way slowly towards the shore. Christopher remained wary of a searching boat, since the current was taking them closer and closer to Ramsen's dock. He heard shouts and occasional shots not too far away, but was beginning to feel they had avoided immediate danger, when suddenly he saw the light of a lantern. It appeared to be heading straight for them.

Christopher froze, hoping that the lack of movement would cause them to be overlooked.

It didn't work…they were caught in the light of the boat's bow lamp. There was an exclamation, "there, over there," then shots were fired.

Musket balls spit into the water nearby. Christopher clamped his hand over Johnny's mouth and pushed himself and the boy underwater.

They surfaced noisily and almost immediately more shots were fired, the balls again coming dangerously close. This continued for some minutes. Finally, Christopher whispered to

Johnny to take a deep breath; and, holding the boy, dove to the bottom, where he half swam and half crawled in the mud for as long as he could hold his breath.

Lungs bursting, he finally surfaced, spewing out water and trying not to have a coughing fit. Listening quiet as he could, he heard the boat, men still yelling, moving away from them. Johnny was quiet and heavy in his arms.

More shots rang out and he could see the sparks from muzzles in the distance. They were firing at someone else.

Christopher finally reached shore, dragging the boy with him, careful to keep his head above water.

Christopher saw that they were some distance east of Ramsen's dock. Resting on the beach, he attended to the boy, who was very quiet. Too quiet. Oh Lord, Christopher thought, did I drown him?

Fidgeting with the boy's limp body, Christopher saw a neat dark hole in his neck. It was not messy, but a mortal wound nonetheless. He turned the boy on his back and pulled his shirt over his head.

After a few minutes, Christopher carefully unwrapped his journal and lead pencil. Forcing his hand not to shake, he carefully wrote,

This is Johnny Heth,
Of Rawlings Regt
Age 14

He tore out the page and placed it on the boy's chest, weighted with a rock. He couldn't even cry.

Christopher rested only a few minutes, then started loping north toward the coast along the East River. After awhile, he turned and headed inland towards Brooklyn. The plan was to get over to New York and, from there, go north a bit before taking a boat over to New Jersey, where it was thought there were no garrisons or pickets. Christopher had enough hard coin to pay his way and buy some decent clothing.

But first he had to put some distance between himself and the prison ship. He continued his fast pace, wanting to get away from Remsen's where he knew the search for any remaining escapees would be intense.

Hours later, in the early morning, as he cut through a field towards the road leading to Brooklyn, he saw two dragoons, splendidly attired, their huge horses clopping along the road.

Before he could hide, he knew that they had seen him. Quickly, he turned and started to pick up large rocks lying in the field and carefully began piling them as if constructing a stone wall.

The dragoons, who were obviously on the lookout for suspicious persons, looked him over closely. Christopher looked at them and uttered a gruff "mornin' gents," and continued his work in the field. Apparently satisfied that he was what he appeared to be, a farmer clearing his field, the dragoons rode on.

Late that afternoon, tired to death, and awfully hungry, Christopher came upon a farm. He foraged for something to eat in the kitchen garden. Then, too tired to go on he went into the barn, hid himself in the loft, and fell fast asleep.

He was awakened when he felt something poking him in his side. He opened his eyes to see a man holding a fowler pointed at him.

"I don't know who ya be, mister, but ya appear ta be a man on the run. My wife has gone to fetch our son, and I've a mind to send him for the authorities. Suppose we jus' sit here 'til we sort this one out."

33

THE INVASION

Head of Elk, Maryland
July - August 1777

ON SATURDAY, JULY 19, Lord Howe's grand army weighed anchor at New York, and the tension built regarding British military intentions for the coming campaign. The Continental Congress had received a warning "that the enemy meditates an Expedition to the Bay of Chesapeak." Additional details indicated that the British intended to land at Head of Elk, Maryland, taking Annapolis and Baltimore on their way.

The pretty brick town of Elk served as a Continental Army depot and terminus of a major supply route between the bread basket of the revolution and Philadelphia, and other points north, providing manpower and subsistence to the main army as it positioned itself to defend the revolutionary capital.

Throughout July and well into August, movements of the British fleet gave rise to consternation, then relief, then consternation again for the inhabitants of the Chesapeake Bay as the enemy appeared, then disappeared along the Delaware coast. Then on August 15, rebel signal guns announced that the British fleet had entered the Bay.

The fleet sailed leisurely up the Chesapeake, indifferent to the fear it was causing, anchoring in the evening with impressive ceremony, and spending evenings peacefully netting huge numbers of swimming crabs.

The threat from a British landing was real to Hannah Williams as she walked towards the landing on a hot, steamy afternoon in August, half expecting to see a British fleet filling the river Elk at the very head of the Bay. But it remained empty of invaders—except for the jellyfish.

Shaking off the silly idea that towering British ships of the line would suddenly appear practically at their doorstep, Hannah continued with three of the younger Alexander children down to the landing. Here, they would spend the afternoon crabbing and picniking.

But not for long, Hannah thought, as gathering clouds threatened the usual summer thunder squall. Still, she would have some time to ponder her predicament while the boys dangled chicken necks tied to strings in the water, and hauled up huge crab after crab.

…Back in March Hannah had received a letter from Christopher. It was much like the most recent ones he had been writing her: thick writing in lead on stained paper, always hopeful but with little really said.

Only this time it told her of his capture and imprisonment.

As devastating as this news was, Christopher's letter was typically hopeful, assuring her that he would be exchanged before long. It contained little additional news, only that he was fine, having suffered only a trifling wound during the recent campaign. He also promised her that he had "no desire to campain ever again." This, at least, gave her something to look forward to.

Then, later that March, she was visited by Rachel Jones.

Hannah's presence had been requested and she entered the manor house sitting room to find Rachel there having tea with Isabella Alexander.

Rachel rose and rather formally said, "My dear Hannah, I have news of your betrothed which he asked me to deliver personally to you."

Turning to Missus Alexander, she politely asked if she might speak to Hannah alone.

"Of course, Missus Jones. I will be in the library and would like to see you before you leave."

Rachel, patting the settee, "Sit here next to me, Hannah."

She noticed Hannah's somewhat confused expression, and laughing, whispered, "Isabella and I have some history in common, which makes our rare meetings a little awkward."

"I see," said Hannah, who understood because she now had her own history, as they say.

Rachel clasped Hannah's hands fondly, and asked, "How are you! You've been missed so much!"

"Oh Rachel," Hannah exclaimed, "I'm happy enough here—under the circumstances, of course...," she added, "truly...but...oh of course you must know that Christopher is a prisoner of the British in New York, and—"

"Which is the reason I am here," Rachel interrupted. "We wanted to make sure that you had received word from Christopher, but also to let you know that we met again with the young officer who delivered the letters. He was also captured—at Fort Washington, I believe—but paroled, which means he can travel between the lines carrying communications between prisoners and family. We sent a package including silver coin, which we were assured he would receive...*if* I understand the protocol correctly."

"Rachel, Chris wrote that he expected to be exchanged quite soon. Mister Alexander told me that that was certainly possible but then emphasized patience...in a manner which I did not think was too encouraging."

Rachel sighed. "War is a ritual, Hannah, with costs that must be contained or even the treasuries of kings will be emptied. A captured soldier—our Christopher—is an expensive commodity that is usually traded for an enemy soldier of like value. Unfortunately, we are rebels in the eyes of the enemy. Treat them like you would soldiers of another power and you tacitly acknowledge independence. See the problem? That, at least, is the explanation I've received. But the accountants will work this out—they always do."

"But they do treat them well, don't they?"

"So I'm told." Rachel wanted to sound convincing, but she had heard ugly rumors.

They continued to talk for sometime until Rachel noted that she had to leave, and as she rose suggested, "Hannah, write a note to Chris while I am paying my respects to Isabella." Rachel smiled and gave Hannah a hug. "We want you and Chris back with us as soon as possible. Please stay in touch."

Later that day. "How do you know Rachel Jones," asked Missus Alexander, trying to sound only vaguely interested.

"Oh, Rachel boarded with Christopher's aunt, Missus Jane Everett. I doubt if you know her. She owns a trimmings shop in Baltimore..." and Hannah went on to give a fair explanation of her friendship with Rachel.

"A very interesting woman, Rachel Jones." Missus Alexander then mentioned that Rachel's past was the subject of considerable gossip in Annapolis. "Too independent for many in society. She was quite close for some time with a wealthy merchant, a Jew, Robert Levy. She tells me she is opening an academy for young women in Baltimore. I think she will provide a great service for the young women of Baltimore."

"I'm sure she will, Missus Alexander," said Hannah, even as she was thinking how interesting it was that her savior, Mister Hyman Cohen, was also a Jew. Mister Cohen worked for a powerful employer and she remembered Rachel's curt dismissal of her curiosity about this man.

Following Rachel's visit, life at Friendship resumed its stately rhythm. As spring gave way to summer, more troops passed through Elk on their way to join General Washington's army. Concern for Christopher and the rumor of invasion constantly occupied Hannah's thoughts.

But the weeks flew by and before she knew it July had come and gone, and Christopher had been away at war for a year....

****

Then came the alarm of August 15. Since then, they had lived in a constant state of fear. The mighty British fleet of more than 200 ships was making its stately way up the Bay. There was no doubt any longer that its destination was Head of Elk, where it would land a vast army to march upon Philadelphia. But first, everyone assumed, the enemy would take the state capital and Baltimore.

With that, there would not be much left of the independent State of Maryland.

Oddly, the growing terror among the community did not seem to be reflected in the manner in which Mister and Missus Alexander responded to the state of emergency. The greater grew the threats, the more relaxed they seemed.

Curious, Hannah questioned Missus Alexander. "What will Mister Alexander do should the British come, Missus Alexander?"

Isabella Alexander looked surprised at the question, "Why, I suppose remain here, Hannah. Why do you ask?"

"I just thought his position as an important patriot made him a wanted man, or put him at risk in some way—" Hannah's voice trailed off...

Missus Alexander stared at her. "I suppose you're right, Hannah. I'll have to talk to Mister Alexander about it." Smiling, she added, "Now, dear, don't worry. The King's soldiers will not hurt this family or you, I can assure you."

How can she be so sure, thought Hannah, who still thought their casualness was a bit odd under the circumstances.

On August 24, word was received that British ships had actually entered the Elk River and that the van of the fleet intended to drop anchor opposite Cecil Courthouse the next morning.

Beachhead
25 August 1777

The very day that the British launched flat-bottomed boats to ferry battalion after battalion of troops ashore, Robert Alexander was hosting General George Washington to dinner at Friendship.

It was a dire situation for Washington and for his army but one he had been expecting for some time. He was here in the town of Elk to try to obtain the most current intelligence as to the British capabilities and intentions, and to see to the evacuation of as much of the military supplies as possible from this once strategic center.

It was a rare pleasure for His Excellency to dine with such a patriot as Robert Alexander, better yet to hear his advice regarding this most immediate threat to the cause of American independence.

General Washington's visit caused great excitement at the manor house. Missus Alexander and Hannah rushed around hastily organizing a splendid meal with a table that would be memorable. The boys, of course, couldn't wait to see the general and his staff, talking excitedly about dragoons and colorful uniforms.

General Washington and his horse guard swept into the front yard; he dismounted and was courteously received by Mister Alexander, who was standing at the bottom of the steps. Hannah, peeking out of one of the windows with Araminta, saw a tall man, dressed in blue and buff, who seemed to have a tight smile—if, indeed, it was a smile he gave as he saluted Robert Alexander.

As they went inside to converse and then dine, the women and servants hurried between kitchen and house, seeing to the comfort of the guests. Handsome cavalrymen lounged in the shade, while couriers came and went.

Hannah again watched from a distance as the general spoke to the entire Alexander family and sincerely thanked Mister and Missus Alexander together for their hospitality, before mounting and riding back to his army.

Even as General Washington rode away, British troops, the object of General Washington's visit to Elk, were coming ashore by the hundreds a few miles away at Cecil Courthouse. While camp was being established there, British light infantrymen, in their short red jackets and plumed caps, were soon seen moving up the road towards the town. The children, anticipating a parade with colorful flags and bands playing, wanted immediately to go to town.

Three days after Washington's visit, Mister Alexander left the house in the family carriage, a resolved smile on his face. He returned later that day and announced that General Sir William Howe had accepted his invitation to use their family manor as his headquarters, adding that he had gladly made available to Sir William and his staff all his stores of fine foods and wines, and to his army, the wealth of his lands in wheat, corn, pork and all else.

Hannah was stunned.

"Missus Alexander," she asked, hoping for a satisfying explanation. "May I ask the meaning of this? It's as if Mister Alexander welcomes this...this invasion of your home."

Isabella Alexander looked sadly at this young woman, knowing the horrid disappointment Hannah was about to experience; akin, she thought, to learning that your lover has been unfaithful.

"Hannah, dear, my husband, like most husbands, does not discuss business or politics with his wife; but I have known for quite some time that Mister Alexander has harbored loyalist sympathies—intense sympathies. And now he has publicly cast his reputation and fortune with the Crown."

Hannah had tears in her eyes. "And you agree with this, Missus Alexander? You have always spoken highly of the cause, and just days ago, William was talking about wanting to join General Washington's staff, and you applauded his patriotism. I don't understand."

Isabella looked kindly at Hannah. "Do I agree with my husband's decision?" She shrugged. "I am his wife and will support my husband in all matters. Whether I agree with him or not counts as nothing. I have no say in his politics—or, for that matter, does William," she added.

That was her explanation.

Hannah was beside herself. Trembling, she announced, "Missus Alexander, I cannot—," She took a deep breath, "—I cannot in good conscience continue to be a part of this family."

She looked directly at Missus Alexander, drew herself up, and said primly, "I request that I be allowed to leave your service, ma'am."

Letting the tears fall, Missus Alexander wanted desperately to hug Hannah. "Oh, dear Hannah," she cried, "I wish with all my heart that there was no such thing as politics! I don't want you to leave me and the children."

Then, Isabella collected herself. "But I understand, Hannah, and I will discuss your request with Mister Alexander."

****

The Friendship manor house had been occupied for several days with the hustle and bustle of a field army headquarters when Hannah's world became undone.

Hannah was carrying a tea service to the sitting room when she saw him. She was so surprised, so overcome by the unfairness of it all, that her arms went limp and she simply let go of the tray, and tea pot, creamer and sugar bowl hit the floor with a ringing sound as silver holloware bounced on the pine boards.

Isabella Alexander rushed by several officers who were self-conscious on-lookers, embarrassed as all were by the mess. "Oh, my goodness! I'm terribly sorry, gentlemen...."

"Madam," quickly interjected the handsome young naval officer, "it was entirely my fault. I was not paying attention and almost collided with this young lady, causing her to lose her balance. My apologies, please, Missus Alexander...and to you, young lady." He smiled at Hannah. "Do forgive me."

Hannah gasped. The handsome young naval officer was Benjamin Harvey.

34

CHRISTOPHER'S ESCAPE

Long Island and New York
July-August 1777

CHRISTOPHER SPENT HOURS talking first to the old man, then to his son, trying to convince them not to turn him in to the British authorities. Finally, it was the woman, after hearing his horror stories about the prison ship, and looking at his wounds, and seeing how boney he was, who decided in his favor.

The Wyckoffs were not patriots, but they weren't loyalists, either. They were Dutch and didn't understand the English, nor did they want to. All they wanted was to be left alone, not to be included in this senseless (in their mind) war. Finally, they didn't want any trouble either, that's why the old man had a mind to turn Christopher in to the authorities. But Christopher's vivid narrative of the living hell aboard a British prison ship was more than they could bear.

The man's fowler had long ago been put aside. They were talking and drinking good Dutch beer all this time in the Wyckoff's huge barn, where at the sides a man could barely stand straight, but in the middle, amidst the dusty stalks on the threshing floor, the height was grand, like that of a church interior.

Once they had accepted Christopher as an honest man, and a man worthy of their hospitality, they invited him into their house. As they walked out of the barn, Christopher looked around and saw a pleasing prospect.

The Wyckoff farm was on a hill not too far from the East River. This part of Brooklyn was not heavily wooded and in the distance Christopher could see the southern edge of Manhattan, buildings and a few church spires visible in the late morning light.

More immediately, he saw the exterior of the Wyckoff's awesome barn, with its high shingled roof, the eaves almost touching the ground. In front of him was the house, an unprepossessing, rambling structure, a story and a half high, he reckoned, made of weathered wood shingles, with a low-pitched gable roof. Two massive chimneys loomed from each gable.

They entered into a long hallway with a door at the opposite end. Missus Wyckoff motioned for him to turn right, and he entered a comfortable kitchen. She invited him to take a seat at a long, narrow table. As her husband and son did the same, she set a huge pot, smoking up a storm, in the center of the table.

As Mister Wyckoff handed him a pewter tankard of beer, Missus Wyckoff placed a Canton bowl and a huge spoon in front of him.

"This'll be a start to puttin' some meat back on that scrawny frame of yours! If you don't know good Dutch cookin', this is a hodgepot—James here," pointing her spoon fondly at her son, "calls it a 'hodge podge.' No matter, it's beef n' pork n' mutton n' bones, more vegetables than ye can count, and a bunch a sweet herbs. Ye never tasted anything better!"

And he hadn't. Even considering the fact that he had been half starved for God knows how long, Christopher had never tasted anything so good. Armed with his long-handled spoon, he helped himself to more and then more.

Over the next couple of weeks, as Christopher recovered from his imprisonment and prepared for the next stage of his return home, he learned that variety in dishes was of little account compared to the quality and quantity of food. He vowed that he was prepared to live forever on hodgepots, oyster loaves, and good beer.

As his strength increased, Christopher worked as hard as he could in the Wyckoff's fields, or threshing corn in the barn, or at any other job needed. In the evening, around the kitchen table, they would eat, drink and talk. Relaxed, the Wyckoffs would lapse naturally into Dutch before catching themselves.

"Everyone speaks Dutch at the fireside, Mister Sims—*even* the colored people hereabouts." Missus Wyckoff laughed. Then turning serious, "but now our children are being forced to speak English in school. While we've not taken sides in this civil war, the British authorities do not seem to care about our support."

Christopher made no effort to persuade the Wyckoffs to support the cause. Instead, he spoke in personal terms.

"Everyone has a reason to support or not support the revolution. I support it because the woman I intend to marry is a bonded servant, and we had no right even to acknowledge our fondness for each other. Her master could even marry her off if he'd a mind to. That's English law for you. I want a law that favors the poorer sort."

They'd work all day and talk half the night, about politics, war, or farming, anything that came to mind, the men smoking pipes and drinking "quince drinks," a potent mixture of hot rum, sugar, and quince marmalade, out of horn cups rimmed in silver.

The war news surprised Christopher. He had missed much as a captive and access to both newspaper reporting and word of mouth in the local community was enlightening.

"I wouldn't put any stock in what the *Weekly Mercury* or the *Royal Gazette* print. It's common knowledge around here that they publish naught but false reports to lift the flagging spirits of local loyalists. We occasionally get the Philadelphia papers, and I'll be happy to pass those on to you. They seem to be objective enough. Mainly, though, we get our most accurate news by word of mouth."

Mister Wyckoff apprised Christopher of the outcome of the New Jersey campaign, assuring him that the revolution was alive and well. "Why, your army drove the British clear outta the Jerseys!" He learned that the Continental Army had wintered at Morristown, safely nestled atop the Watchung Mountains. Now that it was the season for campaigning, there was news of skirmishes in Jersey. The latest news, however, was the most important for Christopher.

"On the nineteenth of July the British fleet set sail from New York harbor. Some say they're going up the Delaware to attack Philadelphia; others agree that the plan is to attack Philadelphia, but the army will be landed at the head of the Chesapeake Bay in Mary-land." When he stated this, Mister Wyckoff had no idea how important this information was to Christopher.

"What? What is the latest intelligence, sir?" Christopher almost yelled the question. "Do we know where the fleet is actually headed?"

Mister Wyckoff was quite taken aback. "Why, the fleet appeared at the entrance to Delaware Bay near the end of July, then disappeared. Now 'tis believed that the fleet is headed for the Chesapeake Bay."

Realizing that Hannah might well be in harm's way, Christopher became anxious. He had to get to Head of Elk as soon as possible.

His announcement that he had to leave immediately took his hosts by surprise. Sensing the hurt he caused by his abruptness, Christopher apologized and then carefully explained his urgent need for leaving. The Wyckoffs immediately understood and did all they could to prepare him for his journey.

"Christopher, Mister Van Brunt, who we helped the other day with his fence, has agreed to take you in his market boat over to Manhattan. From there, you should be able to get passage over to Bergen. You'll need to spend one or two of those silver dollars of yours." Cornelius Wyckoff had turned down Christopher's offer of money, but he was a practical man when it came to other people's wants.

Christopher's prison rags had been replaced weeks ago by some of the elder Wyckoff's old clothes. These were fine for work around the farm but hardly proper traveling clothes. Elizabeth Wyckoff surprised him with a new suit, shirt, and hat, bought during one of her trips to the village. "To get you started out on the right foot, Christopher Sims, and so you look sparkling for your woman!"

Wanting to put off the goodbyes, the Wyckoffs walked Christopher down to the Van Brunt house. There, they had much to drink, one more filling meal, and then it was time to go.

Feeling almost as he had when he left Aunt Jane's to go off to war, Christopher settled into Mister Van Brunt's boat and off they went, two Negroes pulling on the oars, taking him to the New York terminus of the Brooklyn Ferry and its stone stairs, which Christopher vividly remembered. It reminded Christopher of the time the black mariners of Marblehead saved him and the army in the daring escape from Long Island.

This time it was not so daring, but looking at British warships everywhere, Christopher realized he still had a long way to freedom.

Bergen, New Jersey
August - September 1777

It was too easy to think that he was free once he landed on Jersey soil. The truth was, he was more at risk here than he had been on Long Island. Mister Van Brunt warned him about this—stating that the Britishers and the loyalists were far more skittish on this side of Hudson's River, and for good reason. While you could ridicule the idea of militia doing well in a standup fight with the regulars, they could sure raise hell when the odds were on their side. Up and down the Jerseys, they'd appear out of nowhere to strike patrols, capture wagons full of forage, as well as bully or kidnap troublesome Tories.

With Van Brunt's help, Christopher found a periauger, a flat-bottomed sailing barge, going over to Communipau on the Jersey side.

Communipau was a small ferry landing with a fine, broad wagon road to the town of Bergen, an old Dutch community.

Christopher walked cautiously toward Bergen, climbing the tall hills and crossing the marshes on the other side. He skirted the town itself, passing the race track, and continued west toward the Hackensack River.

Van Brunt had given him the name of a friend, a man named Archibald Campbell, who owned a riverfront farm on the Hackensack, who could help him.

"Best way to go," Van Brunt had advised, "is by boat across the Back Bay"—by which he meant Newark Bay—"round to Elizabeth Point, and then by the Post Road to Philadelphia.

"Ah, ye know the route beyond Elizabeth—good! And Archibald Campbell will tell ye who to trust and who not to along the way!"

James Van Brunt had turned out to be a patriot. He had been arrested in mid-1776, but was then paroled to his farm after the Battle of Long Island. Archibald Campbell of Bergen was also a patriot and had helped a number of escaped prisoners to get beyond the British defenses, which were concentrated around the Jersey ferry landings serving New York.

Christopher approached a low, one-story house and knocked at the door. The top of what was a divided door was opened by a pleasant-looking woman dressed in town clothing.

"May I help you, sir?"

"Yes, ma'am. My name is Sims and I have a letter for Mister Campbell from Mister Van Brunt of Long Island.

"Well, now," the woman said happily, "from the Van Brunts, ye say! Why, come in, please."

Turning, she yelled down the wide hallway, "Husband, we have a visitor with a letter from the Van Brunts!"

The Campbells turned out to be a lively, middle-aged couple, whose children were married and off on their own. They were careful about what their children were doing in these times of trouble. Christopher understood and didn't ask any awkward questions. In fact, he was also circumspect about his own history.

Christopher had been shown into their dwelling room, where the Campbell family ate, socialized, and often slept around the cavernous fireplace, as wide as the house, which smelled of fruit pies and stew. They drank beer as they talked.

Van Brunt's letter, of course, contained no compromising information, but the tone was that of asking travel assistance for the son of an old friend from Baltimore.

"Sir," said Archibald Campbell, "I'll be delighted to assist ye on your way to Bal'mer. Now, you can inform me an' the missus on how the Van Brunts are farin' and conditions on Long Island. An' did ye meet any of the Van Brunt's neighbors?"

Later, Archibald Campbell apprised him of the latest war news, which, to Christopher's surprise, was closer than he would've thought.

"Don't know if ye heard the racket or not, but there was an American raid on Staten Island just the other day—August 22, to be exact...no one really knows the purpose behind it; but I'm afraid it ended in considerable loss of our men and boats."

Campbell then added, "I'm told it was Marylanders."

Christopher stared at Campbell. "Marylanders, ye say, Mister Campbell? And ye say they took heavy losses?" Christopher shook his head.

"Well, a goodly number—mostly captured, I hear. But most of 'em got off and they're now hurrying south towards Philadelphia. Latest intelligence is that General Washington is gathering his forces somewhere south of Philadelphia to contest the advance of Lord Howe's army from the head of the Chesapeake. There don't appear to be any sizable American forces north of Trenton. But plenty of British are spreading out across east Jersey."

"Sir, I've got to get to Head of Elk as soon as possible. There's—"

Campbell interrupted him. "I wouldn't try it right now, Mister Sims. Best advice I can give ya is stay here until the situation becomes clearer. Right now, if you try to travel to Elk, ye'll be between the hawk and the buzzard."

They offered him a comfortable bed upstairs in the garret, near the warmth of the great chimney, amidst the family store of apples, nuts, peppers and sausages hanging by strings.

Raised as a farmer himself, Christopher was impressed with the richness of the Bergen County farmland, the great timber growths, and the area known as the Meadowlands, a good place to cut salt hay, fish, hunt and harvest cedar wood.

Whenever there were visitors to the Campbell house, Christopher would be hidden in the root cellar, preferably, or in the garret. On one occasion, some of Skinners' provincial horse made a surprise visit to the Campbell house searching, the leader said, for a "spy."

They were not satisfied with Archibald Campbell's assurances that there were no spies on his property.

"We'll see for ourselves," the leader said, and his men began their search. Outbuildings, cellars...and lofts were prime areas for such searches.

Worried because she had no idea where Christopher was at that moment, Missus Campbell smiled at the man who was in charge and said loud enough for his men to hear, "Sir, as soon as you and your men are convinced that there are no foes of the King on our property, please join us in the kitchen for some good supporn, fresh pies, and a tankard."

"Why, thankee, ma'am," the man said with a genuine smile.

Just as she has hoped, the search for a spy was short-lived and there were no damning shouts of "here he is, here he is!" And before Missus Campbell knew it, the troop was crowding into the kitchen to fill bowls with stew and grab a tankard of cool beer.

Long after the departure of the loyalists, a shaken Mister and Missus Campbell heard Christopher call quietly from outside. They went out on the porch to see a filthy, evil smelling man standing apologetically before them.

"I found a safe hiding place," he said matter-of-factly, "in the tub beneath the necessary house. "Now, I'm going to soak a while in the river...."

Christopher's plan was to get to Elizabeth Town and from there take the King's Highway to Trenton; by coach or on foot—it didn't matter; then cross the Delaware and follow the road down to Philadelphia. He knew he could catch a stage boat at the Crooked Billet Wharf which would take him to New Castle; and from there it was a short walk to Elk.

It didn't turn out quite that way. Further news was received that Howe's grand army had indeed landed at the head of the Elk and was now advancing toward Philadelphia. At the same time, British and loyalist activity around Tappan, Bergen and

Newark Bay increased greatly and made travel in these areas extremely difficult.

With all of that, Christopher still needed to cross the Hackensack and Passaic Rivers, or go south, crossing Newark Bay. Campbell's place included a dock at which a sloop bound for New York stopped once a week.

"Ours is one of the 'little ferries' which abound hereabouts. Now, the sloop carries firewood to the city but takes passengers, too. It also stops at Elizabethtown Point, which is where ye want to go.

"My advice, Christopher, is get to Burlington, then take the King's Highway south to Salem. If that way is cut off, ye can take one of the coach roads, cutting through the "Barrens"—at least there ya won't have to worry about contesting armies—to Bridgetown, then over to Salem. From there ye can catch a ferry boat to New Castle. Once ye get to New Castle...well, I don't know what ye do when ya get there, Christopher Sims."

Mention of the Barrens brought back vivid memories for Christopher: the night march to Princeton and being spooked by dwarf oaks, imagining them in his feverish mind to be Hessians with poised bayonets.

He shook his head, putting the thought out of mind.

Now, however, while the Barrens might not be full of bugbears, it was a sanctuary for Tory refugees, criminals and deserters from his own army; and sadly, Christopher had to fear so-called patriot partisans as well as loyalists, both of whom, Campbell warned him, were not well-versed on the rules of war. "Makes ye wonder...."

Christopher looked at Archibald Campbell. "You're right, sir. Can you obtain a pistol for me?"

35

CHRISTOPHER'S ODYSSEY

Traversing the Barrens
New Jersey
August - September 1777

VIEWED FROM some of the higher hills in Burlington County, people might have considered the Barrens, or "poor land," to be majestic, even beautiful, with miles and miles of pines, and oaks, and cedars, and an occasional picturesque lake or cranberry bog; but traveling through it was a different matter. Most outsiders had no use for the Barrens and regretted the need to pass through any part of it.

Only peculiar people would live in this strange land, thought Christopher. Peculiar, or perhaps the need to hide well away from justice, he concluded.

"You're right to some extent, Mister Sims," his traveling companion noted with a laugh, as he watched Christopher try to peer into blueberry bushes and scrub-oaks and pine seedlings, searching for the dreaded "Pine Robbers."

Christopher started, "Mister Mathis, I didn't realize I was thinking out loud. My apologies. I know that you have connections with this area and did not mean to be insulting."

"Not just connections," the man again laughed. "I grew up somewhere in this wilderness!" He lunged to the left, then to the right, pretending to be lost in a maze.

Both men laughed.

"Actually, my uncle was John Mathis—'Great John' he was called—who made his fortune carrying lumber to the Caribbean and smuggling in his fortune in rum!"

William Mathis's family was not rich like their uncle but they made a good living operating a tavern on the very road Christopher's party was now traveling. William had marched with a militia company from Bridgetown in January following the Princeton fight and again for sixty days just recently to annoy British and loyalist troops still in the Jerseys.

Having done his duty, he was now happily on his way home, telling Christopher, "I know you Continentals distrust us militia, as perhaps you should, but the militia has its virtues, namely getting supplies to you great warriors and ensuring that the loyalists in your rear are held in check."

Christopher considered this, and thought also of men like Van Brunt and Campbell, before replying. "Aye, 'tis a fair argument against what could be an unfair accusation."

After that, the two men were on a first name basis.

Christopher had met William Mathis in Burlington, the old capital of West Jersey, located on the Delaware River. Thinking back on the battalion's march from Philadelphia to New York, he remembered having seen this pretty town from across the river, the sun reflecting off the roof of the governor's mansion.

Learning from William that crossing into Pennsylvania and traveling south was much too risky, Christopher gladly joined him and several other travelers on their way to south Jersey, a lesser but still risky venture.

"The Pine Refugees, as we call loyalist outlaws here, tend to stay close to the edges of the Barrens. Same goes for our own deserters. Place makes them nervous—like it does most outsiders, like it does you." William smiled innocently.

"Ah, but then there are the Pine Robbers. Now these banditti know the land and a good many of the people. They travel in packs, like wolves, often masked, and prey on those weaker than them."

"While we were retreating up New York, in Westchester County, we were attacked by a gang of outlaws, one who was a deserter from my own battalion. This is the kind of place I'd expect that swine to be doin' his devilish work. 'The Boar,'" Christopher said as he looked at William, remembering all the grief that animal had caused him. "That was his nick-name."

"The Boar? Interesting alias."

"He was good with a shiv," Christopher noted.

"City bred? Well, he wouldn't survive in the Barrens. Besides, there are no boars here. So ye can rest easy Christopher!"

William's assurances aside, Christopher did not rest easy. He slept away from the fire, fitfully, his pistol within easy reach. Every noise reminded him of The Boar and his confederates stalking his little party of desperate patriots.

As tired as he was, nodding off was so easy. One moment he thought he was wide awake, the next moment he sensed he was asleep and had trouble waking himself. This dance between consciousness and unconsciousness would have gone on until Christopher's weary mind gave up and lapsed into comforting sleep, to awake refreshed the next morning....

...Except he heard, faintly, man-made sounds coming down the sand road.

Christopher was immediately awake, pistol in hand, crouching behind a pine tree which gave him a view of the bend in the road beyond which the sounds were coming.

Yes, there were noises, all right: the soft thud of horses' hooves on sand, a cough, low murmuring...the sounds indicated that they hadn't rounded the bend in the road yet.

Christopher quickly went to the campsite, noticing that the small fire had providentially gone out, and carefully woke William.

"Shh, horsemen."

William immediately grabbed his musket and was on his feet. He quickly woke the other man in the party, whispering in his ear, then handing him a pistol. There was a woman and her two children with the party, and William signaled that they should be left alone.

The three men moved toward the road and carefully took up positions along its edge.

The noises had stopped and no one rounded the bend. The moon and pale sand would show men and horses plainly, but it continued quiet with an empty view of the road. Christopher and the other two men began to fidget.

Suddenly a voice rang out, bold and authoritative. "This is John Cox. Identify yerselves immediately or we open fire. Hear!" It was not a question.

"John Cox! Easy, now, John. 'Tis I, Bill Mathis."

Silence…then, "Come forward, Bill."

Leaving his musket, William stepped out on the road.

Shortly, a man stepped out on to the road not fifty yards away. "Well, by damn, it is you, Bill. Welcome home!"

"Thankee, John. Now, may I have my party step out also? An' we got a woman and her children still sleeping a bit in back of us."

Once the threat of two spitting cats going after each other was averted, the two parties explained how they happened to be in the same vicinity at the same time to threaten each other.

Cox was leading a posse looking for Joe Mulliner, an infamous Pines bandit. "Raped and killed old lady Elkins, he did, near Helen's Furnace."

"Know of her. Sorry to hear. Are we in danger? We're headed for Bridgeton."

"Naw, you folks are in no danger—generally speakin', y'know." The local inhabitants nodded as if this was a reasonable qualification.

"We think Mulliner has headed east. Oh, by the way, we ran across some Hessians from Prince Town hidin' out. Good men. Sent 'em on their way to Batsto with one of the boys from there. Believe they could be of use to the iron works. If any wander your way, don't kill 'em."

"We'll pass all this on when we get to Bridgeton. Meantime, good luck in huntin' down Mulliner, John."

As Cox and his party continued south, Christopher said with relief, "Thank God, they were honest men."

"Oh, I wouldn't say honest, necessarily. John Cox is a smuggler by trade." William smiled broadly.

"Pineys make their livin' in the Barrens as iron workers, diggers of bog iron—which never rusts, woodcutters and sawyers...and, of course, smugglers. Have a mind to take up the trade myself. With the war, privateers are landing their booty on the shore and having it carted it through the Pines. Profitable, it is!"

Their party continued on without further incident, and a day and a bit later arrived at Mathis Tavern, just before Bridgetown.

The tavern was an unprepossessing two-story wooden frame house set on a stone foundation with chimneys at each end. As they walked into the great room, there were exclamations and shouts of joy. William received a hero's welcome by family, friends and customers, as did Christopher when they learned that he had escaped from a prison ship *and* was one of Smallwood's now legendary Marylanders who had saved Washington's army from certain destruction on Long Island.

Christopher stayed late with everyone else, enjoying good tavern fare and undiluted drinks, telling stories only slightly embellished, until it was time to go to bed. He was given a comfortable bed and slept as soundly as ever he could remember.

The next morning, after helping William with some chores, and consuming a hardy breakfast, Christopher said goodbye to his traveling companion and his family, and set out on the coach road to Salem.

He soon came to Bridgetown, a hamlet of perhaps a dozen houses surrounding a surprisingly pretty brick courthouse with an impressive cupola. He crossed the bridge over the Cohansey River and was on the road to Salem, with a good day's walk ahead of him. Carrying a letter of introduction from the Mathises, he would stay in Salem with the Garrison family. Richard Garrison, the head of the household, was a member of the local committee of observation.

Salem, New Jersey
September 11, 1777

Sitting on the ground with his back to the large sycamore, Christopher had been listening all morning to the sound of cannon, the hollow booming a battle-tested soldier never forgets. The cannon fire had started early with a few tentative reports, the sounds reverberating over Pennsylvania hills and valleys, along rivers and creeks, before radiating out across the Delaware River, to be heard faintly here on the Jersey side.

For some time the reports had followed an almost steady cadence. To a veteran's ear, this was "amusing" the enemy. Later that afternoon, the cannonading broke out in a frenzy of deep resonant sounds—as if every cannon on the battlefield was being loaded and fired as quickly as possible—indicating that one side or the other was advancing.

Lydia, the thirteen-year-old daughter of his host and hostess had come to sit with Christopher, listening in fascination to the angry sounds.

She had first asked if they were thunderclaps.

"No, Miss Lydia, those are the sounds of cannons which hurl iron balls at enemy soldiers."

"Oh, goodness! I was hit by a ball once—it wasn't iron—but it hurt awful just the same. I hope no one is hurt like I was." She looked very concerned.

Christopher smiled at the young girl, appreciating her youthful innocence. Hannah had possessed the same innocence until she was forced to leave Potomac Hundred. Now he thought of her as a worldly woman whose tolerance would be more the level of Rachel's than, say, that of Anne Crabbe, the deceased wife of the Reverend Crabbe. Anne Crabbe was a saint, Hannah had once claimed.

The cannons fell silent in the late afternoon. As he walked back to the house, he wondered: Where had the battle been fought? Who had won? Would the dispositions of the armies allow him to travel to Elk?

It was a short walk to the house, a simple two story structure of brick with a skirt roof. The brickwork was beautifully rendered in blue and red glazed brick; and one of the gables had a wonderful zigzag ornamentation in blue brick, with the date "1754" and the initials "R W" for the builder.

The Garrisons, Richard and Anne, were friends of the Mathis family. Richard Garrison was active in patriot activities. Their son Jeremiah was on active duty with the State troops.

Christopher entered the large front room that served as the dwelling room with a large fireplace on the side, and a trestle table and benches taking up much of the center of the room. A small partly sheathed stair against the partition for the rear room led up to a second floor with a similar two room design. The house also had a garret which served as Christopher's sleeping quarters.

Anne and Lydia were preparing dinner, their largest meal of the day.

This midday meal would consist of oyster stew, roast beef with cabbage salad; another course of chicken; then a selection of jellies; an Indian pudding, good Jersey pears and peaches, raisins and a pungent cheese. There would be plenty of coffee, as well as wine if Richard and Christopher wanted.

The smell of good meat cooking in seasoning! Ever since he lived off the lean, meatless carcasses of beeves provided by the Continental army, or the bits of old, tough pork served out of a barrel on the prison ship, Christopher savored every piece of meat he smelled and tasted. And then there were the breads! Ah the breads. So soft and fluffy. Once he came across one of Anne Garrison's freshly baked loaves of bread and couldn't resist pressing his nose into the warm, yeasty crust.

The conversation at the table was filled with rumors of a great battle in Pennsylvania.

"There's no doubt about it. John Jefferies returned from New Castle this afternoon and said the two armies were facing each other across the Brandywine Creek, near the border between Delaware and Pennsylvania."

Christopher nodded. "Well, Miss Lydia and I sat most of the afternoon listening to the cannonadin', didn't we?"

"We sure did, and a fearful racket it was!" Lydia assured the table.

As he stabbed a chicken breast with his fork, Christopher asked, "When do ye suppose we'll receive news of the outcome?"

"It's on the way now, Christopher," said Richard Garrison. "One of the ferry boats should arrive with the news by morning."

Patriots and loyalists alike awaited this news with trepidation.

Early the next morning, both Christopher and his host hurried through only the most urgent early morning chores, then walked several streets over to Nelson's Tavern on Broadway at the head of Market Street. This was the center of town around which were also located the courthouse, the Friends Meeting House, and the market place, as well as a few fine residences.

They entered a crowded long room just as a man was saying, "It was a clear defeat for our army, but it wasn't a rout. Retired in good order, they did."

"And still between the British and Philadelphia," another assured the audience."

"What are the dispositions?" Christopher asked anxiously.

"Our army is now situated around Germantown, between Philadelphia and the British Army. I've heard that British units have occupied Wilmington," the man reported.

Christopher's heart dropped. *Damn,* he thought, *I'll never be able to get to Elk and Hannah.*

"But, here's some intelligence that I didn't believe when I first heard it, but damn'd if it isn't true: Howe's army has ended its occupation of the upper Bay—in fact all of northern Maryland!"

"What?—"

"You heard me right! Not only that, but the British fleet is also said to be departing the Bay and goin' round to Delaware!"

"Why, that's incredible."

"The British think that the capture of Philadelphia, the rebel capital, will be the end of the war. That's the way it's fought in the Old World: ye capture the capital and the other side sues for terms."

"You don't say! How little they know...."

So it appeared that despite the fact that the British could capture Baltimore and Annapolis, and control the entire Chesapeake Bay and northern Maryland, they were going to settle, instead, for merely occupying Philadelphia.

Richard Garrison looked at Christopher and broke out in a broad smile. "Well, Christopher, which god of war is looking out for you?"

Christopher felt like an eagle should, soaring over land and sea, as he quipped, "Could be Hannah's patron saint, Saint Jude, he of lost causes!"

The locals called it the Port of Salem. Christopher looked disdainfully at the public wharf and the small wooden shanty that had been the King's Custom House. To him, a port was located on a great river or expansive bay, and was not a single wharf jutting a little ways out into the Salem River!

It was now getting to be late September. The two opposing armies were maneuvering about, with the British in the vicinity of Valley Forge, and the Americans guarding the fords along the Schuylkill, trying to keep themselves between the British and Philadelphia. While British and American parties roamed around the Wilmington area, the dispositions seemed good for Christopher to walk in, and with Hannah, walk out of the village of Elk, both of them on their way to Baltimore before the region ended up behind enemy lines.

For one of Christopher's silver coins, Richard was able to obtain passage for him on a hay boat going over to New Castle. The hay boat was not at the public wharf, but at a farmer's dock down the river a bit. Richard, Anne, and Lydia saw Christopher off.

Christopher had become quite attached to the Garrison family. "You know, Baltimore isn't too far from Salem. And keep in mind," looking at Lydia, "I have a dear friend who has an academy for young women just down the street from my aunt. Lydia would be most welcome."

"We'll keep that in mind, Christopher Sims. In the meantime, God be with you and your Hannah."

The ship deposited Christopher and its load of hay at New Castle. Christopher paid to spend the night with a farm family outside of town. Here he learned that there were no opposing forces worth mentioning in the area, and that militia units throughout the region had reorganized and were out in force pursuing loyalists.

"It's peculiar, for sure," the farmer said. "People a lot smarter than I am think the loyalists in the area hereabouts have been tremendously discouraged by the fact that the British army and fleet just up and left 'em."

"Well, I hope that's the case."

The next morning, Christopher set off on the one day walk to Elk.

"Friendship"
Kent County, Maryland
September 21, 1777

Isabella Alexander herself answered the door.

"May I help you, sir?" She looked at the man standing in front of her. He was dressed neatly in a clerk's suit of clothes, carrying a pack slung over his shoulder.

"Are you Missus Robert Alexander?" he asked politely. He did not look like the Committee members who had been coming to the house and threatening her with banishment from her land because of her husband's disloyalty.

"Yes, I am, sir." She stood straight, daring the man to threaten her yet again. To Christopher, she looked tired and defeated.

"Ma'am, I am Christopher Sims, and—"

But before he could finish, she gave a small gasp and stepped back, as if visited by the avenging angel himself.

Surprised, and also shocked at the woman's reaction, Christopher asked, "Madam, are you all right?"

Collecting herself, Missus Alexander indicated she was, "I apologize, Mister Sims, the past month has been quite a burden…and now…well, please do come in, Mister Sims.

She showed him into a pretty parlor and invited him to seat himself in one of the comfortable side chairs. She seated herself on a settee. Christopher declined refreshment.

She looked closely at him. "You are Hannah's young man. She talked so highly of you."

Isabella Alexander sighed. "I might as well be blunt, sir. Hannah is not here. Wait, please…," she brushed aside his interruption as she would that of any lesser person.

Collecting herself, she went on, "My husband to everyone's shock has declared himself to be a staunch loyalist. He—"

Here Christopher rudely broke in. "I am aware of your husband's treachery, Madam, but that is a different matter, of no concern to me right now.

"Where is Hannah?" he demanded angrily.

The question obviously shocked the woman. "I sit before you, sir, as someone who must confess that she has committed a great harm to both you and poor Hannah. Though I would not have wished it, my husband handed her over to the British authorities as a runaway."

Christopher glared at her. "And you did nothing to stop this injustice?"

"I was unable to do anything about it."

Christopher didn't really care if this was true or not.

"Where is she now?"

Isabella rose from the settee and walked over to a window. She turned nervously to face Christopher.

"I don't know. I honestly don't know. She was entrusted to a British naval officer—I was told they are acquaintances—to be returned to a Reverend Crabbe. Her boat set sail several weeks ago. That's all I know, sir. My husband refused to discuss the matter with me." Tears were streaming down her cheeks.

"And Mister Alexander is—where?"

"He departed with the fleet," Missus Alexander said in obvious embarrassment.

Having nothing more to ask of or say to this woman, Christopher rose abruptly, ready to excuse himself and leave, but he hesitated and looking at Isabella Alexander, "Missus Alexander. Hannah spoke very highly of you and your children—and even Mister Alexander, for that matter. And *you* abused her trust in you.

"Good day, Madam."

Christopher was staying at one of the taverns in the village of Elk, and the day after his visit to "Friendship" was sitting in the long room brooding when approached by two young adults. One was male and the other female. Both were well-dressed and very attractive. The barkeep and the few customers looked at them curiously.

"Mister Christopher Sims?" the young man asked tentatively.

"Aye, and who might you be?" Christopher smiled absently.

"I'm William Alexander, and this is my sister Araminta." After making these introductions, the young man was silent, not knowing what to say next.

"Oh!" exclaimed Christopher, "two of the Alexander children. Hannah had such wonderful things to say about you!"

This seemed to break the ice, because Araminta immediately began gushing about Hannah, also pointing out that her brother has "a liking for Hannah," all of which went on until her brother ordered her to be quiet.

"The reason we're here, Mister Sims, is because we think we know where Hannah has been taken."

Christopher looked intently at both of them. "You know where Hannah is?"

"We think so. Araminta, tell him."

Araminta glanced around conspiratorially. "None of us were allowed to talk to Hannah, including Mama, but I just barged in to her room past the guard—who liked me!"

"Araminta!"

"Well, Hannah gives me a hug and we're crying in each other's arms and she whispers in my ear, 'Aramini—that's my nickname—all right, I know...she whispers 'Aramini, people will come lookin' for me and you're to tell them that I've been taken to a place called Smith Island. Can ye remember that?"

"I told her I could remember that, for goodness sake! And then I asked her where this island was.

"She told me that she didn't rightly know. 'It's one of the Bay islands, off the Eastern Shore,' she said.

"Oh, an' she said she'd be staying with Mister Mister's family. She told me to be sure to remember that too."

"Mister Mister? Are you sure?"

"Sure, I'm sure. Hannah said his name is Mister but I forgot his Christian name."

"But his last name is 'Mister.' Correct?"

"Yes," Araminta said impatiently.

Christopher thought about what the two youngsters had told him. It just might be enough. Looking at them, he exclaimed, "You two have made me a very, very happy man."

"And Hannah a very, very happy woman," pointed out Araminta.

"Aye, Miss Araminta, you've made *both* of us very, very happy!"

36

"WILFUL AND MALICIOUS DESERTION"

Smith Island, Chesapeake Bay
November 1777

HANNAH HAD EXPECTED Mister Alexander to be disappointed and, she supposed, maybe even a little angry with her as he addressed her request to leave his employment. Still, as she stood unacknowledged before him as he sat at his desk, she felt afraid. To make matters worse, Missus Alexander was not present for the interview, making it appear more an interrogation than the awkward end to a business agreement gone sour.

Finally, he looked up at her. He looked intently at her as she stood before him, as if seeing something in her he had not seen before. Then, "Missus Williams, you have requested permission to leave my service. Rather abruptly, I might say. Still, I would ordinarily agree to this—sadly, because you have served this family well."

Perhaps it was just her nerves, but Hannah was sure he emphasized "served" as if to make a point.

"However," he continued, "a matter has come to my attention which goes beyond your mere employment with this family, a matter which would have to be addressed whether you stayed with us or not."

Hannah froze.

"You, madam, are a runaway, a bonded servant who willfully deserted her legal responsibilities. Under English law—and we are once again under English law—you must be returned to your rightful master."

"Sir," Hannah said carefully, "I have no master, and I am no one's slave, for that is what indentured servitude is—slavery, which I'm told is against English law. I am a citizen of a free country, the United States of America, a country you, sir, have betrayed."

To his credit, Robert Alexander accepted Hannah's willfulness with grace. "Missus Williams, I regret that circumstances have put you and me in this position, because you do not deserve it and I do not wish it upon you; but the law must be obeyed or we are at the mercy of the beasts among us."

Robert Alexander looked infinitely tired. "You will be returned to the Reverend Crabbe, a loyal subject of the king, to satisfy his complaint against you. Lieutenant Harvey, with whom I understand you are acquainted, has kindly agreed to accompany you to ensure your safe return to the Reverend Crabbe.

"That will be all, Missus Williams."

"I might have known you would betray me, *Lieutenant* Harvey."

"Ah, my dear Missus Williams, I sincerely regret what duty forced me to do. But I shall make up for it, I promise."

"So, Lieutenant Harvey, what are your intentions? May I assume you have no intention of returning me to the Reverend Crabbe?"

"Please call me Benjamin."

"Oh, why not. So, *Ben*, answer my question."

"Well, actually, it would not be possible to take you to the Reverend Crabbe. You see, he's serving with loyalist privateers who have bases on isolated islands and inlets, using uncharted waterways, from which they sally forth to attack rebel vessels."

Ben Harvey looked at Hannah. "You know, Roger Crabbe has gone quite mad. He's as good as abandoned his children and is obsessed with seeing every rebel in hell."

"And just where are the children, Ben?"

"Oh, they're on Smith Island, one of the Bay islands, staying with a Marmaduke Mister, an interesting character, I might add, whose nephew, Stephen, commands an armed loyalist barge working off the Nanticoke River. I am a sort of liaison between His Majesty's naval tenders and our loyalist privateers, and spend considerable time on Smith Island myself.

"Unfortunately, the children have been left to their own devices and are sadly in need of a mother figure." Ben smiled happily at Hannah, "Could you ever have imagined, dear Hannah, that such a place as Smith Island was so in need of your womanly ministrations?"

The next day Hannah was escorted aboard a British Navy sloop. Before she left, she was not allowed to see Missus Alexander or the children. However, Araminta somehow managed to steal into her room to say goodbye. Desperately, Hannah gave the young girl information on her destination, hoping that it would be passed on to somebody who could help.

Hannah was put in a room in the stern cabin. She was treated politely by the officers and crew and allowed to walk on deck. Lieutenant Benjamin Harvey escorted her during her first such walk, acting contrite and being the gentleman.

They stood at the railing, silent for a minute. Harvey made a motion with his arm which encompassed the entire vessel.

"My first command," he said proudly. "Her name is the *Chester*—I have such fond memories of that town!—She's a sloop of war, fifty feet in length. That's a particularly nice stern cabin, well provided with windows for light and air. I trust you found your room to your liking. And you will experience an impeccably set dining table. She carries six swivels now, but I plan to arm her with two six-pounders on each side and a nine-pounder in the bow. I'm looking forward to taking plenty of rebel prizes!

"Look up, Hannah, and you will see a single mast with fore and aft sail, bursting in the wind—a fair fast boat, and she has a centerboard for shallow waters."

After describing his current mistress, he looked at Hannah, kindly, and said, "I have no intention of forcing myself upon you, dear Hannah…not after our sweet interlude in Chester."

Hannah looked at him in contempt. "That was a *sweet interlude?* How quaint."

****

That had been months ago.

Upon being informed that they had arrived before Smith Island, Hannah looked curiously out over the Bay and saw patches of land, or what appeared to be land, floating in a maze of waterways. Though there were clumps of woods here and there on slightly higher ground, it was a flat land of saltmarsh cordgrass and meadows, and black needlerush thickets, virtually awash in brown tidal waters.

The sloop had entered what one of the seamen called "Big Thoroughfare." Here they had dropped anchor and took a small flat-bottom boat up a serpentine little creek to a cove, finally pulling alongside a small dock.

A long boardwalk set on pilings took them to what passed as dry land. Walking along a twisting path, her shoes crunching on a covering of crushed oyster shells, Hannah realized that they weren't headed to town. She asked Ben about that.

"Actually, Hannah, there's not even a single village on the island. But you'll be living in the largest community here. It's called 'North Point' and consists of five families!"

Looking around, Ben almost grimaced. "Indeed, you'll find life here very basic."

Hannah later learned that there were four "communities" on the island consisting of four or five families each. The other inhabitants, perhaps a hundred people altogether, were tucked into the many little coves and creeks along the edges of the archipelago referred to as Smith Island.

Not long after her arrival, a stray loyalist justice of the peace had heard Hannah's case during a visit to the island and found her guilty of being a runaway servant. He sentenced her to one additional year plus time lost, which meant that she had over two more years to serve. And it appeared it would be served on a barren island, swept by winds and misty spume.

What saved her from utter dejection was her reunion with the Crabbe children.

She hardly recognized them as she came upon the two of them doing chores at the house of Marmaduke Mister. Molly would be almost thirteen, thought Hannah, and Peter would be eleven. At their ages, thought Hannah, a year and a half would change both of them considerably...and then it occurred to her that their lives during her separation from them surely had not been easy.

But they immediately recognized the tall young woman walking toward them and flew to her as if wafted by the gentle Zephyr himself.

There were exclamations, and hugs and laughter, and swirling skirts and flying hats as Hannah and the children greeted each other.

With all the unencumbered joy of their reunion, it was quite a while before the inevitable question arose: "Hannah, why did you leave us?"

Molly's question was more desperation than raproach—it was the cry of a young person who had come to believe that no one loved her or her brother.

Hannah realized that their hurt was a raw wound which had festered simply because no one—not her, not their father, nor anyone else—had been there to give them the love and attention they needed in these, the worst of times.

The three of them talked, and talked some more, and came to an understanding.

Hannah's tears fell on Molly's cheek as they clasped each other, both feeling the pull of having grown up together almost like sisters. Peter tried to play the strong young man; but he, too, felt the emotion, and decided that he felt happier now than he had for ages....

Hannah, along with Molly and Peter, lived with Marmaduke Mister and his family in a large house on an enviable patch of lawn amidst wax myrtles and a few loblolly pines. Oddly, or perhaps not so oddly, everyone referred to the Mister homestead as the "Woodlands." Four other families lived in close vicinity to the "Woodlands," and these comprised the community of North Point.

"Woodlands" was home to an extended family which now included a number of relatives from Somers Cove on the Eastern Shore, the nearest town to Smith Island. These family members from the mainland were the women and children of "Refugees," loyalists who had fled their homes because of their beliefs, finding sanctuary on Smith Island, while their men went to sea as privateers.

"They call our men 'picaroons,' one of the women complained, "which I'm told means 'rogue' or 'brigand' in the Spanish tongue. 'Tis a lie! They fight for the Crown. Nothin' more, nor less."

Most folks on the island would agree with this. They were loyal to the Crown if for no other reason than they, as well as their ancestors, had always been English; and they remained happily English to this day—there being no particular reason to change now.

Adding to this sense of ancient loyalties, the families of Smith Island were mostly named Marsh, Evens, Bradshaw, Tyler, and Thomas...that was about it. The Mister family really belonged on the mainland; but Marmaduke had bought property here, and became one of the island's characters.

Marmaduke Mister was a loyalist who was arrested by the patriot authorities every chance they got. Then they would up and let him go free for one reason or another. Marmaduke's nephew was Stephen Mister, who commanded an armed barge, which was having its way plundering Eastern Shore farms and taking small Bay trading vessels. Stephen and some other picaroons brought their captured boats and goods to Smith Island where Uncle Marmaduke would put them to good use or sell them. Cattle and provisions were among the most desired items, sold to British navy tenders supporting cruisers on patrol in the Bay.

War or no war, life on Smith Island went on virtually unchanged.

Ben Harvey had said it was a basic life, and so it was.

In addition to crops and fruits, shellfish and succulent blue crabs, the island raised beeves which fed on the sweet grasses, while finding protection in the brush and patches of woods on higher ground. Fresh water for man and beast came from large dug holes. There were no fences on the island.

There were plenty of chores for everyone all year 'round, but now winter was approaching and preparations were ongoing to collect and store vital supplies. Women and children collected sea'ors—grasses washed up by the tides—used for winter forage, stuffing for cushions and bedding, and, when mixed with a little marsh mud, even served as a good source of heat against the damp cold of a Bay winter.

Molly and Peter taught Hannah how to handle the local skiff, with its blunt stern and low sides rounding to a pointed bow. Soon Hannah was confidently poling this craft up and down the tidal guts and marshy inlets, as they fished, gathered sea'ors, and collected firewood.

Soap Making Day

Life on the island was a struggle, and island families banded together to provide for the comfort and good of all of them.

Saturday mornings were given over to communal work. It could be any one of a number of tasks but this Saturday it was the making of soap by the women, and butcherin' by the men.

After these dreadfully dull chores were finished, the neighbors were ready to frolic. First, they feasted on a variety of foods brought by each family: there would be pots of food, oyster pies, potatoes and succotash, puddings, breads, and fruit pies. Following this feast, the women would visit, the men would play cards, while the children played hide and seek.

Later in the evening, with great anticipation, parents herded their young children upstairs to the big room and put them to bed. Now it was time for the grown-ups to enjoy adult amusements—singing, dancing to a fiddle, and maybe some licentiously festive behavior.

Hannah looked forward to these Saturday evenings more than she wanted to admit. She even came to tolerate—well…perhaps even enjoy dancing with Ben; who she knew, despite her own lack of skill, was very adept in all of the various dances—and he was patient in teaching her his favorites.

Marmaduke Mister would insist upon dancing with her, too. But unlike Ben, Marmaduke was as clumsy as a dancing bear she had once seen on the Chester Town green.

Hannah had met Marmaduke Mister on her third day on the island. From all the things she had heard about him, she was pleasantly surprised to meet an older man, rather oddly dressed in outdated finery, who possessed a happy smile almost hidden by a wild beard. He doffed his plumed hat and bowed extravagantly.

"So, Missus Williams, I presume that you have heard the stories about me—that I am a pirate?"

"I have, sir."

"Well, young lady, that is exactly what I am!" And Marmaduke Mister laughed uproariously. "And," he leaned towards Hannah and whispered secretively, his beard tickling her cheek, "I'd be a pirate even if I wasn't fightin' for the king!" He laughed again, and then stepped back to see what effect he had had on this attractive woman.

Hannah liked him immediately.

"Mister...Marmaduke—may I call you Marmaduke, sir? I can't call you Mister Mister because I'd"—and she burst out in laughter.

"...Because I'd burst out in laughter." Both of them were laughing now.

"My dear young lady. You may call me whatever you want, as long as you share a dance or two with me at our Saturday evening frolics."

So it became a Saturday evening ritual...and more. It was hardly a father-daughter relationship. Hannah was well aware of this, but she was confident she could manage Marmaduke. She quickly realized that he could be satisfied, at least for a time, with little pleasures—a hand on her rump instead of on the small of her back, feeling the press of her pert breast against him as they walked arm-in-arm, a coy display of ankle and calf.

Without fully thinking this through, she hoped to pit Marmaduke Mister against Ben Harvey.

****

They told her that Smith Island lay directly across the Bay from the Potomac River, and, she thought, her once hopeful past. Memories that sent shivers of nostalgia through Hannah's body. But she could not see the western mainland from where she was; so she looked to the east and toward a hopeful future. Hannah would often look eastward, and on a good day she might see the Eastern Shore some nine miles away. She would sigh and turn away.

Benjamin Harvey would look out over the same scene and he would see a distant horizon entirely different than the one seen by Hannah. He would then sail off in his sloop, satisfied that Hannah could not escape.

37

PIRATES ON THE CHESAPEAKE

The uninterrupted depredations committed on Trade being a greviance long and severly felt…It was hoped the States at large would before now have adopted some Measure for protecting the extensive Commerce of this Bay…
Leading Merchants in a letter to
Maryland's governor

Baltimore Town
Winter, 1777-1778

UPON HIS ARRIVAL IN BALTIMORE in late September, Christopher was at a loss as to how to start organizing a rescue attempt to get Hannah safely off Smith Island. To begin with, he had no idea where the damn'd island was.

Finding out its location was easy. "It's ten miles or so off the Eastern Shore of Maryland, Christopher," advised Mary Katherine Goddard. She went over to a hutch in the corner of her print shop and pulled out a folio from which she removed a map. As she placed the map on the table, Christopher saw that it was a map of the Bay and Eastern Shore measured by Charles Mason and Jeremy Dixon.

"I'm told this is a very accurate map…and here is Smith Island, almost directly across the Bay from the Potomac River."

Christopher stared at the map. The island was unmarked on the map but everyone seemed to know that it was, indeed, the Smith Island where Hannah was being held captive.

While finding his destination did not prove to be much of a problem, just getting there, much less rescuing Hannah from the picaroons, seemed impossible. All of his contacts, those that might be helpful, were off to war. Casting about, he realized he had only Rachel to call upon. But then, Rachel had something to do with securing Hannah's freedom; and once again she would prove to be an incredible ally.

"Chris, I have a dear, old friend who may prove helpful. You say that Hannah has been taken to Smith Island? And the Alexander children mentioned a 'Mister Mister'? Well, that would likely be Marmaduke Mister, who, in fact, lives on Smith Island, and is a common pirate. Quite a character, I'm told.

"In addition, I've heard that a number of important merchants in Baltimore want to mount armed operations at their own expense against pirate activities in the Bay. If this is true, perhaps we can kill two birds with one stone…hmm—" she tapped her lips with her forefinger, "let me think on this."

This possibility animated Christopher anew, and he was ready to get started now.

"Chris," Rachel looked sternly at him, knowing his penchant for wanting to act before making proper preparations, "this will take some time to arrange, assuming that my friend agrees to it. I want your complete cooperation, is that agreed? Don't hesitate in answering me, sir."

"Yes, agreed, Rachel," Christopher said, perhaps a little truculently.

Some time later, once the plan appeared feasible, Rachel introduced Christopher to Hyman Cohen.

"Baltimore is called 'The great emporium of Maryland commerce,' Mister Sims, but it is now being strangled by pirates. You may call them what you want—Royal tenders, cruisers, privateers, picaroons—but they are pirates, plain and simple, and they are ruining us."

Hyman Cohen took a sip of his coffee, and collected his thoughts, keeping in mind the purpose of this meeting. "My employer is one of a number of prominent merchants who have requested that the council lend them two row galleys belonging to the State navy, stating their willingness to pay the operating costs of those two vessels for four months in order to go after these pirates where they hide out.

"One of these hideouts is Smith Island—fortuitously, for our purposes. Now understand that my employer has agreed to direct his own resources in search of your Hannah only at the request of Rachel Jones." Cohen looked carefully at Christopher. "You are very fortunate, sir, that you and Hannah have Rachel as your friend."

"I am truly aware of that, sir." Christopher had accepted the incredible debt of gratitude both he and Hannah owed Rachel, and by extension, her patron. At the same time, he didn't see the purpose in Mister Cohen pointing this out, unless it is the businessman in him who disapproves of mixing business and private lives. If he could be of service to Rachel, or her "benefactor" (struck by the euphemism, he suddenly remembered Terry Simon's statement to the effect that only the British would call a cannonade "amusing" the enemy!) he would do so—out of friendship, debt, whatever…why raise the obvious? But he listened respectfully as Mister Cohen went on.

"The expedition will strike Smith Island first in the hopes of capturing or killing several picaroon captains who harbor there. This will provide our own force the opportunity to search for Hannah. If she is on the island, we will find her."

"And preparations will take how long, Mister Cohen."

Cohen paused, thinking. "At least a month or two…let us say around mid-March, depending on the weather. In the meantime, Mister Sims, with your experience in battle, I ask that you act as lieutenant to Mister Crawford—who served honorably as an ensign with the Eastern Shore Battalion. Most of the men are handy with firearms and knives, but untrained in the martial arts." Hyman Cohen chuckled at the idea that his hired thugs might become good soldiers.

"Of course."

"Well, then, I'll take my leave." As he started for the door, Mister Cohen turned towards Christopher. "Oh, and Mister Sims, I had the great pleasure of facilitating Hannah's travel to Baltimore from the Eastern Shore in May of '76…and I," he hesitated, "…well, I am truly glad that we have the opportunity to rescue her."

Ah, now I understand...stern Mister Cohen is smitten with Hannah and wants me to be as grateful as he that his master has agreed to this scheme!

"As we all are, Mister Cohen."

****

While staying in Aunt Jane's little blue house on Lovely Lane, Christopher's bedroom was the one once occupied by Rachel, who later shared it with Hannah after her escape and arrival in Baltimore to join Christopher. There were times when Rachel was away and Hannah had the room to herself....

Christopher would climb the narrow stairs to the landing which led to Rachel's room (in his mind, it would always be Rachel's room), to sleep in the bed that was both hers and Hannah's.

Before he first entered the room, he thought of the memories it would bring to mind. But looking around, he realized the room was empty except for a few simple pieces of furniture: there was the standing bed which nearly filled the room, its familiar bedspread now without the soft comforter which had always lain folded at its foot; a washstand, a small desk with an old mirror above it; a slightly wobbly chair, and a chest of drawers. It was hard for him to realize that it had always been a simple room.

He had walked across the colorful hooked rug, pulled out the chair and sat on it, laying his haversack on the floor by the desk. Sitting in the hard chair, his forearm resting on the desktop, he thought about the bedroom.

It was different, of course. He knew it would be before he walked into it...but he was seeking memories.

He thought of Rachel's small trunk that he carried up to her room that day, and being overwhelmed by the sheer femaleness of this room. A woman's apparel—chemises, petticoats, dresses, hats—hanging everywhere, which the mirror above the desk multiplied in its reflection. A bar of soap on the shelf under the wash basin. Dainty ceramic pots and an array of brushes on the desk. Always a bunch of flowers set in a glass vase. He remembered it as a perfect room.

But above all he remembered its smell. He sniffed the air, his nose quivering like a dog's, seeking that distinct odor of female muskiness, lavender and lovemaking.

Usually, he would be the first up. So he would go downstairs and start the fire in the parlor and boil water for coffee. Then he would lift the card table from its corner spot and place it, unfolded, before the fire. That's where he and Aunt Jane would have breakfast every morning.

Then, over gammon and hominy, with day-old bread grilled over the fire and slathered in strawberry preserves, and between sips of hot coffee, Christopher would begin to tell the rest of his story.

It was the same story of his adventures that he would repeat to Missus Goddard.

"So, ye did make entries in the journal I gave you, Christopher."

Mary Katherine was pleased, even though his entries were tedious rather than colorful, and his use of a hammered musket ball as a writing instrument made for hard reading. Journalist that she was, Missus Goddard's first instinct, after clucking over his safe return and obviously poor condition, was to obtain the firsthand story of one of Smallwood's "Immortals," as they had come to be called.

Christopher apologized for the brief entries and playfully explained that it was only due to the need to save every other page for food. He had meant to be humorous, but obviously Mary Katherine was intent on documenting this epic campaign. "You men resorted to eating writing paper? Good heavens!—but never mind, sit yourself down, Christopher, and tell me about your adventures."

Which meant, he knew, retelling the attacks on Trenton and Princeton.

He might have been wrong here and there, but generally he thought he described events as they happened. He did embellish a bit—naked soldiers and bloody footprints in the snow lent a heroic aspect to their misery, but were, he knew, exaggerated descriptions increasingly used by officers and men to embody their heroic nine-day campaign. And for the same reason, Christopher substantiated these claims: to raise up those poor Continentals who had suffered greatly to save the revolution.

"Now, Christopher," said Mary Katherine with a hint of disapproval after listening to his description of the Battle of Princeton, "we don't want to go and refer to the British soldier as heroic...and let's leave it to the New Englanders to create their own legends, shall we? But other than that, this'll make a good narrative." Thrusting the quill in its holder and putting the stack of papers aside, Mary Katherine was quite pleased with their efforts.

She refilled their cups and gave Christopher one of her intense looks, her mouth set, her eyes full of concentrated energy. "Christopher, you made corporal and led men in battle...so, tell me, is it true that the army has lost faith in General Washington's ability to lead the army?"

Christopher looked curiously at Mary Katherine. "I don't think that's the case. After Trenton and Princeton, most of us consider His Excellency to be an American Gideon or Joshua."

She looked at him with incredulity.

"No, 'tis true, Mary Katherine! Oh, I hear some officers believe he is not so capable as to be our commander in chief, but all the men and the best generals are attached to him."

"Well, that's a relief, because back in December, when all was defeat and gloom, the Congress gave him dictatorial powers even while it questioned his martial skill."

"Well, I don't know why the Congress would give General Washington such powers when that's the very thing we're fightin' against. Surely it would have done General Washington more good if, instead, Congress had given him the men and supplies the army needed."

Mary Katherine laughed heartily. "Isn't that the logical truth."

The war was not going well. The battles of Brandywine and Germantown ended the Philadelphia Campaign with the not surprising loss of Philadelphia. What surprised many on both sides was that the fall of the rebel capital did not have a ringing effect on the war. Then came news from the north that an entire British Army—not a mere detachment of Hessians or a brigade of British—but an entire British army under Gentleman Johnny Burgoyne had surrendered to an American army under General Gates.

Early in the New Year, Christopher ran into Colonel Mordecai Gist at Missus Goddard's shop.

"Why Christopher Sims! I had heard you managed to escape from one of those prison ships off Long Island and were back home safe and sound. Welcome home, sir."

"Thank you, colonel. And I understand congratulations are in store for your recent marriage."

"Indeed! I had the good fortune of Missus Mary Sterett of Baltimore accepting my humble offer of marriage.

"Humble, indeed, Mordecai," laughed Mary Katherine; "but I have to admit you are indeed a fortunate man to have a wife like Mary Sterett."

Colonel Gist was aware of Hannah's current plight. "Christopher, I blame myself for not seeing the obvious, and putting your Hannah in harm's way. I understand there is a plan to take that pirates' nest on Smith Island and in so doing rescue Hannah. I have advised those involved that I fully support this endeavor…I only wish I could participate myself, but, alas, I am ordered to rejoin the division and prepare for the upcoming campaign."

"Thank you for your support, Colonel. What is the condition of the army, sir?"

"Well, so far we have survived a rather harsh winter—you know that the Maryland Division is wintering in Wilmington, while the Main Army suffers at a godforsaken place called Valley Forge.

"But we shall survive and break winter camp a better army then we were. Militarily, I believe we are in a much better position than this time last year. Our victory at Saratoga cannot be underestimated."

"True, colonel, but there are rumblings that General Washington has been overshadowed by Gates and should be replaced by him."

Colonel Gist smiled. "Won't happen, Christopher. Back in December '76, Gage spent too much time in Philadelphia lobbying Congress when all was going to hell. He appears more at home there than with an army. No, Congress'll decide to keep Washington because they can always ignore his letters!"

Waiting for the time when they would finally set out to deal with the pirate infestation in the Bay, Christopher spent his time alongside Jack Crawford training Hyman Cohen's harbor gang in close order drill, platoon firing and use of the bayonet. Christopher knew that no initiative would be taken against the pirates until spring.

So, in addition to training the harbor gang, Christopher also bided his time doing chores for Aunt Jane, Mary Katherine, and even Rachel, who had opened her academy for young women in a modest two-story clapboard house on New Church Street.

Since Christopher had no one with which to enjoy the nightlife of Baltimore, his evenings were sedate. The most excitement he would have usually involved an evening discussing politics with Aunt Jane, Mary Katherine and Rachel.

Since Rachel had just returned from a visit to Annapolis, Aunt Jane asked, "And just what is our new state government doing, Rachel? Are the assembly and senate being civil to each other?"

Rachel carefully swallowed the ham she had been chewing and, putting down her fork, spoke. "Well, sessions are raucous, to say the least. Low manners are the price of democracy. In any event, the conservatives and the radicals fight each other like cats and dogs. The state legislature is, however, carefully dismantling the old government and, I gather, instituting a more progressive one."

Aunt Jane was obviously hoping for more pyrotechnics. Turning to Christopher, "What has been the mood of the army to the new establishment?"

Christopher had a blank look on his face. "It's been some time since I was with the army, but, generally, civil government wasn't much discussed. I suppose many of us figured we had to win the war first, then think about what independence might mean."

Mary Katherine had her opinion. "The process of establishing a new government involves the age-old conflict between haves and have-nots. Other than throwing off royal rule, the conservatives prefer little or no change, while the radicals demand too much, too soon.

"Dependin' on how you look at it, Maryland's new constitution is either a bitter disappointment for the rights of the humble folk or a victory for sensibleness over 'democratical confusion.'"

Christopher was perplexed. "The revolution is supposed to be about liberty and a perfect constitution according to God's Will."

"Many say that's the way of it," interjected Rachel. "But, first, it's about independence from tyranny. Then, it's about the election of public officials who are responsible to the people. It's obvious that we don't quite have the hang of it yet."

****

Soon after his return to Baltimore, Christopher went to district military headquarters to collect his mustering out pay. Having been one of those who stepped forward at the end of December 1776, as well as a prisoner of war, the clerk and Pay Officer were unsure exactly what pay he was due. So, while the bureaucrats were wrestling with this problem, Christopher wandered around the townhouse turned headquarters in the hopes of seeing someone he knew from the old battalion.

Wandering from room to room he came across a man polishing windows like a man possessed. Staring at the man and his industry, Christopher suddenly recognized him.

Christopher walked up to the man. "Walker? Walker Muse! It's me, Christopher Sims."

The man's head jerked up and he peered at the man standing before him. "Christopher Sims? Why, we signed up together in the regular battalion, didn't we?"

"And were messmates with Terry Simon, Davey Lynn and Caleb Hayes," Christopher added.

"Caleb Hayes was the best friend I ever had." Muse shook his head and opened his eyes wide, as a drunk would do to restore his senses. "And I do recollect ye now, Chris Sims...how be you?"

Judging from his slowness Christopher guessed that Walker had some brain damage. Walker and Caleb were severely beaten in an altercation outside their favorite booze den. While Caleb was able to march with the battalion, poor Walker had to remain behind, confined to a hospital bed.

"Fair to middlin', Walker. And you?"

Walker thought about this for a few moments. "Oh, good, mostly. But I get these bilious headaches which pretty much take up most of my time.

"Say, Christopher Sims," Walker decided slowly, "let's you and me go for a drink, and you can tell me all about the battalion, and Caleb, up there in York."

"Let's do that, Walker." They went to a nearby tavern and Christopher told Walker all about the battalion's adventures in New York and New Jersey. He did not tell Walker that Caleb had been struck in the throat by grapeshot, but did confirm that Caleb had been killed.

"But we have no definite intelligence on Terry or Davey," Christopher reported.

"Well, I don't know about Davey," Walker said slowly, "but I do know that Terry Simon is alive."

"*What!* You know that Terry is alive! How do you know this, Walker?"

Unabashed, Walker stated simply, "Why, Colonel Smith said so. I was doing some work at the Fourth Regiment headquarters and heard him talkin' to Terry's father. Why, I don't know the particulars, Christopher, only that he's alive and a prisoner in York. His father is trying to buy his freedom or something like that."

Soon after his meeting with Walker, Christopher visited the Simon house; a large brick townhouse on an expansive street, which attested to Terry's privileged upbringing. He learned that Terry had been wounded on Long Island (not seriously), taken prisoner and incarcerated in a prison in the city. He also learned that, indeed, Mister Simon was actively engaged in obtaining a parole for Terry and was "confident that the British authorities would accept our entreaty and will grant parole to Terrence."

Later, discussing this with Rachel, she laughed in disgust and said that Mister Simon was undoubtedly dealing through loyalist business contacts. "The difference between a revolutionary war and a civil war is as unimportant to merchants as it is to the side which loses...."

But while merchants may flutter like kites in the winds of war, their true course was in the direction of profit. They might make concessions to Old Scratch, himself, but they would never concede to pirates—and the cruisers on the Bay that preyed on merchantmen were pirates, the flags they flew notwithstanding.

38

SETTING SAIL ON A LOYALIST LAKE

Chesapeake Bay
Early April 1778

IT WAS A BEAUTIFUL VESSEL and it was named *The Love of Rachel.*

Hyman Cohen noticed Christopher staring at the name on the side of the ship.

"The name a man christens his personal ship usually illustrates his true weakness."

"And if you had a vessel to name your own, Mister Cohen, what would be her name?"

Hyman Cohen thought about this. *"The Wandering Jew."*

"Oh. You don't feel at home here, Mister Cohen?"

"I could feel very much at home here, Mister Sims; but Jews are supposed to feel like strangers everywhere they find themselves."

"The Revolution is supposed to change that."

"No, I didn't mean it that way," and Hyman Cohen smiled. "Being a Jew is being a member of a tribe, like the Indians here, and like the Indians we have our ancestral land—in our case, the land of Israel."

"I read about Israel in the Bible…but it was a time so long ago, I think. It's difficult to believe that the Israelites still survive."

"More than ye know!"

Overwhelmed by history, Christopher changed the subject. "Is this the ship that brought Hannah to Baltimore?"

"'Tis, indeed."

"She said she felt like Queen Cleopatra sailing down the Nile! We laughed at its design—a 'bugeye!'"

Hyman Cohen had to laugh. "Damn'dest name I ever heard for a superbly designed boat. I'm told 'bugeye' comes from the Scottish word for 'oyster.'"

Christopher looked out over the railing. "And when do we reach Smith Island?"

"Oh, with these winds, in a half-day, but we'll stand off shore and attack in the early morning."

The two men talked on until it was suppertime.

While businessmen paid for this venture, the military would provide the command and firepower.

Following supper, the little flotilla's captains and sponsors met aboard MSN *Baltimore* for a council of war. The captains of the two galleys, *Baltimore* and *Conqueror*, were naval officers, and their men sailors and marines of the Maryland State Navy. The *Rachel*, on the other hand, was manned by civilians and had aboard representatives of those merchants who were sponsors of this operation. She mounted a half dozen swivels and carried an armed complement of twenty men, ostensibly to cooperate in the land attack under military command, but more importantly, to rescue Hannah.

As Christopher boarded the *Baltimore*, he was surprised at how big it was. In fact, both of the row galleys were big and powerful. They were eighty feet in length, ten long sweeps to a side, each manned by two men, rigged as ships, and classed as twenty guns, although neither mounted that many. They did, however, mount several eighteen-pounders, and eight to ten smaller caliber guns, as well as a number of swivels for the rails. Each had a crew of more than sixty men.

The sailors were dressed in civilian garb, while the State marines were dressed in the prescribed navy blue rifle shirts.

They went below to a large room on the rowing platform.

"Gentlemen," opened Captain Tawes, commander of the MSN *Baltimore,* "we have intelligence, tho' it is several days old by now, that the British sloop of war *Chester,* Joesph Wheland's tender, and Stephen Mister and his barge are anchored in the Thorofare. It's also possible that those Tory villains Callalo and Moore are hiding out there also."

"Why, if that's the case, Captain, we can virtually end enemy depredation in the Bay!"

"That remains to be seen, sir. In any event, we will destroy whatever is here at Smith Island, then swing around to invest the Annemessex River on the Eastern Shore. The Somerset and Dorchester County militias are prepared to block any escape inland from the coast."

Hyman Cohen interjected, "I was just recently in those counties with Colonel Gist's force and can assure you that the militias are well-trained and have Continental officers advising them."

"Excellent!"

"Well, gentlemen, we are within striking distance of Smith Island and will attack at first light according to the agreed upon plan. The *Baltimore* will hoist British colors offshore and then enter the bayside channel, blocking Big Thorofare from the west. *Rachel* will support. The *Conquerer* will attack from the main channel on the Shore side. Gentlemen, God bless our cause!"

"God bless our cause," they all said in unison.

Later, Christopher and Hyman Cohen, now on a first name basis, held their own council of war with Captain Lewis and Jack Crawford.

After agreeing on the role of the *Rachel* in the upcoming engagement, Hyman Cohen turned to Christopher and Crawford.

"Gentlemen, as soon as possible, we'll go ashore in the smallboats. We have a man"—he turned to Crawford who nodded in the affirmative—"who can lead us to Marmaduke Mister's house. Unfortunately, he doesn't know the creeks or guts should they attempt an escape and take Missus Williams with 'em. Should that be the case, we'll just have to obtain the cooperation of one of the inhabitants. That shouldn't be a problem, should it, Mister Crawford?

"Very good, gentlemen. Let's drink to success."

"And to Hannah's safe rescue, Hyman."

39

"A RESPITE FROM THE INSULTS
OF THE PYRATES"

Smith Island, Maryland
April 1778

IT HAD NOT BEEN an easy winter. Big storm after big storm stampeded down the Bay, trampling over the island, banging up against the manor house, bending the clapboard-framed structure to its breaking point. On any number of occasions they couldn't risk sleeping in the great room upstairs, but cuddled under piles of blankets on the freezing ground floor. There were times that winter when the wind pushed so hard, Hannah could literally feel the house giving ground.

In addition to the weather being particularly nasty, the political situation was also unsettled and everyone on the island felt its effects. True, it was known that Washington's pathetic little army was wasting away in its winter quarters somewhere up there in Pennsylvania. But news had also been received of a great rebel victory last fall in New York Province, where it was said an entire British army lay down its arms and flags in abject surrender. In addition, privateers brought news, unsubstantiated but worrisome, that France had joined the rebel cause.

At long last, spring finally came wandering up the lower Bay, bringing with it a heady feeling as winter's scrimpy sun suddenly brightened, the saltmarsh vegetation turned greener, and fair weather birds, scurrying egrets and laughing gulls crying *ha-ha-ha*, made their first appearance of the season. Things began to look up for the residents of Smith Island.

While Hannah could inwardly cheer the good fortunes of the patriot cause and outwardly welcome the "rush," as spring was happily called, her own situation was becoming increasingly precarious.

In November, word came that the Reverend Roger Crabbe had succumbed to one of the many camp fevers that afflicted all armies.

The Crabbe children received this news without expression and actually looked to Hannah for some indication as to what this meant.

For Hannah, this was the true tragedy of this war. You have to remind children to grieve. Their mother had succumbed to a disease...which their father had blamed on a rebellion...and had deserted his children to fight...only to succumb himself to a disease caused by men gathered together to fight a war. And the children don't understand.

It was all very confusing.

Ten days later Ben Harvey returned from one of his forays and added what he had learned to the account of the Reverend Crabbe's unfortunate death.

"Roger was doing God's work on Hog Island, which serves as a base for Captain Kidd's command—he has a flotilla of some barges manned by Refugees and escaped slaves—anyway, Roger ministered to their souls and gladly sacrificed his life for the Crown. Terribly sad, but a part of war," Ben Harvey noted primly.

One of the crew members of Lieutenant Harvey's ship had a different story to tell. Talking to some of the islanders over a few drinks, this man casually mentioned that rumor was the preacher had been found with a ball in his heart. "Now, mind ye, I'm not sayin' it's fact, 'cause I didn't see the body. But, I'm tellin' you the reverend was standing tall one day—I seen 'im, I did—and then dies of some fever the next day? I doan believe it! But, then, why would anyone shoot a preacher?" The man could only shake his head.

The fact was the Reverend Crabbe was dead, and it didn't take long for Ben Harvey's plan to become clear.

"Smith Island is really not the place the Reverend Crabbe wanted his children to be raised," Ben stated, sweeping his arm around the flat, featureless landscape. "He wanted them near but out of danger and decided that they would be safe with Marmaduke Mister and his friendly family here on the island." Ben looked at Marmaduke and smiled, as if acknowledging his paternal graciousness.

"But," Ben Harvey continued, "he did make it perfectly clear to me that should anything ever happen to him, he wanted his children to be sent to England."

Ben was really directing his comments to Marmaduke, who appeared to nod in agreement.

"Rather than take this to a British court, I've taken it upon myself to discuss the possibility of indenturing the children to a very fine family from Virginia which has decided to resettle in Jamaica. Jamaica is not England, but it is English—if ye know what I mean. They have agreed to accept the Crabbe children on the best of terms."

Again, he looked at Marmaduke for approval and appeared to get it.

"So, there it is," he concluded. "It's the best we can do under these sad circumstances."

Later, Hannah looked at Ben Harvey in horror. "Jamaica? You're going to send those poor children off to Jamaica? Why, you're not even trying to be believable, are you?"

Ben looked critically at Hannah. "My dear," he said with a sense of weariness (or was it anger?), "The children will be taken care of—far better, I should add, than the 'care' provided in recent years by their sickly mother or mad father."

Then he looked directly at her, with obvious disdain. "And don't forget, young lady, that given the opportunity..." and he jabbed his finger on her breastbone, "you abandoned 'em, too."

Which left Hannah in tears.

The children would not be sent off until spring. Hannah took advantage of this to convince those on the island to allow the children to stay. While some supported this, she saw that Marmaduke, himself, did not appear to be in favor.

The various beds in the manor house were communal and Hannah took to sharing a bed with Molly and Peter, rather than with some of the other women. This was both to compensate for yet another emotional blow to the Crabbe children, and to discourage "displays of affection" as the single women gaily called the habit of a favored suitor slipping into their beds, keeping the other occupants awake and giggling at their lovemaking. This ploy obviously irritated Ben Harvey, even while it seemed to amuse Marmaduke Mister.

Once again the Crabbe children were outcasts.

"Oh, Hannah," cried Molly, tugging on the older woman's skirt, insisting on her attention even as Hannah was self-absorbed and pitying herself. "Oh, dear, dear Hannah. You can't let them do this to us!"

"And I shan't, Molly," Hannah said soothingly, having no idea how she could prevent it.

"We could run away!" proclaimed Peter. "I know how to use the local skiff—I'm fast as the dickens in poling and I know the creeks almost as well as the locals here. We can hide out like the pirates do!"

Both Molly and Peter looked hopefully at Hannah.

"I don't think that's the answer. And…" she began, looking wistfully in the direction of the Eastern Shore, "there's no way we can escape off the island. So," she concluded, looking both of them square in the eye, "we'll have to go about convincin' our neighbors that all three of us ought to stay Smith Islanders."

When all was said and done, though, Hannah knew that it would all depend on Marmaduke Mister. How far was she willing to go to allow the Crabbe children to remain on the island?

****

With spring came judgment time for Hannah. Just when she thought she could stand it no longer, that her world was all but lost, her future all but surrendered, she was awakened early in the morning of April 7 to the sound of cannon and panic in the manor house.

"God almighty, them's State boats out there comin' up the 'Therfer.'"

Despite the tumult and confusion, the mariners among them considered the chances of making it to their ships and fleeing in their shallow-draft craft, to disappear in the maze of channels and dangerous shoal waters; or, perhaps, give the damn'd rebels a fight.

But it soon became clear that they could not reach their ships and would have to flee into the mysterious interior of hidden harbors, fertile stands of trees and dry hummocks, where hunted men had hid out ever since the island was first used as a sanctuary for pirates.

"Wimmen and chil'ren will stay here."

There was no panic as the men carefully prepared to disappear into the marsh.

"Doan forget ta put some rum in tha kitbag o yours!"

Hannah could not believe her good fortune. *Saint Jude is taking care of me, for sure.*

Then she was suddenly grabbed by two men whom she recognized as crewmen aboard the *Chester.*

"You're comin' with us, ma'am."

Hannah struggled and yelled, resisting their pressure. The men hesitated, not knowing quite what to do, when Ben Harvey walked up to her.

Calmly he hit her with the flat of his sword. Stunned, she could only look at him, in fear now, and obey his orders. "Get in the goddamn'd boat, Hannah." She stumbled to the dock, where she was roughly placed into a large Bay canoe.

40

ROGUE'S POINT

Smith Island
April 7, 1778

THE ISLANDERS REALIZED they were being attacked when the lead vessel lowered the Union Jack and hoisted the Maryland State flag, a wild medley of bright colors and bold shapes, leaving no doubt that the enemy was before them.

The raising of the State colors was immediately followed by a volley from the two American row galleys, a huge stuttering broadside from their carriage guns, the sounds of the discharges as varied as their bores, emitting orange and yellow jets vaguely seen through eddies of gray smoke.

There were three ships at anchor in the creek: a gunboat, a small row galley, and the sloop *Chester*. None of them had the time or the men on board to mount an effective defense, and the result was devastating.

The little gunboat was turned into tinder, its single nine-pounder in the bow bouncing off the gunnel and splashing heavily into the water. The galley was barely touched, it seemed, but there was no activity onboard. And the lovely sloop, Lieutenant Harvey's first command, had its side stove in, and its single mast toppled, entangling the hull in a cobweb of cordage.

The attackers then used the swivels and muskets to cut down the few remaining crewmembers that continued to resist. Amidst the crunching of wood and discharges could be heard strident voices, yells, and screams, while shadowy figures were seen leaping into the water.

It was over in minutes. Captains and officers yelled for a cease-fire. The sweeps were used to bring the galleys up against the enemy ships, boarders prepared to leap over railings and take possession of the helpless vessels.

Meanwhile, the *Rachel* headed toward the little wharf next to the cove. From the quarterdeck, Hyman and Christopher saw the destruction of the enemy ships and readied themselves to go ashore. Their armed force, now under some discipline after months of drill, would follow the local guide toward the small cluster of houses located on the Over the Hill Road, as it was called.

Other small boats filled with men were rounding the two galleys and also heading for shore.

Once on land, the *Rachel's* landing party quickly formed in a semblance of a military body and moved off on the ancient boardwalk onto the shell path toward the road that would take them to Marmaduke Mister's house.

There was no resistance. Picaroons and other loyalist combatants were too busy escaping into the interior, hoping to lose themselves in the marsh, to put up any kind of fight. When the Americans reached the houses, they found only women and children, and a few elderly.

Jack Crawford commanded one of the ship's parties, while Christopher, accompanied by Hyman Cohen, led a second party in a frantic search of the manor grounds, and then entered the large manor house, itself, to continue the search.

Tramping through the few rooms on the ground floor, Christopher saw women and children but no Hannah. Then, huddled against a corner, he saw two youngsters who he vaguely recognized.

Approaching them as they cowered against the wall, Christopher exclaimed, "Why Molly and Peter Crabbe!"

At first Molly thought the fierce man was looking past them, and would not stop to bother them, but mention of their names by him caused both to panic.

"Please, sir, do not hurt us," pleaded Molly.

"We are not pirates," was all Peter could think of in their defense.

Christopher realized that the Crabbe children didn't recognize him after all these years. Why should they?

He lowered his musket, and in as quiet a voice as his nervous energy would permit, "Molly, Peter. I'm Christopher Sims from your old home." Seeing the confusion, Christopher said, "I mean I knew you back in Frederick County when ye lived at Rock Creek Chapel. Do ye not remember?"

He could see that suddenly Molly recognized him, and while Peter, who was too young to remember those days, still looked mystified, the young girl smiled and practically threw herself into Christopher's arms.

"Oh, Christopher, of course we remember you," and looking at Peter, nudged him and said, "He was Hannah's beau!"

Peter looked at Christopher in an odd way. "But, Molly, how can he be Hannah's beau?—I thought Lieutenant Harvey was her beau!"

There was silence.

Then Molly carefully said, "No," looking at Christopher and not at her brother. "Lieutenant Harvey is *not* Hannah's beau—He just *wants* to be. I know that for a fact," she assured Christopher.

Now urgently, he demanded, "Where is Hannah?"

The two children glanced at each other. Then Peter blurted out, "They took her with 'em—the pirates and Lieutenant Harvey, I mean."

"She didn't want to go with them," Molly added quickly. "She fought real hard and the Lieutenant stabbed her with his sword."

"No, no, Molly, he *hit* her with the flat of the sword." Looking at Christopher in a manly way. "Girls don't know anything about war." Then he quickly assured Christopher, "I saw her, she was crying, but not hurt...much—" he trailed off.

Molly looked at Christopher with great tears streaming down her cheeks. "You must save her, Christopher."

Excitedly, Peter vied for Christopher's attention. "Look, Christopher, I know where they're goin'...to Rogue's Point, at the very tip of the island...I been there countless times...there's an old pirate village there."

Christopher looked around, seeking adult opinion, then turned back to Peter. "How do ye know this, Peter? We must be right!"

"Young'un's right, mister," came a deep voice from behind him. "There's usual a British cruiser off the point. They'll go thar fer sure."

Christopher swung around to look at the man who spoke. He was old and gnarled and smooth, like a piece of ancient driftwood; and like such wood an ax blade would no doubt bounce of him with no effect.

"Name's James Tyler, if that's a matter. I kin take a skiff or a log canoe an' run through all these miles of gut and creeks faster'n anyone, and thar's no channel or camp ground I doan know...*and* I personally know ever' soft crab and oyster around!"

"With qualifications like that," said Hyman Cohen, who had just joined Christopher, "I'd like to take him foragin' with me—unless you have a better use for him, Christopher."

Turning to the old man with a smile, Hyman said, "Mister Tyler, I'll give ye a gold guinea—no...I'll give ye *two* gold guineas if you will guide Mister Sims here in the pursuit of this Lieutenant Harvey and his prisoner."

The old man thought about this. "Well, they've got maybe an hour or so on y'all. Might still catch'em...Doan know fer sure, a'course." He looked at Hyman. "What'll ye do with 'em if you do catchem? Now, I doan care much 'bout Marmaduke Mister nor that British gentleman, but most o' the others are family, y'know."

"We won't arrest or kill 'em this time. We just want the woman back."

"Oh, that tall young stranger woman with the proud tits. She got haul'd off with 'em. Aye, I'll help ye get 'er back fer two gold guineas.

"Now ta business. They surely wen' O'er the Gut and takin' the straightest creeks to Rogue's Point 'cause they worry 'bout pursuit. There some skiffs and canoes o'er there. One o' the canoes is capped for a small swivel, if you'd like to take one." He pointed off into the marsh. "We'll hafta take my dog, Mathew, 'cause he can sniff out anything. Oh, and we'll take the boy—he knows the creeks pretty well 'cause I taught 'im."

Minutes later, leading three boatloads of men, Christopher, Jack Crawford, young Peter, and the old man and his dog set out in pursuit.

Traveling Over Shimmery Roads
April 7, 1778

It had still been dark when they fled—dark and wet and cold. Hannah shivered, rubbing the pain on her upper arm caused by Ben Harvey's hard smack with the flat of his sword. Looking into utter darkness, the small craft diving into trough after trough—"nosers" Peter had called them—she felt she was crossing that feared river over to Hades.

She nodded off and awoke sometime later when the craft smacked into a deep trough. Becoming aware of her surroundings, she saw a soft morning sunlight on glistening marsh meadows, now a vague but pretty green, with birds floating in the sky and a light breeze brushing the grasses back and forth. It was almost peaceful, she thought.

But once fully awake, Hannah felt the sharp pain in her arm and her awkward position in the boat. She waved uselessly at a swarm of gnats enveloping her head. She realized it was low tide now and the creek they were following was a narrow shimmering ribbon between muddy gray banks. She needed to relieve herself.

Hannah could not imagine a more helpless predicament.

"Here." Ben Harvey tore off a hunk of bread and thrust it at her, then handed her a piece of cheese.

Hungry, she took both the bread and the cheese, even while trying to look disdainful.

"And let's make you more comfortable." Ben guided her to a cushioned seat in the bow. "There."

They were in a log canoe. The name was misleading; actually, it was a sailboat built in the Indian fashion of hollowing out logs, up to three of them fastened with drifts, and the hull then shaped with saw and adz. It was a design peculiar to the Bay, a shallow draft work boat with a low freeboard and ample deck space, carrying one or more masts. It was actually a comfortable boat, even for a prisoner.

Ben looked at her. "Hannah, I apologize for striking you, but you were being uncooperative at a time when we were in great danger from the enemy."

"Your enemy, Ben, not mine."

Ben ignored her statement. "Within a few hours we'll be aboard a British man o' war, and in a day or two we'll land on Hog Island, off the Atlantic Ocean. A silly name, but the island is a British naval base, a place that will never be threatened by the rebels with their little rowboats. There, Hannah, you will have the opportunity to get to know me as a sincere and loving companion."

Despite her hunger, Hannah threw the rest of her food overboard and turned her back on Ben Harvey.

Back a ways was another canoe in which were Marmaduke Mister and a number of other men. While Hannah wasn't aware of it as she continued to look out from the stern, a third boat, which had started out with the other two, was not to be seen.

It must have been two hours later—it was now a clear, bright morning with the sun moving quickly toward center stage and the tide brimming over the banks—when shots were heard behind the two fleeing boats.

The lead boat with Hannah and Lieutenant Harvey was pulled about, allowing Marmaduke Mister's boat to catch up.

"That's rifle fire and…heavy musket—or, sounds almost like a wall gun to me. What d'ya think, Billy?"

"That or a small swivel and it don't sound too far back."

"Must be pursuit and they caught up with the third boat."

"Damn. And not enough wind. They might catch us! Oh, Lordy…."

Hearing this, Hannah made her decision that she would try to escape.

****

Off in the distance, Christopher could see one of the picaroon boats. It was obviously having difficulty in maneuvering. The sail was fluttering, and men could be seen dancing about with poles or sweeps.

"Jack, please, let's be careful not to risk hurting Hannah."

Jack Crawford looked sympathetically at Christopher. "Chris, I've got several excellent marksmen with the long rifle...we'll aim carefully for those men on the poles—you can see 'em clearly. Also thought we'd throw a solid shot towards the boat while making sure we don't hit it. They might give it up. If not, we'll play catch-up without risking the young woman."

The marksmen took careful aim and let off a handful of shots. Looking through a telescope, Christopher saw two men drop, one overboard. "Nice shooting," he said to them.

The swivel had been set up on the bow. It was a small bore of less than two inches, but was all sound and fury when fired. The ball caused a small geyser off the bow of the enemy ship.

A little while later, they came upon the wounded man who fell overboard. He was standing in waist-deep water nursing his forearm.

As he was hauling him aboard, Christopher was in his face demanding to know if Hannah had been in the boat.

"The young woman? Nay—she's in the Lieutenant's boat. No, sir, I don't know if she's hurt or not."

Jack Crawford continued the interrogation of the prisoner as Christopher fumed and tried to estimate if they had gained any distance on the boats ahead.

41

THE UNHOLY BAND

Smith Island
April 7-8, 1778

IT WAS, AFTER ALL, her last chance for freedom. But as far as she could see, there was nothing but twisting ribbons of light brown water and marshes that seemed little more than floating islands of marshgrass.

Hannah hoped that she would know when the right opportunity would come to attempt her escape. Looking at the landscape, though, she was not so confident. She did remember Peter telling her that the creeks and channels were generally shallow enough to wade at low tide; but, at high tide, they could be too deep and fast. She knew it wasn't low tide, but couldn't tell if it was high tide. Somewhere in between she concluded. But where is the dry land?

Then she remembered islanders telling her about the wetlands and how to identify dry land. If you don't immediately see ridges, hummocks or stands of wax myrtle, then look for black needlerush and saltbush, both of which grow above high tide, and then they kind of taught her what to look for. Well, she'd have to depend upon the little knowledge she had absorbed in her short time here.

Her other concern was her dress. She wasn't weighed down with layers of clothing as a woman usually would be. Awakened by the sounds of fighting, she had on only her linen shift. She quickly had pulled the back of the skirt under and up and tucked it in her cord belt. She then pulled on a wool petticoat skirt and grabbed a waistcoat. Making sure that the children were dressed warmly, she completely forgot about her shoes.

In the windy boat, she had tightened the shift's drawstring around her neck for warmth. At some point, Ben had politely thrown a blanket over her while she was sleeping. This she now had wrapped around her.

As scantily dressed as she was, Hannah still couldn't trudge through water in what she had on...and what if she had to spend hours or perhaps even the night in wet clothing? She concluded that she would have to take off her wool skirt and, instead, carry the blanket. Dry or wet it would be better than nothing.

Now it was a question of waiting for the right chance.

And it seemed the right chance came as one of the crew members cried out, "boat coming 'round the bend back there—could be State marines...I caint make out if they wearin' rifle shirts or not."

"Are they dark color or light?"

While this discussion was ongoing, Hannah carefully pulled off her wool skirt and, with a silent prayer, quickly slipped over the side into the water below the bow while all were looking towards the stern.

The cold water took her breath away but she was greatly relieved to find that she stood in waist-deep water. The mud was soft and she sank to her ankles in it. As she carefully slid her foot along the bottom a black cloud rose to the surface.

Ducking beneath the bow, she stutter-stepped as the boat drifted. Now, what should she do? She heard voices but could not distinguish words. Soon they would realize she was gone. Should she strike out now while they were no doubt still concerned about the activity behind them? She quickly looked around and saw ahead a small rivulet no more than a rod away with vegetation that could conceal her.

It was now or never. She struck out for the little stream and the security it offered as it disappeared around a sharp turn. Crouching, she half-walked, half-swam toward the bank. She had put the blanket over her head, hoping it would hide her profile. The muck pulled at her legs, and with each heavy step the taut muscles of her calves felt like they would snap. Still no alarm, and she reckoned it would only be another few feet until she would be fully hidden from the boat.

Just as she found refuge in some tall cordgrass creekside, there was a yell from the boat.

Oh, please, she prayed.

"Hey, that boat's ours!" And a cheer went up.

Hannah breathed a sigh of relief.

Then another, more strident voice cried out, 'Where's the goddamn'd woman!"

"What—?"

Hannah heard confusion and the angry voice of Ben Harvey.

"*Is* she on the damn'd boat, man?" It took only a few seconds to confirm that she wasn't on the boat.

"Then she went over the side…find her, now! Get in the damn water!"

Hannah could hear splashes as several men dropped into the water.

"I want you to head over to the bank, and follow it. Check out all the streams!" All of these orders were coming from Ben Harvey. Hannah slowly moved along the bank trying to put distance and cover between her and the searchers.

"Pull the boat over here." The voice seemed to be closer.

"Lieutenant, Lieutenant," came a voice from further away.

"What is it?" Ben Harvey's voice sounded impatient. It also sounded even closer.

"Tha other boat's come up, sir. They got some wounded, and say there's at least three rebel boats not far behind. What do ya want us to do, sir?"

"I want you," Harvey yelled at the top of his voice, "to find the goddamn woman, so we can get out of here!"

There was movement of a boat in the water, and then a soft smacking of wood against wood. "Hold for a moment, Harvey," Hannah heard Marmaduke Mister call out. "Tha boys say the rebel boats have at least one swivel. Now, as soon as they round the bend back there, we'll be in range. It's time to leave, Lieutenant."

"We'll stay until the woman is found, Marmaduke."

There was virtual silence. Hannah heard the soft swish of tidal ripples rolling against her and the bank to which she clung; and she thought she could even hear the water slapping against the wood hull of a boat.

"Now, here's what I got ta say, Harvey. Maybe you want ta stay around here 'cause ye got a good sniff of it—but enough to die for? Leave her be—do you hear me, Harvey?"

From where she was hidden, Hannah could sense the tension. It was broken by a gunshot, then another.

There were shouts, yells, scuffling sounds, the thud of a man falling, and then another shot echoed down the creek. Hannah could hear groans, and cursing, as if men had been hurt by these actions.

Then, "Don't shoot, don't shoot!" There were no more shots.

"Now," came a hoarse voice, obviously from a man hurt, "we'll stay here and find the woman. And then a command, "You others—go."

Hannah could hear the movement of a boat or boats—she couldn't tell—and, moments later, the movement of water, as if men were again wading. Exhausted and cold in waist-deep water, leaning upon the miry bank, pressing down on soft grass, Hannah simply buried her head in her arms, like a child wishing away the hobgoblins.

"Hannah," he said gently.

She looked up without interest, clearly resigned to whatever fate awaited her.

The man crouching on the bank above her was Marmaduke Mister.

"Here, let me help you out of that muck."

Hannah looked down at herself. Half in and half out of the water, she looked a mess. Her long hair was wet and muddy; her vest barely covered breasts which were not really concealed by a wet shift; and she could only imagine what else might be revealed when she climbed out of the water without her skirt.

"I'm not presentable, sir," but she gave him her hand and allowed him to pull her up to solid ground.

"No, you're not!" Marmaduke laughed, taking an appreciative look at her figure, muddy as it was, before covering her with his ornate coat.

He grimaced as he wrapped the coat over her shoulders.

"Why, you're wounded, Marmaduke."

Marmaduke put a hand on his side, covering a bloody stain spreading on his linen shirt. "Aye, 'tisn't bad—but it does hurt," he was quick to point out.

"Had a disagreement with your lieutenant. We took shots at each other, and both of us hit our target. I regret to say that I wounded him much more seriously than he wounded me, though I do believe he'll live. I sent him and his men on their way."

"Oh," was all Hannah immediately said, thinking of all she had been through because of…and, yes, with Benjamin Harvey. Then she realized the enormity of what had happened. "What's to happen to me now, Marmaduke? Am I to be allowed to rejoin the children?"

"I believe that will be up to the rebels to decide. Shall we go see?" He offered her his arm, "May I?"

Marmaduke's men had brought the canoe alongside the bank and ran out a stout plank to ease their boarding. Once on deck, Hannah was wrapped in blankets and made as comfortable as possible. Sitting on a bench, she realized with excitement that the three boats she saw coming towards them were filled with American patriots, friends and rescuers, and soon she would be free!

As the lead American boat approached, ready to open fire, Marmaduke Mister stood waving on the stern, and called out, "Sir, I am Marmaduke Mister and I and my men will not resist. Also I have a young woman with me and ask that you respect her safety."

"Nice ploy," Jack Crawford noted to Christopher, before answering, "Aye, Mister Marmaduke, we're comin' alongside."

With the other two boats standing off, ready to engage if necessary, the boat containing Jack Crawford and Christopher came alongside.

Knowing Hannah was aboard, Christopher could hardly keep from leaping the six feet that still separated the two craft. Remembering who was in command, Christopher contained himself long enough for Jack Crawford to board first and inform Marmaduke Mister and his men that they were under arrest by authority of the Maryland Council.

"Sir, I submit to the authority of the Council."

With that, Christopher leapt on deck and dashed to Hannah, who was now standing, tears streaming down her smudged cheeks and a huge smile on her face.

Neither had to say a word.

Marmaduke Mister looked with surprise as the two embraced each other. Turning back to face Jack Crawford. "I gather the gentleman and Missus Williams are acquainted!"

Still clutching her, Christopher guided Hannah to the side of the canoe, ready to help her over to the other boat. Hannah hesitated, turned, and went over to Jack Crawford who was standing with Marmaduke Mister.

"Sir, I am Hannah Williams and thank you for reuniting me with Christopher. I request that you treat Marmaduke Mister without rancor. He saved me from a fate worse than death," Hannah added rather dramatically.

She then turned to Marmaduke, who was enjoying the moment. "Marmaduke, thank you, and I should like to speak to you once we are back at the house."

"Your servant, Ma'am."

She returned to Christopher and he helped her across the gunnels to alight on the deck of the other boat with the help of none other than young Peter.

"Hannah, oh Hannah, I'm so glad you're back with us. And I helped Christopher and the others rescue you!" he announced proudly.

"I'm so proud of you, Peter, and so will your sister be when we tell her."

****

Thoroughly exhausted, Hannah, Peter and a much-relieved Molly had gone to bed. Christopher took this opportunity to speak to Marmaduke Mister, first to thank him for preventing Hannah's abduction by Benjamin Harvey, and then to satisfy his curiosity about this fascinating old rogue. The two of them along with Hyman and Jack were sitting comfortably in the great room drinking rye whiskey.

"I'm not really a pirate, Mister Sims. I just claim the title from time to time because it tends to excite women! And I have to tell you, sir, I think Hannah would have taken to me if she hadn't you."

Christopher laughed. "Then, sir, she was rescued just in time from herself!"

"Too true," lamented Marmaduke.

Then Christopher asked, "Why didn't you continue your flight, sir?"

Marmaduke looked at him incredulously. "To where, sir? To a waiting British cruiser and be tried by a court-martial for shooting a British naval officer? Good Lord, man, the worst a reb—er, a state court will do is fine me!"

Christopher looked questionably at Hyman Cohen.

Knowing how things worked in Annapolis and that Marmaduke was likely to get off virtually scot-free, Hyman shrugged and replied, "Oh, indeed, he's right."

Marmaduke Mister and the other prisoners would, however, be taken to Annapolis for trial, and were put aboard The *Rachel* under a marine guard to be transported there. The *Rachel* was returning to Baltimore while the two State row galleys and the captured galley would continue the offensive against the picaroons with the planned attacks on their mainland bases. This was even more necessary since not all of the armed loyalist ships had been at Smith Island as originally hoped.

The *Rachel* weighed anchor on the morning of April 9 and sailed for Baltimore with a thoroughly happy complement.

Also aboard, of course, were Molly and Peter Crabbe. As a matter of course, Hannah and Christopher had discussed what to do with the children. Hannah made it known in no uncertain terms what she expected would happen.

"Christopher Sims," she reminded him, "I, too, was an orphan and I was bound out as a child. You know the trials I have endured to this very day because of that fact. So, what would *you suggest*, sir?"

Not at all surprised by her ferocity on the subject, Christopher simply agreed to do whatever Hannah wanted. While they did not exactly agree then and there that the children would be part of their family, both privately accepted it as fact. She also knew in her heart that they would find happiness in their sudden family; and, with heated anticipation, the enjoyment of adding to it.

42

NO REST FOR THE WEARY

Baltimore Town
Mid-Late April 1778

THEY RETURNED TO BALTIMORE as heroes, as well as loved ones whose safety had been a desperate worry for friends and family.

"Goodness gracious," Aunt Jane had exclaimed shortly after their appearance at her little blue house on Lovely Lane, "We'll need to celebrate with a gathering!"

And for Aunt Jane that meant the guests of honor, of course, all of whom were staying at her house; then Rachel, Mister Cohen, Mister Crawford, Mary Katherine Goddard; and even Henry Murray, Aunt Jane's occasional suitor appeared, his florid face emphasized by a deep scarlet suit in silk.

Nearly everybody in town seemed to wander by Aunt Jane's house that afternoon and drop in to say hello. Jane was obviously reveling in the occasion, but it was Rachel, Hannah and Christopher who ended up running up and down the street to keep Jane's table stocked with meats and fresh breads, and other delicacies. Frowning good-naturedly at Hannah as they went off to pick up yet more pies, Christopher feigned irritation at the unreasonable responsibilities of being a guest of honor.

Once the spur of the moment festivities were over, Hannah and Christopher spent the rest of the evening telling their adventures to Aunt Jane and Rachel. They were sitting comfortably in Jane's parlor, a small fire giving off warmth against an unusually cold night.

The two women were horrified by Hannah's account of Robert Alexander's betrayal and her abduction. Both were fascinated by her description of the Smith Islanders and their piratical way of life. Then they sat on the edge of their chairs as both Christopher and Hannah thrilled them with the fight on the island and her rescue.

As they called it a night and rose to retire, Hannah said with a laugh, "I do hope the two of you enjoyed our tale because you know you will have to listen through Molly and Peter's version of their 'adventures with the pirates of Smith Island.'"

"A child's impression—that should be so interesting," opined Aunt Jane with true enthusiasm.

With less enthusiasm but still with good humor, Rachel nodded, even while saying, "And we shall then judge who told the story best—if not the most factual!"

Finally alone together, Hannah and Christopher talked about intimate things and first hesitantly then with unabashed enjoyment fondled each other.

That's when Hannah realized that Christopher was not wearing the old Spanish coin on the silver chain. "Did ye need it for an emergency?" she asked, knowing now all the dangers he had been through.

"Nay, Hannah, I was attacked by some of our own soldiers in August '76 and they stole it. I came to find out that the man who was behind the attack killed Alma Lynch.

Hannah gasped, and after a silence said, "Tell me about it."

The next morning, Aunt Jane had unexpected news for Christopher. "Oh, Christopher, Jeremiah Smith"—she said his name as if asking a question—"visited here...oh a week ago, I think; said he was a comrade of yours in the army and asked if I had received any word about you. Well, I told him, indeed, I had, that you had escaped from your captors and had returned to Baltimore. I then added that as we spoke you were on a mission to save your lady love"—smiling fondly at Hannah—"and I was hopeful you would be returning to Baltimore with her anytime now. He was very excited by this news, and asked that I have you contact him as soon as you return.

"Now, I have to warn you, Christopher, that Mister Smith is missing an arm."

Christopher's joy turned to shock at hearing this. "Missing an arm? Oh my god."

"Lost it in service to his country, God bless him. Oh, and he said he and his…er," Aunt Jane hesitated, searching for the right word…"his lady companion Mary can be found most afternoons at the Sheathed Sword Tavern; and said ye would know it."

Hannah clearly wanted to question him about this; and later he explained everything about his friendship with Jeremiah and Mary McBride to her.

That very afternoon, Christopher went off to find Jeremiah.

The Sheathed Sword was one of those booze dens along Baltimore's Basin that had no pretenses: it was just there for anybody needing a drink. Nor did its weathered sign, displaying a poorly painted sheathed sword, or its façade of gray clapboard and filthy panes of crudely blown glass, set it apart from any other drinking hole along the waterfront. Its name, however, had once fascinated Private Terrence Simon, who wondered if the owner of such a disreputable establishment could be a well-lettered man. "Did the soldier's sword fit your sheath?" Terry had quoted from *Pseudolus*, a Roman comedy by Plautus. He referred to it as a play on words, but had given up further explanation when he saw the blank looks from his messmates.

Suddenly remembering Terry's fascination with its name, Christopher entered the Sheathed Sword, and immediately spotted not only Jeremiah but Mary as well.

There were heartfelt embraces, and a little awkwardness; but Jeremiah laughed and thumped Christopher on the back with his remaining arm to assure him that a true soldier took his wounds in stride. All three started talking at the same time.

First Christopher had to explain the rescue of Hannah. After that, he recounted his capture, imprisonment and escape. Then it was Jeremiah and Mary's turn, and they brought him up to date as best they could with the Philadelphia Campaign of 1777, during which Jeremiah was wounded in a skirmish just before the Germantown battle.

"I was evacuated with most of the wounded from that battle to the general hospital at Bethlehem, in the Lehigh Valley of Pennsylvania.

"I think it was the largest stone building I ever saw," Jeremiah said in awe. "'Twas built by a missionary group, called the Moravians. Called it the Single Brethren House, a communal residence for all the single men in the town! Strange, but the entire community was divided into groups that lived and worked in segregated fashion. Well, anyway, the army took over the building and turned it into the hospital."

His narrative trailed off after that, but Mary picked up with a description of Jeremiah's ordeal, while Jeremiah looked away, as if in denial of an unpleasant past.

Jeremiah returned his attention to the conversation and actually became animated when his commission as an ensign in the Continental service came up. "Indeed," he said with pride, "General Smallwood himself nominated me for a commission in the Corps of Invalids. Maimed though we may be, we'll provide useful service to the army by providing a school for officers appointed to the marching regiments."

"I'm so proud of him," Mary stated, her eyes watering.

"As well ye should be, Mary," Christopher quickly responded. "And congratulations, *sir!*"

They continued to talk, sitting on benches at a wobbly trestle table near one of the broken windows. Having brought each other up to date on what had happened since their forced separation and on their plans for the future, Christopher happened to mention that he had seen Walker Muse. He said this only because they were accounting for absent comrades, and assumed without thinking that neither Jeremiah nor Mary would much care.

But this reminded Jeremiah of something much more important. "I know, I see Walker from time to time. Oh, by the way, Walker mentioned that The Boar is back in town. Yep, that's what he said.

"No, I don't know for fact that's true," he noted in response to Christopher's question. "I did notify the provost office, but they've got more important things to do than look for deserters."

Christopher was shaken by this news; but he decided against revealing its potential seriousness until he had had time to mull it over. His old company commander, John Stone, recovering from a foot wound at Germantown, might still be in town. Colonel Stone knew the background of this matter; and perhaps he would know what to do.

He realized something had to be done and would look into it first thing tomorrow.

****

It wasn't surprising that The Boar would return to Baltimore. It was his home, after all; and, besides, after his abortive association with those Refugees up in Westchester, home offered a sanctuary and friends with whom he'd been mischief-making since childhood.

He felt through his shirt and rubbed the old Spanish coin, a habit he had acquired since taking it from the Sims fella he had intended to kill in Elizabeth Town. The motion reminded him that there was the possibility of making some real money here if he could kill that bastard. His failure to do so still rankled him. He had been promised good money by the Tory priest at St. Paul's if he succeeded. Well, as far as he was concerned, the offer was still on the table.

And who knows, Sims just might have mustered out and returned to Bal'imer. On the off chance that was the case, The Boar decided to spy on the house of Sims' aunt every once in a while. *'The early bird catches the worm''—or some shit like that, he concluded.*

On an infrequent reconnaissance of the old lady's house, The Boar was surprised and gratified to spot *both* Sims and the Williams cunt, the two of 'em together, for crissake, coming out of the goddam'd house—and, later, he would congratulate himself by being especially abusive to his latest squeeze.

Settling down to business, The Boar made his plans. He found that the Reverend Johnson was no longer associated with

St. Paul's here in Baltimore. The priest Scott, the one who dressed all in black, might still be in Annapolis—who knows. The man who paid him to kill the Lynch woman was the real spy, he knew, but he had no idea how to contact him.

Thinking about it, Thomas Boarman admitted the whole business might be a shot in the dark. But he enjoyed killing people and might as well kill Sims and the woman if he got the chance. If nothin' else, he owed Sims for that business up in Westchester. If it turned out there was some hard coin involved, then good. Forgetting the money, he imagined a huge upward thrust of his shiv into a man's belly, then splitting him open up to his chin. That's how a wild boar does it; and that's how The Boar does it.

****

Unfortunately, Colonels Gist and Stone had already left to join the Maryland Division as it prepared to leave its winter encampment at Wilmington, in Delaware.

Christopher was at a loss as to what to do next. Frankly, the only one he still personally knew in the military establishment here was Walker Muse. Walker could be counted on for brute strength, but nothing else. So, that left Jeremiah, and between them they could probably recruit a number of veterans to hunt down The Boar.

Well, there it was.

It was the next afternoon, seated at their usual table in the Sheathed Sword, that Christopher proposed assassinating Thomas Boarman, alias The Boar.

Looking at Jeremiah, Christopher said solemnly, "Thomas Boarman is more than a deserter," and he then described The Boar's work for the loyalist secret service and his murder of the young counterspy, Alma Lynch.

"I have a price on my head, and Hannah might also because of our contact with Alma Lynch. As in her case, it is likely that Boarman is the sworder hired to kill us."

Christopher looked beseechingly at Jeremiah, "I need your help in killing him."

"Of course, I'll help you, Christopher; but, frankly, I don't even know where to begin." Jeremiah looked helplessly at his friend.

Reluctantly, but because it was so important, Mary confessed, "He's known to me. His dog hole is at Fells Point, which I know like the back of me hand." She looked embarrassed. "I didn't have a proper upbringing like you gents," she said almost resentfully. "He'll be spending a goodly amount of his time in a favorite gin shop; and I shouldn't have a problem findin' out which one it is." Mary hesitated before adding sadly, "I know 'em all...."

Christopher remembered the hellhole that was a Fells Point tavern he and Alma Lynch had been forced to visit, now so long ago. It was while playing their role as loyalist sympathizers meeting clandestinely with a disreputable Tory spy; and the venue and circumstances still made him shutter.

"It would be great if we could count on him being in a certain place, at a certain time. I know Walker'll help and we should be able to find a few men from the old battalion to once again wield a firearm for the cause."

Their plan may or may not have worked. If it had taken as much time to carry out as it appeared it would, Christopher and Hannah would have been killed by The Boar and the gang he had brought together for that purpose. Thomas Boarman was much more efficient in organizing a killing than was Christopher Sims.

Fortunately, though, Christopher had discussed this dangerous threat with Rachel and Hannah, the intention being to agree on how best to protect them.

Hannah just shook her head, not so much in denial but in frustration. "If the past is any guide, running away is not the answer, so *what* is? she said with a sense of doom.

"Stop that this instant, Hannah," commanded an angry Rachel. Turning to Christopher, "You, sir, will do as I tell you—which is to do nothing. Do you understand?"

"But, Rachel," he began...

"Don't you 'but' me, Chris. Once again, I will ask Hyman Cohen to take care of my dirty linen. If he needs your help, he will ask for it." Rachel then looked kindly at Christopher before adding, "Mister Cohen is capable of brutality, while you are not."

"Now," she said softly, "tell me more about Mary McBride...."

Rachel's Ire

Mary was quite contrite and for once spoke softly, as if she was afraid someone would overhear her.

"'Twas the voice of Old Scratch hisself, I swear." She then lowered her voice even more. "Your dear Rachel has an evil benefactor—aye, I discovered this poking around the Fells Point wharves." Mary looked carefully around the tavern, before adding, "Must have raised a few hackles while I was at it..."

She looked defiantly from Christopher to Jeremiah and then back to Christopher. "Well, gents, I was just asking around about The Boar. Then I come to find out word has been put out on him among the riff-raff down at the docks; and gossip is the responsible party is one Rachel Jones, who's close to 'the Man,' as they call him."

Christopher was mystified. "What is this all about?"

Jeremiah provided an explanation. "It appears Rachel Jones has a 'benefactor' who is well-known around the docks. He's a rich merchant who makes his money operating warehouses, a business he made profitable by 'coaxing' misfits and thieves who profess to be dockworkers into a little honest work.

"In short, he's a ruthless man who has mastered, literally, the cut-throat commerce of the wharves."

"And," Mary interjected, "I was made to know just how ruthless by one of his hirelings. Actually, he was very polite in asking me what I knew about a criminal named Boarman, alias The Boar. I told him I didn't know any 'boar,' and ta leave me alone or I'd have a few of me dockworker pals teach him not to accost a lady.

"Well, that was a mistake," Mary admitted, and shuttered. "I could see that my life was in danger and I tol' him everything I knew," she exclaimed with some intended exaggeration.

"Then..." Mary hesitated and took one more look around the room. Satisfied, she continued, "well, then, I asked around some more—namely, who's behind this interest in The Boar. That's when I found out. Chris, you gotta square me with Missus Jones." She looked like she would cry

Christopher's face grew red. "Ah—Mary, I'm afraid that's my fault. And I assure you there's nothing to worry about with Rachel. The other day, I warned Rachel and Hannah and, quite frankly, Rachel warned me off, saying she would have it taken care of." Christopher held up his palms, as if emphasizing his ignorance. "I honestly didn't know anything about her patron...."

Within days of Mary's encounter with Hyman Cohen (it was indeed Hyman as it later turned out), one of Mary Katherine Goddard's news sources reported that Thomas Boarman alias The Boar, a wanted deserter and suspected murderer, had himself been murdered on the waterfront at Fells Point. Missus Goddard told Rachel that the next issue of the *Maryland Journal* would provide a report of his demise, moralizing that this is the usual fate of sworders and deserters. Those responsible for The Boar's death are unknown, of course. Mary Katherine left it at that, but Rachel did not doubt the publisher knew everything that happened in her city.

The demise of The Boar would seem to have brought closure to this tumultuous period in the lives of Hannah Williams and Christopher Sims. Both were perfectly willing to have it so; and Hannah probably expressed it best when she asked, "Christopher, do ye suppose we can be wedded now *and* begin to lead normal lives for once?"

"In revolutionary America?" he asked innocently.

Epilogue

JUST IN TIME FOR A MAY WEDDING

Then Equal Laws let Custom find
And neither Sex oppress;
More Freedom give to Womankind,
Or give to Mankind less.
                    Quoted in
                    The Virginia Gazette

Baltimore Town
May 1778

I

"ON SATURDAY LAST Mr. Christopher Sims, late of General Smallwood's Command, was married to Miss Hannah Williams, an agreeable young lady. The mutual affection and similarity of disposition in this agreeable pair afford the strongest assurance of their enjoying the highest felicity in the nuptial state.   5-28-1778"

The notice, above, which appeared in *The Maryland Journal and Baltimore Advertiser,* told the reader that here was a tale untold—just as Mary Katherine intended. "A young couple should have a little mystery in their past. Makes them that much more interesting as neighbors," she had opined to Aunt Jane.

Hannah and Christopher were married in a Catholic ceremony at the house rented by Rachel Jones on New Church Street. The bride appeared in a muslin gown *a la polonaise* and her admiring groom in a plain French frock in navy. More than thirty guests attended the happy occasion. Among the guests were Jeremiah and Mary, and Hyman Cohen. It took some quick assurances by Rachel (and almost the need for smelling salts) to steady Mary when she laid eyes on Hyman; but they even ended up talking pleasantly to each other.

The tying of the nuptial knot was followed by the wedding banquet at two o'clock in the afternoon, then dancing, the drinking of healths, and general jollity that lasted well into the next day. A cold late evening supper was also served, with punch, wine, coffee, and chocolate, but no tea.

Most of the guests danced until close to four o'clock in the morning, although a few, Aunt Jane and Mary Katherine among them, retired at midnight.

The youngest guests, Hannah's young pupils and some bachelors, tried to steal Hannah's slipper in the hopes of redeeming it for a silver dollar.

And much to their embarrassment, and earlier than they wanted, Hannah and Christopher were actually put in bed and forced to participate in "throwing the stocking!"

"We didn't even get to dance to our favorites," Hannah complained. "Never mind," she decided, turning to Christopher.

Rachel was lavish in her gifts for the newlyweds, but one of the smallest meant the most.

"Actually, Hyman Cohen gave it to me to give to you. You must open it in private," she cautioned. "You will understand."

Much later, after luxuriating in the newness of their mornings together, Hannah cried, "Oh, we must open Hyman's little present as Rachel said!" Straightening her shift, she dashed downstairs and shortly returned with the little present, wrapped in colorful paper and a silk ribbon.

Tearing off the wrap revealed an exquisite box of Morocco leather. Opening it, they both stared in shock at their old Spanish milled dollar on its silver chain.

"You know Hannah, this coin has shared our adventures together ever since we both left Potomac Hundred."

Chris had told Hannah about it turning up missing after being attacked by The Boar. She had actually cried over its loss. Like

Christopher's mother, Hannah truly believed that the coin was good luck.

"Aye, Chris, and it was returned to ensure our good luck continues. Now, I am sure we will have a happy and normal married life together!"

Which was all Hannah Williams Sims wanted out of life.

II

"Marmaduke Mister has permission to return home, he having brought some American Prisoners from the Bay Islands."

The order was signed by the Clerk of the Court for the town of Annapolis. Hyman Cohen was showing Hannah and Christopher the report in *The Maryland Gazette*.

"Oh, and by the way, you two will appreciate this," Hyman added, "the State Council actually *paid* Marmaduke nine pounds for his 'service.' 'Some' prisoners included Molly and Peter, as well as you, Hannah."

They all laughed.

Hyman Cohen shook his head in disbelief. "We might be too innocent to win this war."

III

The war would go on. From 1778, though, the war didn't much intrude upon the citizens of Maryland. The state would be spared from another land invasion, though attacks upon shipping and coastal towns by British raiders operating in the lower Bay would continue. Occasionally the new states of Maryland and Virginia would be irritated enough by these "pirates" to mount an offensive; but usually the two states didn't get along with each other any better than they did with Britain.

The Sims family's sense of well being came to an end with the crisis of the revolution in 1780. The revolution was on the verge of psychological collapse, brought on by the shattering betrayal of General Benedict Arnold, an American icon, and devastating military defeats in the south. The Cause needed the services of every able-bodied man; and so Christopher joined the Additional

Maryland Regiment of 1781 being organized by General Smallwood. By this time Christopher and Hannah had added to their family a little girl and a liver-and-white spaniel to complement Molly and Peter, their children by default.

In 1782, Hannah and Christopher were blessed with the birth of a boy. Hannah was horrified at Christopher's suggestion that they name the boy "Freedom" Sims. With relief, she realized Christopher was having fun at her expense. She had been appalled when she learned that General Mordecai Gist had named his first son, born in 1779, "Independence" Gist. "Of course, you wouldn't be that silly," she said, admitting her gullibility. Interestingly, Mordecai Gist's second son was named "Freedom." Upon learning this, Hannah accused Christopher of giving Modecai the idea.

By 1782, the Revolutionary War was winding down and victory all but assured. On July 4, an ebullient Christopher celebrated Independence Day. Late that night, after the colorful grand illumination had died away and the crowds dispersed, he suddenly thought about Terry Simon (who had yet to be exchanged) and celebrating with him the declaration of independence in 1776. He was reminded of Terry and the first "Independence Day" because on that day, July 11, 1776, together they had watched a grand illumination as they marched with the battalion through Baltimore on their way to New York. It also reminded him of those heady days of 1776 and Terry's comment: "this is just the war of the revolution. If the war is won, only then will the revolution itself truly begin—and then who knows where it will lead us."

*The epic story of Maryland and
her brave men and women
who did so much to help
win the Revolution continues
in*

The Well Fought Day

Volume Three of

The Old Line Chronicles

ABOUT THE AUTHOR

JOHN CONRADIS learned his love of history from his father who was a published author of local Civil War history in Montgomery County, Maryland. He has been a student of the American Revolution since his teens and has spent years researching Maryland's role in the Revolution. He is a member of the Company of Military Historians. He saw active service in the U.S. Army in Vietnam and was a career intelligence officer serving overseas for thirty years. He lives in Bethesda, Maryland with his wife Hazel and son Brandon.

www.ingramcontent.com/pod-product-compliance
Lightning Source LLC
Chambersburg PA
CBHW070216030726
47505CB00006B/1703